For my mother, Mary Gail Cargo.
Thanks, Mom.

Chapter One

It was my habit to arrive home in time for supper with my son. I wasn't always successful, but today we had enjoyed a quiet afternoon. Quiet being a relative term, meaning that things weren't quite as hair-raisingly frantic as usual.

I left the Savoy Saloon and Dance Hall—my own private gold mine—at six o'clock and made my way west along Front Street. The streets were no more packed than usual for early evening, meaning there was a sliver of room along the boardwalks and across the duck boards.

In later years, what I would remember most about Dawson in this summer of 1898 was the mud. The town had been built with no thought for anything other than access to the gold fields. Inconveniences, such as being located on a flood plain on the flats where the rivers jammed during spring break-up, were inconsequential in light of the town's desperate need to be close to the Creeks, where lumps of gold waited to be found. Waiting, as some would say, to be plucked like potatoes in a well-tilled Ontario field, or apples hanging low in a New England orchard.

As long as there were men gullible enough to believe that, there would be women like me, happy to provide them with a bit of comfort when they realized all their dreams had come to naught.

I exchanged polite greetings with a good number of the men I passed on the street. I didn't know most of them from Adam, but they knew me and that I kept "the finest, most modern establishment in London, England, transported all the way to Dawson." My son, Angus, had recently come up with that slogan.

At the intersection of Front and York Streets, close to the mud flats and the swift-moving Yukon River, the most miserable of donkeys struggled to get the back wheels of a cart through the mud and up and over the duckboard laid across the street. The red-faced driver waved his whip about and screamed with so much vigour that I hoped, for the donkey's sake, he'd drop dead with apoplexy.

"Allow me to assist you, Fiona." A hand touched my elbow. It was my friend, Graham Donohue.

"I am perfectly capable of crossing the street."

"I know you are. But imagine the prestige I'll enjoy for a day if I'm seen escorting home the raven-haired beauty of the Klondike." Our admiration was completely mutual. If I was (to heck with modesty—no *if* required) the most beautiful woman in the Territory, Graham was probably the most handsome man. A woman could easily drown in his dark eyes, with only the thick black lashes to hold her up. His face was thin, the cheekbones sharp underneath perfect skin. He laughed a great deal, as he did now, showing off straight white teeth. He was a bit on the small side, but I intensely dislike men who loom over me. I do not care to feel physically vulnerable.

I allowed Graham to take my arm. "Then you may assist me."

The donkey cart driver was almost foaming at the mouth, but the poor beast at last managed to drag the cart over the duck board and plodded away down the street.

"Boor," I sniffed.

"Anyone interesting been in the Savoy lately?" Graham asked.

I laughed. "So your gallantry is nothing but an ill-disguised attempt to extract the latest gossip?"

"You know I have no ulterior motives concerning you, Fee."

I ignored the comment because I knew Graham held feelings for me I was not prepared to reciprocate.

"However," he went on, "if you have some good gossip to share..."

Graham was a reporter for a big American newspaper,

always on the lookout for news.

"It's been a fairly uneventful week, as far as Dawson goes," I said. "Although we've been visited the last few nights by an interesting character."

"Yes?"

"A professional gambler, I would imagine. An American. Flashy dresser. Plenty of money, at least that I can see. He'll probably be back tonight. He seems rather fond of Irene."

"Irene. Aren't they all? You're lucky to have gotten that one, Fiona."

And I was. Irene—she pronounced her name in the French fashion *Irenee*, although she was as American as Graham—was, for this week at least, the most popular dance hall girl in Dawson.

We walked up York Street in companionable silence and soon arrived at Mrs. Mann's boarding house on Fourth Avenue. It was a most unimposing dwelling—built of wood harvested too early and thrown up too quickly—with only one storey and two windows on either side of the plain front door. But in a town where a canvas tent was all the accommodation many families could find, I was happy to live here. For now. I hadn't come to Dawson to live comfortably; the frantic days of the gold rush wouldn't last forever, and I intended to make my money and get out.

"Shall we see if Mrs. Mann has prepared enough supper for a guest, Graham? And then if you'd like a touch more prestige, you may escort me back to the Savoy." Opening the door and stepping into the front hall, I tossed him a seductive smile.

If Graham had owned a tail, he would have wagged it. But he was a man, so he bowed gallantly and said, "It would be my pleasure, Fiona."

I was surprised to see that Graham wasn't our only dinner guest. A small brown-skinned woman sat at the kitchen table, hugging a steaming mug of tea. Mr. Mann was sitting in his usual place at the head of the table, scowling mightily (as usual) while Angus ferried cutlery and plates, and Mrs. Mann stirred the contents of her heaviest cooking pot. Beef and boiled cabbage tonight, by the smell of it. I hate boiled cabbage—I hate cabbage no matter how it is prepared, but after coming through a winter of near starvation, I ate whatever was put on my plate.

Angus didn't look up when Graham and I came in. Instead he ducked his head as though he were trying to hide behind a lock of too-long blond hair. He was only twelve years old but growing into a man too quickly for my liking. He would be passing my height of five foot eight soon, and his lanky, huggable frame would turn hard and firm.

This was a tough town for a boy without a father to learn how to be a good man.

As I plucked a pin out of my hat prior to taking it off, I realized the woman was wearing my dressing gown, my favourite one, made in the Chinese style of brilliant crimson silk with an elaborately embroidered gold dragon streaking across the back. I had bought it in Vancouver and carried it all the way over the Chilkoot Pass in order to have a touch of luxury for my private enjoyment only.

"What the…" I said, my hat half off my head.

"I brought her here, Ma," Angus said.

"Why, it's Indian Mary," Graham said.

"Not proper," Mr. Mann said.

"More tea, you poor dear?" Mrs. Mann said.

"Angus," I said, "what is going on here?"

"Are you all right, Mary?" Graham asked.

"Yes, Mr. Graham," the Indian woman mumbled into her mug. She hadn't looked at me.

"You know this lady?" I said, tossing my hat onto the wooden plank that served as a sideboard.

"I can explain," Graham said.

"I can explain," Angus said.

"Then explain," I said.

Mrs. Mann snatched up the hat, tsk-tsking heartily. It was a plain straw affair, suitable for daytime, saved from total ugliness by a wide satin ribbon of startling midnight blue. "Don't leave your hat there, Mrs. MacGillivray. It'll get kitchen grease on it. Angus, take your mother's hat to her room." She shoved the offending headpiece into my son's arms.

Angus blinked in surprise but took the hat.

Mary got up, not making a sound. Much too long for her, my dressing gown fell in a silken red puddle around her feet. "I'll leave. Thank you for your hospitality, young Mr. Angus, Missus."

"Oh, for heaven's sake. Sit down and finish your tea." I waved my hand. "Graham, tell your friend she needn't leave on my account. Angus, put that hat in my cupboard."

"Is not proper," Mr. Mann repeated.

"Why the poor thing was half drowned," Mrs. Mann said. She ladled up a big bowl of beef and cabbage. "You eat this, my girl. My mother always said there's nothing like a hot dinner to put a man—or a woman—to rights."

"Helga," Mr. Mann said, his thick German accent falling heavily on the single word.

"Will Mr. Donohue be having supper?" Mrs. Mann asked, the ladling spoon held high in her hand. "We can probably stretch the meal to accommodate another. With enough bread."

"No. Thank you, Mrs. Mann, but I've remembered an appointment. Most important, must dash. Perhaps I'll stop by the Savoy later, Fee." He tipped his hat to Mrs. Mann and disappeared with unseemly haste out the back, the door to the yard slamming shut behind him. How odd.

Angus said, "Mary fell into the river, and I happened by and helped her out. She couldn't go home so wet, so I brought her here to get dry. Mrs. Mann hung her dress on the line, so I gave her your robe to wear while she warmed up." He stopped talking and looked at me. "Please, Mother."

"I'll be leaving. I don't want to cause any trouble," Mary said. A healthy helping of defiance filled her black gaze; defiance with a generous amount of contempt and perhaps a touch of fear lurking beneath. I remembered what it felt like, hating someone who, for no reason but a circumstance of birth, had power over you.

"Fell in the river, did you? Must have been dreadfully cold. That cabbage smells heavenly, Mrs. Mann. I've always loved cabbage. I am simply starved. Let me wash my hands, then you can tell me something about yourself over dinner. Mary, is it? I should be able to find a housedress you can wrap a belt around a few times to make reasonably respectable. It will do in a pinch. Angus, why is your hair wet?"

*   *   *

Angus MacGillivray instinctively touched his hand to his head. His hair didn't feel wet. He patted down a slick at the back and avoided his mother's questioning eyes.

He glanced at Mary, who was pulling the long sleeves of the dressing gown back to reach for a spoon.

Angus had found Mary in the river.

Someone said they'd seen a bear a couple of miles outside town, fishing in the river. Angus and his friends, Ron and Dave, were hoping to get a look at it. They'd been trying to walk carefully, without making any noise, but Dave could never stop complaining for long. He was telling them that that his father said the bear was dangerous and should be shot before it got closer to town. Guns weren't allowed in Dawson: Dave's father had a lot to say about that also.

Angus had been out in front, tired of Dave's whiny voice. He came to a stop so quickly the other boys bumped into him. "Shush," he warned.

Something was in the river. Not big enough to be a bear. A dog perhaps, or a wolf—that would be almost as good as a bear.

Tendrils of long dark hair moved across the top of the brown water. A head bobbed to the surface, a wave washed over it, and when the wave passed, the head was gone.

The three boys ran to the bank. "A woman, I think it's a woman," Angus said.

They'd been warned that this spot got very deep, very fast. Without stopping to think, Angus MacGillivray jumped into the swollen river.

It was late June, after an exceptionally hot spring, but this was the Yukon River. The shock of the cold took his breath away. His boots, which he hadn't thought to remove, pulled at his legs, trying to drag him under. The water was over his head. But he was young and well-fed and a good, strong swimmer, and she was only a few yards away. In seconds he reached the churning water where the woman had been. Her skirts billowed up behind her, and she was easy for his reaching arms to locate. He hauled her to the surface and set off in a one-armed crawl back to shore. She was small. Even waterlogged, she felt like a doll in his arms. She fought him and cried out for him to let her go.

When they reached shore, Ron and Dave grabbed the woman by the arms and dragged her out of the water. Angus crawled onto the bank and collapsed onto his back, gasping for air.

While the woman retched up a goodly portion of the Yukon River, Angus struggled to his knees and crawled over to her. She was lying on her stomach where the boys had placed her. Ron and Dave sat on their haunches, wide-eyed, as unsure of what to do now as Angus. He touched her back lightly.

She groaned and rolled over. "You stupid boy." Her flat nose and dark eyes were red, and her breathing was laboured. "Why did you do that? I'm not worth you risking your life." She began to cry.

The boys watched her. Eventually she struggled to her knees, then to her feet, and without another look at her rescuers, took a wobbly step toward the river.

"No!" Angus jumped up. "Nothing is as bad as that."

She looked over her shoulder, naked pain in her eyes. "What do you think you know about life, child?"

"I know I don't want to go swimming again," he said. "The water's cold."

Ron and Dave watched through wide eyes, saying nothing.

The edges of the woman's generous mouth turned up slightly. "Then not today. Not here. But there are other days, other places. And you won't be there, young boy." Her English was almost perfect, but a bit too stiff, too formal, as if she had been taught it in school, not in life. She touched the cheap cross hanging from a chain around her neck.

"Look," Angus said, "you're soaking wet; it's getting late. Why don't you come home with me? My ma'll have something you can...put on." He almost said "wear", but his mother was so much larger than this slight figure, nothing she owned could possibly fit. "Until your clothes dry, I mean."

Her dark eyes travelled down his long, thin body. "You must be older than you look. You think I'm going to pay you in return for my life?" She raised her eyes to look directly at him.

Ron tittered, and after looking confused for a moment, Dave let out a bark of an embarrassed laugh. Angus flushed. The boys had been running unsupervised on the streets of Dawson long enough to know exactly what she meant.

"I don't want you to die of chill, that's all. My ma will be home soon, and if she isn't, Mrs. Mann, our landlady, will be there."

"Angus," Ron said in whisper, "let's go. It ain't none of our business what she does."

Angus half-turned away from the woman and tried to keep his voice down. "She might try it again if we walk away and leave her here."

"You can't take her home, for God's sake!" Dave said, not bothering to whisper. "Your ma'll tan your hide if you let her put a foot in the house."

"Why would she do that?" said Angus, whose mother had never so much as paddled his diaper, never mind tanned his hide.

"She's an Indian, you idiot. You can't invite a squaw into a white woman's house."

"Indian?" Angus asked, feeling like a fool. When they'd come over the Chilkoot Pass last year, his mother had hired Indian packers to carry their goods. He'd seen a few women working as packers, but only from a distance. They'd all been heavy-set, muscular, bundled up in clothes suitable for the high mountain passes. This woman was tiny, frail almost, but the dark complexion, black hair, and flat cheekbones should have told him. Would it have made a difference if he'd known it was an Indian woman throwing herself into the cold Yukon?

He turned to face her. She had begun to slowly pick her way back towards town, dragging sodden skirts behind her, shivering with cold in her light blouse.

"Wait," he shouted, running after her and catching her by the arm. "You can still come with me, at least long enough to get dry and warmed up. Our landlady always has lots for dinner, to make our lunches the next day, so she'll have enough to set an extra place."

She turned and smiled up at him. She had a nice smile, he thought, kind. And sad. Her face was wet, river water mingling with her tears. "You're a nice boy." She touched his cheek with one small brown hand. "You go home to your nice mother. She doesn't need any trouble."

"It's no trouble."

"If you take me in, you'll get a great deal of trouble from Mrs. LeBlanc."

"Angus," Dave called. "The squaw can look after herself. All that talk about supper's makin' me hungry. You comin'?"

Angus ignored his friends. "Mrs. LeBlanc? You mean Joey LeBlanc? Nothing my ma'd like more than to set Joey LeBlanc straight." He held out his hand. "I'm Angus MacGillivray."

She didn't accept his hand. "White people call me Mary."

Chapter Two

Mary didn't speak a word over dinner; she stared into her plate and moved the food around. Mr. Mann huffed a bit and maintained his scowl, but he never had much to say to me at the best of times, so I ignored him. Mrs. Mann, on the other hand, seemed to love having a distressed guest and encouraged Mary to eat up. She declined politely. She looked seriously underfed to me, but I suppose near-drowning has a negative effect on one's appetite. Angus spent the meal watching Mary, while trying not to appear to be doing so, and looking quite pleased with himself. I suspected there was a good deal more to the day's events than her slipping daintily into the river and my son offering her a gallant hand up, but I said no more about it. I would get the full story soon enough.

"That was a wonderful supper, Mrs. Mann," I said at last. I rarely lie, but sometimes it is indeed the lesser of two evils. "Come with me, Mary. I have to be getting back to work, but first I'll find a dress you can borrow."

Head still down, after a mumbled thanks to Mrs. Mann, Mary followed me into my bedroom. Angus and I rent three small rooms in the Mann's home. My bedroom faces the street with a tiny sitting room between me and the kitchen. Angus is across the hall. I've lived in back alleys of Silver Dials and in the townhouses of Belgravia, so I can say in all honesty that I'm not terribly particular. Mrs. Mann keeps a spotlessly clean house and, having no children of her own, has become very fond of Angus. Mr. Mann tries hard not to approve of me, but during a recent crisis he came perilously close to showing some degree of emotion over my fate. His wife's English is much, much better than his, which has somewhat shifted the centre of power in their home. Much to his dismay, I am sure.

I rustled through my closet looking for a plain housedress. I manage not to own many garments fitting that description. "There, this should do." I produced a cotton print day dress and a plain shift. "As it is probably about six inches too long, you can use this belt to hold the whole thing up and in. Don't be shy. Try these on. You can't go home in my dressing gown."

Mary tossed me a look, but I made no move to turn away. She snatched the clothes out of my hands and half turned her back. She tried to wriggle out of the dressing gown while at the same time pulling the shift over her head. She couldn't keep herself wholly hidden, and I wasn't terribly surprised to see a row of fresh red welts criss-crossing the knobbly spine at her lower back and the tops of her thin buttocks.

I looked out the window into the scrap of back garden where Mrs. Mann hangs the laundry she takes in. Working men's shirts and trousers flapped in the breeze beside a cheap red dress, torn petticoats, and a set of bloomers, all of which had seen better days.

"You don't have to stay with him," I said to the window. "In Canada you have some rights, particularly if you aren't married. The law can help you."

"What do you know, rich white lady?"

Mary looked like a child playing dress-up in my cheapest dress, far too big for her, the belt holding the excess fabric.

"I'm not rich. I've had a man's hand raised to me. I vowed it would never happen again, and it hasn't. I can guess why my son came across you in the river, and I will help you, if only because of him."

"Your son." She gave the belt a strong tug. "A good boy."

"You can have our help, if you want it. Or you can leave now and return tomorrow to collect your clothes. I doubt they will fit me."

She fingered the edges of the belt. "Rich white lady,

there is no help you and your nice son can give me. I thank you for your kindness, but I don't want you to have trouble on my account. My troubles are not for you."

"I have some influence in this town." I turned my back and made an effort to straighten the contents of my closet in order to give Mary a bit of privacy. She seemed like a proud woman; it wouldn't be easy for her to accept my charity. Though why it would be harder than crawling back to an abusive man, I didn't understand. I've taken charity when I had to—and been darn happy to have it. "I can make your man sorry for what he's done."

She threw back her head and laughed a cold, bitter laugh. "I belong to no man, rich white lady. Mrs. LeBlanc, she is not afraid of you, I am sure."

I sucked in my breath and turned to face her. "Joey LeBlanc. You…work for her?"

Her head dropped as her shame won out over her pride. "I'll return your dress tomorrow, Mrs. MacGillivray."

"Bugger the dress." I sat on my bed and patted the counterpane beside me. The window had been left open to let in a bit of air, and, as usual, a thin sheen of sawdust covered everything. The cursed sawmills in this town never stopped working. "Sit," I commanded.

Mary sat, back stiff and head bent.

"You work for Mrs. LeBlanc, do you? If my son hauled you out of the river, I suspect you're not happy in your employment. Is that correct?"

The last piece of her pride crumbled. She lifted her hands to cover her face, her thin shoulders shook, and dry sobs racked her flat chest as she began to talk. "Mrs. LeBlanc owns me. There are some men who like Indian women, she says. So they have to pay well. But not many such men, so she says I am not making them happy."

I stroked her luxurious black hair—unbound, it fell almost to her waist—and peeked at the watch hanging on a gold chain from my belt. It was well after seven—long past time I should be back at the Savoy. And I hadn't yet dressed for the evening. The stage show began at eight, and, as supervision of the dancers was my responsibility, I needed to be there to make sure they all showed up—on time and reasonably sober.

Once she started to talk, Mary was like the spring break-up of the Yukon River. Nothing could stop her. The gist of it was that she was from Alaska and believed herself to have been sold to one Mr. Smith, a man heading for the Yukon, in payment for some nebulous debt owed by the uncle of her widowed late mother. Mr. Smith had tired of her, and on arriving in the Yukon, he'd passed her on to the infamous madam, Joey LeBlanc. She was honour-bound, Mary told me, to stay with Joey in order to see the original debt paid in full. But the shame was so great that it had eventually taken her to the banks of the Yukon River and the timely intervention of my son. Even now she wanted only to return to the solace of the river, even though the fathers had taught her at school that to take one's own life was the darkest of sins. Through her tears she asked that neither Angus nor I interfere with her again.

I took a deep breath and lifted her chin with two fingers. "You don't have to go back to Mrs. LeBlanc if you don't want to, Mary."

Her dark eyes searched my face. "But my uncle's debt? There is no one else to repay it. I belong to Mrs. LeBlanc. If I don't complete my time, she will tell Mr. Smith, who will return to extract payment from my uncle."

"Your uncle can pay his own debt. Or not. As he wishes. If they told you you're bound to Mrs. LeBlanc, they lied. I know this. I have friends in the Mounties. You know the Redcoats?"

"Don't condescend to me, Mrs. MacGillivray."

I stood up and began unbuttoning the bodice of my day dress. "I mean no insult, Mary. Your English is perfect, your manners beyond reproach. But if people have told you wrong for their own selfish gain, I am not condescending to you if I attempt to set you straight." I opened my wardrobe and peered in. The wooden cabinet, missing one set of hinges, which housed my entire ensemble, was substantially smaller than what in times past would have stored my shoes or undergarments. I didn't often miss what I'd left behind, but sometimes... I ran my fingers through my gowns, hoping something forgotten yet perfectly lovely would be waiting to be found.

"What do you think I should wear tonight? The green satin is the nicest, but I've worn that rather a lot lately." My best dress, a genuine Worth, presented to me in London at the original Savoy Hotel, guarded across seas and continents, carried over the Chilkoot Pass, had recently died an ignominious death. Mrs. Mann was still attempting to salvage something of the crimson silk, the ostrich feathers, and the Belgian lace. Nothing, I feared, would ever replace that gown.

"Everything you have is lovely, Mrs. MacGillivray," she said in her soft voice. I knew she was talking about more than my clothes.

I looked at the garments in question and pulled out the green satin. "What I'm attempting to say, Mary, is that if you think you belong to Mrs. LeBlanc because of someone else's arrangements, then you've been deceived. For heaven's sake, it's 1898, and this is Canada. I'll contact my friend in the Mounties, and he will ensure you don't have to return to the likes of Mrs. LeBlanc."

"Even an Indian woman has to eat," Mary said, picking at loose threads in the counterpane.

I dressed quickly, draped a length of fake pearls around my neck, arranged my hair, settled a hat onto my head, thrust several hatpins through it, and regarded myself in the cracked mirror on the wall. I do not succumb to false modesty: if I wasn't the most spectacular woman in Dawson tonight, I would...what would I do? I would eat the hat on my head.

I turned to face Mary. "I have decided. Mrs. Mann has only recently begun this foolish enterprise of running a laundry. She complains non-stop about the amount of work, combined with keeping Mr. Mann looked after and caring for this boarding house, although Angus and I are the only residents. She's been trying to find an assistant, but willing women are scarce on the ground. You will take employment beginning tomorrow as helper to Mrs. Mann in the laundry. Now I must be off." I slipped pearl earrings through my ears and patted a touch of rouge on my cheeks.

Mary stared at me. "Mrs. LeBlanc…" she said.

"If Mrs. LeBlanc has a concern about these arrangements, then she may speak to me. Do you think these earrings match? Perhaps the gold ones would be best?"

"The pearls," Mary said.

"I agree. Let's tell Mrs. Mann of our arrangement."

Mary cracked a small smile. It went a long way towards putting some life into her pinched face. "I'd like that," she said.

I'd had a few encounters with Joey LeBlanc, and none of them had been pleasant. Prostitution was technically illegal in the Yukon. Then again, so was gambling, yet the Savoy operated an extremely lucrative casino. But Dawson was a town full of prospectors from every corner of the world, so the police, wisely in my opinion, decided to let vice have its way as long as they could control real crime. Joey ran a stable of prostitutes, mostly operating out of the cribs of Paradise Alley, along with a handful that were a touch more respectable. The Mounties turned a blind eye: after all, women were as eager to enjoy the residue of a prospector's dreams as was anyone else. But slavery, indentured servitude, whatever it was called these days, Her Majesty's North-West Mounted Police would not approve of that one little bit.

I don't know why I liked Mary so much almost immediately upon meeting her. I'd hired Indian packers to take us over the Chilkoot. They had been, by and large, efficient and taciturn. They kept a respectful distance from me, although on the trail and around the campfire Angus had hounded them for stories from their tribal history and information about their customs. Our packers were Tagish, he'd told me. I had no idea if Mary was of that tribe or another. Other than working as packers and the occasional guide, the Indians kept pretty much to themselves in the

Yukon. They weren't allowed in the bars and dance halls, and there were so many white (and some black) men looking for work in Dawson there was no need to hire Indians. Mary was the first Native I'd seen in town.

How lonely she must be. And caught in the talons of Joey LeBlanc to boot.

Everyone looked up as I came back into the kitchen. Mary followed, dragging the overlarge dress behind her like a bridal train.

"Angus," I said, "I have to be at the Savoy. Go with Mary and find Constable Sterling. Ask him to accompany you to get Mary's belongings from her place of…residence."

"We don't need…" Angus began.

"Yes, you do. Don't go there without a Mountie. There might be some opposition to her leaving, and I want this entirely above board. Then take her to one of the empty rooms at the Savoy. I don't think we have anyone in residence today. Use the back stairs."

Occasionally some of the bartenders or croupiers who are temporarily short of accommodation are permitted to sleep in the upstairs rooms beside the offices. Good customers, who collapse over the bar or fall asleep over their cards, we put up in a cot in the big room at the end of the hall. Poor customers, and certainly those who are winning, we toss out into the mud of Front Street.

"I have no money," Mary said.

I waved a hand. "You can pay your rent out of your wages. Mrs. Mann, I have found you a helper for the laundry. I'm sure you can come to an agreement when she arrives for work first thing tomorrow morning."

"My friend owns a laundry," Mary said to no one in particular. "On Fifteenth Street. She works hard, but she makes good money."

What Mrs. Mann thought of this arrangement, it was impossible to tell. I was thrusting a complete unknown—not to mention an Indian—at her. But she simply said, "Be here at seven."

Mr. Mann stood up. He cleared his throat. I half expected

him to throw Mary out on her ear, and me after her for suggesting that such a woman come and work for his wife. For him it would be enough that she was an Indian— without even knowing her (former) occupation. "I go with Angus," he said. "Help carry."

I smiled at him. "Thank you, Mr. Mann."

He almost blushed and turned away.

My suggestion that Mary take employment in Mrs. Mann's laundry and residence in the Savoy wasn't entirely altruistic. I was rather delighted at the idea of having a confrontation with Joey LeBlanc, while knowing that the law was, for once, on my side.

I can be such an idiot sometimes.

Chapter Three

Constable Richard Sterling settled his broad-brimmed hat on his head, said goodbye to the corporal in charge of the Dawson town detachment and opened the door. A lanky blond boy, a tumble of too-long arms and legs, stood in front of him with his hand extended towards the latch.

Sterling grinned. "Angus, what brings you here? Looking for me?"

"Yes, sir. Well, we're looking for a Mountie, that is."

"We?" Sterling said, before noticing two people watching the exchange from the bottom of the steps. He nodded to the man. "Mr. Mann."

"My ma said we had to get a Mountie. Let's go."

"Hold up, Angus. Where are we going?" Sterling touched the brim of his hat. "I don't believe I've been introduced to this lady." Which was factually true, although he knew well enough that she worked out of a crib on Paradise Alley and handed her earnings over to Joey LeBlanc.

Seeing the recognition in his face, the woman lowered her eyes.

"Oh, right," Angus said. "This is Mary…uh…just Mary. My friend."

"Sterling," Mr. Mann said. "Weeze wasting time. Youze gos now." He made a sort of shooing gesture with his hands towards the woman, and she set off down the street with long determined strides that belied her short legs. She was wearing a dress far too large for her and made of considerably better fabric than most of the cloth one saw in Paradise Alley.

"What are you and Mr. Mann doing in the company of that woman, Angus, and where are we going?" Sterling asked as they fell into step behind the German man and the native woman.

"To get her things," Angus said. "She's moving into the Savoy."

"She's moving into the Savoy!" Sterling almost stopped in his tracks. Angus kept on walking, forcing Sterling to take a skipping step to keep up. "Does your mother know about this?"

"Of course. It was her idea."

"Of course. Do you know where this...Mary lives?"

"Second Avenue, I think."

"That's right. Angus, before we go any further, you'd better tell me what you're doing and why you need a police escort to do it."

They turned the corner, and Mary picked up her pace. She scurried through the street with her head down, looking at nothing but the ground in front of her feet. This part of Second Avenue was popularly known as Paradise Alley, for obvious reasons. Although Sterling's father, a stern, strict preacher who ruled his flock, and his family, like an old testament prophet expecting judgement any moment, would have had more than a few strong words to say about such blasphemy. The street was narrow, full of mud and debris, lined with two neat rows of nearly identical narrow wooden dwellings. These were the cribs, where women plied their trade, peak-roofed, wide enough for only one long thin window beside the door, their frontage not much more than a few feet wide. A few sported an awning over the door, presumably to keep the customers dry while they waited their turn. In the early evening there weren't many men around. A few women, with worn faces and tired bodies, tattered dresses and cheap jewellery, stood in their doorways or gathered together on the strip of boardwalk, exchanging gossip and watching the passing traffic. No one spoke to Mary as she marched down the middle of the street, mindless of several inches of her ill-fitting dress dragging through the mud and ignoring the men and boy following her.

She stopped in front of one of the shacks. "Here," she said. It was no better, and no worse, than any of the others.

Angus stepped forward, ready to go inside with her. She lifted a hand. "Please wait."

Sterling stood in the street with a scowling Mr. Mann and a red-faced Angus, feeling conspicuous in his red tunic, broad-brimmed hat, and high black boots. The women watched with expressionless eyes. The few customers on the street stayed well clear.

He could see them coming from a long way away. Two toughs with many-times broken noses, calloused hands, good clothes and a practiced swagger. As they approached, the women disappeared into their homes, slamming doors behind them as if a skunk were coming down the road with tail raised. A small woman in an unadorned brown housedress stood alone on the far side of the street, watching.

One of the men stopped several yards short of Sterling, and the other approached with a friendly smile that didn't touch the steel in his eyes. Sterling doubted the man had given anyone an honest smile since he ceased to be a toddler. "Help you, Constable?"

"No."

Mary came out of her home, clutching a cloth-wrapped bundle to her chest. Mr. Mann took the package then handed it to Angus. His arms hung loosely at his sides, but his body was as tense as wire on a range fence, and Sterling was glad the German would be on his side if worse came to worse.

"We're in no hurry. Get the rest of it, Mary," Angus said.

"There is no more."

"This is all you have?" He sounded as if he couldn't quite believe it. Considering he was the son of Fiona MacGillivray, Sterling had no doubt the boy truly didn't believe a woman could get by with so little.

Then Mary saw the two men. Her colour didn't change and her expression didn't waver, but Sterling saw the tension crawl into her neck and shoulders.

"Leaving?" the man asked in a voice as polite as his false smile.

"Yes," Sterling said.

The man took one step to stand in front of Mary. She stared at her feet. "Mrs. LeBlanc would like you to stay." Mary's eyes flicked towards the woman in the brown dress watching the exchange. "Go back inside, and there'll be no hard feelings."

"Mary doesn't want to stay," Angus said.

"Angus," Sterling said, "be quiet. Shall we go, Mary?"

The big man was solidly in her path. She took a tentative step to one side. Without appearing to move, he shifted slightly and blocked her. "Mrs. LeBlanc says you owe a month's rent on your cabin, Mary."

She looked up. Her eyes were dry and clear. "I don't have so much money."

"Then you can't leave."

"If there's a dispute about monies owning, tell Mrs. LeBlanc to take it to the magistrate," Sterling said. "Judge'll hear her case in due course. Angus, why don't you take Mary's arm. Mr. Mann can carry her things."

Mr. Mann grabbed the bundle, and Angus slipped his arm through Mary's with a shy smile. The little party started to move away, Sterling leading, followed by Angus and Mary, Mr. Mann and the bundle of meagre possessions bringing up the rear. The second tough slapped his fist rhythmically into the palm of his meaty hand. A small crowd had gathered at the end of the street. Curtains twitched in the windows of the nearby cribs.

"You got something you want to say?" Sterling asked. The slapping stopped. The tough looked at his partner.

"Mrs. LeBlanc believes that ladies can sort out their problems without going to court. She's asking you not to leave, Mary, until she's had a chance to talk to you. All nice and lady-like. Proper. If you still want to go, Mrs. LeBlanc'll probably let you out of paying what you owe her, and off you can go. Now don't that sound better than dealing with the redcoats and the white man's courts?"

Mary hesitated and looked up the street at the unsmiling woman standing alone. Sterling feared she was about to give in, to take her bundle from Mr. Mann, mumble goodbye to Angus, and return to her miserable dwelling and whatever despair had resulted in her wearing Fiona MacGillivray's cast-offs.

"I'd like to go with Angus," Mary said. Her voice was soft, but it didn't waver. She lifted her head and looked the man in the face. "Please, get out of our way, Mr. Black."

"You think your word will stand up in court against a white woman's, Mary? You're a fool."

"You're full of nonsense," Angus shouted. The boy had remained silent as long as he could. "Mary's word's as good as anyone's in a proper Canadian court. Isn't that right, Constable Sterling? And anyway," he continued without waiting for an answer (the honesty of which Sterling would have been reluctant to affirm), "if Mary owes Mrs. Leblanc some money, she can pay it out of her wages without living here."

"I don't want any trouble," Mary said.

"You're free to come and go as you like without worrying if it causes some folks trouble or not," Sterling said. "The North-West Mounted Police will see to that. Shall we go?"

"Yes, sir," she said. She lifted her head high and patted Angus's hand.

"You'll regret it, stupid squaw," Mr. Black said. His partner spat into the street, barely missing Mary's feet.

"Take Mary and Angus to the Savoy, Mr. Mann," Sterling said. "I want a word with Mrs. Leblanc. I'll make sure those two don't follow you."

Joey LeBlanc remained on the other side of the street as she watched Angus, Mary, and Mr. Mann disappear around the corner. A flicker of anger moved behind her small black eyes before she recovered her composure and extinguished it. Her face returned to its customary empty expression. It was rumoured in this town of a thousand rumours that there had once been a Mr. Leblanc, but Joey had knifed him in St. Louis for doing irreparable damage to a piece of merchandise belonging to the family business, so to speak. Sterling questioned the veracity of the story but not that Joey was perfectly capable of it. He crossed the street while keeping one eye on the two toughs, although neither of them seemed inclined to follow Mary or indeed to have any idea of what to do now, without their boss issuing an order.

"Lovely evening, Constable," Joey LeBlanc said, gathering her shawl around her shoulders

"It is, and I'm sure it'll stay that way, Mrs. Leblanc, quiet and peaceful."

"That chit of a squaw 'as humiliated me in front of my employees and my customers." Leblanc's accent held strong memory of Montreal French. She spoke in an even tone, as if they were discussing the weather. "I don't care for that."

"The North-West Mounted Police don't give a damn what you care for, Mrs. LeBlanc. As long as you keep it to yourself."

"Really, Constable, such language. But perhaps that is why a promising, but not-so-young, fellow such as yourself remains *only* a constable?"

The barb struck home, and Sterling could tell by the expression on the whore-mistress's face that she knew it had.

"You and your friends," he glanced at the two hired toughs, "are to leave Mary alone."

"*Mais, monsieur,* she owes me money." LeBlanc shrugged and held out her arms. "What is a poor widow to do to get justice?"

"Take it before a judge, madam. But if any harm comes to Mary, I'll know where to come looking."

"'arm Mary? Who would do such a thing? A damaged whore is no good to me. She'll return of 'er own free will, Monsieur Sterling. The world is a frightening place for a woman on 'er own."

"Perhaps," Sterling said. He walked away without bothering to say goodbye. In his wake the street returned to life; whores opened the doors of their cribs and men crept out from alleys and side streets.

*   *   *

It was well after eight when I arrived at the Savoy. Most of the dance halls in Dawson are open twenty-four hours a day, six days a week. Even in the early hours of the morning or in the middle of the night—or what passes for night this far north in late June—the croupiers are spinning the tables and dealing cards and calling out their magic words, the bartenders are pouring rivers of liquor, and the dance hall girls are kicking up their heels for a dollar a dance and selling champagne by the wagon load. But at eight o'clock in the evening, something special settles over town as the musicians and callers come out onto Front Street, set themselves on the boardwalk, or in the middle of the street, and announce with much fanfare that the show is about to begin.

Then they all troop back inside, hopefully followed by a crowd of eager cheechakos and sourdoughs, every one of them begging for the chance to spend their money.

Tonight the stage at the Savoy was presenting scenes from the plays of Mr. William Shakespeare, a goodly number of heart-wrenching songs specially designed to have the lonely miners weeping in their dust-encrusted handkerchiefs, and a rather poor vaudeville act, which would have to do until I could find something better. At midnight the stage show ended, the percentage girls stepped forward to dance, and the performers changed their stage costumes for evening wear. The dancing would go on until six a.m., at which time the girls would cash in their drink tokens and stagger home.

They were in the middle of the opening dance when I walked into the hall. I counted the girls in the row: all present and accounted for. They kicked up their heels and flashed their petticoats and the crowd roared in approval. Ellie stepped forward to begin her song. She was the oldest of my girls by far. Sometimes she struggled to keep up with the younger ones, particularly at the end of a long night. But the men liked her, and that was all that counted. Perhaps she reminded them of dead mothers and abandoned wives. She acted as a mother hen, looking out for the other girls, which relieved me of some of that chore.

I stood at the back, inches away from the wall—it would never do to lean—and watched. Ellie finished her song, gave a deep curtsy in exchange for thunderous applause, and the dancers trooped out again. I made a mental note to tell the second girl from the left to give her petticoats a good wash before stepping onto my stage again. Chloe was so bad tonight that only nimble movement on the part of the dancer next to her avoided several collisions. Drunk, I suspected. In my dance hall, as in all the others, the girls were expected to accept drinks from the customers once the dancing began, and more than a few would be quite tipsy by the end of the evening. But to show up drunk for the stage show? That was not at all acceptable. Chloe had always been a problem—a generally miserable, lazy, pasty-faced, skinny piece of flotsam who didn't have any apparent talents. She wasn't popular with the men, and I would have shown her the door long ago if she wasn't such good friends with Irene. Irene, stage name of *Lady Irenee*, liked having Chloe around, and as long as Irene was the men's favourite, I would keep her happy. I thought that Chloe served as a substitute for the fussy lapdog with ribbons in its fur theatrical women like to carry around. That wouldn't be too practical in Dawson: such a creature would disappear into the mud the first time its mistress set it down, if it avoided being eaten once the bigger dogs got a look at it.

Now that I was thinking about it, I realized there had been a chill between Irene and Chloe over the last few days. Perhaps they'd had a falling out. Maybe I could cut Chloe loose while Irene was angry with her.

Soon a hush settled over the room; the audience knew what was coming. It was time for Irene's first song. She slipped onto the stage hidden behind two enormous crimson fans carried by two crouching dancers, who looked rather silly doing so. Only her feet, clad in satin slippers, were visible, but as one, the men sighed with delight. The music of the five-piece orchestra rose to a crescendo, the crimson fans were swept to one side with a flourish, and Irene stood in centre stage, her face hidden behind a smaller version of the two fans. The men roared. The fan was lowered slowly, provocatively, and Irene peeked out. She was well into her thirties and somewhat stocky, but still pretty despite a face scarred by the effects of bitterly cold winds and a hard life. On stage and on the dance floor, she conveyed such a cheerful enthusiasm that all the men loved her. She was easily the most popular dance-hall girl in Dawson, which did wonders for my business.

Unfortunately, my business partner, Ray Walker, also loved Irene. Too much, I feared.

She flicked her fan back and forth across her face, and the men went wild.

"You know how to play with fire, Mrs. MacGillivray." Constable Richard Sterling moved so quietly, even in his heavy boots, I hadn't heard him come up beside me. Although I knew full well he only wanted to speak to me without everyone in the room hearing, I took an involuntary step back. At a good deal more than six feet with the bulk to match, Sterling always seemed to stand too close for comfort. He smelled of pipe smoke, boot polish and the mud of the streets.

"My son found you?"

"We settled the lady in a room overhead. Mrs. LeBlanc's gentlemen employee tried to talk Mary out of leaving. I suspect you'll find Mrs. LeBlanc on your doorstep tomorrow; she recognized Angus."

We have a rather awkward relationship, Constable Sterling and I. I am, of course, not attracted to him at all, but somehow early in the morning, which is when my mind struggles towards sleep, I find myself thinking about him more than might be considered reasonable, and when he stands near me, my heart skips a beat or two, before wisely settling back into a sensible rhythm.

"I don't waste my time worrying about Mrs. LeBlanc," I

said, concentrating on the activities on the stage, where the girls were flittering about behind Irene. Definitely time to get rid of Chloe—she tripped and barely avoided a collision with Ellie, who tossed her a filthy look. "You realize the situation the poor girl finds herself in?"

"Not that she said a single word to me, or even looked me in the eye. Angus didn't understand why they needed a police escort. I sent him home, by the way."

"Thank you. I have offered her my protection, for what it's worth."

"It's worth a good deal, Fiona." Sterling straightened his perfectly straight wide-brimmed hat in a gesture I recognized as meaning he was about to take his leave. "If removed, it would be much worse than never given. Good night."

He took a step towards the door, hesitated and turned back. "That is a striking dress. Most becoming. Excuse me." And he was pushing his way through the crowd.

If I were an imaginative woman, I might believe that the proper Constable Sterling had actually blushed.

Chapter Four

At closing time, the girls trooped upstairs to my office to be paid for the drinks they'd convinced their "dance partners" to purchase. The bartenders gave them a small disk to mark every drink sold, and the girls stuffed the disks into the tops of their stockings. By the end of a good night, the legs of some of the most popular girls resembled baby elephants'. Chloe brought up the back of the line. As usual, her night's takings were as slim as her talent.

Shortly after four o'clock, Irene had slipped outside for a bit of fresh air. I followed her and told her I was disappointed with Chloe's performance that evening. I suggested Irene have a friendly word with her. Irene told me, biting off every word, that she would never again have a "friendly word" with Chloe.

Oh, goodie, I thought.

Outside my office window, Dawson was warming up to the day's commerce. Men shouted, women chattered, horses and donkeys stepped through the ever-present mud, and loaded carts rattled down the street. The loud whistle of a steamboat announced its arrival. Ever since break-up in May, the waterfront had been clogged with boats beyond count, everything from luxury steamboats to muscle-powered rafts made out of green wood, pulling into the makeshift harbour on the mud flats. All were full to bursting with men and women in pursuit of a dream that would more often than not bring nothing but frustration and disappointment. A steady stream of people was already leaving the Yukon, their dreams shattered by the reality of life in a northern mining town thrown up out of trees, mud and muskeg, and mines that were staked and claimed before word of the strike reached the outside.

Chloe placed a handful of disks on my desk.

I pulled a thin envelope out of my drawer.

She peered at me through red-streaked eyes and a badly cut fringe of greasy brown hair.

"I'm sorry, Chloe, but you are dismissed." I held out the envelope. "You were drunk when you got on stage. If I'd been here when you arrived, I wouldn't have let you get that far. These are your wages, and I'll count out the money owing for your disks."

"What?" she asked, blinking as if trying to make out my face through a fog.

"I said you are dismissed."

"You can't fire me. Ma'am."

The girls who were on their way out the door, or who had remained behind to chat for a few moments, stopped dead. You could almost hear the ears pricking up.

"Sobriety is a condition of your employment, which was explained to you."

"I need this job."

"You should have thought of that before taking a drink. Good day."

"Please, ma'am. Gi'me another chance. I've the toothache, you see. I needed a sip to dull the pain. That's all." She rubbed the side of her face with her fingers.

The girls were watching me. A few more drifted back down the hall and stood outside the door listening, Irene among them. I shoved the envelope towards Chloe again. "Your employment is terminated. Please leave."

She snatched the money out of my hand. Her eyes narrowed, and her mouth drew into a flat line. Most unattractive. She spat at my outstretched hand. My reflexes are still good, and I managed to pull back in time. The onlookers gasped.

Chloe clutched her pay envelope to her chest. "They say you're the hardest woman in the Yukon. Nothing but a black-hearted bitch under that fake Lady-Muck-Muck accent."

"I've been called worse by better people than you." I gathered up the remaining coins as if to slip them into the drawer where I kept a good solid billy club. "It would be better if I don't have to call Mr. Walker to have you thrown out."

"Bitch," she repeated. She turned and walked away. The dancers parted and watched her pass.

The blob of spittle was beginning to sink into my desk blotter. I scooped it up with my handkerchief and dropped the mess into the waste basket. The silent crowd of watching girls scattered at a look from me.

"I can assure you there is nothing at all fake about my Lady-Muck-Muck accent," I said to no one in particular.

Ray came into my office lugging a bag brimming with our take for the evening. I was happy to see that he was struggling with the weight. Like every business in Dawson, we accepted gold dust as legal currency. "Trouble?" he growled as the last of the girls slipped away.

"No," I said as he dropped the bag in the desk drawer, which he'd reinforced with a cage of steel bars. I'd never lived in a more law-abiding town, but we didn't take any chances. I locked the drawer and slipped the key into my reticule. Time to go home and sleep. I'd do the books and banking later.

"Young Murray might work out as head bartender," Ray said, standing back while I locked the office door.

"I hope so. That'll take some of the pressure off you." Our previous head bartender had left town abruptly. We needed a new man to put in charge, but Ray was having trouble finding someone he could trust with not only the earnings but also the liquor.

The male employees, the bartenders and croupiers, were Ray's responsibility. I managed the percentage girls—who came in at midnight when the stage show ended to dance with the men—and the performers. I also kept the books.

Mary came out of her room as we walked down the hall. Her black eyes glanced down to avoid looking at Ray.

"Good morning, Mary," I said. "I won't ask how you

slept, as I'm sure the racket kept you up all night. I hope you were comfortable."

"I slept fine, Mrs. MacGillivray," she whispered. "I can ignore the noise."

"A useful talent. Mary, this is Mr. Walker, my business partner. Ray, Mary is beginning employment in Mrs. Mann's laundry today, and I offered her a room until she finds something more permanent. And a good deal quieter."

"Pleased to meet ye, Mary," Ray said, with a surprised look at me.

Mary blinked.

"He said he's pleased to meet you," I told her. Ray hailed from the teeming tenements and shipyards of Glasgow, and his accent could be almost indecipherable to the uninitiated. He was a tough little Scotsman with a nose mashed flat enough to spread out in several different directions and a mouthful of broken or rotting teeth. He stood barely five foot six and didn't carry an ounce of perceptible fat or muscle on him—the visible heritage of a hard Glaswegian childhood.

"If you're ready, I'll walk with you to Mrs. Mann's, Mary. You can get something for breakfast there."

"I have no money," she said.

"I'm sure your meals will be included as part of your wages."

The downstairs rooms were empty, save for Irene sitting primly at a big round table by the far wall under a not-very-prim portrait of a lush nude with somewhat unrealistic bosoms. It would never hang in the National Portrait Gallery, but the customers liked it. She—Irene, not the painted nude—stood up as we approached.

I looked from her to Ray and raised one eyebrow. He blushed. "I've invited Irene for a wee breakfast, Fiona. Do ye want ta join us?"

I almost said "yes" just to see the expression on his face. I resisted the temptation.

Irene looked Mary up and down and turned up her nose. "Heard you had trouble upstairs, Mrs. MacGillivray," she said with an unnecessary amount of relish.

"It was nothing I can't handle. Enjoy your breakfast. Come, Mary, mustn't keep Mrs. Mann waiting."

I was half-afraid a bitter Chloe would be waiting for me outside. But fortunately—for her—she had taken her leave. I doubted I'd see her again. There were plenty of dance halls in Dawson, and she'd find employment in another one soon enough. If she kept on drinking, which it was almost certain she would, she would be fired from each one, gradually descending the ladder of what passes for respectability in the Dawson demi-monde, forgetting about me as new resentments crowded in.

The fancy gambler I'd been telling Graham about earlier was standing outside our front door. He was dressed in a crisp suit, diamond stick pin too large to be real, cravat as white as snow on the Ogilvie Mountains in February. His dark hair was slicked back with oil, and the ends of his heavily-waxed handlebar moustache pointed towards the sky. I gave him a second look and could see the signs of genteel wear: ground-in dirt on the edges of his white cuffs, a line of stitches holding together the knee of his right trouser leg, the strain around the waist as an ill-fitting shirt tried to stretch over his sizeable belly.

He'd had a good night in our gambling hall, bent over a hand of cards at the poker table, not pausing to watch the stage snow or joining in the dancing. All for the good— he'd be more than eager to return.

He tipped his hat to me. "Good morning, madam. May I compliment you on the quality of your establishment?" American. Very Boston Brahman. He spoke to me but watched Irene out of the corner of his small, dark eyes.

"You certainly may," I replied. "We're closing temporarily, but I hope you'll do us the honour of a return visit this evening."

"It would be my pleasure. Allow me to introduce myself. Tom Jannis, late of Boston, Massachusetts."

"Mr. Jannis." I stepped around him, my hand on Mary's arm.

"Lady Irenee," he said. "If you would allow me a small

indulgence, I'd like to offer you a small breakfast."

Ray growled. I kept walking: let them sort it out.

"Thank you for the offer, sir," Irene said, in a simpering voice, "but I'm having breakfast with my boss, Mr. Walker here."

"Some other time perhaps," Jannis said.

I didn't hear any more. Ray would not be pleased at being identified as Irene's boss, as if breakfast with him were an obligation.

Poor Ray. I suspected Irene had a secret lover. Almost certainly a married man, as she kept him so much under wraps that she'd been prepared to go to jail rather than use him as her alibi when she'd recently come under suspicion of a particularly heinous crime.

Ray continued to live in hope.

Don't we all?

*   *   *

Angus MacGillivray hated working at the hardware store. His mother had insisted that he spend every morning, six days a week, helping out in Mr. Mann's shop. The waterfront consisted of a sea of stores operated out of filthy canvas tents thrown up as soon as the spring floodwaters receded. They called the instant road Bowery Street. The floodplain beside the Yukon River was prime retail territory, catering to men who staggered off the boats, took one look at the town they'd given their all to reach and sold everything they owned at pennies on the dollar to raise enough money for the return journey south. Mr. Mann did a roaring trade buying hardware, mining equipment and personal items cheap before turning around and selling them at a handsome profit to men who'd come prospecting but somehow neglected to equip themselves with the proper equipment. The whisper of gold seduced a lot of foolish people, Angus's mother had told him, and there was no shame in taking advantage of their stupidity—as long as one remained within the boundaries of the law and common decency. Angus was only twelve years old, but he'd sometimes wondered about his mother's definition of legality. He had a clear memory of being roused out of his warm, comfortable bed in the dormitory of his exclusive boys' school in the early hours and bustled through ice-covered streets to catch the next train leaving Toronto's Union Station. Somewhere in the back of his mind, he thought he could remember England and making an equally rapid departure from his beloved nanny and their London townhouse for the ship that took them to Canada.

Right now he wished he could make a rapid departure from Mr. Mann's store. A huge mountain of a man had dumped a donkey cart full of crates at the entrance. He and Mr. Mann had negotiated a price, money was exchanged, and the man left. It was Angus's job to lug the crates into the side tent and unpack everything for Mr. Mann's inspection.

He'd rather be at school, but there wasn't a school in Dawson, although his mother hoped someone would open one soon. Over the winter, when everything moved slowly because no one had much of anything to eat and nothing much to do, his mother had attempted to teach him herself. She could speak a schoolgirl sort of French and Italian, could read classical Greek and Latin, and could paint amateurish watercolours and embroider a beautiful lace handkerchief. She could also play a simple tune on a piano. She knew nothing of mathematics, or science, or even geography. In short, she could teach Angus almost none of what he wanted to know.

Most of all, Angus MacGillivray wanted to be a Mountie some day. Mounties were not required to embroider or to translate the *Iliad* from the original Greek.

He hefted a particularly heavy crate and grinned at the sudden image of the police calling upon the only man they could think of, one Angus MacGillivray, to decipher a clue hidden in the writings of Virgil or of Homer.

"Yous a good boy, good worker," Mr. Mann said from behind the wooden counter, mistaking the smile of a boy's daydreams for enjoyment of his work.

Mr. Mann's shop was so profitable that he owned two tents. The smaller one had an awning stretched between two poles driven into the mud on either side of a low wooden table where the best merchandise was displayed. Other goods were piled in the back of the tent, where the customers could see them and beckon to Mr. Mann or Angus to pull them out for a closer look. The larger tent, off to one side, mostly contained goods in great quantity— yesterday there had been case upon case of canned beef, all of it sold by this morning—and stuff waiting to be examined by Mr. Mann's bargain-hunting eye.

As Angus came out of the back tent for yet another crate, two ladies stepped hesitantly up to the wooden counter. A mother and daughter, he guessed. The younger one looked as if she hadn't had the sun touch her face in her lifetime. He knew a pale complexion was supposedly a sign of good breeding and great beauty, but as his mother was as dark, with black hair and black eyes, as he, Angus, was fair, he never associated paleness with beauty. This woman was as scrawny as a scarecrow on the cornfields back in Ontario, and her washed-out blue eyes flittered around the interior of the shabby shop like an exotic butterfly in a net trying to find its way to freedom. The overabundance of birds and feathers on her large hat had been tossed about by the wind so they now resembled a pair of crows building a nest. Her tiny, delicate shoes were caked with mud. Her dress was very fine, although Angus, who'd lived closer to a woman than most boys of his class ever would, recognized hasty stitches and mismatched patches on the sleeves and around the hem. But where the young one looked like she might blow away in a middling-strong wind, the older woman was bold and buxom, with a prominent nose that came to a sharp point. She was dressed in a travelling costume of practical tweed, a no-nonsense hat, and heavy boots.

"This looks quite the place, doesn't it, dear. How exciting; we're here at last! What an adventure that journey was. You, young man, we're in search of mining supplies and were told we could find them here."

Angus gaped. "Mining supplies, ma'am?"

The woman winked at him and dropped her voice to a theatrical whisper. "We're in search of people who are buying mining supplies. This looks like exactly the sort of place to locate them."

Mr. Mann had finished serving one customer, having sold an old sourdough a pair of almost-white longjohns, and bowed slightly. "Ladies, I help?"

"I am sure you can, sir." The woman's accent was middle-class English, and Angus imagined she might have been the sort of formidable governess his schoolmates told stories about. "I arrived in Dawson this very morning and am scouting out the town, as you might say. I am," she announced after a heavy pause, "a writer."

Unimpressed, Mr. Mann said, "Yous wanting to buys or sells?"

"My dear man, I want to observe. You go about your business," she flicked her fingers at him, "and pretend we are not here."

Mr. Mann shrugged and tucked the coin he'd received for the underwear into the cash box.

"Do you work here, young man?" the governess asked Angus.

He was somewhat ashamed to admit it but could think of no way to avoid the question. "Yes, ma'am."

She carried a large straw bag, and from its depths she whipped out a small notebook and the stub of a pencil. Angus took a step back. An outside reporter had caused his mother a good deal of trouble recently, and Angus knew things about his mother's friend, the American newspaperman Mr. Donohue, that he could never tell her. He was not in the frame of mind to be friendly to newsmen—or women for that matter.

"I am Miss Witherspoon, and this is my companion, Miss Forester. Your name is?"

"Angus, you left before Mrs. Mann finished the baking." Angus's mother bustled into the shop, looking like a pearl lost in a barnyard. She wore a light green day dress with a touch of lace the colour of sea froth circling the hem. Her straw hat was trimmed with matching ribbons, and sapphire teardrop earrings peeked out from beneath the brim.

She nodded to the two women. "Good morning. Don't let me interrupt your business, Angus. I'll put your treat here behind the counter, shall I? Mr. Mann, I've brought biscuits for you as well."

Mr. Mann grunted and tried not to look pleased.

"Are these real gold pans?" While the older woman had been introducing herself, her companion had been poking about the goods with an air of mild disinterest. She spoke for the first time as she pulled the top pan off the pile and turned it over. It was brand-new, never used, as shiny as the day it was made. It had been purchased by some low-level bank clerk, diary farmer, or unemployed labourer who hadn't the slightest idea what real gold prospecting involved. And once he arrived in Dawson, discovered he had no desire to find out.

"Indeed they are," Angus said, trying to look like a man of business and wishing his mother would leave. Constable Sterling's mother didn't follow him on his rounds.

"Did you bring these things all this way?" the lady asked. "It must have been quite a feat."

"Gee, Ma, uh, Mother, Miss Forester sounds exactly like you," Angus said. "The same accent, I mean. Maybe you're from the same town back in Scotland. Where did you grow up, Miss Forester? My mother is from Skye. That's an island."

Miss Forester looked up from the gold pans. Fiona was staring at her quite strangely. Miss Witherspoon glanced from one woman to the other.

"Forester?" Fiona said. "Euila?"

"That is my name. Do I know you, madam?"

"I think you might. I'm Mrs...Miss...Mac...I'm Fiona."

"Fiona." Miss Forester exhaled the word in a long sigh. "Fiona. Good heavens..." She crumbled to the street in a dainty, although scrawny, heap.

Chapter Five

I might have joined her in the dust of Bowery Street myself had I not been concerned for the condition of dress and hat. Euila Forester. I wouldn't have recognized her at all, had not Angus pointed out the similarity of our accents then called her by her surname. Euila Forester. Of all people. Here in Dawson, Yukon Territory, Canada.

Men ran from all over. So many eager hands reached out to help Euila to her feet, she was in danger of being trampled. Angus crouched beside her, unsure of what to do. Mr. Mann kept a wary eye on his property, and Euila's companion, a formidable lady of more advanced years, stood out of the way and scribbled in her notebook.

"Give her some air. Stand back, you fools!" Graham Donohue pushed his way to the front of the crowd. "Angus, unbutton the lady's collar," he ordered.

Angus gasped. "I couldn't!"

I looked around the crowd, hoping to find a female amongst the onlookers. None but Miss Witherspoon, still writing furiously. "For goodness sake, I'll do it." I knelt beside Euila, cursing the dust as it settled into my skirts. At least it hadn't rained in a few days, nor had a horse recently left evidence of its passing.

Euila's dress was done up to her chin by a formidable row of tiny mother-of-pearl buttons. My fingers fumbled, and after seemingly endless effort, I managed to release one. Throwing propriety to the winds, I grabbed either side of the fabric and pulled. Mother-of-pearl flew in all directions. Euila moaned, and her eyes flickered.

"She's coming around," a man shouted. "Fiona saved her."

"Fiona?" Euila whispered.

Someone placed a cup of water in my hand, and I lifted Euila's head to help her take a cautious sip. She sat up, grabbed my hand and drained the cup.

She seemed to be in no danger of collapsing again, so I got to my feet. "Graham, Angus, help her up," I ordered. The front of my dress was an absolute mess—streaked with dust and spotted with mud and I-hated-to-think-what from knee to hem. I made a few feeble swipes, hoping to wipe it all off, to no effect.

While I examined my garment, Angus and Graham each grabbed Euila by one arm. As she began to stagger upright, two other men got behind her and pushed, and the four of them managed to get the poor thing to her feet with about as much dignity as if they were unloading a reluctant cow from the belly of a steamship.

"Three cheers for Fee!" someone shouted. I smiled at no one in particular and waved my right hand as the crowd took up the cry. I hadn't done anything, but I never miss the opportunity to be the centre of attention.

"What should we do with her, Ma?" Angus asked.

"Don't call me that," I said, automatically. "You know I hate it." One of the too-eager helpers had a firm hold on Euila's bottom. I whacked his arm, and he sheepishly released his grip. "I don't know," I said. "Take her to lie down, I guess."

"Where are you staying, miss?" Graham asked. Euila blinked at him. I will admit that she looked even worse than I. The back of her dress was filthy; the neckline was torn almost to the top of the breastbone; one of the unfortunate birds on her hat (what could she possibly have been thinking when she purchased that hat!) tilted precariously, and a good deal of her hair had escaped its pins. Her hands and face were covered in dust.

"Miss?" Graham repeated. "Can we take you to your hotel?"

Miss Witherspoon dropped her pencil and notebook into her cavernous bag. "We have reserved rooms at the Richmond," she announced. "Take her there."

"Are you well enough to walk, miss?" Graham asked.

Euila blinked again. "I think so." She gave Graham a rather sickly smile. He tucked her arm under one of his. Angus did the same on the other side.

"Angus," I said. "Get back to work."

"Zee boy help," Mr. Mann said.

"No."

"But, Ma... Mother..."

"No buts. Back to work. You." I pointed to one of the helpers, the one who hadn't taken advantage of the opportunity to grab a handful of Euila's scrawny bottom. "Assist Mr. Donohue."

"My pleasure, Mrs. Fiona, ma'am." He leapt forward to do his duty. And the little procession, led by Miss Witherspoon with her head held high, made their way through the parting crowd into town.

"Mother, I don't see..."

"I must go home and change, Angus," I said. "Enjoy your biscuits."

I almost broke into an undignified run as I took the long way around, down the street towards the water instead of following Euila, Miss Witherspoon and Graham towards Front Street. My mind was in such a tempest of emotion that for once I didn't know what to do. All I could think of was that I had to prevent Angus from having any more contact with Euila Forester. I had succeeded in that for the time being. What I would do next, I had absolutely no idea.

*   *   *

Angus seethed for the rest of the morning. His mother had embarrassed him in front of the whole town. He had been trying to do a good deed, to help a lady in distress, and his mother had ordered him to return to the shop, even though Mr. Mann said he could go. Everyone in town had seen him humiliated.

He weighed a bit of gold dust on the scales in the front of the shop beside the cash box, then he handed a customer a sack of nails in exchange.

"Thank you, lad. A fine woman, your mother, a fine woman, the way she stepped in to help that poor young lady what had the fainting spell. Very noble o' her."

Angus didn't even try to force a smile. Sometimes it was difficult being the son of the most famous woman in town.

"Fainted, eh?" came a familiar voice. "Word on the street is that a lady choked on a lump of meat, and your mother singlehandedly wrestled the offending piece out of her mouth." Constable Richard Sterling fingered a rough flannel shirt as the old miner shuffled off, chuckling to himself, his bag of nails tinkling cheerfully. "This might do come winter," he added.

"A lady fainted, that's all," Angus muttered.

Sterling smiled. "No doubt by midnight the lady will have been attacked by a pack of rabid wolves, and your mother will have driven them off with a single well-aimed shot between the leader's eyes."

Despite himself, Angus grinned. "That's Dawson," he said.

Sterling laughed. "I'll take this shirt." He pulled a few pennies out of his pocket. "Lesson day, isn't it?"

Angus's grin grew wider. "Yes, it is, sir."

"Thought I'd walk over to the Fort with you, if you're ready to go."

This time Angus's grin almost split his face in two. "That would be grand, sir." He proudly pulled his watch out of his pocket. The watch had been owned by his mother's father. It was the only thing of his grandfather, also named Angus, they had. She'd given it to him only the other day, having decided now that he was working, he was ready to carry it. "Mr. Mann, it's five to one. Can I leave? Constable Sterling wants to walk with me to the Fort."

* * *

Sterling hid a smile at Angus's choice of words. It was no secret to him the boy worshipped him. A bit of hero worship never did a man's ego any harm.

Mr. Mann came out of the back tent, wiping his hands on the front of his trousers. "Go. Have good lesson."

The fact that Angus was taking boxing lessons from Sergeant Lancaster, the former, to hear him tell it, champion of Manitoba and contender for all of Canada, was a secret carefully kept from Angus's mother by Lancaster, Mann and Sterling. If she heard of it, she would probably forbid it—so why inconvenience her by letting her know? Sterling could see the outline of sinew and muscle lying dormant under the lanky twelve-year-old frame, waiting to burst out into the sun like a hibernating bear at first signs of approaching spring. Angus was growing into a big lad, and before much longer, his bulk would be the target of men who needed to prove themselves and wouldn't hesitate because of an unshaven face, friendly blue eyes and soft blond hair.

"Did Mary get settled in?" Sterling asked as they made their way east on Front Street, where the bars and dance halls were already doing a roaring trade, towards the NWMP's Fort Herchmer.

"She showed up for work at Mrs. Mann's on time."

"Mary seems like a nice woman."

"She is," Angus said, with a touch of proprietary pride.

Helen Saunderson, the Savoy's cleaner, came out of the dance hall wielding her formidable broom and sweeping all before her. It was a hopeless job; the more Mrs. Saunderson swept, the more mud and dust seemed to get tramped through the Savoy's doors.

She took a moment to rest her heavy bosom on the broom handle. "What's this I hear, young Angus, about your ma gettin' a woman's heart started what had stopped from shock the moment she laid eyes on Dawson?"

Sterling and Angus laughed. "It was amazing, Mrs. Saunderson," Angus said. "Why, Ma swept the goods right off the table in front of Mr. Mann's store and sliced open that woman's chest with a hunting knife that was for sale."

"Are you making fun o' me, Angus MacGillivray?"

Sterling tossed her a wink. Mrs. Saunderson shook her head and chuckled through her mouthful of missing teeth before bending her head to her sweeping.

"Let's walk down Paradise Alley," Sterling said. "Make sure everyone's behaving themselves."

They cut down Queen Street, heading for Paradise Alley. As they turned into the Alley, they could see a crowd of men up ahead, laughing and jeering at something Sterling couldn't see. The mood was vicious, ugly.

"Stay here, Angus," he said. "If you think I need help, run for the Fort. Understand?"

"Understood, sir," Angus said, his blue eyes wide.

"What's going on here? Break it up! Move out of the way." Sterling waded into the crowd.

"Nothing to concern yerself about, Const'ble," a man said.

"No business o' the Redcoats," said another.

"I'll be the judge of that. Move aside." Sterling practically tossed a neatly dressed gentleman to one side.

A man lay in the roadway, curled into a ball, his arms and hands attempting to protect his head as two heavy-set dandies took turns kicking him.

"Hey!" Sterling shouted and grabbed the man nearest him, the one about to place another boot into exposed ribs. The dandy turned. His face was twisted in rage, and blood-lust filled his red eyes. Furious at missing his mark, he was prepared to strike at the new target that had suddenly presented itself. Sterling grabbed the oncoming arm and twisted. "You don't want to do that, fellow."

The onlookers shuffled back. The other man turned to see what was going on. Puffed up like the bully he was, he visibly deflated at the sight of the red tunic and broad-brimmed hat.

Sterling gave the wrist he was holding another firm twist. "Want to tell me what's going on here?" he said pleasantly. He might have been inquiring about the weather.

"No concern of yours, Constable," the second man said. He, like his friend, was well dressed, in black waistcoat and jacket and houndstooth trousers. A black bowler hat was perched on top of his head. He was considerably overweight and very pale—his small dark eyes looked like raisins in a bowl of Christmas pudding batter. When he held out his hands in a gesture of surrender, he showed nails perfectly trimmed and spotlessly clean. A brown wool scarf was draped several times around his neck. "Tom Jannis is the name. Sam and I are settling a private matter. Nothing to worry the law."

"I'll be the judge of that. Someone get this man onto his feet. Quickly now!"

The onlookers rushed forward to help the man they had only moments before happily watched being kicked to a pulp.

Sterling faced Tom Jannis. "What's the story here?"

"This fellow lied to us. Told us he knew where we could find a good whore, then brought me to this fat tart." Jannis gestured contemptuously at the single woman in the crowd. It was the prostitute they called Fat Fanny.

"That weren't no lie," Fanny shrieked. "I'm a good whore, ain't I, boys?"

The onlookers shouted their agreement.

The victim staggered to his feet. Sterling stifled a groan. He was drunk—and an Indian. Not much point in trying to arrest Jannis and his friend. As likely as not, the judge would only want to know who'd sold liquor to an Indian.

"You all right, fellow?" Sterling asked.

The Indian swayed. His eyes were unfocused, his long hair stiff with dirt and grease. Layers of stale vomit stained the front of his ragged shirt. He didn't look like he'd suffered too much damage from the kicking; Sterling had probably arrived in time. The man would suffer more from a hangover than from the attempted beating.

"Drunken Indian," the first man said, spitting into the dust. "Arrest him. He tried to cheat us."

Sterling looked at Fat Fanny. "You know this man, Fanny?"

"Na," she said. "Never seen him before."

"He bring these men to you?"

She looked at the crowd. She looked at the two well-dressed men then at Sterling. Her thoughts passed across her face. She wouldn't want to offend potential customers, particularly ones as well-heeled as this pair, by calling them liars. But then again, judging by what they'd said about her, they didn't seem too inclined to bring their business her way. It didn't do to annoy the police. A working lady might need the goodwill of the Mounties some day. "Na," she said. "He were just standin' here leanin' up ag'in that wall, not doin' nothin' but bein' drunk. And them two started in on him. Ain't that right, boys?" She looked to the crowd for support.

They gave it to her.

"The Indian weren't even talking to them," someone said. "And they started punching at him."

Sterling raised one eyebrow and looked at Jannis.

"Stupid Indian wouldn't get outta my way. Where I come from, an Indian doesn't stand in a white man's way, not if he knows what's good for him."

"Perhaps you should go back to where you came from," Sterling said. "Now get out of here before I'm tempted to take you in for disturbing the peace." The Indian was struggling to focus and looked as though he were about to settle back into the roadway. Sterling grabbed his arm. "You'd better come with me, buddy. You don't belong here."

The Indian groaned, and a tiny dribble of spittle leaked out of the corner of his mouth. He looked up at Sterling. He was a good deal older than the Mountie had first thought. It was the eyes that gave his age away—they'd seen altogether too much. Under the dirt, his hair was a snowy white, and deep lines were carved into his cheeks and through the delicate skin under his eyes.

He staggered, and Sterling caught him under the arms. A wave full of the smell of old drink, unwashed clothes and the weight of a tired old body washed over him, but he held on. "Let's go," he whispered. "Let's get you some help." He tossed the old man's arm over his shoulder.

"Indian lover."

Out of the corner of his eye Sterling saw the blow coming. Weighted down as he was by the old man, he couldn't move fast enough to get out of the way. The man Tom Jannis had called Sam had pulled a metal bar out of his jacket, and with an angry shout swung it at Sterling's head.

The bar never connected. Instead Sam dropped the

weapon, clutched his lower side and crumbled to the ground, all in one smooth movement.

Angus MacGillivray stood over him, rubbing his right fist.

"Angus," Sterling said. "Thought I told you to run for the Fort if there was trouble."

"Didn't think I had enough time, sir."

"Here, you help this gentleman, and I'll take care of the other one." Angus took over the support of the old Indian, and Sterling dragged Sam to his feet. "Assaulting an officer of the law. It's a blue ticket for you, if I'm not mistaken." He looked at Jannis. "Coming with your friend?"

Jannis shrugged his expensively-draped shoulders and straightened his cravat. "Never laid eyes on this ruffian before today."

"That was quite the punch," Sterling told Angus as they led the two moaning men, one carefully, one with much less consideration, to Fort Herchmer.

"To the kidneys, sir. He was wide open, lifting that bar up that way. Sergeant Lancaster told me a good solid blow to the kidneys will bring a man down every time."

"Not very sporting."

"Sergeant Lancaster told me that too, sir. He said you never hit a man below the belt in a fair fight."

"Well, that wasn't a fair fight. You did good, Angus. But next time—if there is a next time—run to the Fort, will you?"

"Yes, sir. What will happen to these two now, sir?"

"This one will get a blue ticket and be out of town by nightfall. Permanently. The old Indian? I'll send someone to fetch one of the ladies from St. Paul's. They'll give him a hot meal and a bed in the church for the night and see he gets home to Moosehide tomorrow."

"But he'll drink again. Why won't he stop drinking?"

"Don't judge, Angus. The white man took everything from his people and gave them only disease in return. Alcohol is as much a disease for Indians as smallpox or typhoid. It takes longer to kill them, that's all."

Chapter Six

I was in a fine temper when I got home. A bird flew overhead as I crossed the yard. It was a tiny thing, lost and confused amongst the noise and bustle of Dawson, no doubt searching for a tree to nest in, but she was out of luck—the trees had all been chopped down for lumber and firewood.

I stormed into the laundry shed and stripped down to my bloomers—even my petticoat was filthy—right there and then. Mary and Mrs. Mann watched me with wide eyes. Huge vats of boiling water steamed over open fires, and acres of sheets were being rung out on a wooden press ready to go on the line, which was already filling the yard with men's undergarments and shirts, billowing in the wind. The whole place smelled of a disgusting mixture of lye soap, filthy water and unwashed men's clothes.

"If this isn't the most God-forsaken town," I shouted, bundling the dress into a ball and stuffing it into Mrs. Mann's arms. Mary was holding the huge wooden paddle they used to stir the laundry in the hot water as if this were a tennis court and she were about to return my serve. "I might as well go to work in sackcloth and ashes. I expect you to take care of that dress, Mary. It has scarcely been worn."

"Yes, Mrs. Fiona."

I had to cross the yard to get back to the house. I snatched a clean sheet off the folding table and wrapped it securely over my corset, bloomers and stockings. "I'll bring this back," I snarled as I stalked out. I had once worn a sheet to an extremely daring party at Lord Alveron's Welsh country house. The party was so daring, in fact, that it could only have been held as far away from London, and Alveron's grandmother, as he could get. The sheet was supposed to represent a classical Roman toga. I wore an expensive set of pearls with the sheet—Alveron's great-grandmother's pearls. They'd come in handy not too many months later when I'd sold them to secure Angus a place at a good school. The memory of my somewhat less respectable days did nothing to improve my mood, and I grumbled heartily as I stomped through the house to my rooms, tore off my hat and washed my hands and face. The water was cold, slimy with the residue of the morning's soap scum; Mrs. Mann had not yet changed it. Fortunately my hat was unscathed. It had cost almost as much as the dress. I struggled into my old day dress with no easing of my temper. The dress didn't go with the nice hat or the paste-sapphire earrings I'd carefully selected for the ensemble. Dawson was proving to be hard on my wardrobe. If I ever sold the Savoy, I might consider going into ladies' apparel. I bravely faced myself in the mirror as I tore out hairpins and attempted to repair my hair.

My anger began to dissipate under the slow, rhythmic action of the brush against my hair. I'd been afraid Euila would notice that my son carried my maiden name. I didn't give a whit about my reputation, and most of the townsfolk of Dawson would care even less, but I had led Angus to believe I'd been married to his late father. When he was born, I didn't even consider giving my son his father's—if I weren't a lady, I would spit on the floor—name. Angus MacGillivray had been my father's name, and a kinder, gentler man I had yet to meet.

Fiona was my mother's name. Sometimes, if I close my eyes and concentrate very hard I can hear my father's voice saying "Fiona" in his rich Scottish brogue. He was full of adoration for my mother, full of fun towards me. Regardless of where I happen to be, whenever I hear that rough, beautiful accent, I fly through space and time back to our crofter's cottage on Skye. It's a cold winter's evening, snow blowing outside, peat fire burning in the hearth,

Father bouncing me on his knee and asking my mother if I weren't the bonniest wee lass.

When I calmed down at last, under the steady stroke of my hairbrush, I realized I was worrying for nothing. Euila had probably never known my surname. Even the house servants only called me Fiona. Euila hadn't met my parents in all the years they'd lived on her family property, other than to nod a polite but distant good day as she passed. There were people from London and Toronto who would no doubt still be searching for me—thus, I tried, most unsuccessfully, to keep a low profile—but none of them would be able to trace me through Euila.

I sighed happily. All would be resolved. I had recently joked to Richard Sterling that I expected everyone from the king of the Zulus to our own dear Queen to pass through Dawson one day. But I hadn't expected Euila Forester.

I tucked the last strands of wayward black hair into their pins and chewed on my lips to bring up a bit of colour, deciding to drop in on Euila for old times' sake. Although I wouldn't go so far as to let my son anywhere near her.

I took the sheet back out to the laundry shed. A wave of steam erupted from a huge cauldron over the fire. "I'm returning the sheet I borrowed, Mrs. Mann," I said, waving my hand in front of my face. "How's my dress?"

She stepped out of the steam like the fairy maid of legend emerging from the mists of Avalon. Although Arthur's Lady was unlikely to have had hands and face so red. "It will come clean like new," she said. "With good soap."

"Do you have good soap?"

"No."

"Where would you get good soap?"

"Mrs. Bradshaw on Harper, near Seventh Avenue. She keeps a small supply of good soap for special customers."

For special, read high-paying. "I'm late enough for work, I might as well walk all the way up to Mrs. Bradshaw's," I said with a heroic sigh.

"Good idea," Mrs. Mann said, as if she hadn't thought of it herself.

*　*　*

Seventh Avenue at Harper Street was uphill all the way. Grumbling, I made a quick detour and stopped at the Savoy to collect Helen Saunderson, who could ferry the precious soap back to Mrs. Mann.

"Heard ye had a wee bit of excitement down at Bowery Street this morning, Fee," Ray said as I waited for Helen to hang her apron in the storage room-cum-kitchen which served as her domain. "Saved a lass from drowning by jumping into the river all by yourself."

"Oh, shut up," I said.

Helen wanted to hear the whole story, so I related it to her as we walked. I kept to the truth and put that way, it did sound rather boring compared to the tales that were flying around town.

It was past midday, and once we got away from the teeming waterfront, the streets were almost empty. All the respectable folks were at work, the layabouts snoring it off somewhere, the whores taking a well-deserved nap, the gamblers and drinkers back in the bars.

Helen huffed and twitched and cleared her throat, until I finally said, "Do you have something you want to say to me?"

"Not my place to be telling you what to do in your own place, Mrs. Mac," she said, with a nervous cough, "but I think maybe you don't know, being a foreigner and all..."

"Know what?"

"That woman you've got living upstairs. It ain't proper."

"She's behaving perfectly respectably, Helen," I said. "You may rest assured I wouldn't stand for anything illegal or immoral going on up there."

"I don't mean that. Mrs. Mac, you gotta know she's an Indian. Ain't proper to have Indians living with white people. Men start hearing you've got an Indian in the Savoy, they'll stop coming."

I doubted very much that anyone drinking in the bar, dancing with a percentage girl, or dropping a thousand dollars in the gambling room would care if a tribe of Hottentots took residence on the second floor of the Savoy. I was about to tell Helen so when she carried on.

"I'm sorry, Mrs. Mac, but long as she's there, I won't be able to bring my girls 'round to help with the upstairs cleaning." Helen had four children, the eldest the same age as Angus. "I can't have my children wondering if it's proper to have them living amongst us. Send her back where she came from. It's for her own good, mind. They're not happy living with us, you know."

That gave me pause. I didn't care one whit whether Helen cleaned the upstairs rooms herself or if her daughters helped her. I paid the same regardless. But if Helen thought that way, what about the other supposedly respectable townspeople? I didn't need anyone asking questions about the type of establishment I kept.

"Isn't that Miss Irene up ahead?" Helen said, glad of the chance to change the subject. She opened her mouth to trill a greeting.

I clamped my arm on hers. "I don't think she wants to be disturbed."

It was Irene all right, standing under an illiterate sign advertising a "Dresmakers" shop. Her back was to us, but I could tell by the set of her neck and the rigidity of her spine that a friendly interruption would not be welcome. She faced an older woman whom I did not know. The other woman wore a stiff homespun dress, an unadorned straw hat, and no jewellery. She was older than Irene, very thin, with plain no-nonsense features. Her eyes filled with emotion as she put her hands on Irene's shoulders. She was so short, she had to almost stand on her toes to reach. Her sixth sense, if it were that, caught me watching, and she looked up. Her face was set in hard, tight lines, and her eyes flashed with what I thought might be a warning.

"We've come the wrong way," I said to Helen, dragging her down Sixth Avenue.

"You said it was up ahead. And ain't that Miss Irene over there?"

"No," I said. "That wasn't Irene. Looked a good deal like her though. Oh, look, that must be the street." I plunged down the nearest alley. A man relieving himself against a wall tried to stuff himself back into his pants.

"I'll have the Mounties on you, if I witness that again," I shouted, still dragging a bewildered Mrs. Saunderson. "Imagine, frightening proper ladies."

The man almost took flight, his shirtfront trapped in his trouser buttons.

"Mrs. Mac, what in heaven's name are you doing?" Helen wheezed.

"There we are," I almost shouted. "Seventh Avenue. Look for Mrs. Bradshaw's shop. Remember, I want only the best soap. Bugger the cost."

Mrs. Saunderson gasped, as well she might. I had chosen my words carefully in order to distract her from my rather odd behaviour.

I suspected I now knew the identity of Irene's secret lover.

For, as the woman in the homespun dress reached for Irene and looked into my eyes, my best girl, the most popular dance hall girl in Dawson, had leaned forward in anticipation of a kiss on the lips.

Chapter Seven

It had not been a good lesson. Angus had been so thrilled at how he'd helped Constable Sterling in the fight in Paradise Alley, he'd let his mind wander and his guard down. Sergeant Lancaster moved in with a single-minded determination that put the dazed boy flat on the sawdust floor in seconds. Angus struggled to his feet, shaking his head and wondering what had happened, encouraged by the few Mounties who stood around the makeshift ring which had been thrown up behind the kennels.

"If your mind's not on it, boy," Lancaster said, playing to the audience, "you're gonna lose. Every time."

After the lesson, they ducked their heads into barrels of rainwater and were towelling off when Angus explained to the sergeant why he'd been late.

Lancaster rubbed at his face with a scrap of towel. "Indian, eh?" the boxer said. "They're always causing trouble. Watch out boy, Sterling's got a reputation as an Indian-lover."

When he left the Fort, Angus headed for the river to meet up with Ron and Dave. He could hardly wait to tell them the whole story. He was almost bursting with pride at the way he'd brought down that man who was about to make a cowardly attack on Constable Sterling. Maybe he'd embellish the story a touch. Have the man put up more of a fight. Angus made his way along Front Street towards the boys' gathering place on the other side of town, turning the whole incident over in his head. You didn't see many Indians in Dawson. And here he'd met two in two days. First Mary and now the old drunk. Sterling had called drinking a disease. Angus didn't see how that could be—lots of white men drank. And most of them went back to work or their families when they'd slept it off, although there were some who couldn't hold down a job because of it. Angus's mother ran a bar, and she told him what she thought of some of her clients. But people said Indians took to drinking so bad, the bars weren't even allowed to sell liquor to them.

"My dear boy! Isn't this a most fortuitous encounter!"

Angus looked up to see Miss Witherspoon and Miss Forester bearing down on him. At least, Miss Witherspoon was bearing down; Miss Forester glided behind as if she were caught in a strong draft.

"Ma'am." Angus doffed his cap politely. "I hope you're feeling better, Miss Forester."

"She is, she is," Miss Witherspoon said. "A short nap, and she's as right as rain. Aren't you, dear? We've come from visiting your lovely shop to thank you for your noble efforts, but your employer said you had left for the day."

"Uh..." Angus said.

"Now, now, young man, don't say it was nothing. You were terribly quick to react." She pulled her pencil and notebook out of her bag. "Your mother called you Angus. What's your last name?"

"I don't want to be in the papers, ma'am," Angus said. He meant it. His mother was particularly averse to having her exploits recorded, and Sterling had told him that a Mountie never sought glory for his own sake.

"Nonsense, all boys want to be famous."

"I'd rather not, ma'am."

"Very well, Angus will do. I am not a newspaper reporter. I am a book writer."

"Books, ma'am?"

Miss Witherspoon tucked her writing implements away and slipped one arm through Angus's. "I am here in the Yukon to research a book I intend to write about the gold rush. People in California and New York are dying for news about this wonderful place. They want much more information than they get from a few newspaper accounts. I want to see everything, and meet everyone, and tell all about it in my book. Isn't that exciting?"

"Yes, ma'am." Miss Witherspoon had a contagious eagerness about her. When she talked about her project, her voice rose and her eyes glistened, and Angus couldn't help but be caught up in her enthusiasm.

"I was saying to Miss Forester that we must find ourselves a guide to this exciting town. Didn't I say that, Euila?"

"Yes, you did, Martha," Miss Forester said softly. She, for one, didn't appear to be too caught up in Miss Witherspoon's enthusiasm.

"How does two dollars a day sound?"

Two dollars a day sounded great! Angus opened his mouth to say "yes", but then he remembered he had responsibilities. Miss Witherspoon remembered also. "Your employer told me you work at the shop every morning. So you are free in the afternoons and on Sunday to show us around, isn't that right?"

"Uh, would that be two dollars for the afternoon, or only one?"

"Two."

Ron and Dave wouldn't care too much whether he showed up or not, and two dollars a day was as much as a man might make, more than a constable earned. And for only an afternoon's work at that. "Sure," he said.

"Wonderful!" Miss Witherspoon nodded. "Before we begin, I am simply starving. And so is Miss Forester, I am sure. What would be a nice place for afternoon tea?"

"I don't quite know about tea, ma'am. Maybe your hotel? Or the Regina Café serves good soup and light lunches, I've heard. I'll show you where it is."

"You will eat with us."

"Uh, I don't have any money."

"Did I not mention that all your expenses will be paid while you are in my employ? Come along, lead the way to the Regina Café."

The walk to the café took a long time, as Miss Witherspoon

wanted to stop and look at everything then ask questions about everything she stopped to look at.

She paused in front of the Monte Carlo. "Tonight I want to go to one of the dance halls. It is not at all a place for a respectable lady, so you'll have to remain in the hotel, Euila. As I will be in my capacity as a writer, I'll venture in. Will you accompany me, Angus?"

"I'm sorry, Miss Witherspoon, but I'm not old enough to go inside. The police are strict about things like that. I can only go into the Savoy because my mother owns it."

"Tell me about your mother. Such a gracious lady. So quick to help Miss Forester. She owns a dance hall? Most convenient. What would be a good time?"

"The dance hall opens at eight, although the bar and the gambling rooms are open all day."

"Then eight it will be. How did your mother come to be the owner of a dance hall? The Savoy, you called it? Named after the hotel of that name in London?"

As they settled into a table by the window, Miss Witherspoon plied Angus with questions. He chattered on about Dawson, about the Chilkoot trail, about the Savoy and Ray Walker, his mother's business partner. He talked about Mrs. Saunderson, tragically widowed then cheated out of her claim by her own brother.

Miss Witherspoon jotted everything down in her notebook while she consumed every scrap of beans, boiled potatoes, and pork chop on her plate. Miss Forester said almost nothing and picked at her lunch with an expression of distaste.

"Tell me, Angus," Miss Witherspoon said, placing her knife and fork neatly across her scraped-clean plate. "I've heard the words sourdoughs and cheechakos. What's the difference? Would you care for pie?"

"Yes, ma'am! A cheechako means a newcomer. A sourdough is an old timer. Although a sourdough doesn't have to be old—he only has to have spent a winter in the Yukon."

"So you're a sourdough?"

Angus had never thought of it that way. He rolled the

word around inside his head. "I guess I am. It was some winter, let me tell you. There was talk of Dawson being a starvation camp."

He was scraping up the last of his pie when Miss Irene, his mother's best dancer, came into the café. She was with a plainly dressed older woman, and they made for a table in the dark back corner of the room, although there were window tables still available. Angus waved cheerfully as Irene and her companion crossed the room. Irene tossed him a friendly smile and gave his companions a curious look.

Miss Witherspoon followed his gaze. "Who is that?"

"That's Miss Davidson, Lady Irenee is her stage name. She's the headliner at the Savoy. The main attraction in the dance hall, I mean. My ma tells me she's popular with the men. Worth her weight in gold, my ma says. Don't know the other woman, though."

Miss Witherspoon watched the two women settle at their table. Irene fluffed her skirts around her and drifted into her chair like the first leaf of autumn falling graciously to the ground. Her companion plunked herself down and looked around. She saw Angus and Miss Witherspoon watching. She gave Miss Witherspoon a sharp look before turning her attention back to Irene.

Miss Witherspoon flushed and turned away. "Waiter," she cried, snapping her fingers. "Our account, if you please."

She fumbled in her bag, searching for money. "Now, Angus dear, you must get Miss Forester to tell you what caused her to faint at your shop this morning. She refuses to say a word to me."

"There is nothing to say, Martha. I told you. It was the heat and the mud and all those men gathered so closely. Quite unbearable. I knew it was a mistake to come here."

"Euila spent her childhood on the Isle of Skye. Didn't you mention that's where your mother originated, Angus dear? I find that rather hard to believe because they both have such proper English accents. Almost identical, one might say."

Angus remembered his manners. He hadn't spoken to

Miss Forester during the entire meal. "Are you a writer also, Miss Forester?"

"Heavens no." Miss Forester looked quite startled, whether at being mistaken for a writer or being spoken to, Angus didn't know.

"What brings you to Dawson, then?" he asked, simply trying to be polite. His mother hated men who only talked about themselves.

"The fishing fleet," Miss Witherspoon said, carefully counting out the money for the bill.

"Fishing? The salmon'll be running soon. We weren't here last year for the salmon run, but they say it's really something. I can't see that you'll... I mean, you don't look like..." Angus fumbled for the words.

"Martha," Miss Forrester said, "please be quiet."

"Nothing wrong with it, my dear." Miss Witherspoon waved at the waiter once again. "The fishing fleet, Angus, is what they used to call the pack of Englishwomen who set sail once a year for India in search of a husband."

"Oh."

"Miss Forester is looking for a husband. A wealthy one. Fallen on hard times, haven't you, dear? Such a tragedy when the great families can't pay off their debts."

Miss Forester turned an unattractive shade of red and gathered her gloves. "That is none of the boy's business, Martha."

"We met in San Francisco," Miss Witherspoon continued, as if her companion hadn't spoken. "Euila's brother was most grateful to find her a respectable companion to take her off his hands. *He* was no match for the Klondike, let me tell you. Now, where shall we go next? You may lead the way, dear boy. But remember: I want to see everything!"

Chapter Eight

Helen Saunderson and I collected the good soap, which cost an absolute fortune, and walked back to town. Mrs. Saunderson was telling me something about one of her children who was having problems with a tooth. I scarcely heard one word in ten. What did Irene think she was doing! Having an assignation—and with a woman at that!—on the street. She must be mad. We sold dreams as much as dances and drinks in the Savoy. The men paid to see the show or to have a brief turn on the floor with one of the girls because they needed some happiness in their generally miserable lives. They admired Irene on the stage and imagined, however foolishly, that one day she might be theirs. Let a little reality into the room—such as a female lover—and the effect would be like a magician telling the audience everything he was doing. Illusions once shattered can not be put back together like a piece of old china. Irene would no longer be the most popular dance hall girl in the North. She would be lucky to be able to make a living as a percentage girl.

What would Ray have to say if his illusions of living happily ever after with Irene were so brutally shattered? He'd probably fire her on the spot. And let everyone in earshot know why.

I sighed so heavily, a passing man paused in the act of lifting his hat to me. I tossed him a self-conscious grin and shrugged slightly. Mrs. Saunderson chattered on. The man walked away with a huge smile on his face. He was perfectly ugly and desperately in need of grooming and the attentions of Mrs. Mann's laundry, but his eyes were kind, and I was pleased to have made his day.

"Madame MacGillivray, how pleasant to run into you."

Joey LeBlanc, the most notorious whoremonger in Dawson, had planted her tiny self firmly in front of us, blocking the boardwalk. There was nothing pleasant about the look on Joey's face. For some reason she'd hated me since the day she arrived in town—only a week after Angus and I—although I don't recall having done anything to offend her, other than hold my nose (figuratively speaking) whenever we passed. She was less than five feet tall, and her bones were so fine, I sometimes wondered if she would be carried away by a middling wind. As though defying anyone to guess at her occupation, she dressed in the plainest of clothes. Her grey hair was scraped back so tightly that the skin beside her eyes stretched upwards, and her head was topped with a straw hat about two sizes too small. She wore no jewellery save a woman's simple wedding band, although there was never any sign of a Monsieur LeBlanc.

I didn't bother to be polite. This was no London drawing room where one cooed over the cut of one's worst enemy's new dress ("My dear, I simply loved that frock when I saw it on Lady Morton last month") or her husband's new position ("So nice for you that he will be able to dine at home regularly") and where the sharpest battles were fought with words that could wound more deeply than swords.

In Dawson, I could be so much more blunt. "Get out of my way, Joey."

She looked at me with eyes as cold as the frozen earth out of which the men pulled their gold. "Is that any way for a lady to talk?" She took the thickness of her Quebec accent up a degree.

I wasn't about to stand there all day wondering who would step aside first. I lifted my skirts and stepped off the boardwalk, carefully avoiding a recently deposited pile of dog droppings. From an extremely large dog. I tugged on Helen's sleeve, and she reluctantly stepped into the road beside me. Helen could be even more blunt than I, and I didn't want a scene.

"You 'ave something what belongs to me, MacGillivray," Joey said.

Despite my better instincts, I turned around. "I beg your pardon?" I asked in my best dealing-with-the-peasantry-voice, something that I've noticed a Canadian or an American can't quite pull off.

We were attracting a crowd. Some people in Dawson had far too much time on their hands. Joey lowered her voice. "The Indian bitch is mine," she hissed. "Bought and paid for."

I wiped spittle off my face. "No longer, it would appear." I turned and started to walk away, still tugging at Helen's sleeve.

"I want 'er back."

This time I kept walking.

"And 'ow are you, 'elen?" Joey called after us pleasantly, her voice back at a normal street level. "Enjoying your employment at the Savoy?"

I whirled around. "Is that a threat, Joey? If you have anything to say, you'd better say it to me."

"Me?" Joey said. "I make no threats." This time it was her turn to walk away, head held high under its plain straw hat.

"I've encountered the likes of her before, Mrs. Mac," Helen said. "Not fit to walk on the same sidewalk as decent women, she ain't. Imagine forcing a lady such as you into the street!"

"I'd rather walk in the mud than engage in a contest of wills with her and create a public spectacle."

"What do you suppose that was really about?"

"Nothing good, Helen. Most certainly nothing good. If you see her around the Savoy...if you ever see her anywhere near Angus, let me know right away, will you?"

"You think she'd harm Angus?" At the very thought, Helen Saunderson looked ready to go after Joey and clobber her with the package of good soap.

It was an exceedingly hot day, but I felt a shiver under the strings of my corset. Against the likes of Joey LeBlanc I had few defences. It was unlikely she would be reduced to blubbering idiocy by a witty yet scathing comment about the style of her hair or worry overmuch about being cut out of polite society by a well-placed whisper of scandal. "I think she'd do most anything to harm me. If she could. Take that soap to Mrs. Mann. Tell her I expect to wear the dress tomorrow."

I didn't tell Helen that my earlier misgivings about letting Mary stay at the Savoy had disappeared the moment Joey LeBlanc stepped in front of me. It might not be in my best interests, but I wasn't about to give LeBlanc the satisfaction of letting her think she'd won.

Nor did I mention that someone had been watching the scene with a far greater degree of interest than the majority of the bored crowd. Chloe, the dancer I'd fired the night before for drinking, reversed her direction and headed up the street after Joey, a look of malicious glee filling her sharp face.

*   *   *

When I arrived back at the Savoy, men were lining up at the bar five deep. From the back room came the wonderful noise of cards being dealt and the roulette wheel spinning. The sound of money falling into my pocket went some way towards taking my mind off the triple troubles of Irene, Joey and Chloe.

There were two bartenders serving the customers. Murray, the newly promoted head bartender, and another fellow whose name always managed to escape me. "Mrs. MacGillivray." Murray waved me over. "Thank goodness you're here. Man's thrown up under the roulette wheel, and Mrs. Saunderson ain't around."

I looked at him. "Have you shown the gentleman the door?"

"Shown him the mud of Front Street, more like."

"Has a beautiful fairy arrived to clean up the mess with her magic wand?"

He looked at me, his shiny face blank. A lock of clean blond hair flopped across his forehead. "No, ma'am."

"Then you'd best clean it up yourself, hadn't you? Certainly before I see it."

"Ma'am?"

"You are in charge here in Mr. Walker's absence, are you not, Murray?"

"Yes, ma'am."

"Then please act it. Either clean up the mess or have someone do it, whether Mrs. Saunderson is here or not." I tossed my head towards the bartender who was Not-Murray. Comprehension slowly dawned behind the eyes of our new head bartender. I'd have to ask Ray to re-think that appointment. "I'm going up to my office for about five minutes. Then I intend to tour the gambling hall. If I am not assailed by the invigorating scent of clean sawdust, and nothing else, someone will be seeking new employment."

I walked away, smiling to my left and right and greeting customers graciously. I've had some experience in mingling with minor royalty, and I even moved in the Prince of Wales's social circle for a brief time (but quite long enough, thank you very much), so I know how to put on airs. The men seem to like it. Makes them feel special, perhaps.

It was early afternoon, and although the place might appear to be full, it was only an illusion. Wait until the show ended at midnight, the dance hall doors opened and men spilled out of the back room. Then I'd scarcely be able to breathe as I made my way through the crowds. In some situations that might prove somewhat dangerous for a lady, but in Dawson the majority of the men were so homesick, so lonely—so sad, some of them—that most of them treated me like a hothouse flower. And for those that didn't, there was the very long arm of the NWMP. As well as the hefty billy club Ray kept behind the bar.

I walked up the stairs, wondering if I should tell the Mounties that Joey LeBlanc had threatened me. But what could I say: Joey had asked Helen Saunderson if she liked working for me, and I took that comment to mean I should run for the law? Or that an ex-employee had changed her mind and headed north when she'd originally been going south? I'd be laughed out of the station. But not by everyone. There was always Constable Sterling. I pushed that idea aside. I didn't want to be beholden to Richard Sterling.

At that moment, as though summoned by my very thoughts, Sergeant Lancaster walked through the doors of the Savoy. As usual, he was all puffed up and walked like the emperor penguin in a photograph I'd seen of such an animal captured on an expedition to the Antarctic.

Also as usual, he made a beeline in my direction. Sergeant Lancaster had recently expressed his entirely honourable intentions towards me. It had been a most uncomfortable situation, and I considered myself fortunate to have escaped without causing any hard feelings. This afternoon he was wreathed in smiles across his battered old face all the way up to the cauliflower ears. He sucked in his stomach as he got close.

"Mrs. MacGillivray. May I say that you are looking particularly lovely this afternoon?"

Of course you may.

"A touch of our northern sun does wonders for a lady's complexion, I've always said."

I refrained from rolling my eyes.

"I said to your son…"

I took his arm. "I was hoping to have a word with you, Sergeant." I led him away from the crowd, but no further than the back of the saloon. I was afraid if I took him up to the privacy of my office, Sergeant Lancaster would drop to one knee and burst out a proposal of marriage once again. We stood under a painting of a voluptuous, pale-skinned, redheaded nude lounging languorously on a red velvet settee. Some patriotic soul had driven a pair of Stars and Stripes into either side of the heavy gilt frame. Rather than offend our American customers, I had let the flags remain. I myself had attached a considerably larger set of Union Jacks to the picture beside it.

"Is there a problem, Mrs. MacGillivray?" Lancaster was getting himself ready to mount up and ride into battle on my behalf.

"I'm sure it's nothing, Sergeant," I said. "I've recently taken a young woman under my protection. A woman of most unfortunate circumstances—I'm sure I don't have to explain them to you?"

The big man turned a bright red. He tugged at the buttons on his tunic. "Of course not, Mrs. MacGillivray."

"I am concerned that...certain people...might be anxious to return her to her...previous employment."

"I assure you, Mrs. MacGillivray..."

I raised a hand and touched him lightly on the chest. "Or to take some...action...against me."

"Mrs. MacGillivray!" Lancaster was truly shocked. His fellow officers held him in high regard; I thought him a bumbling idiot. But I was hoping that through him the Mounties would extend me protection without my having to humble myself by asking for it.

Foolish pride. Better I should have crawled on all fours and begged for their help.

Chapter Nine

After leaving Angus MacGillivray at his boxing lesson with Sergeant Lancaster, Sterling continued on his rounds. He walked through saloons and dance halls, checking for crooked tables, clumsily-poured drinks, gold scales out of alignment, underage drinkers, men spoiling for a fight, indecency, all of the detritus of a gold rush town where the innocent sometimes made it as hard to protect them as it was to prosecute the guilty. The drunken Indian played on his mind.

Eventually his heavy black boots led him down Church Street to St. Paul's.

He took off his hat as he opened the church doors. It was a rough wooden structure, looking exactly like what it was— a building thrown up out of the wilderness in a few short weeks. But it was also a rarely-visited sanctuary offering an island of serenity in an ocean of turbulent humanity. The minister's wife was polishing the arms of the pews, a thankless task. In Dawson, dust and sawdust continually fell in a fine rain on everything indoors and out.

She put down her rag and wiped her hands on her apron while walking towards him with a welcoming smile. "Constable. How nice to see you. Come to check on your Indian friend?"

"Yes, ma'am. Did you fetch him then?"

"My husband has taken him down to Moosehide." Moosehide was a small island in the Yukon River, not far from town, where the Han Indians lived. Moosehide was also the name of the ancient rockslide that had long ago taken an enormous chunk out of the side of the hill looming over the town.

"Thank you." Sterling tipped his hat. "I'll be off then."

"Have you time for a cup of tea, Constable?"

A lot of dust got into a man's throat on a hot day walking rounds in Dawson, but he couldn't accept the friendly offer. Sterling's father had been a preacher, a stern, cold, hard man, who had slowly drained every bit of joy out of his timid wife, until she was almost as much of a shell as he. Richard Sterling had been raised in a cold, hard home. It was irrational, he knew, but he could never make himself comfortable in the presence of a man or woman of God.

"Another time perhaps, ma'am." He walked back out into the sunshine and the dust.

He'd never expected it to get so hot this far north. They were almost at the Arctic Circle, yet the temperature had to be close to a hundred degrees, and the sun beat relentlessly on his wool tunic. Two drunken cheechakos were shouting bawdy songs at each other and slapping backs so close to the riverbed, it was likely one or both would be in the water pretty soon. He shook himself clear of the cobwebs of memory and went to suggest they take their frivolity somewhere safer.

* * *

I went home for a much-too-short afternoon nap, had dinner with my son and changed into evening dress. The nap had been disturbed by hammering on a new house being put up across the street to replace the tent that had been there yesterday. Dinner had been dreadful—stew from a ptarmigan that must have died of an extremely ripe old age. A bone on my best corset snapped, leaving me in danger of being impaled. I'd ripped off the offending garment and struggled into an older one. Tonight I was again wearing the green satin dress. It had a plain, unadorned front and a high neckline, so I wrapped yards and yards of fake pearls around my throat. Instead of wearing a hat, I tied my hair back with a generous length of ribbon salvaged from material discarded when the dress was cut down as the bustle went out of fashion. The high neckline was so proper as to be out of place in a dance hall, but the lack of a hat made up for the shock factor.

Angus had been particularly quiet during dinner, scowling into his lumpy mashed potatoes and ubiquitous serving of beans that accompanied the foul fowl. He'd cast glances at me throughout the meal and asked if I was planning to be at the Savoy that night. Where on earth else would I be? He ate only one bowl of canned strawberries for dessert and asked to be excused.

"Zee boy up to something," Mr. Mann said, leaning back to let his wife clear his place and set a cup of tea in front of him while he measured tobacco into his pipe.

I hoped Angus wasn't interested in pursuing a life of crime or gambling: his poker face couldn't fool a blind nun.

As I was saying goodbye to the Manns, Mary appeared at the kitchen door to say she was finished for the day and to collect her wages. Her hands were red and chapped, her face flushed with heat, her hair damp and hanging lank down her back, and the front of her dress was soaking wet. I invited her to walk with me to the Savoy.

A dead horse lay in the intersection of Fourth Avenue and York Street. It didn't appear to have been there for long, as not many flies had yet gathered. I lifted my skirts with a sniff. I didn't often think fondly of London or even Toronto, for I had come to love the Yukon (most of the time), but one didn't have to contend with carrion in the better streets of London. Mary stumbled, and I grabbed her arm. She was obviously exhausted. She looked at me with red-rimmed eyes and mumbled her thanks.

"Have you found accommodation yet?" I said, trying to sound cheerful.

"You're asking me to leave the Savoy, Mrs. MacGillivray?" she asked.

"No," I said, "but you can't stay there permanently."

"Why not?"

"Why not? Because the Savoy isn't a hotel."

"You let white men stay."

"Well, yes. But only our customers. Men who spend money in the dance hall and play at the gambling tables."

"Not Indians."

"Indians are not my customers. What's the matter with you, Mary? I can't let out those rooms nor put up any drunken gamblers while you're living up there. now can I? That wouldn't be at all proper, nor would it be safe for you. I explained yesterday that you can stay in the Savoy until you find alternate accommodation."

"There is no accommodation for an Indian, Mrs. MacGillivray."

"Mrs. Mann pays you well, doesn't she?"

"Yes."

"Then by the end of the week you should have enough money to find someplace to stay. This is Dawson; money is all that matters. I'll ask some of my acquaintances if they know of a respectable woman with rooms to rent."

"Yes, Mrs. MacGillivray," Mary sighed. I did wonder if I was being overly optimistic. If even kind-hearted Helen didn't want Mary around, would any other "respectable" Dawson matron be willing to take Mary under her roof? Perhaps Mary should just leave town, go back where she came from, as Helen suggested. That would relieve me of the burden of caring for her, which, truth be told, I was only doing to annoy Joey LeBlanc.

We arrived at Front Street. The evening crowd was beginning to gather, and men greeted me effusively. My neighbour stood outside the small bakery at which she and her elder sister sold coffee and waffles for twenty-five cents. Business was slow right now, but after a night of entertainment and dancing, men would be lining up for refreshment. Twenty-five cents would be all that many of them had left until their next pay-day, or until they dug up more gold. I'd bought one of their waffles once and found it dry and almost tasteless, but the sisters provided the scent of a warm oven and quality ingredients, and it was likely the men ate at the bakery as much for the smell of home as for the food.

"Lovely evening, isn't it?" she said in her heavy Dutch accent with a warm smile that revealed an overabundance of healthy teeth.

I paused for a moment. "It is." All the summer evenings were lovely in the Yukon. The heat of the day moderated a fraction, leaving the air warm and fresh. (Well, as fresh as it could be, considering the dead animals in the road and the hygiene of some of the miners.) The frantic activity in the sawmills died down enough that noise and dust abated. We paid heavily for these lovely evenings come winter, when the sun barely rose above the horizon all day, and even when it did, it didn't contain a smidgen of heat.

I was about to wish her a good evening when, to my shock, she pulled a tobacco pouch and cigarette papers out of her pocket and began to roll a cigarette. In London, I'd seen barely-acceptable women (the sort who performed on stage and later joined the prince and his friends for supper) smoke cigars. But even in Alaska or the Yukon, I'd never seen a woman smoke a cigarette on the street. I had heard that some of the dancers and prostitutes did so in the privacy of their, or their customer's, rooms.

She struck a match against a box she pulled out of her pocket and lit the end of her cigarette. She took a deep breath and sighed with satisfaction.

"How does that taste?" I asked, curiosity getting the better of good manners.

"Heavenly." She blew a stream of white smoke out of her nostrils. It put me in mind of a horse blowing air after a hard ride on a cold day. "You should try it, Fiona."

"Perhaps I will," I said, although I had no intention of doing so. Tobacco cost money, and I'd managed to live without it all my years.

I remembered my manners. "Anna-Marie, this is Mary... uh... Mary. Mary, Miss Vanderhaege. Mary is living at the Savoy temporarily and has found employment with my landlady, Mrs. Mann."

"You must try this, Fiona." Anna-Marie said, as if I hadn't spoken. She didn't even look at Mary. "It's avant-garde now, but one day every woman will be doing it." She blew a ring of smoke through rounded lips.

"Perhaps I will. Have a pleasant evening," I said.

"You also." She watched her smoke ring slowly dissipate in the air.

"That was rude," I said to Mary as we walked away.

She barely moved her thin shoulders. "Good night, Mrs. MacGillivray."

"Good night, Mary." I watched her round the building towards the stairs at the back. Her back was stooped and her tread heavy.

I paused for a moment, wondering what it would be like to wash clothes all day long. I never allow myself to forget how I was able to escape the filth of Whitechapel and Seven Dials and men who would control my fate. If not for a proper education, good bone structure, and most of all a generous helping of luck, I might now think myself fortunate to spend the day in Mrs. Mann's laundry shed.

I looked out over Front Street towards the swiftly-moving brown river and the tent-dotted hillside beyond. And there she was: Chloe, standing on the sidewalk, watching me. She made no gesture, no movement, didn't wave or smile or even pull out a gun. She only watched me, her face expressionless.

I stepped off the boardwalk, ready to confront her and demand to know what she thought she was doing. A heavily laden cart clattered past, going much too fast for the road conditions. Did the driver think he was on parade in Pall Mall? I shouted abuse at him, and he shouted back over his shoulder, not even watching where he was going, flicking the reins to make the horses go faster. They clattered down the street and disappeared around a corner. Damned fool. He'd be lucky if he didn't kill someone, or get one of his horses injured. Judging by the condition of the horses—if I'd had enough time, I could have counted every rib—he didn't care over much about them.

When I looked back across the street, Chloe was gone. She could be anywhere—ducking between tents on the mud flats that served as the centre of commerce; lost in the teeming crowd surging up and down Front Street; doubled back and slipped up an alley; heading for the docks and the next steamboat out of town, if I were lucky.

"You know that...lady, Fiona?"

I whirled around, startled. "Graham Donohue, do you always have to sneak up on me?"

He grinned most charmingly. Graham at his handsome best. "I wish I could, my dear."

I tried to look stern. "Don't be naughty."

"Seriously, Fiona. That woman was watching you, and not because she was admiring the cut of your dress. Have I ever told you it is the most handsome dress?"

"Every time I have worn it, but you needn't stop. As for that woman, I fired her recently. She was drunk on stage. I've seen her, more than seems coincidental, several times today. You'd best step back quickly, Graham."

The orchestra came spilling out of the doors of the Savoy, and Graham scooted out of their way, conveniently putting one arm around my waist to guide me to one side. They weren't much in the way of musicians, my orchestra. A violinist, a clarinet player and one trombonist. Inside we had a piano, but the pianist could scarcely carry that out to the street, so he acted as caller. I stood in the doorway, flashing a gracious, welcoming smile while the three instruments played a few tunes. Graham didn't remove his arm, and I allowed it to remain, enjoying its warmth. All down the street, the dance halls sent their musicians out. It made a considerable racket: talent was no requirement for a musician's job in Dawson. Eventually my men shuddered to a halt, and the caller lifted his bullhorn to announce to the entire population of the Yukon Territory that the Savoy, "the finest establishment west of London, England", was open for their entertainment.

The orchestra gathered up their instruments and trooped back inside, followed by an eager pack of customers. I smiled at Graham. He tightened the arm around my waist and bent forward. His lovely hazel eyes moved under their heavy lashes. "Fiona, I..."

"Show time," I said cheerfully, wiggling out of his grip. "Let's go and see what trouble Dawson can get up to tonight, shall we?"

His face twitched above the generous moustache that overpowered his boyishly handsome face. "Yes, let's do that."

I nodded to Ray, who was standing behind the highly polished mahogany bar pouring rivers of whisky. He gave me a wink, indicating that all was well. Graham and I were waylaid by an old miner named Barney, eager to relate another story of his pals Snookum Jim, Taglish Charlie, George Carmacks, and the discovery at Bonanza Creek. Barney, bleary-eyed, badly dressed, scruffy as could possibly be, stinking to high heaven, had, for a brief time, been one of the richest men in Dawson. He'd been prospecting at Forty Mile when news of the strike spread and he'd had made it to Bonanza Creek in time to stake a good claim. As for almost everyone else, those who'd struggled up from San Francisco, Seattle, Edmonton, maybe even London, Amsterdam or Johannesburg, the good claims were gone before they'd so much as booked passage. Barney quickly spent all of his fortune, most of it in the saloons and at gambling tables. He loved to treat everyone, particularly the stage performers and dancers, when he was in the money. Now he occasionally bought the odd bit of mining equipment and talked about going back to re-work his claim, but mostly he hung around bars, telling tales in exchange for a glass of whisky.

"Why don't you buy Barney a drink, Graham," I suggested. "He'd love to tell you stories about the discovery that you can write for your newspaper."

"Ain't never been a day like it, let me tell you, lad," Barney said, dragging Graham towards the bar. Graham tossed me a filthy look. The first time he'd heard this story, he'd dutifully written his copy and sent it to his newspaper. When the story appeared, his paper, the *New York World*, had the best single-edition sales in its recent history, and the name of Graham Donohue became synonymous with

"Klondike Gold Rush" to eager readers. The following hundred times Barney related the story, Graham ignored it. He didn't look happy at a hundred-and-one. I wiggled my fingers at him, leaving him to it.

I liked Graham a good deal. If I were looking for a husband, I might cast my eye his way. He was good-looking, charming, well groomed, and highly successful in his profession. But I wasn't looking, so that was the end of that.

I went into the back, to the performers' dressing rooms. I'd meant to arrive early and get a chance to speak with Irene, but the broken corset had put an end to my plans. The girls were a hurricane of preparations as they put on stage costumes, applied make-up, checked hair and stretched limbs.

Irene was pulling on a pair of long red gloves. Tonight she was going to do King Lear. For reasons unknown to me, the men loved Shakespeare. Particularly as, in a considerable switch from historical precedent, it was all acted by women. The vaudeville performers were onstage, warming up the audience and giving the girls time to dress and get ready for the first act. A lively chorus-line dance, while Ellie belted out a song, would precede *King Lear*. It was perhaps not as Shakespeare imagined it, but it was the way Dawson wanted it.

Satisfied everything was under control, I ducked to avoid a flicking red boa and glanced at the watch I kept pinned at my waist. Almost eight thirty. I didn't hear gales of laughter coming from the front of the house. I didn't even hear snickers. The vaudeville comedians were supposed to be in the middle of their act. I slipped out of the dressing room.

They were onstage all right, in front of a stony-faced audience. The two men ran about, tripping over their own feet and shouting lines of dialogue at each other. No one was laughing. Miners and cheechakos will laugh at almost anything, I have found, and they'll weep buckets of tears at the worst song cranked out by the worst voice you've ever heard, but they weren't laughing at this show.

I walked to the back of the room and leaned against the

wall. Lots of running around on stage, lots of shouting. One of them fell over a chair—that earned a round of chuckles.

"Where on earth did you find those two, Mrs. MacGillivray?" Constable Richard Sterling stood beside me.

"They brought letters of recommendation from theatres in the east."

"I should arrest them for impersonating comedians," Richard said.

I lifted one eyebrow. "I believe that's the first time I've heard you tell a joke, Constable."

"I wasn't joking, Mrs. MacGillivray," he said, but the gold streaks in his brown eyes twinkled with something approaching mirth.

Together we watched the show. The next skit involved the mother-in-law of one of them arriving at a dig and setting about organizing the mining activities. The audience chuckled at first, and before the end they were roaring with laughter. The mother-in-law character insisted on inspecting each piece of gold with her white gloves, and one miner fell off his bench in appreciation.

Richard chucked, then his voice dropped, and he was once again all business. "How's Mary doing?"

"Fine."

"She worked at the laundry today?"

"All day long."

"I don't mean to interfere…"

"Then don't."

"She can't make a life for herself in Dawson, you must know that."

"She will be safe with Mrs. Mann and me."

"Fiona." He turned to face me, full on. His eyes were now dark and serious. "You mean well, but I don't know if you understand what it can be like for the natives. No one will accept her, at least no one other than Joey LeBlanc and her customers."

"Precisely my point. I hope these fellows' second act is better than the first. Perhaps I'll see you later, Constable."

I edged my way through the rows of chairs as the vaudeville performers left the stage to a round of boos, and the chorus line danced on to a round of enthusiastic hooting. I didn't worry about the boos. The audience always booed the male performers and cheered the females.

Chapter Ten

Angus peeked through the door of the Savoy. Mrs. Saunderson often gave him a second breakfast or an after lunch snack; he visited his mother regularly, and sometimes he did his school work in her office. He considered Ray Walker to be a good friend and knew most of the dancers, bartenders and croupiers by name. The older of the dancers in particular seemed to like patting him on the head or pinching his cheeks while murmuring, "Isn't he such a dear." And as long as he wasn't working for the establishment, drinking or gambling, the NWMP didn't mind him being there, although Constable Sterling would sometimes roar for Angus to get out if things were getting a mite wild.

Tonight he was with Miss Witherspoon, and he had a feeling his mother would not be pleased, even though he was earning money escorting the English lady.

Miss Witherspoon paused at the doorway and took a deep breath. She'd changed into something approaching evening dress, although not what Angus was used to seeing his mother and the dance hall girls wear. Angus knew enough about women's clothes to know that her dress, with its enormous bustle and tight sleeves, was very out-of-date. His mother hadn't worn a bustle since they'd lived in Toronto. The dress was a dark, rich plum, draped with lace across Miss Witherspoon's majestic bosom and around the high collar and the hem. Matching lace and plum silk and a cluster of fake plums made up an enormous construction of a hat. She wore spotless white gloves that climbed past

her elbows and gripped her overlarge and quite out of
place brown leather bag (into which she had stuffed
notebook and pencil) in quivering hands.

"Here we are, Angus dear. Let us go in." She marched into
the Savoy with firm steps, looking neither left nor right. All
conversation stopped as everyone watched them make their
way across the room. Miss Witherspoon walked up to the bar
as the crowd parted politely. She hesitated only for a moment
when she caught sight of the two nudes that hung on either
side of a portrait of Her Imperial Majesty.

Her steely gaze fixed resolutely on her equally steely
Queen, Miss Witherspoon called for a whisky. If her voice
broke, perhaps only Angus, pressed up against her bustle-
bound rear end, heard it.

Ray abandoned the customer he was serving and stepped
around Murray. "Angus," he said, "is this lady a friend of
yours?"

"Yes, sir," Angus mumbled. Ladies were not supposed to
be in the bar, but on that matter, as so much else, the NWMP
kept quiet for the sake of keeping the peace. Miss
Witherspoon in her ancient plum dress and tattered hat,
gazing at her Queen to gather courage, was about as out of
place as a grizzly bear who'd wandered in and ordered drinks
all around. "This is Miss Witherspoon, sir. She's a writer."

Miss Witherspoon leaned over the bar and grasped
Ray's hand. "Pleased to meet you, sir. From Scotland, are
you? I can always tell. My grandmother was a Scottish lady,
a Miss MacDonald. More than a few Miss MacDonalds in
Scotland, I dare say." She laughed heartily. "I trust you have
proper Scottish whisky. I'll have one of those, please. And
a lemonade or something for my young companion."

Ray poured the drinks and slid two glasses across the
surface of the bar.

Miss Witherspoon swallowed her whisky in one gulp. She
gasped, her eyes welled up with tears, and she coughed.
Angus patted her discreetly on the back.

She slapped her glass back on the counter. "Another," she
croaked. Ray raised one eyebrow to Angus but obligingly

poured. The entire room watched Miss Witherspoon.

"Can I help you with something, miss?" Ray asked politely. This time Miss Witherspoon raised her glass cautiously and sipped. "I am a writer," she explained. "I am here to collect material for a book about the Klondike and this uh... establishment looked like a promising place to begin."

Miss Witherspoon didn't appear to have a single idea about how to begin. Angus cringed in embarrassment and looked over his shoulder to see if he might make a quiet escape. He was hemmed in by a solid mass of humanity, either pushing forward for a drink or to hear what the lady newcomer had to say for herself.

His mother's friend, Graham Donohue, watched them, a bemused expression on his face. "Mr. Donohue," Angus waved frantically. The newspaperman made his way through the crowd. He leaned against the counter and rested one boot on the footrest running the length of the bar.

Angus made the introductions and suggested that perhaps Mr. Donohue could help Miss Witherspoon with the gathering of information.

Miss Witherspoon nodded with enthusiasm, the basket of plums on her hat wobbling dangerously.

Donohue stroked his moustache as his eyebrows drew together in concentration. "See, Angus, it's like this: a good newspaperman doesn't reveal his sources. If I told everyone and his brother who was giving me the best information, then I wouldn't have any exclusives for my paper, now would I?"

"The heck with that nonsense, Donohue." A huge man stepped forward. He was almost seven feet tall, with chest and shoulders to match and an enormous moustache waxed to turn up at the ends. He was perfectly dressed in a custom-made suit with a showy red cravat pierced with a stickpin made up of a gold nugget the size of the end of Angus's thumb and a grey hat with a white headband. He carried a bag containing his outdoor boots. It was Mouse O'Brien, who always changed his shoes whenever he came in off the street. He was called Mouse not because of his size but in memory of the time a field mouse had darted across his path on the road to Bonanza Creek. The big man had screamed in terror and practically flown into the branches of a nearby tree. When his companions stopped laughing, they'd anointed him with the name. "Everyone in town knows where you get your stories, Donohue, those you don't make up at any rate." He politely doffed his hat and nodded to Miss Witherspoon. "Welcome to Dawson, ma'am." He raised his voice. "Barney, come and meet this here lady."

Various drinkers propelled Barney off his stool. He burped through a mouthful of whisky and rotten teeth. Miss Witherspoon tottered but managed to maintain her composure.

"This here is Barney, ma'am," Mouse bellowed in his normal speaking voice. "There's nothing happened in the Yukon in the past ten years that Barney don't know. He'll help you, won't you, Barney?"

Barney grinned and burped again. "I come north in '86," he said. "Weren't like it is now…"

Mouse nodded to Miss Witherspoon. "Don't you let the likes of Graham Donohue tell you anyone's stories are private. Stories in Dawson are like gold—just waitin' to be dug up."

"I was only joking," Donohue protested.

"I'm late tonight." Mouse stroked the ends of his moustache. "I've probably missed hearing my favourite girl sing and all. If you want to talk to me one day, ma'am, most folks know where to find Reginald O'Brien. Not that I've got stories like these old-timers."

Mouse tipped his hat, bowed graciously and took his leave.

Miss Witherspoon blinked in astonishment, watching Mouse's head and shoulders pass above the crowd of drinkers. Several of the men filled the space he'd vacated and shouted that they'd be happy to talk to her too.

Angus realized it was time to earn some of his pay. He straightened up. At twelve years old, he was already taller than a good many of these undernourished, poverty-raised men. "Miss Witherspoon'll be interviewing Barney this evening," he said. "But if you'd like to make an appointment with me, we can accommodate everyone who has a story to tell." He pulled out a sheet of paper he congratulated himself on having had the foresight to bring.

Miss Witherspoon was still blinking. Barney had stopped talking and was staring at her hat. He wasn't holding a glass, and his fingers twitched.

"Perhaps we could find a table," Angus suggested.

"A table?"

"A place to conduct the interview and make appointments for later?"

"A table! An excellent idea," Miss Witherspoon blinked one last time and focused on Angus. She leaned over to whisper in his ear. "Who was that remarkable man?"

"They call him Mouse O'Brien, ma'am. I've never heard anyone call him Reginald. He's here most nights. I'll ask him if he'd like to make an appointment, if you like."

"An appointment?"

"To be interviewed by you?"

"An appointment. Yes. An appointment." She almost visibly shook herself. "Time to get to work then. Secure us a table, young Angus. You, bartender, I don't think I want the rest of this drink. I'll have a lemonade instead."

Ray, who'd been listening throughout the entire exchange, because everyone else was listening and no one was buying drinks, grinned and slipped the full glass of whisky under the counter to have once her back was turned. He poured a glass of what passed in Dawson as lemonade, rather horrid, terribly sweet, canned stuff, the colour of dog piss.

Miss Witherspoon accepted the glass with a weak smile and turned away from the bar. Angus had managed to magically snare an empty table and waved her towards it.

Barney didn't move. He looked at Ray Walker, who had gone back to serving customers. "Are you coming, Mr. uh, Barney?" Miss Witherspoon inquired.

Barney looked at the row of bottles against the back wall. His eyes followed Murray as he poured drinks.

"Mr. Barney?" Miss Witherspoon repeated.

Murray leaned over the counter and attempted to speak *sotto voce*. "Barney expects a drink in exchange for a story, ma'am."

Miss Witherspoon scrambled in her bag for money. Murray accepted the cash and handed Barney his drink.

"So I said to George," Barney said, making his way to their table, "look here, George, there ain't no gold..."

Angus MacGillivray could always tell when his mother was about to enter a room. The men standing by the door fell silent, some of them attempted to slick their cowlicks down, some straightened their tie or suspenders or checked that their shirts were tucked in, and some sucked in their stomachs, while an almost invisible path formed where moments before there'd been a solid line of drinking men.

She floated into the saloon on a cloud of satin of such a pale green, it reminded Angus of the icebergs they'd seen from the first-class deck on their voyage to Canada. He wondered if she knew how the atmosphere in the room changed the minute she approached. She smiled at the men and stopped for a brief moment to chat with a few of them and accept compliments. She seemed to be able to make every man feel he had her full attention, but all the while her black eyes were flitting about the room, noticing everything, missing nothing.

And, eventually, those black eyes settled on her only son, who was trying very hard to make himself invisible.

Her smile didn't falter, but she waved her hand at a man who was in mid-sentence and stalked across the room. Angus remembered how one of the icebergs had calved as they watched; a great roar and an icy hunk had broken off into the heaving ocean.

"Good evening, Mother," he said, politely getting to his feet. "You remember Miss Witherspoon?"

"What on earth are you doing sitting at a table in the middle of the saloon?" Fiona looked up with a brilliant smile at a man walking dejectedly out of the gambling hall, shaking his head in disbelief. "Good night, Martin. Please do come again soon. Angus, I'm talking to you."

"Mrs. MacGillivray, please join us. Angus, fetch another chair for your mother." Miss Witherspoon's notebook was covered with chicken-feet scratches that didn't look anything like English to Angus. He'd been kept busy alternately jotting appointment times on his scrap of paper and ferrying glasses back and forth between the bar and Barney, who hadn't stopped talking since they'd sat down. Barney burped heartily in greeting.

Fiona settled herself into the chair Angus provided and fluffed her green skirts. "How is your companion, Miss Witherspoon?"

"She is resting at our hotel. I thought it improper to bring a delicate lady into this sort of establishment."

"Quite. And what brings you here?"

Miss Witherspoon explained while Angus shifted uncomfortably in his chair, and Barney's eyes began to close. Fiona's smile was as icy as her gown.

"Angus," she said, once Miss Witherspoon's narrative came to an end. "I believe it's time you were going home."

"Oh, surely not," Miss Witherspoon said. "We are coming along simply famously. I can't possibly remain here by myself, and Barney has ever so much more to tell me, don't you, Barney? Barney?"

But Barney's head had hit the table, where his cheek rested in a pool of whisky. Fiona raised her arm and snapped her fingers. Murray came running. "Take Barney home," she said.

Murray tucked his bartender's cloth into the waistband of his trousers and lifted the old miner under the arms. Fiona was fond of Barney, and he was always taken care of in the Savoy. If anyone else collapsed, they'd be tossed out into the street with little regard for what might be concealed under the mud or any vehicle that might be passing by.

"It would appear," Fiona said, "that your interview is over, Miss Witherspoon. Angus, escort Miss Witherspoon to her lodgings. And then go home."

Miss Witherspoon gathered up her belongings and dug

through her bag for two crisp dollar bills, which she thrust into Angus's hand. "Do you have my appointments for tomorrow evening, young man?"

"Yes, ma'am. Starting at eight o'clock."

She pulled out a man's heavy pocket watch and held it in front of her, stretching her arms to almost their full length. "Close to midnight." The watch snapped shut under the force of her approval. "I'd say that was a most successful evening. Make my last appointment for eleven. This seems to be late enough for me." She pushed back her chair and patted the front of her dress. Her white gloves were stained with spilled whisky, pencil lead and a good coating of dust. "Would you care to join us for tea tomorrow, Mrs. MacGillivray? Say two o'clock at my hotel? An improper hour for tea, I know, but that's when your son starts work, and I expect we'll be busy for the remainder of the day. I've noticed that in Dawson people are somewhat relaxed in consideration of proper social convention, therefore the early hour will be of no consequence. Euila's most anxious to talk with you. Until tomorrow, good evening."

Miss Witherspoon sailed out of the Savoy, looking a great deal more confident than when she had entered. Angus gave his mother a glance before running after Miss Witherspoon.

He didn't often see his mother at a loss for words.

*   *   *

Once I got over my initial shock at seeing Angus in the company of Miss Witherspoon, I decided I was rather pleased with the boy. As a girl, I'd lived in comfortable rural poverty on Skye, when my parents were alive, and grinding urban misery in the worst slums of London after their deaths. Whenever my son got too satisfied with the life I provided for us in Dawson, I reminded him quickly enough that bad fortune is always lurking around a corner. I was rather proud that he was showing initiative and earning money. I would have preferred it weren't from Miss

Witherspoon, having been determined to keep Angus and Euila from meeting again, but other than tie him to his bed until they left town, I had no way of preventing him from associating with them. Any direct order to stay out of their way would only make the boy curious. I would try, somehow, to indicate to Euila at tea tomorrow that she should not tell Angus about our mutual past. I'd always been able to manipulate her into doing anything, and Euila didn't appear to have grown any more backbone since our childhood.

It would be nice to spend some time with Euila Forester, I thought, but I wasn't too keen on having tea with her and Martha Witherspoon in the company of my wide-eared son. As it happened, I managed, with no conniving on my part, to get out of it.

I slept through the appointment.

When I woke from my afternoon sleep at the regular time of three o'clock, I stumbled into the kitchen in search of a cup of coffee. A note sat on the counter, propped up against a light blue can of Old Chum smoking tobacco, in which Angus explained that he didn't want to disturb me and would offer my excuses to the ladies.

I poured a cup of the thick, black, far-too-strong coffee which Mrs. Mann had left on the back of the stove, and smiled at my good fortune in having such a thoughtful son. After tasting the coffee, I dumped it into the bucket that served as a sink and got ready for the second half of my day.

The Savoy was quiet when I arrived. Not-Murray was filling the big barrel of drinking water behind the bar. Helen Saunderson came out of her storage closet/kitchen lugging one of the enamel spittoons, temporarily clean. Barney slouched against the counter and lifted one hand in lazy acknowledgement of my arrival. I stopped to chat for a few minutes with a table full of old timers who were still covered in a thick layer of mud and dust from the Creeks. They were as excited as schoolboys at the start of half-term break at getting the opportunity to tell me all about their lucky strike. They opened their bags and let me take a peek at the pile of gold dust and the handful of nuggets inside.

I offered my congratulations, wondering how long it would be before the gold found its way out of their bags and into my bank account.

Excusing myself, I headed for the gambling rooms. A rotten floorboard squeaked under my weight. The place was so badly made that even though it wasn't yet a year old, the floorboards were already protesting. The poker tables were empty, but a few games of faro and roulette were in progress. The fat American gambler named Tom Jannis stood at the roulette table, shouting at the wheel to land on red. His face was very round and very red and dripped with sweat. The crispness of his clothes was wearing off, and his cuffs were showing more than just dust. He wore a wool scarf, too hot for this weather, which I assumed hid a tattered collar.

"No more bets," Jake, our head croupier, called out, and the wheel settled slowly to rest on red. Jake raked in a few of the white twenty-five cent chips belonging to the other players but slid a good-sized pile of blue five-dollar ones towards Jannis.

Chloe stood at Jannis's elbow, squealing enthusiastically while the wheel turned. Her faded purple dress had a layer of dried mud around the hem and a tear through the elbow. The lace protecting her scrawny bosom needed a wash.

"Get out, Chloe," I said in a low voice.

She turned, and her eyes narrowed.

"I'm here with a gentleman, Mrs. MacGillivray. As his guest." She tried to lift her chin, but her eyes watered, and her attempt at a ladylike sniff came out more like she had allergies.

With single-minded concentration, Jannis divided his winnings into neat piles.

"Hey," Chloe screeched, "are you gonna let *her* throw me outta this dump?"

Jannis studied the table, debating where to place his chips. I was about to call for a bouncer, when he said, "Her dump, you do what she says." He arranged his chips across the board, concentrating on the lower numbers with a big pile on zero. Jake spun the wheel.

"Get out, Chloe," I said.

She glared at the back of Jannis's uninterested head.

"No more bets," Jake said.

Chloe turned and stomped out of the room. I was the only one who watched her leave.

"Twenty-five," Jake said.

Chapter Eleven

The rest of that day and through the next, I kept glancing over my shoulder, expecting to see the miserable Chloe haunting my steps. Leaving the house on Thursday evening, I caught a flash of purple at the side of the building across the street. But by the time several overloaded carts had rumbled past, there was no sign of her. There was, however, a patch of purple fireweed growing amongst the stumps of trees that had been levelled to create the street. The flowers were not the same colour as Chloe's dress, but I convinced myself I might have been mistaken in thinking I'd seen my former dancer.

Nevertheless, I told Ray to tell the men to keep Chloe out and to let me know immediately if she turned up again.

It was nearing closing time, and the dance hall was a mass of humanity; all the percentage girls were dancing, and men were lined up waiting to have the opportunity to pay a dollar for a single minute of their company. Irene had spent most of the night dancing with Tom Jannis, unfortunately keeping him away from the tables where I could earn more off him than a dollar a minute. I dragged her away with a weak excuse and told her to go upstairs and sit in my office for a half hour or so. However, instead of going into the gambling hall, he disappeared. I cringed as a bow scraped across the violin strings. The orchestra was getting tired, and they were starting to make mistakes. Murray was climbing down the stairs from the balcony carrying an armful of empty champagne bottles, for which we charged forty dollars a quart. Mouse O'Brien leaned over the railing and waved to me. Mouse had had a rare poor night at the poker table, but unlike most of our customers, he knew when to cut his losses and seek other entertainment. I waved back.

A spot behind my right eye was beginning to throb. If I didn't get some fresh air, I'd spend the rest of the night with a headache.

I slipped out the back door and stood in the narrow, grubby alley that separated the Savoy from the mortuary and dry goods shop behind. The light was dim from the rays of a sun that had only dipped behind the hills for a moment before rising again for another twenty-two hours.

I picked my way through the muck in the alley, stretching my legs and enjoying the fresh air, what there was of it above the scent of dog urine, human vomit and assorted trash. A man and a woman were arguing in the shadows towards York Street. I couldn't make out the words, but the tone was unmistakable. None of my business: at this time of night, in the alley, they couldn't be much else but a whore and either her pimp or her mark. As I started to turn around, the woman raised her voice, and I recognized the well-educated, properly-enunciated accent.

I tiptoed forward and peeped through the gloom. Tom Jannis had Mary pressed up against the wall. "You know you want it," he said while his hand fumbled with her skirts, which were gathered up around her waist. Whether she was trying to push his groping hand away, or help him to release her undergarments, I couldn't tell.

"Stop that!" I shouted, in my best Lady-Muck-Muck accent. "Release that woman."

Jannis stepped back. The dim light revealed Mary's half-unbuttoned shirt. She hesitated, not knowing what to do first: straighten her skirts or fasten her bodice. In her embarrassment, she did neither.

"Oh, Mrs. MacGillivray," she said.

"Haven't you got anything better to do than hang around back alleys looking for people to interfere with?" Jannis said. His round face was red with anger and the residue of excitement.

"No," I said. "It looks like it's a good thing, too."

His clothes were dishevelled, and his hat was lying in the dirt. He straightened his tie and scooped up his hat. "Regardless of what this might look like to you, madam, I am simply trying to get value for my money."

"No," Mary said, fumbling to do up her buttons. "That's not true."

"Get inside, Mary," I said.

Jannis dusted his hat in a lazy gesture, and Mary ran past me, her face averted.

"Best you be on your way," I said.

"Or?" His eyes wandered boldly down the front of my dress.

"I am not without friends and influence in this town."

"I've no doubt of that. I don't care much for Indians anyway." He put on what he probably considered to be a hard man tone in an attempt leave me no doubt as to what he preferred. He was trying to be intimidating, but I've stood up to men a good deal tougher than he. And many a good deal more powerful.

"You're banned from the Savoy," I said.

"That's no hardship." He placed his hat neatly on his head. "Plenty of joints like it. But I'll be seeing *you* around soon. Mrs. MacGillivray."

He touched the brim of his hat, smirked and walked away, down York to Front Street. The skies were clear, and it was a warm, humid night. A drop of sweat ran down the small of my back and under my corset, while a knot of red rage boiled up in my chest. I'd allowed Mary to stay in the Savoy, against the advice of everyone from Richard Sterling to Helen Saunderson, and now it looked like they were right after all. Mary could come back inside to collect her belongings, then she could get the hell off my property.

As I turned, I caught a whiff of cigar smoke. A red spark burned in the shadows, a man's face behind it. Someone was watching me. The spark faded as the man retreated further into the gloom. Someone else out for the air, I assumed. Tonight, at least, the back streets of Dawson were no place to be if one was in need of privacy.

I hurried after Tom Jannis, wanting to make sure he didn't try to come in through the front door. He sauntered across York Street and joined the line at the Vanderhaege sisters' bakery. He must have known I was watching him, but he didn't look around; he said something to a group of men, and they laughed. A couple of drunks came swaying down the boardwalk towards me, their arms wrapped tightly around each other, singing in surprisingly good voices about someone named Johnny whom they hardly knew.

Out of the corner of my eye, through a momentary break in the crowds, I saw a skinny figure weaving its way through the mob, heading south. When I looked again, she'd disappeared in the mass of men.

Chloe. No doubt about it.

This was getting ridiculous. Next I'd be finding her in my bed. I considered chasing after her and having it out, but I next considered what "having it out" might mean for Chloe. I couldn't afford to ruin another dress. I wasn't particularly concerned about myself; what could a miserable chit like her do to me? But if I ever found her anywhere near Angus...

My break had not improved my mood, and I returned to the Savoy in a rage. There was only one reason I could think of for why Mary would be out in the alley. It was not uncommon for dancers and percentage girls to earn extra on the side; some dance hall proprietors encouraged it, and the Mounties ignored it unless it became too obvious. Ray and I most emphatically forbade the custom: it helped to keep our dancers popular and our prices high if the girls were considered unobtainable. But Mary was an Indian, and the Mounties were trying to keep the Indians away from white men's vices. If the authorities thought I was prostituting her, I'd be closed down before I could shout "respectable". And if it wasn't bad enough that she was using my hospitality to continue in her old profession, she was risking a lot worse than my anger by going freelance in the face of Joey LeBlanc, who knew everything that went on in the alleys of Dawson.

And then there was Chloe. She was watching the Savoy—to what aim I couldn't imagine. Unless simply to annoy me, at which she succeeded magnificently.

The throbbing spot behind my eye had now taken possession of my entire head.

It was six o'clock, and Ray and the men were ushering our customers out. One or two protested and tried to point out that the other saloons and dance halls were not closing. As if Ray hadn't noticed. As usual, he mumbled something about "the boss", laying all the blame on me.

Which was fine, as in turn I usually put the blame for everything the customers didn't like on him.

"Feeling all right, Fee?" he asked once the last straggler had been evicted.

I touched my head. "No." No matter how bad I felt, I still had to go upstairs, settle the women's drink chips and prepare to lock up our night's takings.

*   *   *

It was going to be another hot, dry day. If the rains didn't turn the streets into rivers of mud, the dust choked everything and everyone it touched. Only in the winter did the mud and the dust go away—then you couldn't walk as far as the outdoor privy without so much clothing, you resembled an Eskimo. Not that I'd ever seen an Eskimo, but I had seen pictures of them standing beside their ice houses with nothing showing but noses and happy smiles. What on earth, I asked myself, was I doing in this cursed country? Tomorrow I would tell Ray he could buy me out, and Angus and I would take the next steamship south.

As I mumbled and grumbled, earning a strange look from a properly-dressed woman on her way to begin her day's work, I knew Angus and I were staying. In no place I'd lived had I ever felt as alive as I did every day in Dawson, nor was I able to make so much money. Legally, that is. Although considering the pain that was throbbing through my miserable head, I could do with a touch of numbness right about now.

Before collapsing into my most welcome bed, I would have to speak to Mary. She could continue working for Mrs. Mann, if Mrs. Mann wanted her to, but she was to vacate the Savoy immediately. If she couldn't find alternative accommodation, she could sleep in the street.

The laundry shed was beginning to steam as Mr. Mann fired up the stove, and Mrs. Mann sorted through piles of filthy clothes.

"Where's Mary?" I said.

"Not here," Mrs. Mann said.

"She late, she not get pays." Mr. Mann straightened up from the fire, holding a fist to the small of his back, his face red with the heat and the exertion of carrying wood from the big pile beside the shed. "She very late, she fired. My wife not do all zee works herself. Stupid Indian."

"She was prompt yesterday," Mrs. Mann said, holding up a shirt for inspection that was scarcely more than a rag. She tilted her head from one side to the other. "Wash this, and it'll fall apart."

"Is Angus up?" I asked.

"He was eating his breakfast when I left the house. How do you suppose this shirt got all these little holes in it?"

"I truly do not want to know."

"Perhaps Mary slept in. Can you ask Angus to go around and fetch her?"

Angus was in the kitchen, eating porridge and bacon, and bread fried in dripping while reading a penny dreadful. I asked him to go to the Savoy and pound on Mary's door to get her up. Considering that I'd seen her not much more than an hour before with her dress around her waist in a back alley, it was unlikely she was in any condition to get up and face a day's work. But I'd been the one who'd arranged for Mrs. Mann to hire her, and I'd make sure she faced her commitments.

Angus sopped up the last of his dripping and stood to give me a greasy kiss on the cheek. "You look dreadful, Mother. Go to bed."

So I did.

I had scarcely untied my hair, washed my face (the water was lovely and hot; Mrs. Mann knows my schedule), removed my jewellery, struggled out of dress, petticoat, over-corset, corset, stockings and undergarments, and pulled on my night-gown, when Angus was hammering on my bedroom door to tell me there was no answer from Mary's room.

I sighed and told him to come in.

We debated for a few moments—Angus insisting that something had happened to her and we had to go in search of her; me attempting to remind him that this was a small town in terms of geography, but bigger than many cities in terms of population. Angus suggested I could at least check Mary's room to make sure she wasn't sick or dying, then we could ask at the hospital and Fort Herchmer if they'd had news of an accident.

I knew where I'd look first, but I didn't want my son going there on his own. He'd taken to Mary, and his lovely face was pinched with worry. Against my better judgment, I shooed Angus out of my room and told him to wait in the kitchen. While I struggled back into undergarments, corset, over-corset, stockings, petticoats, and day dress, pinned my hair and selected a hat, I developed a plan. We'd check Mary's room, then Angus could go to the hospital and the Mounties while I went to Paradise Alley and discretely asked around. If I found her there, I could at least tell my son that Mary'd decided the life of a laundry maid wasn't for her, and she wouldn't be back.

Dressing completed, I sat on my bed to lace up my street shoes. It shouldn't be much of a mystery to anyone why Mary would so quickly go back to her old life. Mrs. Mann paid two dollars a day, plus three meals and the occasional cup of tea, for twelve hours spent in a stifling hot, steamy and quite dangerous (with all that boiling water and open fires) laundry shed, sorting through working-class men's disgusting clothes and sordid undergarments. I cringed merely thinking about it. I'd heard that some Paradise Alley prostitutes could get ten, twenty dollars per assignation, of which they gave fifty to seventy-five per cent to their manager. Mary was an Indian, so she wouldn't command top rates, but it had to be a lot more than a laundry maid got. Perhaps even enough to endure the beatings I'd seen evidence of on her back.

I'd once been faced with similar choices. I'd decided to accept neither of them and find my own way.

It was the thought that Mary was searching for her own way, like a young, frightened, but dreadfully cocky Fiona MacGillivray, that had me out of my nightgown and back into my street clothes.

Chapter Twelve

Angus's friends often complained about how long it took their mothers and sisters to get ready to face the world, but his mother always seemed to be able to get herself decent in not much more time that it took some men. On the Chilkoot trail, he'd seen the amount of clothing she wore, and the many more layers she'd brought for when they reached "civilization". It always amazed him that she was able to get dressed in under several hours.

This morning, he'd scarcely finished another chapter of his book before she was in the kitchen, in a crisp, lacy white blouse with a big blue bow and a dark blue skirt. Her hair was perfectly arranged, and her hat, featuring a huge blue feather and a cluster of fake plums, was properly in place. Only the hint of dark circles under her black eyes indicated that she hadn't yet slept.

"We'll go to the Savoy first," she declared. "And if Mary isn't there, you can inquire at Fort Herchmer and the hospital. I will…uh…search elsewhere."

Angus had not the slightest doubt as to where "elsewhere" might be. Nor did he doubt that he would not allow his mother to search Paradise Alley on her own. Mary had been a prostitute; Angus knew what that meant. He also knew that people like Mrs. LeBlanc, who controlled prostitutes, considered them not much more than property. So someone might well have taken poor Mary against her will from her room in the Savoy under cover of the noise below, or even snatched her off the street.

At the Savoy, Angus pounded on the door to Mary's room.

The sound echoed throughout the empty building. When no one answered, his mother cautiously opened the door.

The room was plain, with a narrow bed and a small dresser to hold the chipped wash jug and basin. The walls and floor were cheap wood, and there were no pictures on the walls. A scrap of red cloth covered the single window to serve as a curtain. The room was neat, the bed made, the basin wiped out. A single stem of fresh purple fireweed sat in a water glass on the dresser beside a pocket bible. Fiona shut the door. A plain dress hung on the hook at the back. She pulled out a dresser drawer to reveal a few scraps of neatly folded undergarments and stockings. The sum total of Mary's possessions.

"Looks like she hasn't moved out," Angus said.

"No."

"Is something the matter, Mother?"

"No."

They left the Savoy and stood outside on the boardwalk. One half of the town was starting to come to life as men walked to work, stores opened, and respectable women went about their family's errands. The other half was closing down as men staggered out of dance halls and less respectable women stood in the shadows. The line in front of the Vanderhaege sisters' bakery stretched a good way down the street.

"Are you looking for someone, Mother? Someone other than Mary, I mean."

"Certainly not."

"It's just that you keep looking around, and you seem nervous."

"What a ridiculous idea," Fiona said in that haughty tone which, Angus had come to recognize, meant he was right.

"Go to the hospital and then to the Fort," she said. "I'll look...elsewhere. We'll meet up at home."

"I'll go with you."

"Certainly not."

"Mother, I know you think Mary has gone back to Mrs. LeBlanc, and you're going to Paradise Alley to find her. But she hasn't. Remember, I was there when we collected Mary's things. She hates Mrs. LeBlanc. And Mrs. LeBlanc was really mean, told her to never come back."

"Angus, dear. Sometimes people don't always do what they want to do. Or even what's best for them. I'll check to set your mind at ease. Then I really do have to be getting to bed."

"I don't want you going there by yourself, Mother."

Fiona looked quite astonished. "Angus…" She started to say something but changed her mind. "I don't want you there at all."

"I know what happens in Paradise Alley, Mother. I know about men paying women like Mary used to be to make love with them. I know what sex is, Mother."

Two men, out-of-luck old timers by the look of them, stopped dead on the boardwalk. They looked at Angus through red-rimmed, bleary eyes. "Good for you, lad," said the first one. "I was almost twice your age 'afore I figured it all out."

"Wouldn't have been tellin' my ma, though," the second one said, his words slurred almost beyond recognition. "Times are changin', eh, Roy."

"Do you mind, this is a private conversation," Fiona snapped. "Stand aside." She pushed the one named Roy off the boardwalk. They chuckled and went on down the street, talking loudly about what the times were coming to.

"We will discuss that particular matter later," Fiona said. "Now, go to Fort Herchmer."

"I would like to accompany you, Mother," Angus said, trying to sound grown-up and formal. "It is my responsibility to protect your reputation."

To his surprise, his mother threw back her head and laughed. "Where on earth did you get that idea?" she said once she could speak again.

"Sergeant Lancaster told me if a boy's father isn't around, it is his responsibility…"

"Oh, yes. Sergeant Lancaster. You can take his advice with a grain of salt, Angus; he does have an ulterior motive."

"Yes, Mother."

"All right, you win. You can show me where you got Mary's possessions, Angus. The girls around there might tell us if they've seen her."

They walked up York Street to Second Avenue and headed south towards the heart of Paradise Alley. It was morning, and the night's business was coming to an end. A few girls still stood in the doorways, but most of the cribs looked to be closed for the day. Despite what he'd said to his mother, Angus didn't really know much about what went on behind those cheap wooden doors. His friends whispered about it sometimes, and Dave had told everyone that he'd visited Big Bessie's crib with his dad lots of times. But no one believed him, particularly because Dave couldn't describe anything that happened after Bessie took off her clothes. He didn't even seem to know that women wore a corset to give them that funny shape, all kinda pulled in and pushed out at the same time. Dave thought they were made that way, probably because he lived alone with his dad, who was a bartender at the Horseshoe.

The women watched them pass.

A man came out of a crib, doing up his tie and straightening his hat, and stepped directly into their path.

"Fiona, what on earth?"

"Graham! What are you doing here?"

Donohue flushed and left his tie askew.

"Fiona. Angus. This hardly seems like the time or place to run into you. Not that it isn't a pleasure, as always."

Fiona's dark eyes blazed. Angus almost thought he could see a flicker of a red ember in their depths. "I asked what you are doing here, Graham."

The newspaperman took her arm and dropped his voice, forcing Angus to strain to hear. "Working on a story, Fiona. A big one. Some of these unfortunate ladies are being kept here against their will. It seems..."

"Tell me another time." Fiona pulled a lace-trimmed handkerchief out of a tuck in her dress and rubbed at a smudge on Donohue's cheek. "Why do you have lipstick on your face?"

"The dear lady," Donohue's eyes clouded over, and he nodded towards the crib from which he'd emerged, "is afraid to speak to me openly in case her boss sees us. She was so grateful to me for listening to her story that she honoured me with a kiss."

Angus snorted, but Fiona smiled at Donohue. "It is a disgrace what goes on in some of these places. The poor girls are treated like cattle. I'm sure your story will do a great deal of good, Graham."

Angus couldn't believe what he was hearing. His mother had accepted Donohue's nonsense? Just when he thought he understood women, they went and did something completely stupid.

"Whatever you're doing here, Fiona, I suggest you consider your reputation, and Angus's young sensibilities." Donohue attempted to steer Fiona back in the direction from which they'd come. Fiona, never one to be steered anywhere, resisted. A minor tug of war took place over her arm. They sort of danced up and down the street, and Angus bobbed and weaved as though he were in the boxing ring, trying to keep up with them.

Eventually Fiona tired of the struggle. "Graham, I insist you unhand me." She wrenched her arm out of his grip. She stumbled backwards into a tiny opening between two of the cribs.

Angus heard a cry, and a crash, then a good bit of bad language.

"Fiona, are you all right?"

"Mother?"

Graham Donohue and Angus MacGillivray peered into the darkness. It was daylight, but the space between the buildings was so narrow, the sun couldn't poke its probing rays into the alley. Only the white froth of Fiona's petticoats was visible in the gloom.

"You fool, help me up. If I've ruined another dress, you'll pay for it, Graham Donohue. Be careful, there's something there, and it tripped me. It's sort of soft and squishy. I most certainly hope it isn't a dead dog."

Donohue stepped forward. "Hard to see anything," he muttered. "Hold out your hand, Fiona. Oh, god."

"Are you going to assist me or not? Angus, come here. Graham seems to have found something of greater importance than helping me."

"Angus, get your mother up." Donohue's voice was flat. "Keep against the right hand wall. Get her out of here and don't look down."

Angus looked down. The shape at Donohue's feet started to take form as his eyes became accustomed to the lack of light.

A woman lay on her back with her skirts twisted around her body so that her stockings were showing up past her knees. Angus averted his gaze and immediately wished he hadn't. The eyes were wide open and staring directly at him, and her head lay in a patch of mud that hadn't dried after the last rain. A fat fly buzzed loudly as it flew past his ear, and there was a strange smell, sort of sickeningly sweet, filling the alley. Angus looked again and realized that it wasn't mud at all. The dirt under the woman's head was soaked with blood.

Chapter Thirteen

What on earth is the matter with men these days, I thought. I was practically flat on my back, struggling like an overturned turtle to get up, and Graham and Angus were studying something at their feet. Flies and mosquitoes buzzed around and the smell was dreadful. There must be a dead dog in the alley. Most unpleasant, and if I got any of it on my dress, you can be sure Graham Donohue would be promising to buy me a new one before the sun was much higher in the sky.

By the incredibly squeamish way they were behaving and the rather unsettling sounds they were making, you'd think that Donohue and Angus had never been inside a butcher shop.

Then, as if the school bell had rung, they sprang into action. Between them, they actually lifted me off the ground and carried me out of the alley. They weren't fast enough, and I still had my wits about me, so I saw what they were lifting me over.

"Put me down immediately. Angus MacGillivray, put me down, or you'll spend the rest of the month on bacon and beans." An idle threat, as Mrs. Mann did all the cooking, but the only thing I could think of on the spur of the moment.

I was unceremoniously dumped in the street. No thanks to my rescuers, I managed to retain my balance.

"Keep it down," a voice called from the nearest crib. "People is sleepin' round here."

I took a deep breath and steadied my shaking limbs. I looked at my son—he was white around the mouth, and his eyes were round. Graham shook his head slightly and tried to step in front of me. I pushed him aside and forced myself to look.

Bile rose in my throat, but I pushed it down. I'd allow myself to be sick later, in private.

My first thought was relief. It wasn't Mary, as I'd feared, lying there at my feet with her eyes wide and staring as a fly landed on a lid. I reached behind me and fumbled for someone's hand. I clutched it and hoped it was my son's.

It wasn't Mary lying there, but it was someone I knew.

"Go for the Mounties, Angus," I said.

"Okay, but let Mr. Donohue take you home, Mother."

"No." Women were sticking their heads out of their cribs. A few men gathered at the street corners, wondering what was going on. "If we leave...it...her alone, every ghoul in town will be here. Not to mention every fly and stray dog"

Angus gulped, turned and ran.

Graham took my arm. "Why don't we stand over here, Fiona? We can be out of the way and keep others away at the same time." I allowed him to lead me a few short steps back into the street.

Seeing that one of us had left and the others weren't doing much, the bystanders lost interest. Women slammed their doors, and men drifted off.

"She looks a mite familiar," Graham said. "Hard to tell though, with the bl...mess."

A mangy dog, all bones and matted fur and shaking legs, crept towards us. Graham snatched up a stone and hurled it. His aim was good, and the creature squealed once and disappeared. I thought I could hear vermin crawling out from under the buildings, and I held my hand over my mouth and tried to think about what plans I had for the day ahead. I had been told there were no rats in the Yukon. I didn't know if I believed it: where there are people, there are bound to be rats.

Angus was back so soon, he must have found Constable Sterling in the next street. Which turned out to be the case.

The light was getting better as the sun climbed, and it was easier to see into the alley. Richard stepped forward and crouched down. He didn't touch anything, just looked. With a sigh he got to his feet, wiped his hands on his trousers and faced us. "Angus, go to the Fort and get Inspector McKnight."

"Yes, sir!" Angus rushed to do as he was asked.

The arrival of the Mountie brought the curious back out. Some of the bolder men edged forward, necks craning to see what we were looking at. Richard ordered them to stand back, and with ill grace and some muttering, they did so.

Graham smiled at me. It lifted the corner of his mouth but didn't reach his eyes. He took my hand and squeezed it. I was pleased he was writing a story about the conditions in which some of the Dawson prostitutes were kept, although I doubted if any newspaper would be so daring as to publish it.

Graham nudged me lightly, and I realized Richard was speaking. "Sorry, Constable, I'm a bit, uh…"

"That's understandable, Mrs. MacGillivray. You know this lady?"

"She's one of my dancers. That is, she was one of my dancers; I fired her on Tuesday. Or was it Monday? Can't have been Sunday, of course, we're not open on Sunday. Wednesday, perhaps. No Tuesday. Hard to tell sometimes, the way the days all run into each other without true night time. Her name is Chloe. I don't know her surname, but it will be in my files back in my office if you need it."

"We probably will."

The rapidly growing crowd edged back fractionally to let Angus through, and behind him came Inspector McKnight.

McKnight was a small man whose red jacket didn't quite fit, making him look like a boy playing dress-up in his father's old uniform. His spectacles were so thick, he must have been nearly blind, but they served to emphasize the keen intelligence in his eyes and the way they were always moving, always watching everyone and everything. He was besotted with Ellie, one of my dancers, and would hang around the Savoy hoping for a smile or a nod.

He touched his hat. "Mrs. MacGillivray, a pleasure."

"Unfortunately, Inspector, the pleasure is not at all mine. If you don't mind, I am feeling quite unwell and need to go home and lie down." I've often used the delicate, fainting female trick to get out of unpleasant, or exceedingly boring situations, but this time it was no trick. I desperately needed to get some sleep and to stop the throbbing in my head, which was now accompanied by the churning in my stomach.

"If I have any questions, I know where to find you."

"Thank you, Inspector. Angus, you may take me home."

"Mother!" Angus protested.

Before I could argue with my son, everyone's attention was distracted by a cry of deep grief as Joey LeBlanc, of all people, dashed out of the crowd and threw herself into the alley. So sudden was her appearance, neither Sterling nor McKnight had the presence of mind to stop her. Her tiny body fell to its knees beside Chloe, and she wailed and cried out in French. Something about youth cut down and innocence destroyed and vows of retribution. She tore at her hair and grabbed the front of her dress, careful not to rip anything, and moaned and sobbed. All in all kicking up an unseemly fuss: wasn't that just like a Frenchwoman!

The crowd was growing exponentially as people were attracted by the noise and the general excitement of a mob gathering for something—anything. Mounties came running from all directions and attempted to keep some sort of order. Puffing and panting with the exertion of getting there, Sergeant Lancaster arrived and asked no one in particular what was happening.

"Angus," I ordered, "you will take me home."

"Yes, Mother," he said, so meekly I thought I might have misunderstood.

"*You.* You did this," Joey LeBlanc stood in front of me, although at a considerably lower level. Her scrawny chest was puffed up with indignation, and her face was mottled red with rage. She poked her forefinger into the front of my lovely clean white blouse.

Of course, I should have simply walked away. But, of course, I didn't. Instead, I removed her finger from my bosom and tossed it back at her. "Pardon me, but you have absolutely no idea what you are talking about."

"You toffee-nosed bitch," she shouted. Joey's English is excellent, but when she gets upset, the Quebec accent tends to take over. Which is fortunate, as I believe that she went on to offer opinions on my ancestry and my motives for being in Dawson.

"Now see here, madam," Graham said.

"How dare you talk to my mother like that," Angus said.

"Really," Sergeant Lancaster said.

The crowd edged closer. A well-dressed dandy made a break for the alley to get a better look, but a Mountie headed him off and told him to get out of the way, or he'd spend the rest of the summer chopping wood at the Fort.

"I suggest, Mrs. LeBlanc, that you step back." Constable Sterling said. "If you have something to tell the Inspector, he will be conducting interviews shortly."

"Are you going to talk to 'er?" she demanded, sticking that damned finger in my chest again.

"If we think it's required. If you'll step over here, please." He grabbed her arm and, very politely of course, almost jerked her off her feet.

Joey is no favourite of the police. They put up with her while waiting until they get a complaint they can act upon. Which never comes, her customers being generally satisfied and her girls being generally frightened into submission.

Joey tossed me a look, more crafty than nasty. Instead of meekly shutting up, she turned to the crowd. She shook her arm out of the constable's grasp and waved it in a great arc that encompassed Constable Sterling, Inspector McKnight and me. "They'll protect 'er," she said, speaking to the back of the crowd like a good theatrical actress. "Sweet Chloe, lying there, brought down like a dog, they don't care about the likes of 'er and me."

That was so patently ridiculous, I wanted to laugh. A few of the men in the crowd exchanged glances and muttered. Newcomers mostly—you could tell by their clothes they had recently stepped off the boats. Americans likely, ready to believe everything they were told about police corruption and influence. But the old-timers laughed. Even the whores snickered.

"Joey, the only sweet thing you seen the last ten years was a child's lollypop," a voice in the crowd shouted.

"Yeah, what you stole from him and then charged a dollar to give it back," someone else joined in. I couldn't see who the speaker was, but the voice sounded a lot like my favourite of the regulars, old Barney.

Joey's face turned red. It was unlikely she was blushing. She whirled on one of her whores, a fat old thing with a pasty face puffed up from too much drink and not enough good food. "What are you laughing at? You get back to work or I'll…"

The whore ran, leaving the threat unfinished.

I took the opportunity to grab Angus's arm and slip away. Graham followed. I was well liked in this town, and Joey generally wasn't, but a friendly crowd can turn into a howling mob in no time at all.

Behind us, the Mounties were asking everyone to move along. The crowd grumbled and complained, but in Dawson most everyone did as the Mounties asked.

We scurried back to Fourth Street, moving against the crush of people hurrying to find out what all the excitement was about. Who on earth would care enough about poor, stupid Chloe to kill her? I thought. At a quick guess, I'd say she'd tried turning tricks on her own, and someone had proved to be a-not-very-good customer. Which was, thankfully, none of my concern.

"What about Mary, Mother?" Angus said. "Aren't we going to find her?"

"Not now, Angus. We have enough worries for one morning."

"You mean Indian Mary?" Graham asked. "What about her?"

"She didn't come to work this morning," Angus explained. "Mother is worried about her."

I didn't bother to mention that it wasn't I who insisted on stomping through the streets of Dawson in search of a single small woman. "How do you know Mary anyway, Graham?"

"Uh," he said, tugging at his tie, "I interviewed her for my exposé on the conditions of the Dawson fairies." He used the local slang for a prostitute.

"That's great!" Angus said. "In the process of your... interview...you might have learned something about her habits, the places she likes to go. So you can help us search."

"Later, dear. Please."

*   *   *

I collapsed into a chair at the Mann kitchen table. Three loaves of bread that had been left to rise sat on the counter covered in cloths. The whole house smelled, as it always did on baking day, of fresh yeast and old grease. My stomach churned. Angus stoked the fire under the stove and moved the kettle onto the hob. Uninvited, Graham dug through the shelves. He found a tin of biscuits and put them on the table.

I picked up a biscuit and nibbled on the edges, realizing that my headache was gone. Now I knew what to do the next time one comes on—trip over a dead body and be accused of being the killer in front of the entire citizenry by the nastiest madam in town. Realizing I was starving, I downed the rest of the biscuit.

Angus busied himself with the tea things. "Why did Mrs. LeBlanc think you had something to do with this business, Mother?"

"Because she wanted to kick up a fuss," I said, snatching the tin out of Graham's hands before he could help himself to the largest biscuit. "And generally cause trouble and embarrass me. She can't be the least bit concerned about the death of a stupid slag...uh, woman...like Chloe."

"Seems out of character for Joey," Graham said. He placed his hat on the table and loosened his tie. Making himself quite at home, Graham was. "To draw attention to herself, I mean. Joey keeps to the shadows. Where she belongs."

"True," I said as Angus poured water into the big, chipped brown teapot. "Please go and find Mrs. Mann and tell her I'd like lunch early."

"I'm sure Mrs. Mann is busy, Mother. I'll fix you something." He took a slab of bacon out of the icebox and pulled a can of beans down off the shelf. Once I leave the Yukon, I will never eat bacon and beans again. I poured three cups of tea.

"Thanks, Angus." Graham said. He hadn't been offered lunch. He alternately sipped his tea and stroked his generous moustache. "As for Joey, what do you suppose her relationship with Chloe was?"

"Cobra and mesmerized mouse," I snapped, suddenly weary of the whole subject. "I don't want to talk about it." I stood up, clutching my teacup. I was deathly tired, but I'd never be able to sleep. Although I'd heartily disliked Chloe, no one deserves to die abandoned in a back alley, left for the insects and the rats. And then to be mistaken for a dog—I felt a frisson of guilt over that. Poor Chloe, now reduced to nothing but a lump of meat, leaking blood into the good Yukon earth. "Angus, I'll be in my sitting room. Good day, Graham."

I dropped my teacup, not caring if it landed on the table, covered my mouth with my hands and dashed for the privy rather than the sitting room.

When I finally returned to the kitchen, Angus handed me another cup. Graham cocked one eyebrow but wisely said nothing. Bacon was hissing and popping in the big iron frying pan.

"I don't feel much like lunch any more, dear," I said and made my way on unsteady legs to my sitting room.

The Manns' boarding house is very small and very plain and will not withstand a strong wind, but in this town that almost literally was thrown up overnight, a good many people lived in accommodations a good deal worse: one-room cabins with gaps a healthy rat could fit through or tents clinging precariously to the hillside. Angus and I have bedrooms at the front of the house, one on either side of the front door. Angus's room is slightly larger than mine, but I have a cosy sitting room where, theoretically, I can entertain guests. The kitchen, on the other side of my sitting room, and the Manns' bedroom, next to Angus's, takes up the back of the house, and that's it. The privy is in the yard, next to the improvised laundry shed, almost leaning up against the back neighbours' privy.

I have a tendency to leave town quickly, usually with the forces of the law on my heels, so I tend not to accumulate too many material possessions. But I keep a precious photograph of Angus as a baby, all frilly white dress and lacy cap, and another of the two of us enjoying a boating adventure one lazy summer Sunday in High Park when he was four and dressed in a sailor suit with an over-large straw boater. I'd placed the two pictures on a wooden tea crate, covered with a linen cloth carefully arranged so the scorch mark left by an iron was not visible. It served as my tea table. I'd managed to purchase a comfortable chair for reading and kept a colourful quilt, made out of scraps of fabric in every shade of blue imaginable, tossed over the back in readiness for chilly winter evenings. A big iron stove took up almost half the room, leaving not much space for any visitors I might wish to entertain. It suited me perfectly.

On the wall opposite the stove, I'd hung a painting that supposedly depicts the Black Cuillins of Skye. Either my memory of my childhood home is poor, or the artist wasn't skilled, but I'd bought the picture on a rare sentimental whim off a wooden slab down at the waterfront. A mirror, missing the top right-hand corner, hung beside the painting. I examined the back and sides of my skirt carefully, terrified of what I'd find, but there appeared to be only a bit of dirt on the hem and on my right hip.

I picked up the book sitting on the table: *Anna Karenina* by Tolstoy. I'd started it in Vancouver, almost a year ago and was almost finished. I read the same page over and over while Angus served up beans and bacon in the kitchen, and Mrs. Mann came in to find out what was going on and scolded Angus for not calling her in to do the cooking. She asked if he'd found Mary, then went back out to the laundry. Graham ate his lunch, no doubt enjoying my portion as well, and attempted to engage Angus in conversation. Angus had lately turned against Graham, although I didn't know why, and his end of the conversation was strictly monosyllabic. Graham finished his meal and thanked Angus for it.

As they left the kitchen, they stopped in front of the sitting room door. "I'll pop in for a quick moment and say goodbye to your mother," Graham said.

"She doesn't want to be disturbed." Angus's tone was so disapproving, it sounded like he'd reached puberty in the last ten minutes.

"She won't mind if it's me," Graham said cheerfully.

"I'd rather you didn't, sir."

"Graham, go away!" I bellowed in the manner I'd learned from fishmongers in Covent Garden.

"Tell your mother I'll call when she's feeling better," Graham said in his rush to get out the door.

I checked my watch. It was mid-morning, and regardless of the fact that I hadn't had any sleep, it was almost time to get to the Savoy.

I decided to read *Anna Karenina* for a while more. Maybe the book would have a nice happy ending that would take my mind off the ending of poor Chloe.

But it was not to be. A heavy pounding sounded at the front door. Angus opened it. Not at all to my surprise, I heard Inspector McKnight announcing he wished to speak with me.

Angus escorted them into my sitting room. Between the small inspector, the burly, gone-to-seed Sergeant Lancaster, the looming Constable Sterling, and my son, who, tall as he was, at least didn't take up much horizontal space, there was scarcely room for anyone to breathe.

I carefully marked my place in the book and laid it on the table. "Gentlemen," I said, "I'd ask you to sit, but as you can see..." I smiled graciously and indicated the cramped room with my hand.

"Quite all right, Mrs. MacGillivray," McKnight said.

Richard pulled a badly torn notebook and a pencil stub out of his pocket. I could guess why Lancaster was here—

feeling protective of me, he'd tagged along, and no one had the heart to tell him to go away.

"Tea, gentlemen?" I asked.

McKnight started to refuse, but Lancaster was faster. "That would be nice, Mrs. MacGillivray."

I nodded to Angus, and he slipped away. He was a good boy, Angus, none better. As far back as he could remember, we'd always had a full complement of servants: lady's maid, upstairs maid, cook, kitchen maid. Sometimes even a butler, a downstairs maid and a boot boy. But as soon as we'd set off for the Yukon, where a lady's maid was as rare as a trophy elephant and a butler even rarer (he would be off to the gold fields with a shovel over his shoulder the moment the boat docked), Angus knew he had to pitch in, which he did without a word of complaint.

"I'd like to ask you a few questions, Mrs. MacGillivray," McKnight asked, "about the events of this morning."

I told them about Mary not showing up for work and Angus being concerned. About going in search of her and my suspicions that she might have returned to Paradise Alley. I mentioned running into Graham, who was doing research for his story about the exploited women of Dawson. At that point Angus held the door open for Mrs. Mann, who was bearing the tea tray, and Richard, who appeared to be on the verge of a coughing fit, rushed to help her lay out the things on the table.

"You need anything more, Mrs. Mac," Mrs. Mann said, "I'll be in the kitchen." She didn't approve of a young man such as Angus making tea for visitors.

Ever the gracious hostess, I poured.

"You didn't find this woman, Mary?" McKnight asked.

"No," I said. "Milk, Inspector?" Milk being a relative term, as all we had was the horrid canned stuff.

"Yes, please."

"With all the excitement of finding poor Chloe, we abandoned the search and came home." I passed the inspector his cup. It wasn't a proper tea presentation by any means: the heavy brown teapot, the mismatched mugs, the sugar still in the tin it was sold in. Not to mention canned milk. In Dawson one makes do.

"As soon as Ma, I mean Mother, leaves for work, I'm going to look for Mary," Angus said. "You haven't seen her, have you?"

The men shook their heads. "Sorry, Angus," Richard said. He declined a cup of tea, indicating the paper and pencil in his hands.

McKnight didn't seem the least bit interested in Mary. He asked me about Chloe: who might not have liked her (no one, I assured him), who her friends were (all the dancers, I said), why she had been fired (reduction in staff, I said, with a tinge of regret in my voice).

McKnight put his mug down. "Thank you for your time, Mrs. MacGillivray. If you think of anything else, I'd be obliged if you'd contact me."

"Certainly." I stood to show my guests out.

"One more thing," McKnight said, reaching into his pocket. "Have you seen this before?"

It was a tiny tin-plated cross hanging off a thin chain with a broken clasp. I shook my head, trying to appear thoughtful. "It isn't original, nor at all valuable," I said at last. "Probably a good many like that around."

"It's Mary's," Angus said. "She must've lost it." He held out his hand. "Thanks, Inspector, I'll see she gets it back."

McKnight put the jewellery into his pocket. "Sorry, son. I'll hold on to it for a while. Why don't you sit back down, Mrs. MacGillivray, and you and young Angus can tell me more about this Mary."

Angus and I looked at each other. "Not much to tell," I said. "Constable Sterling knows the story." I sat down.

McKnight glanced at Richard, but he spoke to me. "Why don't you tell it to me, Mrs. MacGillivray?"

So I did. The whole story. Leaving out the matter of finding Mary in the shadows behind the Savoy with Tom Jannis and her running off, which I couldn't see was any of their business. I simply said she hadn't come to work that morning, and Angus was concerned.

There was a long silence after I finished speaking. I sipped my tea. Sergeant Lancaster attempted to give me an encouraging smile. Richard wrote in his notebook, carefully avoiding both Angus's and my eyes.

"You're sure this necklace belongs to Mary, Angus?" McKnight said at last, pulling the object back out of his pocket and turning it over in his hands. His hands were like a lady's, soft, uncalloused, the fingers long, the nails neatly trimmed.

"Looks like it. But as Mother said, it's a common enough type."

He dropped the cross back into his pocket. "If you find this woman, Mary, bring her around to see me would you, Angus?"

"Why?" Suspicion crept into Angus's voice.

"I want to talk to everyone who might have seen something suspicious in Paradise Alley this morning."

"Sure," Angus said.

McKnight put his hat back on his head. Lancaster and Sterling did likewise.

I rose from my chair, but I couldn't pass the men in order to get to the door to show them out. Instead we all jostled and shifted and spilled out into the hallway. We found Mrs. Mann standing by the sitting room entrance, where she no doubt had been listening. More jostling ensued as Angus opened the front door and the police filed out. Sergeant Lancaster came last.

I lifted my hand to my forehead and swayed with the slightest of moans. The sergeant took hold of my arm as a look of concern crossed his beefy features. "Mrs. MacGillivray?" he said.

I waved my hand (the one that wasn't pressed to my forehead) and swayed once again. "I feel quite faint. Sergeant, if you don't mind." Angus rolled his eyes and followed the police out the door, asking Richard Sterling what would happen to Chloe's body. Mrs. Mann went into the kitchen. Abandoned by my natural protectors, my son and landlady, who apparently know me too well, I leaned on Lancaster's arm. "My chair, please," I breathed.

He almost carried me into the sitting room. I collapsed

delicately into the chair and arranged my skirts around my legs. I opened my eyes wide. "A glass of water, perhaps," I whispered.

Lancaster bolted from the room.

When he returned with the water, I accepted it graciously. "Do pardon me, Sergeant," I said, a touch of strength returning to my voice. "The events of this morning have been most distressing."

He picked up my empty hand and patted it. "Quite understandable, my dear. As I've told you before, I simply don't understand how a gentle lady such as yourself can continue to mix with the more undesirable elements of society."

I managed to avoid copying Angus and rolling my eyes. Lancaster had indeed told me his opinions on the proper milieu for a lady such as me: making his dinner and washing his socks.

I pulled my hand away, politely, and sipped the water. "Thank you for your gallantry, Sergeant. Due in no small part to your courteous attentions, I am feeling a good deal better." I have learned that it's simply impossible to go too far in praising a man's concept of his own chivalry.

He smiled hugely. Lancaster's nose appeared to have been broken on more than one occasion, but he still had most of his front teeth. "I'd best be on my way then," he said, reluctantly.

I smiled and placed the glass on the table. "Perhaps you should. But before you go could you tell me why Inspector McKnight is carrying that cross around." I refrained from batting my eyelashes.

"He found it..." his voice dropped "...on the body of the dead woman."

I gasped and held my hand to my forehead once again. Lancaster grabbed the water glass and pressed it back into my free hand. "So it was hers then, Chloe's, how sad."

"It wasn't on her body, as in around her neck, Mrs. MacGillivray." Lancaster bent forward so as to whisper. "It was clutched in her hand. Like she'd ripped it from the woman who'd killed her."

I didn't bother to gasp again. I'd suspected as much. The only question was whether Chloe had been gripping the cross and chain before or after Joey LeBlanc had bent over her body.

Chapter Fourteen

"What do you know about this Mary, Constable?" McKnight asked as they headed back across town towards Fort Herchmer.

"Not a great deal, sir," Sterling said. "Nothing more than what Fiona...Mrs. MacGillivray told you. Mary's not from the Yukon, so she's far away from her tribe. I think she's a Christian; there was a bible among her belongings, so I wouldn't be surprised if the necklace belongs to her."

"The necklace seems to be the key, wouldn't you say?"

As they walked through the streets, men stepped aside to let them pass, nervous eyes watching them go. News of the finding of the body had swept through town on the wind. Miners tended to be a superstitious lot, and no one wanted to cross the path of men who had so recently been in the presence of death. McKnight and Sterling had questioned the onlookers, but none of them, to no one's surprise, had seen or heard anything unusual. Apparently no one—whore, customer, or passerby—had laid eyes on Chloe before.

McKnight liked to talk out loud, to hear his thoughts as if they were part of a conversation. Sterling found it fascinating.

So deep in thought was McKnight, he didn't notice the tall, scrawny figure of Angus MacGillivray tagging along behind.

Lancaster hadn't been seen since he'd fallen for Fiona's fainting trick like a pig trotting after the farmer to the slaughterhouse, tail waving. Sterling could take a guess as to what Fiona was up to—trying to find out more about the investigation—particularly as her protégé Mary appeared to be involved in this mess. He hoped she'd stay clear. A murder investigation in a community as isolated as Dawson was difficult at best, without the added complication of the lovely but somewhat headstrong Fiona MacGillivray trying to take charge.

Sterling felt the edges of his mouth curling up in a secret smile.

"Constable?"

Sterling tore his thoughts away from an image of Fiona MacGillivray in red serge and crispy ironed jodhpurs tucked into shiny boots issuing orders to the investigating officers.

"Uh, sorry, sir. Didn't hear." Sterling gestured to a passing wagon, loaded down with crates, the driver of which seemed to be under the impression that screaming at his miserable nag of a horse would make it go faster.

"I said that the necklace is most interesting. What do you think about it?"

"Seems rather conveniently placed to me, sir," Sterling said, managing at the last minute to avoid a pile of recently deposited, steaming horse dung.

"Sometimes the easiest solution is the answer all along," McKnight murmured, as much to himself as to Sterling. "Don't go looking for complications if you don't have to, that's what I always say. And I'm usually right. But I'd be more comfortable had that bloody LeBlanc woman not interfered with the body before we had a good look at it. Don't suppose you noticed this necklace before LeBlanc's performance, did you, Constable?"

"No, sir. I didn't."

"Too bad." McKnight stopped abruptly in the centre of the intersection. "I'm assigning you to assist me in this investigation, Constable Sterling," he said, heedless of the traffic forced to detour around him.

"Sir?"

"You heard me. I'll speak to your sergeant." McKnight

pulled the cross and chain out of his pocket and handed it to the startled constable. "Ask around, find out if anyone's seen LeBlanc with this thing. Can't imagine that if it belongs to LeBlanc, and it innocently broke from around her neck when she fell over the body, how it would wind up clutched in a dead woman's hand, but we have to ask all the questions. Then find this Indian Mary. I want to talk to her. You can use young MacGillivray here; the woman might show herself if she sees him. Should have asked Mrs. MacGillivray if she knows where this Chloe lived. I'll find out and head over to talk to anyone who knows her."

Without another word or a backward glance, McKnight carried on up the street.

Sterling and Angus looked at each other. A man staggering under a weight of crates marked "canned tomatoes" almost collided with them and yelled at them to "Get the 'ell out o' the way, bloody fools."

Angus was grinning from ear to ear. "Did Inspector McKnight ask me to assist you, sir?" he said.

"I believe so. But you're not coming with me to talk to any of Joey LeBlanc's associates." The boy's smile disappeared. Sterling dangled the necklace by its chain, watching as the cross twisted in the wind. "You're pretty sure this belongs to your friend, Mary?"

Angus grimaced. "It looks exactly like the one she was wearing when I pulled her out of the river. There must be lots of crosses like that one around, like Ma said. It's not as if it's covered with diamonds or nothin'."

"Or anything," Sterling said. "You know how to talk properly, so don't pretend you don't."

"Sorry, sir. Inspector McKnight did think it might be Mrs. LeBlanc's necklace, right? Accidentally torn off when she fell over the body. I bet that's the answer. Mrs. LeBlanc has the same necklace as Mary." Angus grinned, happy to have solved the problem of his new friend's possible guilt.

Sterling didn't bother to correct the boy. Let him think, for a while, that Mary was in the clear. If Joey LeBlanc hadn't planted the necklace, and he reminded himself he had no reason—other than his own intense dislike of the Québécois whoremistress—to think so, and if the necklace found clutched in Chloe's dead fingers belonged to Mary, the Indian woman would almost certainly hang.

"We have to find Mary," Sterling said. "Are you working this afternoon?"

Angus's eyes opened wide, and the colour drained from his face. "Oh, no. I forgot. Miss Witherspoon invited Ma for tea, and I forgot to tell her. What time is it now?"

Sterling checked his watch. "Quarter past one."

"Miss Witherspoon has appointments with men...I mean appointments to interview men about their experiences in Dawson, I mean, their experiences with mining and..."

"I know what you mean, Angus."

"She's paying me two dollars a day to show her around town."

"Escort your mother to tea and tell Miss Witherspoon you have to assist the North-West Mounted Police for a while this afternoon. She'll have to excuse you. I'll meet you at four o'clock in front of the Savoy, and we can start our search for Mary then."

"But she pays me two dollars a day!"

"Two dollars, or service to her Majesty, Mr. MacGillivray? Whether Mary did this or not," he held up one hand to silence Angus's objection, "she's probably hiding and won't be forthcoming to the police. Inspector McKnight is right: she might come out of hiding if she sees you."

"Four o'clock it is then."

"Good boy."

Angus dashed off.

Despite what he'd said to Angus, Sterling knew they had very little chance of locating Mary. A white woman would be easy to find; she'd have to confine herself to the few square miles that made up the city of Dawson. A few square miles of light and noise, laughter and tears, surrounded by the northern wilderness. In the early hours of a rare night, when the drunks quieted down and the dance hall singers and musicians paused to take a break, and the noise in the street stopped, you could hear the wolves howling in the hills. Mary was an Indian. Even without the support of her tribe, she should be able to survive, at least until winter, in the wilderness. If she were guilty, she'd have been long gone, probably before Fiona MacGillivray tripped over Chloe's body. And even if she had nothing to do with Chloe's death, as soon as she heard, as everyone in town would soon hear, that the Mounties wanted to talk to her, she would leave town.

He'd liked Mary, in the brief time he'd known her. She had a lot of fight in her.

Sterling dropped the necklace into his pocket. He'd spend a few hours in the cheapest of the saloons that backed onto Paradise Alley asking a few innocent questions. Joey LeBlanc normally wore dresses as prim as his own mother's, but occasionally they would be cut with a bit of a neckline. If she'd worn this necklace, someone would have noticed it.

* * *

Once everyone had left, I discovered that I was simply ravenous. The house was quiet; Mrs. Mann had returned to her laundry shed. I considered summoning her to fix me something but decided I would try to be an independent Canadian woman. There was a good-sized piece of last night's tough, stringy roast remaining in the ice box and a nice fresh half-loaf of bread in the bread box. I sliced off a generous hunk of the meat and cut, after several attempts, two rather crooked slices of bread, then added plenty of mustard. I put all the ingredients away and rinsed the dirty knife in the water bucket. Standing in front of the counter, I took an enormous bite of my sandwich, feeling quite proud of myself, as well as a bit avant-garde eating while standing over the sink.

The front door slammed, and Angus shouted for me. I grabbed a plate from the shelf, slapped my sandwich onto it and collapsed into a proper sitting position at the kitchen table. I was dabbing mustard off my lips with my handkerchief when Angus came in.

"Good," he said. "You're still here. Ready for tea?"

"Tea? Why should I want tea? Would you care for a sandwich, dear?"

He glanced around the kitchen, perhaps expecting Mrs. Mann to be hiding behind the stove.

"I made it myself," I said. "Would you like me to make you one?"

"I'm sorry, Mother, but I may have forgotten to tell you. Miss Witherspoon and Miss Forester invited us to join them today. At two. It's one thirty now."

"Angus, I can't possibly have tea with your friends today. What were you thinking? I'm exhausted. And this dress is not at all suitable for tea."

He picked the sandwich off its plate and handed it to me. "Finish your lunch, Mother. You'll feel better. You've told me many times that no one here worries about following convention. That dress will do. Although the skirt is a bit dirty around the...uh...middle bit."

"Perhaps we can have tea tomorrow," I suggested, biting into my sandwich. A piece of beef refused to budge under the force of my teeth, and I shook my head back and forth to wrestle it from between the bread.

"It's our duty, Mother, to keep an appointment. I told the ladies we would join them. I myself should probably change."

I hate it when he's right.

* * *

Euila and Miss Witherspoon were waiting for us. They were staying at the Richmond, which tried to be the best hotel in town, but somehow everything managed to fall short. Not far away, Belinda Mulroney was building the Fairview Hotel, which was due to open next month and which promised its prospective guests the best of everything. Belinda and the Fairview were the talk of the town, People were saying the hotel would even have electricity!

The drawing room of the Richmond always reminded me of a country estate gone to seed. The sort of place the heirs of medieval bandits could no longer afford to keep up, but tried terribly hard. I'd been to a few places like that when I'd travelled with the Prince of Wales's party. The family would literally bankrupt themselves to put the Prince, his household, and useless hangers-on (like me) up for a week or a month. It was no fault of the Prince that I'd relieve the long-suffering family of the smaller pieces of silver and some of her ladyship's jewellery the night before we all grandly took our leave.

But I wasn't at the Richmond Hotel in Dawson, Yukon, on this pleasant day in June 1898 to steal the cutlery.

The moment we walked through the hotel's drawing room doors, Euila was on her feet squealing like a schoolgirl. She threw her arms around me and hugged me heartily. Trapped under the force of her embrace, I patted her back a few times. At last she released me, only to go through the same performance with Angus. He stood as still as a Greek statue under the power of her greeting. The entire drawing room watched us. Angus's face was as red as my late-lamented Worth gown, and Euila was sobbing heartily.

My son and I scurried to take our seats.

Euila collapsed into hers without looking. Fortunately no one had moved her chair in the meantime. She was dressed like an English lady making her afternoon calls in a gown, somewhat out of date, of pink satin and white lace topped by an extravagant hat crowned with a garden of pink flowers. I hadn't seen a hat quite so elaborate since I'd left Vancouver.

Martha Witherspoon, in contrast, wore what appeared to be her usual ensemble of stiff brown tweed suit and porkpie hat. She wore no jewellery, not even earrings, save a heavy watch pinned to the centre of her prominent bosom.

The waiter hovered over us. He was young and fresh-faced, with shaggy hair slicked back, dressed in a neat black suit and tie with a long white apron (on which there were

only a few stains) wrapped around his waist. He smiled as if
he genuinely wanted to please us.

Martha Witherspoon ordered tea for us all and
whatever they had in the way of sandwiches and cakes.

"Fiona," Euila said, as the waiter went to place the order,
"after all these years." She sighed happily and simultaneously
sniffed into her handkerchief. It was trimmed with lace,
and "EF" was written in the corner, the letters embroidered
in a fine pink hand. Like the waiter's apron, the
handkerchief was marked with stains that were never
coming out. "You're so...so...beautiful," she said. "I always
knew you would be."

I smiled in return; it *was* nice to see her. I shouldn't have
been so apprehensive about this reunion. "Euila, how have
you been?"

"Lonely, always lonely. I missed you so dreadfully, Fiona."
Water gathered in her eyes. "How could you leave me like
that? Without a word. Didn't you care about me? Your
parents, how could they be so horridly selfish as to take you
away from me? Alistair told me I shouldn't have expected
anything better from people of your parents' class, but
you...you were like one of us."

I stared at her. The waiter arranged cups and plates at
each place. Angus's mouth formed a question, but no
sounds came out. Miss Witherspoon leaned across the table
and waved her hands in front of my face. Euila droned on,
her voice high-pitched, complaining. Now I remembered:
Euila had always been complaining. *Alistair,* she was saying,
your class, your father, unfair. Unfair.

I hadn't slept properly in days; I'd tripped over a dead
body; I hadn't even finished my beef sandwich. *Alistair.
Your father. Unfair.*

I fainted.

For real this time.

I found myself on the floor, with an anxious Angus peering
into my face, Miss Witherspoon calling for cool cloths, the
enthusiastic waiter waving his apron over me, and all the while
Euila whined on about how Alistair had warned her against

becoming too close to people of "your class".

My son looked so worried, crouched on the floor beside me, patting my hand, calling for water, that I thought I should let him know I was perfectly fine. I started to get up, but it seemed like so much trouble, I decided not to bother.

Chapter Fifteen

I am the only living child of my parents. My mother had numerous pregnancies before and after my arrival, but they all ended the same way—in blood and tears. So they doted on me, the precious only child.

It was different up in the big house where Lady Forester cranked out a baby a year. To the delight of Sir William Forester, the Eighth Earl of Sleat, they were usually boys, but to Mrs. Forester's despair, there was, amidst eleven sons, only one daughter: Euila. Sickly from birth, not terribly bright, eager to please. Euila.

We lived on the Isle of Skye, off the west coast of Scotland. Not a very hospitable place, Skye. The big house was more of a castle, with a few modern bits tacked on over the years, which had escaped being burnt to the ground when the Forester ancestors had, through pure dumb luck, consistently chosen the right side (whatever that side might be) in the never-ending battles that plagued Scotland throughout the previous centuries. They certainly had been on the right side in the great uprising that ended with the terrible battle of Culloden, and an appreciative King George had added to the family's estates by handing them the property of those neighbouring landowners who'd supported the Bonnie Prince. My own family, the MacGillivrays, as my father never tired of reminding me, fought like true Scotsmen—to the last man—in the cause of the Prince. Thus, according to my father, we lost all our lands and barely escaped being sent off to the colonies. As my father told the story, a young Lord Forester was hunting companions with a young Master MacGillivray and persuaded his father to let the MacGillivrays remain on the land as crofters.

All of which may or may not be true and is of no relevance to the story of Euila and me and our strange friendship. My father had been groundskeeper of the estate, which they called Bestford, and was held in high regard by Sir William, who would occasionally sit by the peat fire in our neat white croft house, sharing a dram of whisky, and talk about preparations for a hunting party, what to do about poachers, or whether the salmon were less plentiful than in previous years.

My mother would take a chair at the well-scrubbed table and sew, and when I was very young I would sometimes be allowed to sit at the Earl's feet. He would stroke my hair and politely ask how my day had been. I would mumble something and enjoy the scent of him, of whisky and tobacco, horses and leather, with not a whiff of peat clinging to his clothes.

As I grew older and bolder, I had the run of the estate and would often end up in the big kitchen at the castle, where Cook offered me bread and dripping or the occasional oatcake. Euila, with no one but brothers to play with and a mother who always seemed to be about to give birth or recovering from the last one, would tiptoe into the kitchen to beg a treat from Cook. And so Euila and I became as good friends as our social structure would allow.

One day in late fall, when the cold rain had been lashing across the bare hills of West Skye for days, bringing tidings of winter soon to come, the Earl rode up to our door. I was helping my mother in the garden, trying to get the last of the vegetables in before winter came to stay. The Earl removed his hat and made a small joke about the weather. He was always excessively polite to my mother: it was a great shock to me the first time I understood that not all the nobility treated women of no status with such respect. Then he turned to me with a smile and asked if I'd ever thought about going to school. I told him quite honestly that I would love to, and my mother scolded me for talking such foolishness.

Sir William had decided I would join Euila in the day nursery every morning for lessons with her new governess. My parents were easily convinced to allow me to do so.

Euila loved the governess, Miss Wheatley, but hated the lessons. I hated Miss Wheatley and lived for the lessons. The horrid woman never let me forget for a minute that I was daughter of the help, and I should think myself fortunate to have the opportunity to improve myself. Although I was two years younger than Euila, I outperformed her by leaps and bounds. We learned to read Greek and Latin, to speak French, to paint in watercolours, and some English history. (Miss Wheatley slapped me across the face when I asked if we were going to learn Scottish history.) It was only in music that Euila did better than I. Where I was all thumbs, like the crofter's daughter I was, seated at Lady Forester's dusty, out-of-tune piano, Euila could coax beautiful notes out of the keys and into the evening air without appearing to try. Only Miss Wheatley seemed to mind that the charity case was better at almost everything than the daughter of the house. Lady Forester never paid much attention to anyone or anything, Euila least of all; the boys certainly didn't care what we got up to; and I suspect Sir William was happy to see me thriving. As for Euila, she adored me and never seemed to have a moment's envy of either my intelligence or my life, which was so much more carefree than hers. Euila spent the afternoons confined to the house and the gardens, often with embroidery or her Bible, while I wandered across the brown and purple heather, waded through streams bursting with fish, and climbed the barren hills of the Cuillins with my father as he told me the story of how the MacGillivrays had lost all for the Bonnie Prince and Scotland. And would do it again, he always concluded.

When I remember those years, I think of Miss Wheatley with no ill will, for she inadvertently gave me the greatest gift I could have ever received: she constantly (and sometimes literally) beat a "proper" English accent into me. Miss Wheatley had a passionate hatred of Scotland and all things Scottish, which expressed itself in her determination to rid me of any trace of a Scottish accent. She would have preferred to instill the accent of a cockney kitchen maid into me if she had any idea of how to do so, but Miss Wheatley was a niece of minor aristocracy and had previously spent all her life in fashionable London drawing rooms. The only example of proper speech she could teach me was her own.

My son is annoyed with me when I scold him for using colloquialism and not bothering with proper grammar. The way I speak is what lifted me out of the gutter, more important than my beauty, my intelligence, or even my formidable luck. If Miss Wheatley hadn't beaten the sound of generations of Skye crofters out of me, I don't want to think of where I'd be today. Certainly not owner of the most popular, most profitable dance hall in the Yukon Territory.

When I was nine years old, and Euila eleven, Sir William took very ill. The second son, Alistair, was called home from London to manage the estate. Alistair was, to put it mildly, not his father. He hated Scotland almost as much as Miss Wheatley did and hated the life of a country landowner even more. Being the second son, he wouldn't even get to be Earl some day.

At home, my father's face was often grave, and he and my mother would stop talking when I walked into the house. But I overheard bits and pieces of things I'd never known before—of gambling debts and selling off pieces of the land.

Alistair paid no attention to Euila or me, and for another year our lives carried on much as before, although I did miss meeting Sir William out on the road after lessons, when he would pull his big bay to a stop and ask me, as I patted the horse's velvet nose, what I'd learned that day, and give me an apple for the horse and a piece of shortbread for me.

My mother had been a great beauty. Even in her homespun dresses, smelling of the peat fire, her face dusted with dirt from the vegetable patch, and her hands coated with mud from the soil of Skye, she was more beautiful than Lady Forester or any of the fine ladies who visited in their jewels and English clothes. I'm called the most beautiful woman in the Yukon, and when I say that, I'm not being vain, because I know I'm but an imitation of my mother.

After he'd been home for about a year, Alistair Forester started visiting our cottage. Not cheerful and friendly like his father, ready to pull out a flask of whisky and sit by the peat fire, but to sit on his horse and try to talk to my mother while she worked. I did notice that he rarely came around when Father was home. Alistair had no interest in the running of the estate, only in what it could offer him and his wild London friends in the way of sport.

It was November of 1879, a few days short of my eleventh birthday, when Miss Wheatley bent over to pick up a pencil Euila had thrown across the day nursery in a fit of temper and found that she couldn't straighten up again. She put up the most dreadful fuss: moaning and wailing, yelling at us to do something. Euila ran around the room, managing only to wrench Miss Wheatley's back even more when attempting to force her into a chair, and I went downstairs to fetch Mr. North, the butler.

They got Miss Wheatley to her room, with no small amount of trouble. Classes were cancelled for the remainder of the day. I was disappointed at missing Latin but pleased at the idea of having lunch at home with Mother.

I tried to be quiet approaching our house, thinking I would surprise my mother. I peeked through the peat-smoke-darkened window to check if she was inside. Because of my father's favoured place as groundskeeper, our cabin was a good deal grander than most crofters' cabins. It was bigger and sturdier and didn't let in much rain at all, even on the worst days. My mother had a few nice things, such as good dishes, curtains for the windows and thick blankets on the beds. There was a mirror and a painting of Culloden Moor in a proper frame hanging on the walls. But, like most crofters' cabins, it was really one long room, with a thatched roof, whitewashed interior walls and an ever-burning peat fire in the middle of the floor. A small alcove at the back served as my parents' bedroom, and I slept on a shelf set into the wall of the main room.

I could smell mutton stew cooking in the large iron pot suspended over the fire.

Alistair Forester had my mother pinned against the wall. Her long black hair was half out of its knot, and her face was red all down one side. He held both of her hands in one of his, over her head. His free hand fumbled at the front of her dress, and he sort of twitched all over. My mother opened her mouth and screamed, a scream that echoed through the Black Cuillins and had the ravens lifting into the air and the sheep looking up from their fodder in alarm.

Then my father was in the room, pulling Alistair away from my mother. My father hit Alistair in the face, and Sir William's son stumbled and fell onto the floor. My mother threw herself into my father's arms, sobbing.

I wanted to cry out. I wake up in the night sometimes, crying out. Warning them.

I am always too late.

Alistair's long, thin aristocratic fingers touched the iron poker with the big hook on the end that was used to lift the pot from the fire, and while my parents clung to each other, and I watched, he got to his feet, and brought the poker down once on the side of my father's head. My father collapsed and lay perfectly still. Mother didn't scream again. She held her hands to her mouth, her eyes open wide, and she stared directly at Alistair Forester. He knocked her to the floor with one blow from his free hand, then the poker rose and fell as it struck her head time and time again. Bright red blood leaked through her hair, splashed up against the clean white walls, and pooled in the dirt floor, where it mixed with the blood leaking from the gash on the back of my father's head.

I was still standing by the window when Alistair came out of my home, his shirt spattered with blood. He was holding the poker. He looked at me, looked at the poker and walked towards me. At last I came to my senses and I ran. I was only ten years old, eleven in a few days, and he was a young man, but he was weak with drink and rich food and idleness, and I'd run in these hills since the day I could first walk.

A group of gypsies found me a few days later. Or rather I found them, shocked, frightened, cold and wet, drawn out of the hills like a starving rabbit by the scent of meat roasting over their campfire.

At first they thought, by the way I spoke, that I was the daughter of the big house and were all set to take me home and claim some sort of reward. But they'd learned over the generations never to act hastily. A few careful inquiries revealed that the daughter of the house wasn't missing. However, this entire side of the island was full of talk about the sudden disappearance of the MacGillivrays, who had packed up and left without a word, after fire destroyed their home.

When his son told the story to Old Yuri, leader of the band of travellers, Old Yuri stroked his beard and asked me one question only: "What's your father's name, girl?"

"Angus MacGillivray," I replied, lifting my head high. "Our ancestors were at Culloden."

"Time to be moving on," Old Yuri said to his youngest wife.

I lived with the travellers for almost two years.

Chapter Sixteen

When I opened my eyes, all I could see, floating in front of me in a hazy whirl, was an ocean of white faces. Angus was holding the back of my head while Miss Witherspoon held a glass of water to my lips. I blinked, and the faces swayed once then drifted back into focus. Some concerned, some curious, some trying to peer down the front of my blouse.

"Allow me through, allow me through, please." The doctor crouched beside Miss Witherspoon and held his hand to my chest, no doubt checking that my heart was still beating. Any fool would have been able to tell by the look on my face that I wasn't dead. I swatted his hand away. "Leave me alone, you idiot. Angus, help me to stand."

"Are you sure, Mother?"

"Of course, I'm sure. Get this fool of a doctor out of my way."

"Allow me, please." Mouse O'Brien swept through the crowd and gathered me into his arms as though I were one of the straw dolls my mother had made for me so long ago. He carried me over to a somewhat worse-for-wear settee lining the tea room wall and laid me down without even trying for a grope.

"Thank you, Mouse," I said.

Miss Witherspoon was there, still holding the glass of water. "Mr. O'Brien," she said, smiling up at him, her eyes blinking as if the reflection off his shining armour might blind her. "How terribly kind of you." Blushing to the edge of her high, tight collar, she extended the glass of water. He accepted with a slight bow and took a drink.

Wasn't I the patient here?

Miss Witherspoon tore her eyes away from Mouse. "Everything seems to be under control," she said to the onlookers, more of whom were arriving off the street every minute. "Mrs. MacGillivray is perfectly fine."

"Go back to your tea, folks," Mouse said. "You lot…get out of here before I have you arrested for trespassing." He herded a mixture of dust-coated sourdoughs, ragged street urchins, well-scrubbed gamblers, and one scrawny black dog out of the hotel.

The waiter brought another glass of water, and at last I was able to have a drink. Under Mouse's orders, most of the diners had returned to their tables, although a few bolder souls stood about, shifting from one foot to the other, hoping for further excitement, no doubt.

"I can't imagine what came over you, Fiona," Euila said with a giggle. "I was merely asking why you left without even saying goodbye. It wasn't like you to faint when we were girls. I was always the fainting one."

I swung my feet to the floor. Angus tried to push me back down, and Miss Witherspoon protested that I must rest.

"I'm getting up now; it's long past time I put in an appearance at the Savoy."

"Shall I bring your tea out now, ladies?" the waiter asked.

"None for me," I said. "I'm late."

"Very well," Miss Witherspoon said. "Tea for three, please."

"Two," Euila said. "I'll go with you, Fiona. I would like to see your Savoy, and as it is only two thirty in the afternoon, I'm sure it's quite respectable."

"Two," Miss Witherspoon told the young man. "And then Angus and I have appointments to keep, do we not?"

"Oh, sorry, ma'am. I have to help the Mounties with an investigation this afternoon."

I was gathering my gloves and reticule, but that caught my attention. "What?" I said, loudly enough that I once again attracted the notice of several of the diners. "What?" I whispered.

"Inspector McKnight told Constable Sterling I'm to help him find Mary," Angus said, puffing up with pride. "I'm probably the only one she'll come out of hiding for." The three gentlemen and two ladies seated at the table closest to us had stopped talking and were leaning rather obviously in our direction. I glared at them, and with a clatter of teacups and enthusiastic munching of sandwiches, they went back to their own business.

I groaned. My son was spending far too much time with the Mounties as it was. Now he thought he was an important player in their investigation. If he kept this up, he'd never become the banker, industrialist or lawyer I had my hopes set on.

"How exciting," Miss Witherspoon said, leading Angus back to their table. "I will accompany you after we've had our tea."

"But, ma'am…"

"No 'buts', young man. I am a writer, and this presents the perfect opportunity to get a peek at the grislier side of Klondike life." She arranged her napkin on her lap.

Angus was mumbling something into his fish-paste sandwich as I left the tearoom.

I slipped my arm through Euila's as we walked towards the river and the Savoy. My memories of home were always painful, but none of it was Euila's fault.

We walked in silence for a few minutes. Women nodded at me in greeting and men touched their hats.

"You seem to know everyone in town, Fiona."

"Pretty much. Tell me, Euila." I pulled her out of the way in time to avoid a squealing dog that had just been kicked in its very visible ribs by a furious man. The man caught sight of me and tipped his hat. He was a regular at the Savoy and not nice to people either. I glared at him— he was a cheap regular—and he slunk away, no doubt to find another dog to kick.

I continued talking as if nothing had happened. "How is your father? Your brothers? Alistair?"

"Oh, Fiona," Euila sighed. She dug in her reticule and pulled out the pink embroidered handkerchief. "Father died only a few months after you left. Mother is still living in the house, but…well…"

"Yes," I said, trying not to sound too terribly interested. If the family were doing well, it was highly unlikely that the only daughter would be in the Yukon, wearing a dress two years out of date and carrying a stained handkerchief.

"I remember you never liked Alistair, Fiona, and you were entirely correct. I hate to talk ill of my own brother…"

"But…"

"It was perfectly dreadful! Alistair did a terrible job of running the estate after Father's illness." The dam of propriety and keeping a stiff upper lip and maintaining class distinction broke, and the story burst forth. Euila could barely talk fast enough.

Alistair had mismanaged the estate into the ground. To all who would listen, he blamed my father for ruining the hunting and fishing by being in the pay of poachers and running off when he was about to be apprehended. Shortly after my parents' supposed disappearance, Dougal, the eldest son, an officer in an Indian regiment, was killed, and when Sir William died, Alistair became the Ninth Earl. Once he owned the estates, and the town house in London, and the businesses his father and grandfather had built, Alistair's drinking and gambling and extravagance knew no bounds.

"The most dreadful people would come and stay for weeks on end," Euila sobbed into her handkerchief. "Loud men and painted women of the most disreputable sort. I came across a couple doing…doing…what animals do…in the library. They weren't embarrassed in the least; they laughed at me, and the man asked if I wanted to join them. Oh, Fiona, they broke so many of Mother's lovely things and drove the best of the servants away. Alistair fired Miss Wheatley without a word to Mother or to me. One morning, she was just gone. After the library incident, Mother and I hid in our rooms whenever Alistair had people to visit."

We reached the Savoy, but I kept on walking. I didn't want to miss the end of the story. Murray was standing outside having a cigarette, and he watched me pass with a look of confusion .

Euila's monologue faltered.

"And then…" I encouraged.

"Oh, Fiona, it was simply too dreadful for words. Richard and William and Ian and Percy and…the others…tried to stop him. But what could they do? Alistair owned the property; younger sons and daughters have no rights. Even my mother couldn't legally demand that Alistair's guests leave. It was all so dreadfully unfair. The boys tried to have Alistair declared unfit, but the judge who heard their case had recently spent a week hunting with him. He threw the case out."

When we reached the bend in the street, where the Klondike River flows into the Yukon, I turned us around. Euila scarcely seemed to notice we'd changed direction.

"So Ian and Henry and Graham and…the others have moved away to take jobs or join the army. Alistair can't sell the house, because it's entailed, but that's all we have left, the castle and the grounds that were the original estate. Alistair wanders the property cursing his fancy friends because none of them accept his invitations any more. They've all abandoned him now that most of our money is gone. He has a manservant he brought up from London who keeps him in whisky. Mother says that he, the manservant, stays because he is helping himself to the silver and the paintings and the old weapons. Things that belong to the estate that Alistair can't sell. They're hanging in the hall one day and gone the next. Of all the old servants, only Cook stayed to look after Mother. Alistair and his manservant leave Cook alone, because they need someone to feed them."

"Is there nothing the family can do?" We passed the Savoy once again. Helen had to have cleaned the windows that morning; I could see inside. The front room was almost full.

Euila shrugged daintily. "I heard Ian telling Mother he had found a lawyer in Edinburgh who would take our case, but what good can he do? He can't recover what Alistair has lost. Naturally the boys won't tell me anything, except that any hope of a dowry, and a good marriage, is gone."

"I am sorry, Euila." I patted her hand uselessly as we reached Albert Street. In the west, dark clouds were gathering behind the hills on the other side of the river. A light rain is a delight; it settles the dust, washes some of the filth off the boardwalks, but a downpour also turns the streets into impassable rivers of muck. These clouds didn't look like they held anything light. I turned Euila again, and we headed back to the Savoy.

"Where is this establishment of yours, Fiona? You said it was close, but we seem to have been walking forever." She touched her handkerchief to her eyes, but the tears had stopped. Euila had spent enough hours crying over the fate of her family; she was all cried out. I was delighted to hear that Alistair had earned something in the way of his just reward. Unfortunately, he'd taken the whole of Sir William's family down with him. "We're almost there, but first you must tell me how you ended up in the Klondike, of all places."

"Percy moved to America, to San Francisco. He married a lady with some money and a father with a prosperous family business. So as my...prospects...in Scotland seem non-existent, Mother and some of the boys decided I would visit San Francisco for an extended stay." Meaning until her brother found her a husband.

"I've been in America for almost a year, and what with this dreadful depression they're having, there haven't been many prospects. I don't get on at all with Elizabeth, Percy's wife. Percy decided it was time for me to return to Scotland, but then word arrived of the gold rush. He suggested I might want to visit the North while I'm here. His father-in-law owns a publishing company, and Miss Witherspoon had approached Mr. Featherstone, Percy's father-in-law, about travelling to the Klondike to write about it. Naturally, it wouldn't have been proper for Martha to travel unaccompanied, and she was having difficulty finding a suitable female companion. Percy decided I would enjoy travelling with her."

Percy was obviously doing all the deciding. Poor Euila—unwanted, penniless, unskilled, trolling the Yukon in search of the only thing that could provide her with a decent future—a husband.

"Here we are," I said cheerily. Euila looked at the Savoy. She didn't appear too disappointed—no reason she should be, as every establishment in Dawson looks much the same. An unpainted building hastily constructed of horizontal slabs of wood, much of it still green, a wide doorway, open in the nice weather, leading to a dark interior. A huge wooden sign hung above the door, stretching across the entire front of the building, on which the print was fancy script with the "S" and "y" all curly. Only last week Angus had painted a banner in giant capital letters drawn in his most careful schoolboy script, which proudly stated: *The finest, most modern establishment in London, England, transported to Dawson.* Ray and a couple of the bartenders and croupiers had hung it across Front Street.

It didn't look like much—there are pubs in Whitechapel that look more presentable than my Savoy, but there are not many drinking establishments, anywhere on earth, making more money.

"Oh, Fiona," Euila sighed, wringing her handkerchief in her gloved hands. "You own this…this wonderful place of business?" And to my surprise, she threw her arms around me.

"Well, yes," I mumbled, trying to keep the dusty feathers on her hat out of my mouth. "My partner and I do."

"I simply must have a look inside." Without waiting for an invitation, Euila barged straight ahead.

The drinkers watched us enter. Ray raised an eyebrow at my companion. The rain clouds in the west had covered the morning's sun, and Helen was filling up the kerosene lamps dotting the room.

If Euila hadn't been properly raised by Miss Wheatley, no doubt her mouth would have been hanging open. Her eyes widened at the sight of the lewd pictures adorning the walls, then she noticed that everyone in the room, excepting Helen Saunderson, clearly a servant, was male. "Goodness, Fiona, are ladies permitted in here? I mean…the women in those paintings!"

"In Dawson, ma'am," Ray said, wiping his hands on his bartender's apron prior to offering a handshake, "ladies do almost anything they like."

After a moment of hesitation, Euila extended her gloved fingers.

"This is Ray Walker, my business partner," I said.

"Pleased to meet you, Mr. Walker," Euila said in her daughter-of-the-Earl-meeting-the-help voice.

"Ray, this is Miss Forester. We were friends as children."

"I coulda guessed that. She talks like ye, Fee. Although without the London tinge and the bit of roughness around the edges."

"Really, Ray, I have no roughness around any edges."

A sudden roar came from the gambling rooms. Followed by the sound of glass breaking, furniture flying, men shouting, and Jake bellowing.

Without excusing himself, Ray bolted for the back room, a rotten floorboard groaning as he stepped on it. Someday, someone will fall into the foundations.

Under her pink hat, Euila had turned an alarming shade of greenish-white.

"Then again," I said, "perhaps the Savoy isn't always the best place for a lady." I waved Helen over and asked her to escort Euila back to her hotel. Euila politely muttered her goodbyes and ran for the street almost as fast as Ray had run to break up the fight in the gambling rooms.

"On your way back, Helen," I called, "can you stop at the café and purchase a bowl of their chicken soup. A very large bowl." Not even four o'clock, and it had already been one hell of a day. I imagined the shocked look on Miss Wheatley's face at my choice of words. "Hell of a day," I said out loud.

Thunder cracked across the river.

"Sure will be, Mrs. Fiona, when that rain hits," one of the customers said.

Ray and Jake emerged from the back, each with a firm grip on one of two gamblers who were so busy screaming at each other they didn't appear to notice they were being evicted.

"Hell of a day," I said to Ray as he returned to the bar. He attempted to straighten his perpetually crooked tie. "I'll be upstairs."

Chapter Seventeen

Unfortunately, I wasn't able to get much peace and quiet while waiting for my soup. I had scarcely seated myself and opened the accounts book—the rows of numbers swam behind my tired eyes—when a soft knock sounded on the door. Irene's voice said, "Mrs. MacGillivray? Mr. Walker said we could come up."

"Come in," I called. Whatever Irene wanted with me in the middle of the afternoon, it couldn't be good.

Irene's clothes were generally on the cheap side—cheap in appearance and cheap in cost—but lately she'd been dressing a good deal better. The dress she wore today was a striking midnight blue, with a row of appliquéd lace flowers at the level of her knees and again at the top of the bodice. The bodice itself was fashionably pouched, and the waistband thin and pointed at the front, which showed off her lush hourglass figure to perfection. The dress was perhaps too fancy for afternoon wear, but I doubted that Irene cared about the intricacies of the appropriate use of women's fashion. I wondered if she'd be willing to surrender the name of her new dressmaker. She was flushed a deep red, and her chest moved rapidly. She twisted her hands together and glanced over her shoulder as she stepped into the room.

A woman stood behind her. This was no dance hall girl. She wore a plain homespun dress in shades of mud brown and a perfectly hideous yellow, the whole effect looking like Front Street after a heavy rain and the passage of a pack of undisciplined dogs. Her hair was pulled tightly into a knot behind her head, and an ugly straw hat with a flat top and a wide brim was perched on top of it all.

It was the woman I'd seen the other day, about to be kissed by Irene.

She settled, without being asked, into the visitor's chair. Irene shut the door with her foot and remained standing. My office is completely utilitarian—it is where I conduct business (and count all my lovely money) and nothing else. There were no pictures on the wall, just a single small mirror behind the door so that I could check my hair before going downstairs; the cheap wall boards were unpainted, and the rug served only to keep splinters out of my stockings if I happened to discard my shoes at the end of a long day. It does have one rather rickety couch, the springs of which are always threatening to make good their escape, for those occasions when I need a quick nap and don't want to take the time to go home. The same couch on which Graham Donohue has, so far unsuccessfully, attempted to help me "relax".

"I have business to discuss with you, Mrs. MacGillivray," the woman said, not bothering with introductions.

"You have me at a disadvantage, madam," I said.

"Huh?"

"I don't know your name."

"I'm Maggie Brandon."

Maggie was about forty, with the rough, wind-blown complexion and scarred hands that spoke of a youth spent scratching a living out of rock and dirt. Her accent was American, mid-west probably, and quite rough, indicating an informal education, at best. She was barely five feet tall and very slight, but her thinness had a good deal more to do with being wiry than undernourished. Her unblinking pale blue eyes glittered with intelligence and determination. The bags under those eyes weren't much smaller than ones I have used to carry belongings.

She reached out to shake my hand, and I accepted. The tips of the thumb and the first two fingers on her right hand were so heavily calloused, they felt like old leather.

"If you're looking for employment, Maggie, I have all the percentage girls I need right now, but I can take your name."

"I'm here to represent Irene," she said. She looked over her shoulder at the woman leaning against the wall. Maggie's eyes were so full of affection, I almost turned away in embarrassment.

I swallowed. "Have you asked this woman to speak for you?" Irene nodded.

Maggie pulled a piece of paper out of her skirt pocket. "Irene is making a hundred fifty dollars a week here. The Boston Brahman is making two hundred over at the Horseshoe. So we figured Irene should get two hundred and twenty. At least."

"Two hundred and twenty dollars a week," I spluttered. "I've never heard of such a thing." I knew full well how much the Boston Brahman, the stage name of the headliner at the Horseshoe, was pulling in—two hundred and fifty dollars.

"I'm guessing it's time you heard about it."

"Irene is also making a sizeable twenty-five per cent on drinks," I reminded them. "She does very well." I smiled at Irene. "That must bring in a nice sum."

"Two hundred and twenty, or Irene leaves," Maggie said.

I'd never had to negotiate with my employees before. Rates were standard in Dawson, and no one had yet worked anywhere long enough to ask for more. In the past I'd negotiated with men—lots of them—for favours, jewellery, status, even my freedom, but I'd never done business with a woman. I looked at Maggie's steady eyes and decided that my old tricks wouldn't be worth much.

"Irene," I said, "who is this person?"

Irene traced a gap in the planks of the wooden floor with her toe.

"Irene's engaged me to act for her." Maggie said. "Ain't that right, Irene?"

The dancer nodded, still studying the flooring.

I did quick calculations in my head. Irene brought in more, by an order of magnitude, in a night than they were asking for in a week. But I didn't want to create a precedent here. Suppose all the girls starting asking for more money? And then the bartenders and croupiers. Even the Sunday watchman and Helen Saunderson.

"Do you trust Miss Brandon to speak for you, Irene?" I said, although I knew the answer well enough. Judging by the fond looks Irene gave her, she would trust Maggie with a great deal.

Poor Ray.

Poor me, if word got out.

"One hundred and seventy-five," I said, tucking my big ledger back into the desk drawer. "And that's only because I'm most dreadfully tired and don't want to argue."

Irene moved away from the wall with a slight smile turned up at the edges of her mouth. Maggie had her back to Irene, but she seemed to know what was happening behind her; her arm gave a short chop, and Irene fell back.

"Two hundred," Maggie said. "We could get more at the Monte Carlo, but Irene likes it here, although I don't know why."

"We? I don't believe I am offering you anything, Miss Brandon."

Maggie relaxed, not rising to the bait. "Two hundred."

"One hundred and eighty-five," I locked my desk drawer and dropped the key into my reticule. "That is my final offer. Good day, ladies." I got to my feet.

Maggie didn't move. "One hundred eight-five," she said.

I relaxed. Which was probably a mistake.

"Plus thirty per cent on drinks."

"Thirty per cent?" I shuddered. "Most certainly not. Oh, all right. Two hundred dollars a week. But twenty-five per cent on drinks."

Maggie rose to her not-very-considerable height. She held out her hand.

It was like holding the claw of a baby bird. I could have crushed Maggie's hand in mine with no effort at all. Instead I shook it carefully.

Irene clapped her hands. "Oh, thank you, Mrs. Mac-Gillivray," she said.

"Sit down." I unlocked my desk drawer once again. I pulled out a bottle of excellent whisky and three glasses. "And tell me what else is going on here."

Maggie Brandon accepted her drink with no hesitation, but she didn't relax one iota and watched me warily.

I wondered what line of work she was in and what had brought her to the North. She clearly knew her way around a business deal. Irene stepped forward and accepted her drink. "See, Maggie," she said, "I told you Mrs. MacGillivray would be reasonable." She beamed at us both.

Maggie took an indelicately large mouthful. "Good stuff, this," she said. She finished the drink. I poured more. "Don't know what you mean about their being anythin' else, Mrs. MacGillivray."

"Don't you?" I said, enjoying the taste of my own drink. It was real Scottish stuff, made in the Highlands, just like me.

"No," Maggie said. "So I guess we'll be off." She threw back her second glass and got to her feet.

"Your personal relationship with Irene. It could be that Irene isn't worth twenty dollars a week, never mind two hundred."

"Mrs. MacGillivray! What are you saying? I've always been…"

"Shut up, Irene," Maggie ordered, her voice perfectly calm. She held out her glass, and I refilled it. Irene's mouth snapped closed. "If'n you have somethin' to say, say it, Mrs. MacGillivray," Maggie said. "Otherwise thank you for the refreshment. Good stuff this."

"You and Irene have been seen, in public, in a position that if she were with a gentleman, I would consider to be compromising."

Maggie's eyes narrowed before she looked at the cuff of her sleeve and adjusted it slightly. "And?"

"And coincidentally, I have lately been wondering what secret lover Irene has that would have made her willing to go to jail over that business earlier this summer rather than reveal his name. Heavens, this is Dawson, everyone is fooling around with everyone else, and no one much cares. Unless the secret lover is someone like the priest. Or a woman."

Irene's hands flew to her bosom. The whisky glass trembled but remained upright. "Mrs. MacGillivray, we'll be discreet, I promise. But if you insist, if necessary, I won't see Maggie for a while."

At that, Maggie's face paled and her cool façade momentarily slipped. "Don't talk nonsense, Irene. She's fishing."

"Your romantic interests are no concern of mine. However, I suggest you be a bit more discreet from now on. You might not understand, Irene, but Maggie does, I'm sure. What do you think your worth would be in this town if everyone knew that you are...unnatural, shall we say?"

"Shouldn't matter." Irene started to cry.

Maggie stood up and put an arm around the dancer's shoulder. She pulled a handkerchief out of her pocket and wiped at a tear trickling down Irene's cheek.

"I have no interest in revealing your secret to anyone." I put the whisky bottle back in the drawer and locked it. "I'm advising you both to take care, that's all. Now I have to be going home."

Maggie looked at me. Her eyes were clear, and her chin held high. "I appreciate your concern, Mrs. MacGillivray. And I thank you for it."

"Don't thank me for anything," I walked them to the door. "If Irene's worth to me drops to less than two hundred dollars a week, she'll be looking for alternate employment."

Irene allowed Maggie to precede her into the hallway, then she hung back for a moment. "It isn't that easy to find someone who loves you, you know. I mean truly loves you, for yourself, not expecting anything but love back," she whispered. "Haven't you ever loved, Mrs. MacGillivray?"

"Irene," Maggie said, "let's go."

Irene scurried away in a rustle of midnight blue silk and a flurry of ribbon.

I'd forgotten to ask for the name of her seamstress.

As to her question: Yes, I'd loved. And sworn I'd never do so again.

I shut the office door and dropped into my chair. So that was *Lady Irenee*'s lover: a common-or-garden midwest farm girl. Wouldn't that set the egos of the men of Dawson on edge? I debated telling Ray he was fishing in the wrong pond—like trying to catch tuna in a freshwater lake. I discarded the idea soon enough. I wasn't Ray's mother, and even when I'd thought Irene liked men, Ray didn't seem to be high on her list of potential partners.

The dynamics of Irene and Maggie's relationship seemed no different than those I'd observed between men and women. Irene was quick enough to be willing to discuss temporarily giving up her relationship with Maggie Brandon if I insisted, although I doubted that Maggie would have gone along with that. When Irene talked to me about love, she noticeably considered herself to be more on the receiving end than the giving.

What do I know about love? Or care, as long as it doesn't interfere with my profits at the end of the day?

Chapter Eighteen

Angus and Miss Witherspoon stepped aside as Ray Walker and Jake tossed two men into the street. Jake aimed a careless kick at one of them and missed by a good margin. He spat into the street instead and went back inside.

"Goodness," said Miss Witherspoon.

"Ma'am." Ray touched his cap. "Help you, Angus?"

"We're meeting someone."

"Constable Sterling arrived moments later. "Glad to see you're prompt, Angus," he said. "If you'll excuse us, ma'am."

"Oh no, Constable," Miss Witherspoon protested. "Young Mr. MacGillivray has kindly invited me to observe your investigations." She dug through the ample pockets in her skirt.

"I don't think…" Sterling began.

Miss Witherspoon produced her notebook and pencil with a flourish. "In my capacity as a writer, of course. Murder in the…uh…" she struggled to find a suitable alliteration. "Gold fields," she finished with a disappointed sigh.

"We won't be going to the gold fields," Angus explained. "No reason Mary woulda gone there."

"Our readers don't have to know that. Shall we be off? Which way, Constable?"

"I don't think…"

"Do you have any ideas, Angus?" Miss Witherspoon asked.

"Well, yes, sort of. I was thinking about it earlier. But…"

"But what, Angus?" Sterling asked.

"You see, sir, I'd feel bad if I get Mary into trouble."

"If she's innocent of this, you want to give her the chance to clear her name, don't you?"

Angus looked at the ground and nodded.

"And if she's guilty, then you won't be getting her into any trouble that she didn't bring upon herself."

"I guess so," he mumbled.

"If you want to be a Mountie, Angus, sometimes you have to do things that don't seem right at the time. The law is the law, and we have to respect it."

"Yes, sir."

Miss Witherspoon was scribbling furiously. "Well said, sir, well said. Can I quote you?"

"No. You want to tell me about your idea, Angus."

The words came out in a rush. "Mary told us she has a friend who takes in laundry. It's the only friend she mentioned, and if she isn't there, I don't know where she might be. Left town, probably."

"That she left town is a definite possibility. She's a long way from her own people, but it's summer, and she can no doubt manage in the wilderness. Although far as I know, she doesn't have any equipment, like a good knife or even proper clothes. If she is still here, we need to find her. Most police work is mundane stuff, Angus. Nothing but a lot of walking and pointless questions. Did Mary say what the name of this friend is?"

He shook his head. "Just that she keeps a laundry on Fifteenth Street."

"That's a beginning. Let's see if we can find it."

The town of Dawson had outgrown its natural boundaries. A handful of people made accommodation for themselves in boats anchored in the river, and the outlying streets were climbing higher and higher up the steep hills. Sterling, Angus and Martha Witherspoon walked up Princess Street, which formed a gentle slope as far as Tenth Street. There the hill abruptly met the town, but the street stretched on regardless. Miss Witherspoon was panting heavily once they reached their destination.

Few of the homes on Fifteenth Street were actually

houses. Mostly they were white canvas tents, with a few rough lean-tos scattered around.

They looked both ways. A handful of filthy children tossed a ball to a scrawny dog and shouted with glee every time the animal caught it in midair.

"This town changes so fast," Sterling muttered to no one in particular. "Man can't keep up. I've no idea where this laundry might be." He approached the children. The dog eyed him suspiciously and growled from around the ball in its mouth while backing away, hackles high.

"Do you fellows know where the laundry is?" Sterling asked.

"Might do," the largest of the boys said. The smaller ones edged away, two-legged versions of the dog.

"Why don't you tell me, then?" Sterling asked.

The boy looked at Angus, hostility written across his dirty face, and Angus was uncomfortably aware of his reasonably clean, well-mended clothes, neat haircut, and belly full of tea, sandwiches and cakes. "Whatcha gonna give me?" the boy asked Sterling.

"A night at Fort Herchmer, waiting until your father comes to get you," Sterling said.

The boy blanched, and Angus knew it was the mention of a father that put the fear into him, not the prospect of a night in the Fort.

"Don't matter to me," the boy said. He spat, missing Angus's foot by a few inches, and pointed to their right. "Over there." He ran after his friends.

A drop of water disturbed the dust in the road, and Angus looked up. Overhead the sky was black. One more drop fell on his hand, then the clouds opened and the rain began.

"Goodness," Miss Witherspoon said. "We must seek shelter."

"Not even a twig of a tree left standing, and no one's likely to invite us into their tent," Sterling said. "You'd best head back to town, ma'am."

Miss Witherspoon puffed up her chest. "Certainly not. Lead the way, Constable." She slipped her notebook back into her pocket and pushed her hat lower on her head.

They came to a hand-drawn sign advertising Maybelle's Laundry. The premises consisted of a canvas tent with a stove pipe poking through the ceiling and a sheet of canvas stretched between two poles to protect the fire burning beneath a big iron pot. A pile of roughly hewn logs lay in the inadequate protection of the canvas awning. Lines of rope were strung among a forest of poles, full of drying laundry. A woman bustled from one line to another, feeling the clothes and pulling the dry and almost dry items off the line.

"Pardon me, ma'am," Sterling said.

She glanced over her shoulder. She was tall, dressed in a wet and dirty dress patterned with fading flowers. The sleeves were pushed up past her elbows. Her hips were wide and her arms as thick as a man's. Her short black hair curled in tight corkscrews above high, flat cheekbones, and her skin was the colour of rich coffee with a splash of good cream added. Her eyes were even darker than Angus's mother's.

"Can't you see I'm busy," she growled in a voice as thick and sweet as brown sugar waiting to be added to the coffee. "Gotta get the dry laundry in."

"My companion will do that for you." Sterling nodded at Miss Witherspoon. "While we talk."

Miss Witherspoon glared at Sterling, but once he had returned her glare and muttered something about going back to town, she went to help.

The laundress handed Miss Witherspoon her laundry basket. "Now mind you don't collect the ones what's still wet out of the pot," she said. "Little rain won't hurt them none." She placed her hands on generous hips and laughed heartily. "Ain't that a sight. White woman in a silly hat doin' my chores."

"Only in exchange for some answers, Miss...?"

"Maybelle. Just Maybelle. Don't know what you'd be wantin' with me, sir. Maybelle just be doin' the laundry."

"I'm looking for a woman you might know. Name of Mary?"

Maybelle's dark eyes shifted fractionally in the direction

of the tent. She wiped her hands on her apron.

"Lotsa women in town name o' Mary," she said, taking a few steps towards the street, scratching at the skin at the cleft of her bosom.

Sterling turned to watch her. "We've been told Mary is a friend of yours."

Maybelle studied her bare feet. The toes were long and knobbly, the nails yellow and broken. "Maybelle don't have friends. Too many white people in this town."

"Mary isn't white," Angus said. "She's an Indian, and she's my friend. I want to help her."

Maybelle looked at the boy for the first time. "White people don't have Indians and Coloureds as friends," she said. "I gotta be getting back to my laundry. Lady in the hat movin' so slow, she gonna ruin my business."

"She *is* my friend," Angus protested.

"Angus," Sterling said in his no-nonsense Mountie voice, "let me handle this."

"It's all right, Maybelle." Mary stepped out of the tent. "They know I'm here. And I'm happy to have Angus as my friend."

"Mary, you're a fool if'n you trust the redcoats and a yellow-haired boy what thinks he can help you."

Miss Witherspoon handed Maybelle the laundry basket. Rainwater was collecting in the brim of her hat, and her skirts clung to her legs. She wiped drops from her face. "Perhaps we could talk inside," she suggested.

They all ignored her.

"Thank you, Maybelle," Mary said. "I won't forget your kindness." She lifted her chin high. "I imagine you've come to arrest me, Constable?"

"Why do you think that?" Sterling asked.

"Don't play games with me," Mary said. She lowered her chin. "Sorry, sir. I heard you found something belonging to me on that dead dancer's body. I'm an Indian, so you assume I must be guilty. Isn't that the way the police think?"

"Not the NWMP, we don't," Sterling said. "The Inspector wants to ask you some routine questions."

"Don't worry, Mary, I'll stay with you," Angus said.

Mary smiled, a tiny one that turned up the corners of her mouth but didn't touch her eyes.

Maybelle huffed. "Day's worth o' laundry soakin' wet. Now get outta here. I got work to do. If'n they let you go, Mary, you come back here."

"Thank you."

"Mary," Sterling said politely.

"I didn't kill that dancer. I didn't even know her."

"Then it will all get straightened out, you'll see." Angus tried to sound positive.

"You take care," Maybelle said to her friend.

Without another word, Mary started walking at a determined pace back towards town. Sterling and Angus followed.

Miss Witherspoon scurried behind. Having taken off her useless hat, she was using it in an attempt to shield the pages of her notebook from the rain while she made notes on all that had transpired. She was having difficulty balancing hat, notebook and pencil while writing and walking fast enough to keep up with the others. Every tree within shouting distance of Dawson had been cut down for firewood or building lumber, with the result that whenever it rained, the run-off created instant creeks that poured down the hillside. Miss Witherspoon failed to notice that the terrain they were crossing was different from when they'd come this way only half an hour earlier. She stepped into a rushing river. When the cold water flowed over the edges of her shoes, chosen for afternoon tea, she shrieked and tried to jump out of the water. In her haste, she slipped on a rock and pitched forward, downhill, into the middle of the stream. Rather than save herself, she chose to heroically hold her notebook high above the dirty water.

Angus turned at the sound of the scream and splash. Miss Witherspoon was fully stretched out in the middle of the road, flat on her front, while the new river rushed downhill as though it were a sourdough heading for the nearest saloon. Her skirt had risen above her knees, and she thrashed about on her belly, feet and legs kicking at nothing but wet air, like a fish on a line. She was only wearing one shoe. She let go of her hat, and it floated away. She lifted her head and handed Angus the notebook. He tucked it into his jacket pocket and asked, "Can you stand up?"

She mumbled something positive, as Angus grabbed her by the arm. She rose out of the mud with a sickening squelch.

"I seem to have lost my hat," she said once she was standing on her own two feet. She looked down. "And one shoe." The entire front of her dress, from hem to high collar, was covered in mud. Mud dotted her cheeks and nose like freckles.

"I have your notebook," Angus said.

"Good lad. There it is." Miss Witherspoon limped across the road to rescue her shoe. The heel dangled uselessly as she examined it. "Do you think this can be repaired? You follow your friends; they seem not to be waiting for us. I'll make my way back to the hotel, lest my appearance frighten small children. No, you keep that," she protested as Angus reached into his pocket for the notebook. "I have no way of keeping it dry. Come to the hotel when you're free. If I've gone out, I'll leave a note at the desk. I didn't care much for that hat anyway." She set off down the hill, hobbling on one shoe, holding the other, clutching her ribs, hatless, filthy, but keeping her head high.

Angus passed her as he ran to catch up with Constable Sterling and Mary.

* * *

The NWMP post of Fort Herchmer had come into existence in the early years of the gold discovery, before there was much of a town, and thus it occupied a good slice of precious Dawson real estate. Rows of wooden buildings containing the men's barracks, officer's quarters, jail, offices and storage rooms surrounded a large parade square with a Union Jack fluttering on top of a tall flagpole in the centre.

The Fort took up several city blocks near the meeting place of the Klondike and Yukon rivers, which proved not to be a very fortuitous location when the square was knee deep in dirty brown water during the flooding of the spring run-off.

Sterling stopped at the entrance to the Fort. Passersby, the few that hadn't headed for shelter from the driving rain, observed them with interest. "You'll have to leave us now, Angus," he said.

"I want to stay with Mary."

"I'm sorry, son, but you won't be allowed in. The inspector'll want to talk to Mary in private."

"I'm not leaving." Angus almost stamped his foot, looking very much like the twelve-year-old boy he was.

"Angus, I'm ordering you to go home. If you want to be a Mountie…"

"Maybe I don't want to be a Mountie any more. Not if I have to arrest innocent people like Mary." The boy was trying hard not to cry.

"Angus." Mary placed one small brown hand on his sleeve. "You go home. Give your mother a message from me: I don't want her to think I was abusing her trust. The other night, when she saw me in the back of the Savoy, please tell her I was just out for some air. I couldn't stand being in that place. The noise, the horrible music, the air so dirty with smoke. I couldn't sleep, so I went outside. That man…that Mr. Jannis, he thought I was there, well, for another reason."

"Tell her yourself. I'm not leaving you."

"Go home. I trust Constable Sterling to protect me."

Sterling shifted uncomfortably. He wouldn't be any protection for her, not if McKnight intended to arrest and charge her. He couldn't imagine that this petite, polite woman was a murderer. He had no doubt she'd defend herself if she, or someone she loved, were under attack. But to kill a woman, a dancer like Chloe, whom she barely knew? He didn't believe it, but his unsubstantiated opinion would carry no weight with the officers in charge.

"Come on, Mary," he said. "We need to get you dry." Her thin homespun dress was so wet, he could see the sharp bones of her shoulders and hips beneath the fabric. The end of her long black braid dripped rainwater. She shivered.

Angus knew he was defeated. "I'll tell Mrs. Mann you'll be on time for work tomorrow," he said. "The laundry's too much work for her all on her own."

Mary smiled, whispered, "Thank you," and turning, walked towards the flagpole with a straight back and proud chin. The Union Jack hung limp and sodden in the driving rain.

Sterling almost had to break into a run to catch up with her. "This way, ma'am," he said, steering her towards the offices.

It went as he'd feared. McKnight asked him to show Mary the necklace found on Chloe's body and asked her if she recognized it. She told them it looked like one she'd lost. McKnight then arrested her for the murder of Chloe Jones. A constable was summoned to escort her to the cells. Mary didn't look back as she was taken away.

Dawson was so isolated and, particularly in wintertime, the environment so harsh, the Mounties in the Yukon had considerable leeway to adapt the law for their needs. There were normally only two punishments meted out, no matter how severe the crime. Either a sentence of hard labour, which meant a month or two chopping wood to feed the stoves, or a blue ticket—banishment from the territory. Murder? Even in Dawson, that was a hanging offence.

"She didn't do it, sir," Sterling said, once the door to Inspector McKnight's office slammed behind Mary and her guard.

"You have proof of that, Constable?"

"No, sir, I don't, but there's no reason why an Indian woman would murder a white woman she didn't even know."

"She's a known prostitute."

"Sold into prostitution, sir, and trying her best to get out of it."

"There hasn't been slavery in the Empire in almost a hundred years, Sterling; they don't even have it in the United States, or so I've been told. It takes a certain type of woman to become a prostitute, circumstances be damned.

That sort of woman is capable of doing almost anything if she thinks there's profit in it."

"What options do you think a woman like Mary has? It takes a certain type of woman to starve on the street, but I think better of a person… man or woman…who finds a way to survive. That has nothing to do with the fact that you don't have a single reason for why she would kill this Chloe."

McKnight stood up. "Look here, Sterling." He waved his index finger in the air as though he were lecturing a class of naughty schoolboys. Sterling barely managed to refrain from grabbing it and shaking the man at the other end. "The woman is a prostitute, and that's the end of it. She was offered a respectable job at a laundry and chucked it in after a few days. If you hadn't found her, she'd be turning tricks by nightfall."

"We don't know why she didn't show up at her job this morning. Christ, Inspector…"

"Watch your mouth, Constable, or I'll have you up on charges."

Sterling almost said something a good deal stronger, but at the last moment he bit back a retort. His once illustrious career had suffered enough damage at the hands of his temper. But he damn well wouldn't apologize. "If there is nothing else. Sir."

McKnight could have reprimanded him for his tone alone, but instead the inspector sat back down. "I'm not ending it here, Sterling. I want to talk to Irene Davidson about her relationship with the Jones woman. I've heard they had an argument a couple of days ago. We'll be sure to find her at the Savoy tonight. Meet me here at seven thirty, and we'll head over there."

"Yes, sir." Sterling turned and placed one hand on the door knob to let himself out.

"Oh, one other thing, Sterling. It's common knowledge that you're soft on Indians. Don't let that blind you to this Mary's character."

Sterling shut the door behind him with great care. It was the only thing he could do other than rip it off its hinges.

Chapter Nineteen

Although the afternoon's rain didn't last long, it was enough to turn Front Street into an almost impassable sea of mud. Men's trousers were thick with it up to the knees, the shorter men's at any rate, and women's hems deposited black globules of muck across the floor.

I felt a good bit better, having gone home for a long-awaited nap after spending an hour in the afternoon, trying to do the accounts while gorging on the chicken soup Helen brought me.

When I got back to the Savoy, the bar was full of talk about Chloe's death, everyone having an opinion as to the cause of the matter. Men were asking Murray about her, and I told Ray to order his staff not to discuss it. We were busy that night, the increase in custom largely due to the notoriety the Savoy had obtained by its relationship to the dead woman.

The more theatrical of the dancers and performers insisted they needed an armed police escort when walking home after work. I managed to calm them down by implying, without coming right out and saying it, that Chloe had been up to no good.

The orchestra were in the back warming up (a relative term, as most of them do their "warming up" in other bars) prior to advertising our evening's performance, when Inspector McKnight and Constable Sterling arrived at the Savoy. It was Sterling's job to keep an eye on the dance halls up and down Front Street, but I wasn't happy to see McKnight with him.

I approached them with a welcoming smile. "Inspector

McKnight. How nice to see you this evening. The show will be starting shortly." Richard tossed me a warning frown. I ignored him. "Would you care for a drink before taking your seat?"

"Regretfully, I'm here on business," the inspector said without preamble. "I want to talk to Irene Davidson."

"I don't believe Miss Davidson has arrived yet." The words hadn't even left my lips when she walked in, tossing smiles right and left, along with hair and shoulders.

Richard nudged McKnight, and the inspector turned.

Irene tried to duck around a group of drinkers when she saw McKnight, Richard, and me watching her. McKnight had a soft speaking voice, but he could raise it when he wanted to. Perhaps he'd been a drill sergeant at one time.

"Miss Davidson," he called, "might I have a word?" She could hardly pretend she hadn't heard; every man in the saloon looked up from his drink, and a few stuck their heads out of the back room.

Irene attempted a smile, but the edges were brittle and her eyes wary. She had changed her dress and was wearing another wonderful gown: a jet black silk with flashes of scarlet in the skirt panel, the folds of the sleeves, and across her breasts. The dress was so well made that the fashionable forward-tipping waistline took about three inches off her more-than-adequate middle. Ray was pouring a glass of whisky as he watched Irene cross the room. He watched…and watched…and watched…until the liquor spilled over his hand onto the bar. I felt the first uncomfortable stirrings of jealousy—Irene was dressing better than I! The only way she could possibly afford such extravagance would be if she had a rich lover. Could she be seeing a man as well as the woman Maggie?

Ray shoved the overflowing glass towards his happy customer and came to glower within ear shot of us.

All business, McKnight didn't pause to appreciate the beauty of the black and red gown. "I have a few questions for you, Miss Davidson."

Beads of sweat broke out above Irene's upper lip, and

she wiped her hands on her hips. Her eyes settled on the middle of McKnight's chest.

"Perhaps later," she said to the buttons on his uniform jacket. "I've got to prepare for the show. We're doing scenes from *Macbeth* tonight."

"Mrs. MacGillivray, if we could make use of your office..."

"Uh," I said.

"What's this about, anyway?" Irene asked, in a poor attempt to sound indignant. I hadn't hired her for her acting abilities.

"Now see here." Ray stepped forward, bristling with manly concern. "Miss Davidson doesn't have to talk to ye, if she doesn't want ta."

"You were friends with Chloe Jones," McKnight said.

"That's none of..." Ray said.

"Stay out of this, Walker," Richard said.

"No," Irene said.

"Perhaps we should all go upstairs for some privacy," I said.

"Good idea," McKnight said.

"Ray, tell Ellie that Irene might be late. They're to go on with the first dance, and then that dreadful act with the dummy. Move Ellie's song forward. Irene will be ready to continue with the show at that point."

"Why don't you speak to Ellie," Ray said. "I'll make sure these officers don't browbeat Miss Davidson."

"Don't be ridiculous. Irene can't be unchaperoned in the company of three men!"

Even Irene raised her eyebrows at that.

"You can fetch Helen on your way," Ray suggested sensibly.

"Perhaps Miss Davidson would prefer Mrs. MacGillivray's company while we talk," McKnight said, cutting off debate. "Ladies." He gestured to us to go ahead.

Irene tossed Ray a weak smile which went some way towards soothing his disappointment at not being allowed to act as protector. I considered sticking my tongue out at him, but we'd made enough of a spectacle of ourselves for one evening.

No one made themselves comfortable in my office. Irene walked behind my desk and stood by the window to stare out onto what must have been a miserable sight, what with all the mud. Richard stood with his back against the door, and McKnight planted himself in the middle of the floor. The room was electric with tension between the two Mounties. I wondered how I could turn their problems to my own advantage as I sat on the couch. A spring poked into my bottom.

McKnight pulled a handkerchief out of his pocket and began cleaning his glasses. "I want to ask you about your relationship with Miss Jones. Then you can get to your show."

"I didn't have a relationship with Miss Jones. I didn't even know that was Chloe's last name," Irene told the window.

"I've been informed you were good friends. Was that not the case?"

"Sorta," Irene said. "Until we had a falling out."

"Oh?"

"Well, not really a falling out. More like we drifted apart. We weren't that much of friends to begin with. Isn't that right, Mrs. MacGillivray?" Irene turned to face me.

"Uh…" I said. So this was what had Irene so spooked. I'd assumed McKnight wanted to ask her who Chloe's friends were, if she had any enemies, any bad habits, that sort of inanity. Instead he wanted to know why Irene and Chloe had argued only a few days before her death. Heavens, women argue with their friends all the time. A few days pass, then everyone is crying and hugging and saying how sorry they are. Not that I would know—I've never had any female friends. Not since Euila and I were children.

"'Inseparable' is how your friendship was described." McKnight held his glasses up to the dim light coming in through the window. Not satisfied, he rubbed at them again. "Perhaps you can think of a reason why your 'inseparable' friend met her untimely end?"

"I'd like to know who's been gossiping about me. Who was it? I'll set her straight, no matter who it is." She glared at me. Truly innocent, I shook my head.

"That's of no consequence." McKnight plopped his glasses back onto his nose. "I am asking you what happened between yourself and Miss Jones to end your friendship."

Irene collapsed into my chair in a storm of black silk. Her scarlet bosom heaved. "I thought she liked me, but she only made friends with me because she thought I'd get her better parts in the show. She was horribly jealous of me." Irene held a red handkerchief, a perfect match to the scarlet in her gown, to her face. "When I told her I couldn't do anything to help her, she took a knife to one of my best costumes. The Helen of Troy one. She was a mean, nasty girl. I'm not sorry someone killed her. So there." Irene burst into tears.

McKnight and Sterling had the grace to look uncomfortable.

The whole building started to shake. It wasn't an earthquake, it was the men below us hooting and stamping their feet. The music had started in the dance hall.

"Do you know where Miss Jones was the night before her death?" McKnight asked.

"No." Irene spoke into her handkerchief. "I didn't see her after Mrs. MacGillivray fired her."

"Do you know where she lived?"

Irene peeked out from behind the square of cloth. "She had lodgings on Harper Street."

"She vacated those rooms on Tuesday around noon, without informing her landlady that she was leaving. She didn't even collect what remained of the rent she'd paid in advance."

"I didn't know that."

"Very well, Miss Davidson, that's all for now."

"I didn't like her," Irene said, "but I didn't kill her."

"Thank you, Miss Davidson."

Irene sat there, blowing her nose into her handkerchief.

"Do you have anything further to tell us, Miss Davidson?" McKnight asked.

"Irene," I said, "the show has started. Throw some cold water on your face and get downstairs."

"Yes, Mrs. MacGillivray." She scurried away.

"If you gentlemen have nothing more…" I said, standing aside to ensure they understood I was asking them to leave. "I have a business to run."

They put their hats back on their heads.

"Who told you about Irene and Chloe having a disagreement?" I asked, following them to the landing. "I'd scarcely think girl talk of that sort would be of interest to the Mounties."

"Everything is of interest to the Mounties," McKnight said in his most pompous voice.

Richard Sterling lifted one eyebrow at me as he headed for the stairs. All through the interview, he'd looked miserable.

I watched them descend to the main floor. As I mulled over what I'd heard, the door at the end of the hallway opened, and a bleary-eyed, pot-bellied, hollow-chested, heavily-bearded, probably infested, naked man stumbled out into the corridor. I had never seen him before. We looked at each other. He scratched the blanket of hair coating his chest and politely touched one hand to his head as if he'd forgotten he wasn't wearing a hat. "M'm," he burped.

Just another miner, one who'd hit paydirt, and was now desperate to spend every last cent he'd scratched out of earth and rock.

"Go back to bed."

"Yes, m'm," he said. He only collided with the doorframe once on his way to his room.

*   *   *

Angus kicked stones all the way to the Richmond Hotel. He was furious at the way in which Sterling had so casually dismissed him. As if he hadn't been a great help to the Mounties before.

The look on Mary's face when she'd been led away haunted him. He couldn't bear thinking about it. He didn't know Mary well, hadn't set eyes on her before a couple of days ago, when he'd pulled her out of the river. She'd have been better off if he'd left her alone. Better to drown than be hung for a murder she hadn't committed. He'd heard a saying once, something about being responsible for a person's life if you saved it. He'd saved Mary, and now he was responsible for her.

And failing.

He asked the desk clerk to tell Miss Witherspoon he was there and sat in the single horsehair chair in the reception area to wait.

The clerk returned to say Miss Witherspoon would be down momentarily. He held his hand in front of Angus's face, expecting a tip. Angus considered spitting in it, but being thrown out of the hotel wouldn't help Mary.

He settled back in the lumpy chair and ignored the clerk, who soon went back to his desk.

"Angus, what are you doing here?" Miss Forester stood beside his chair. Angus struggled to get up. So many springs were broken the chair almost devoured him.

"I'm waiting for Miss Witherspoon, ma'am."

"You needn't sit down here. We have a sitting room. You can wait for Martha there."

Their sitting room was small, only two chairs, a table and a small writing desk. Two doors led off the room, and Miss Forester knocked on the door to the right. "Angus is here, Martha. Please, take a seat."

Angus sat.

Miss Forester took the other chair. She said nothing for a few minutes, simply studied Angus from all angles. "Your features are like your mother's," she said at last, "but the colouring is all wrong."

Angus blushed under the force of her inspection. "My father was fair with blue eyes," he said.

"Where is your father now?"

"Dead, ma'am. He died before I was born."

"How sad. I knew her when she was your age."

"I guessed that, ma'am. You talk so alike."

"Do we? I hope Martha is almost ready for dinner.

Terribly early for dinner, but it seems that in Canada no one gives much mind to convention."

"Yes, ma'am." Angus strained his ears towards Miss Witherspoon's room, hoping to hear sounds of her coming out.

"Horrible place, Canada. Some of my brothers live in London. I'd like to live in London, it's so exciting. I was there once, for a few days, before catching the ship for America. Still, Canada is nicer than dreary old Skye. At least it doesn't rain all the time in Canada, although it gets exceedingly cold, they tell me."

"No, ma'am. Yes, ma'am."

"Tell me, is Constable Sterling married?"

"What?"

"Constable Sterling, the nice Mountie your mother and I met earlier today. Such an attractive uniform, that red jacket, the big hat and shiny boots."

"Uh, no."

"You don't like the uniform?"

"I mean, Constable Sterling isn't married."

"Still, only a constable. What about Mr. O'Brien? He seems to be prosperous, well dressed."

"I don't know if he's married or not."

"If you find out, I'll give you a dollar," Miss Forester said with a wink. Rather, she sort of scrunched up one side of her face and closed one eye—it didn't look as if she had much experience at winking. "What about your employer at the shop where we first met? He's old, but one can't be too fussy. Is he married?"

"To my landlady."

"Really, Euila, the boy is busy enough without asking him to search town for a marriageable gentleman." To Angus's great relief, Miss Witherspoon came out of her room. She was dressed in an outfit almost identical to the one she'd been wearing earlier. Her hair was tied back in its neat knot, and she'd replaced the frivolous shoes with practical, sturdy lace-up boots.

"You have the notebook?" she asked.

Angus produced it.

She examined it carefully. "It doesn't appear to be too badly damaged. A writer must always protect his notes, Angus. Nothing more important than one's notes. One must never rely on memory. It can be so deceiving. I had the foresight to bring a healthy supply of notebooks, so we can allow this one to dry off." She placed the damp book in the middle of the writing desk.

"Yes, ma'am."

"Well, we're off. It's almost eight. Men will be arriving at the Savoy, ready and eager to be interviewed."

"I was hoping we might have a bit of supper first, Martha," Miss Forester said. "I haven't eaten since breakfast."

Supper sounded like a wonderful idea to Angus, but his hopes were soon dashed. "No time to waste, Euila. I'll speak to the boy at the desk; he can have something sent up for you. Turn the pages of that notebook every half hour or so. I don't want them sticking together as they dry."

Miss Witherspoon plopped another flat brown hat onto her head, gripped a fresh notebook and headed out the door.

Angus followed. They were halfway down the street when he reminded Miss Witherspoon to arrange for Miss Forester's meal.

Chapter Twenty

I found my partner by the roulette wheel observing the festivities. "There is a naked man wandering around upstairs."

"Big loser," Ray said, watching the wheel go around. "Arrived around noon and dropped about a thousand dollars at poker. When he fell asleep at the table, I offered him a room. Gotta keep him in the house."

Jake shouted, "No more bets."

"We can't have him on the loose. Suppose he came downstairs dressed as God made him when the Mounties were here?"

"I'll lock him in," Ray said. "His room doesn't have a window, so he can't do much damage to himself if he wakes up and tries to escape."

The roulette wheel stopped turning. Jake gathered up most of the chips and counted out a small pile for the winner. He added them to the two lonely chips that were all the man had left in front of him. The gambler picked them up. He held them in his palm, enjoying their weight, making sure everyone in the vicinity saw them. He moved as if to put one down my décolletage. I grabbed his hand in mid-air. "Touch me and you're banned," I said softly, giving his wrist a twist for emphasis before releasing him.

"Jesus, lady." He dropped the chip back on the green felt table as though it had burst into flames. "Calm down."

"Mounties hear that talk, ye'll be off to the Fort for using vile language," Ray warned the gambler. He spoke to me under his breath. "I'll check on our guest upstairs."

I walked into the dance hall as Ellie's song came to an end, accompanied by cheers and stomping boots. Now that the audience was nicely warmed up, it was time for Irene and some of the girls who made at least a pretense of being able to act to perform scenes from *Macbeth*. Ellie, who was playing the Thane of Cawdor, slipped out from behind the curtain, half-tripping over the wooden sword stuck through her belt. She looked rather silly with her dress tucked into her belt to reveal a large pair of bloomers, but we had to observe propriety, and I wasn't going to waste money on costumes. Anyway, the men didn't mind seeing Ellie's bloomers.

Satisfied, I stood against the back wall to watch the performance. The audience had fallen so quiet, I could hear a mouse moving in the walls.

Irene had glided out onto the stage, watered-down red paint dripping from her hands, to begin the famous attempt to wash them, when a man came to stand beside me.

"Mrs. MacGillivray," he said.

"Mr. Jannis. I thought I'd banned you from my establishment."

"Only for one night, I believe you said."

"I doubt that. But as long as you don't cause trouble…"

"Oh, let me assure you, Mrs. MacGillivray, I'm here to cause trouble."

I lifted my hand to beckon one of the men over to show Mr. Jannis the street.

"You'll want to listen to what I have to say before you try to have me thrown out." His voice was low and serious, his tiny eyes fixed on me. I dropped my hand, although it itched to slap the smirk off his podgy face.

"If you have something to say, sir, please say it. And then leave."

On the stage, Irene howled her madness. She fell to her knees in a piece of overacting that would have them demanding their money back in London. But this wasn't London, and the Klondike audience moaned in sympathy. For those who weren't completely caught up in the drama, it was enough that the dress was made of layers of sheer fabric representing a Queen's night-gown and that in her despair, Irene tore at the false stitches sewn nightly through the front of the bodice.

"She's popular, your Lady Irenee," Jannis said. "With the men, I mean. All of them thinking they have a chance if they can only spend enough money to catch her interest."

"That's part of the attraction: always wanting, never achieving."

"But still achievable."

"There are numerous other fine dance halls in Dawson. Please take your patronage to one of them."

"You're a smart woman, Mrs. MacGillivray," he said. There were people all around, including men Ray employed to keep troublemakers away, but no one could hear us above the lamentation of Lady Macbeth and the encouragement of the crowd.

A line of sweat had broken out on Jannis's upper lip and across his receding hairline. All I had to do was walk away, and his attempt at blackmail was finished. But was it blackmail? Was he saying what I thought he was?

"Very smart," I agreed. "And very busy. If you'll excuse me."

"Irene Davidson is a lover of women. She has a female companion. Some men like that, or so I've heard. The idea of two women naked and rutting gets them excited."

"Pardon me, Mr. Jannis, if I'm not interested in your immature fantasies. I'll remind you that I can have you arrested for talking to me like that."

"Most men don't care for it. They want their favourite for themselves, and they'll take their business elsewhere if such news were to become general knowledge."

I looked at Tom Jannis. His suit was well cut, and the diamond stickpin thrust through his tie was bold and shiny, but the collar on his shirt was beginning to fray and had not been washed recently. The buttons on his waistcoat were mismatched, the knees of his trousers a mite shinny, and one could buy a tie like his on the waterfront for a few cents.

"The most popular dancer in Dawson and a highly respected businesswoman on one hand, and a down-and-out-Yankee trying to make a buck without working for it on the other. Who will men believe? Don't take me for a fool, Mr. Jannis. You have nothing to threaten me with. Please leave quietly, or I will have my men throw you out, with some considerable loss of dignity on your part."

We only performed a few choice scenes from Shakespeare. It was now time for Banquo to do his haunting of the banquet bit. The already dim lighting went down a fraction.

Jannis's face grew dark right before me, his eyes narrowed and his lips compressed into an ugly line. I moved my hands into position and settled onto the balls of my feet, expecting him to lash out.

If he'd cried, he couldn't have surprised me more. All the bluster exited him like air escaping from a child's balloon popped too early. "Okay," he said, "it was a bad idea, but I'll tell you this for nothing…"

"Wasn't that the day, Fiona?" Graham Donohue almost elbowed Jannis out of the way. "I've prepared some great copy for my paper."

Tom Jannis melted away. The last I saw of him, he was slinking out of the dance hall as Macbeth called upon MacDuff to "Lay on, and damned be he who first cries hold, enough." The men loved seeing the women dancing around the stage in their bloomers waving wooden swords at each other.

"Pardon me, Graham," I said, "I was in the midst of an important conversation there."

"With that son-of-a-bitch?" Graham laughed at the idea. "Sold his watch this morning, I heard."

"Really, Graham. You hear everything."

"The lot of a newsman, madam." He tossed me a wink of such exaggeration, I laughed out loud. "Tell me, my dear, do you suppose the audience would care if Lady Macbeth recovered from her unfortunate death and charged onto the battlefield to save her husband, lover and liege lord at the last moment?"

"They'd love it," I said. "But the staging would be a bit awkward considering that the same actress is playing MacDuff."

"Find a new MacDuff. Then you can present it that way. I won't even bill you for my creative advice."

"I would be much too afraid that the ghost of Mr. Shakespeare would come charging across the Chilkoot Pass to avenge himself on us," I laughed.

"Do you suppose the Mounties at the summit would allow a ghost into Canada without the required year's supplies?" Graham pondered the idea carefully. "Ghosts don't eat too much, I reckon, so they might make an exception in Will's case."

I touched his arm. "You are a dear, Graham Donohue. But you'll have to excuse me; I should tell Ray to keep an eye out for Mr. Jannis. I don't trust him any more than I believe that diamond in his tie is real."

Chapter Twenty-One

After meeting with Irene Davidson to ask about her friendship with the late Chloe Jones, McKnight dismissed Sterling for the rest of the evening. As he'd been temporarily removed from his duties of keeping the town of Dawson somewhat respectable and law-abiding, Sterling returned to barracks to change into civilian clothes. The necklace that had caused so much trouble was still in his uniform pocket. He held the gold chain up to the thin stream of light coming in through the barrack room window. It didn't give up any secrets, and he tossed it into his shirt pocket. Too bad he couldn't throttle the truth out of Joey LeBlanc.

He went into town in search of Angus MacGillivray. Sterling could think of nothing he could do to help Mary; perhaps Angus, who knew the woman better than anyone else, might remember something.

Mrs. Mann told him Angus had not come home for his supper, but before he could say "thank you and good evening," she also confided that she was concerned about Mrs. MacGillivray.

"The poor lady," Mrs. Mann said, leaning against the open front door, "simply doesn't get enough sleep, and she doesn't stop for her meals. It's no good eating on the run, you know. A civilized person needs to sit to table and enjoy her supper properly."

Sterling mumbled his agreement and attempted to back away. "Now," Mrs. Mann said, "if a man is intent on courting a lady, he should ensure she cares for her health. Though goodness knows," she rolled her eyes to the heavens, "it's hard enough for man or woman to mind their health in this place. I'm not complaining, mind. The Klondike's made Mr. Mann and me most welcome and provided us with an income that's the envy of my family, but…"

"Mrs. Mann, ma'am," Sterling interrupted, "Mrs. Mac-Gillivray and I aren't courting. I can't possibly talk to her about her…uh…sleep patterns." He felt so hot, he might well be standing in front of a blazing wood stove in full winter uniform rather than on the Manns' front porch on a pleasant evening.

"Nonsense," the lady said. "Some things may be different here in the North, but I can tell when a man and a woman fancy one another. Sleeping is an inappropriate topic, but you could still hint at the importance of proper meals."

Mr. Mann came out of the kitchen, puffing on his pipe and adjusting his suspenders. "Ah, Sterling," he said noticing that for once the Mountie was not in uniform. "Wees go for zee drink. One moment."

"I don't have time right now, Mr. Mann," Sterling said, unsure as to whether he should be happy that Mrs. Mann had stopped talking about that embarrassing subject or concerned that Mr. Mann apparently wanted to be pals.

Mr. Mann eyed Sterling's clothes. "You not working," he said. It was not a question.

"Not officially," Sterling stammered. "I'm looking for Angus. I have to talk to him about…things to do with a recent case."

"Angus good boy," Mr. Mann said. "I get mine hat, we goes."

Mrs. Mann smiled at them both, looking pleased that her husband had found a respectable drinking companion in this most unrespectable of towns.

With Mr. Mann in tow, Sterling next checked the Richmond but was told that Miss Witherspoon and the blond boy had gone out.

They found Angus at the Savoy, seated at the centre table with a glass of lemonade while Miss Witherspoon conducted her interviews. Angus shouldn't be in the Savoy in the evening, but so long as he only drank lemonade and stayed out of the gambling rooms and the dance hall, Sterling decided to say nothing. Besides, he wasn't working for town detachment tonight, was he?

Angus looked up when he saw Sterling and dashed over to ask the Mountie what had happened to Mary.

"I'm sorry, son," Sterling said, keeping his voice low. "She's been arrested. I'm sure we can…"

"How could you? How could you let that happen?" Angus shouted. It seemed to Sterling that every man in the saloon turned and stared at him with accusing eyes. Mrs. MacGillivray hurried out of the back room at the sound of her son's raised voice.

Sterling wanted to explain, but Angus, trying to hide tears that had sprung into his eyes, hurried back to Miss Witherspoon's table. Ignoring her young assistant, that lady waved Sterling and Mann over to join them. She was momentarily between appointments and was anxious to get an interview with a real Mountie. Sterling told her that he couldn't discuss police business with a reporter. "A writer," she corrected.

Mr. Mann brought over a round of drinks, including lemonade for Miss Witherspoon and Angus, and the moment she heard his thick German accent, Miss Witherspoon insisted he sit down and be interviewed about the immigrant experience.

Sterling clung to his single whisky all night, thoroughly uncomfortable under Angus's reproachful looks.

At midnight, Miss Witherspoon gathered up her writing materials, and a relieved Sterling went to gather up Mr. Mann, who'd wandered into the back rooms. He found the man standing against the wall in the gambling hall, staring wide-eyed at the quantity of money passing across the tables.

"Fools," was all he could say when Sterling told him it was time to leave.

Somehow they managed to collect Mouse O'Brien on the way out the door. Mouse had a silly smile on his face and took Miss Witherspoon's arm as she chattered like a chickadee about all the material she'd gathered. Angus stared at his feet in a thorough sulk. Mann mumbled to himself and finally spat out: "Crazy mens to waste much money. But they makes good business. Good for Juergen."

They deposited Miss Witherspoon at the door of her hotel. Mr. Mann said his goodnights with old-world charm. After a rather drawn-out farewell to Miss Witherspoon, Mouse slapped Sterling on the back and suggested they return to the Savoy: it was time for the dancing. Sterling knew he'd missed his chance of talking privately with Angus, so he excused himself and headed back to barracks, thoroughly despondent.

* * *

The stage show ended at midnight, as it always did. The girls streamed backstage to change out of their costumes, the benches were pushed up against the walls to clear the big room, and percentage girls moved out of the shadows onto the floor. The waiters ran up and down the stairs leading to the private boxes, bearing full bottles of champagne and carrying away empties. The orchestra leader called out, "Grab your partners for a long, slow, juicy waltz," and swung into a tune that resembled a waltz only in that it could generously be described as music.

I went backstage in search of Irene. Her last performance, the one that closed the show every night, consisted of a languid, sensuous dance performed in yards and yards of multi-coloured chiffon. The Savoy doesn't provide the dancers with their costumes, other than the odd accessory they tearfully insist that they need: Irene had lugged all that chiffon over the Chilkoot. It was worth the trouble—the men absolutely loved it, and the dance made a great ending to the show. The audience always leaned closer to the stage hoping that, just this once, the last bit of chiffon would float free.

The dressing room was tiny, scarcely larger than Mrs. Saunderson's kitchen, packed with women in every stage of dress and undress. The air was thick with cheap scent, heavily applied over drying sweat. The women tossed clothes all over the place, either in search of comfortable going-home shoes or their sauciest blouse. Some of the stage performers were finished for the evening, and some, those who needed or wanted the money, would stay behind to join the percentage girls in dancing with the customers for a dollar a minute. Not that they kept the dollar, of course. They got a quarter of that, the musicians got another quarter, and Ray and I pocketed the rest.

Irene dropped the black and red gown over her head. Ellie laid the neatly folded cloud of chiffon aside and helped with the fastenings running down Irene's back.

"Wonderful show, Irene," I said.

She took a deep breath to pull her diaphragm in a fraction and give Ellie a bit more room to work.

"I wonder if I might have a word with you. In private," I said.

"We've had enough words of late, Mrs. MacGillivray," Irene replied, not bothering to look at me. The girls stopped what they were doing to stare at this incredible breach of manners and good sense—I am the boss, after all.

I swallowed my sharp retort, reminding myself that I was here to beg a favour. "Perhaps we could talk once the rest of the ladies have left. If you have a few minutes." I glared around the room. Everyone returned to what they were doing in a flurry of hair, fabric and chatter.

Eventually the dressing room was empty save for Irene and me.

"So," she said, "talk."

"I didn't ask the police to interrogate you, Irene. Don't blame me if your friendships are causing you difficulty." This wasn't the friendly, just-us-girls tone I'd planned to take.

She turned her back to me and looked at herself in the room's single cracked mirror. Her shoulders drooped under the rich silk. "Sorry, Mrs. MacGillivray. Everything's getting me down these days."

If I were the motherly sort, I would have hugged her. Instead I said, "I would appreciate an introduction to your dressmaker. The clothes you've been wearing lately are truly lovely."

Irene ran a red satin ribbon through her fingers. "I've been most fortunate," she said to her reflection.

I agreed.

"A lady's dressmaker is somewhat like a lady's lover. Not something one wishes to share." Still trying to be the actress, Irene had discarded her middle-American accent in favour of one she obviously considered to be more snobbish. Mine. It was a poor imitation.

I considered pretending I didn't care one way or the other. I could dress in the cast-off clothes of a miner who'd hadn't been to town for a year, and I'd still be the most beautiful woman in Dawson. But I wouldn't feel like I was. "Very well. Thirty per cent on drinks."

Irene turned from the mirror with a smug expression . Most unattractive. "Thirty per cent it is, then. Starting tonight." She hitched up her skirts as if she were back on the farm and about to go feed the hogs. "You've met her already. Maggie. For thirty per cent, I'll even take you to her store."

I remembered the sign: Dresmakers Shop. Where I'd first seen Irene with Maggie.

"I know where it is."

"If you walk through the door, Maggie'll show you right back out of it. She thinks you're a stuck-up aristocratic English bitch who doesn't have any business being in America. Of course, I don't agree with her."

Of course not.

"I'll meet you outside the store at four tomorrow afternoon, shall I?" she said, trying not to smile too broadly. "Thirty per cent, Maggie will be pleased."

Irene left in a swirl of black and red silk and cheap perfume.

Let her enjoy a day or two of feeling smug; I'd find a way to get my own back. Once my new clothes were hanging in my wardrobe.

Chapter Twenty-Two

It had been a bad day at Mr. Mann's store. Everyone was in a foul temper at having to slog their way through the mud that filled the streets after yesterday's rain. A woman had been examining a pair of men's long underwear when her child tripped and fell face first into the mud. The woman hadn't even bothered to put the garment back on the table but dropped it into the muck as she yanked the child up by one arm and gave him a good swipe across the bottom. Mr. Mann insisted she pay for the underwear that would now need cleaning—it hadn't helped that the child had stomped across it in his attempt to avoid his mother's blows—and the woman refused.

"Weren't even clean to begin with," she said.

"You wants clean," Mr. Mann said, "go to San Francisco. Buy or give me a dollar for cleaning."

"A dollar! Never!" the woman shrieked. She grabbed her mud-encrusted offspring and stalked away, German curses following her.

Angus pulled the offending garment out of the mud and held it outstretched between thumb and forefinger. "What should I do with this, sir?"

"Take to Mrs. Mann for zee laundry." Mr. Mann checked his pocket watch. "Time to leave."

Meaning that it was one o'clock, and Angus's shift was over.

"All right if I take that pot, sir?" Angus asked, nodding towards a big iron cooking pot sitting half under the table.

"Why?"

Angus held up the underwear in explanation. The woman had been right—they hadn't been at all clean even before their encounter with the street.

And so Angus carried a pair of dripping, muddy longjohns home in an iron pot with a broken handle.

He deposited the underwear in the laundry shed and exchanged a brief greeting with Mrs. Mann before going in search of lunch. Mrs. Mann was so busy without help in the laundry, she hadn't had time to prepare a cooked meal. Instead she'd left him half a loaf of bread, a tin of sardines, and a can of peaches in syrup. Angus struggled to open the fish with the little metal key that came attached to the tin and thought of Mary. The only way he could help her would to be to find out who was responsible for Chloe's death. Between working at the store in the morning and helping Miss Witherspoon all afternoon and into the night, he barely had enough time for sleep, never mind trying to do the police's job for them. Perhaps he could interest Miss Witherspoon in helping him find the killer. She was looking for a good story, wasn't she? Pleased with his idea, Angus munched on his bread and sardines. His mother would have a few words to say if she could see him eating like a common labourer, standing over the bucket on the wooden plank that served as a sink. But his mother wasn't here, was she?

Promptly at two o'clock, he arrived at the Richmond. A man sat slumped in the single chair in the lobby, his legs stretched out in front of him. His hands were neatly folded over the bowler hat in his lap, and his head drooped forward. He was asleep, but he looked uncomfortable. The desk clerk was nowhere to be seen.

Angus stepped forward to check on the fellow and see if he needed anything. With a start, he recognized the scarf wrapped around the man's neck as belonging to Tom Jannis, whom he'd last seen beating up an old Indian in the street. With a sniff of disapproval, so like his mother's he would have been embarrassed to know it, Angus went upstairs to the ladies' suite.

Miss Witherspoon was standing at the window when Miss Forester opened the door. His employer turned to him with a toothy smile. "I simply cannot believe the state of those streets, my dear. I have dressed in my oldest skirt and put on my sturdiest boots." She lifted her skirt a fraction to demonstrate. "And I simply cannot wait to get out and record this scene. Why, I saw a wagon get so stuck in the mud right outside this window, they had to completely unload it, and even at that a good half-dozen men put their backs to it before the horses could move an inch. Most exciting." She placed her hat onto her head. "Now, Euila, you mustn't venture out of doors with the streets in this state."

"But Martha…"

"You have plenty of paper? Good. If you need more, send the clerk for some. Euila is transcribing my notes," Miss Witherspoon explained, stabbing a lethal-looking hatpin through her hat. "Shall we go?"

The desk clerk gave them a bored glance as they descended the stairs.

"I say," Miss Witherspoon said, "is that man all right?"

Angus and the clerk looked at the man snoozing in the lobby chair. The clerk shrugged and returned to his ledger. "Hotel guest. He can sleep it off there if he's too drunk to make it up to his room."

"Perhaps he's ill." Miss Witherspoon took a step towards the man in the chair.

"Leave him," Angus said. "He's nothing but another drunk."

Miss Witherspoon shook the man's shoulder. "Sir, are you in need of assistance?" she asked in her no-nonsense voice.

Very slowly, the man toppled forward. He slid off the chair, face first, and crashed down beside Miss Witherspoon's practical boots. "Good Heavens," she said. "Angus, help me get this man up. You, sir," she ordered the desk clerk, "assist us."

The clerk grimaced, but he put down his pen and left the desk, muttering something about drunks and bossy Englishwomen.

They stood over the man, wondering what to do now.

"Hold on a minute." Angus dropped to his knees and lifted the scarf away from the back of the man's neck.

Miss Witherspoon gasped and took a stumbling step backwards, her hand raised to her mouth. The clerk swore.

Blood had dripped onto the scarf, leaking from a small wound high on the neck, at the base of the skull.

Angus rolled the man onto his back. Glassy brown eyes pinched between pouches of fat stared up at him. He touched the neck. Nothing moved under his fingers.

"I'll go for the police," Angus said, standing up. He looked at Miss Witherspoon; she was pale and swaying on her feet. He took her arm. "Perhaps you should go," he said to the hotel clerk. "I'll stay here."

The clerk looked none too well either. He swallowed heavily.

"Get the Mounties," Angus said. "They'll be patrolling Front Street, that's probably the closest."

The clerk tore his eyes away from the body and looked at Angus. A ribbon of sweat ran across his upper lip, and his eyes were wild. He wasn't much older than Angus.

"Hurry!"

The clerk managed to recover some of his senses and ran out the door. Angus could only hope he was running for the Mounties, not heading for the hills.

Like a tree felled in the forest, Miss Witherspoon gave a slight moan, swayed from side to side and crumpled slowly. Angus caught her. He looked at the dead man, stretched out across the floor. He looked at Miss Witherspoon, trying to stay on her feet. He couldn't leave the body to take her upstairs; he couldn't expect her to stand around while he guarded the body. He didn't know what to do.

His mind was made up for him when a piercing scream came from behind. A lady had come in off the street and seen the empty-eyed body sprawled across the lobby. Her two companions, dance hall girls judging by their dress and the amount of rouge on their cheeks, simultaneously tried to prevent her from falling and see what was going on. The first lady hit the floor in a faint, and her friends started to scream. Men streamed in from the street, pushing and shoving to get a good look. Euila Forester hurried down the stairs, drawn by the noise.

Angus MacGillivray held Miss Witherspoon in his arms, looked pleadingly at Miss Forester, tried to hide the body from the view of passersby with his own, calculated how long it might take until the Mounties arrived, and wished his mother were here.

Chapter Twenty-Three

Most of the day passed in a state of high excitement, as I thought of little other than my appointment with the dressmaker. I decided upon the purchase of one day dress and a minimum of two evening gowns. First thing in the morning, I'd sorted through my jewellery box—sadly depleted since my glory days in London and Toronto—to consider coordinating fabric, colour and texture.

"You're looking pleased with yourself this afternoon, Fee," Ray said when he arrived for work.

I peeked at him through the corner of my eyes in a way that I knew to be most flirtatious. "And what is there not to be pleased about on a beautiful spring day such as this while our coffers overflow with money." I swept my arm in an arc to indicate the entirety of our business.

"Beautiful day, it may be," he said, eyeing my skirt, "but ye ken ye've got mud all across the bottom o' that dress. Turn around, it's no doubt splattered up the back too."

My partner never did let me get away with being too cheerful. I stuck my tongue out at him.

"Not to mention that we've got the suspicion o' murder hanging over our workers," he continued.

"Oh, stop it," I said. "Soon you'll have me crying in my drink." I'd been about to tell him about giving Irene thirty per cent on drinks (he is my partner, after all) but decided to hold that bit of information back, for no reason but to be difficult. It would come out soon enough. Like good partners should, Ray trusted me to keep the books, but he examined them carefully every Monday morning.

Joe Hamilton, who made an occupation out of hanging around the docks collecting news, burst through the doors. "Did you hear?" he shouted.

Every man in the saloon looked up.

Joe crossed the room to the bar. "There's been another murder," he announced.

We all waited for further news. None was forthcoming.

"Let me buy you a drink, lad," one of my regulars offered.

"Don't mind if I do."

Men gathered around, waiting for Joe to spit it out.

Ray poured a drink, and Joe tossed it back in one swallow. He slammed the empty glass down on the bar. His benefactor gestured for Ray to serve another.

When he had the full glass clutched safely in hand, Joe took a deep breath. "Man found dead at the Richmond minutes ago."

"What kind of news is that?" the man sneered, regretting the cost of two glasses of good whisky. "Folk dead all over town from sickness, bad food, bad drink. Bad life."

Joe tasted his second drink with more care. "Blood all over the floor. Ladies fainted straight away soon as they saw it."

"Where? When?"

"Hotel lobby. No more than half an hour ago. The hotel clerk came tearing down Front Street shouting for a Mountie. Pissed his pants too."

Half the men in the saloon headed for the door.

"Know who the dead fellow is?" someone asked.

"Nope."

"How's he killed?"

Joe grudgingly admitted he didn't know that either. It was looking as if he'd had his two drinks' worth. Those who hadn't rushed out at the very mention of the words "blood" and "fainting ladies" turned back to whatever they'd been doing.

I wanted to go upstairs and check the ledger one last time before I left for my dressmaker's appointment.

"Mrs. MacGillivray?" Joe Hamilton said in his soft, always polite voice.

"Yes?"

"I came to the Savoy first because I thought you would be particularly interested in the goings on at the Richmond. You have friends staying there, do you not?"

"Yes, I do."

Even in a town of poor sanitation, Joe Hamilton emitted a particularly unpleasant odour. His clothes had been torn and mended then torn and not mended. And they probably hadn't seen a soap flake since leaving the factory. He came into the Savoy occasionally, when he'd managed to gather some money together, and nursed one or two drinks all night. He usually spent the night watching me. He was always unfailingly polite and respectful, and I sometimes felt a bit sorry for him.

"Your son, Angus, he visits your friends at the Richmond regularly?"

"Yes." I signalled to Ray to pour Joe another drink. This had better be worth it: I was not feeling quite so sorry for Joe Hamilton at this particular moment.

"Angus MacGillivray found the body," Joe said.

The rest of our customers rushed for the doors.

I was ahead of them all.

*   *   *

If there is one thing nice about living in such a small town, it is that one can cross distances in a matter of minutes. I made it from the Savoy to the Richmond Hotel on Princess Street in record time. A good-sized crowd had gathered in front of the hotel; a handful of Mounties struggled to keep them back.

"Sorry, ma'am," one of the redcoats said to me, "you can't go in there right now."

He looked too young to shave and was new to the Yukon. I swatted him aside. "I am Mrs. MacGillivray and I am needed inside." I pushed my way past him. I have found that if you convincingly pretend you belong somewhere, almost anyone will believe you.

The lobby of the Richmond Hotel was crowded. Inspector

McKnight was there, observing everything through his thick glasses; a doctor (a real doctor, not that fool who always seemed to appear whenever I was feeling faint) ministered to a dance hall girl while her friends fluttered uselessly about; Richard Sterling knelt by the body, which had dispensed much less blood across the floor than Joe Hamilton's theatrics led me to expect; Sergeant Lancaster was doing nothing but trying to look important; halfway up the stairs, Martha Witherspoon wrote in her notebook while Euila clung to her. My son leaned over Richard, observing everything and peppering the constable with questions about such delightful topics as lividity and rigor mortis.

"Oh, Fiona, thank heavens you're here." Euila launched herself off the staircase.

Angus looked up and saw me, wrapped in a sobbing Euila. He straightened, leaving Richard to his inspection of the body. "Mother," he said, "you shouldn't be here."

I patted Euila on the back. "And neither should you." I peered around my son's attempts to block me from viewing the body on the floor. "Oh, it's Tom Jannis. No harm done, I must say. Other than to that floor."

"You know the gentleman, madam?" Inspector McKnight asked. I thought I'd spoken quietly. Apparently not quietly enough. Perhaps one day I'd learn to control my tongue.

I decided to speak my mind—Jannis's untimely demise clearly being none of my doing. "Nasty fellow this. Goes by the name of Tom Jannis. If I were you, Inspector, I'd start investigating in the less respectable gambling halls."

"Well, you are not me, Mrs. MacGillivray, and I don't need your advice, as well-intentioned as I'm sure it is."

I blinked. Was McKnight insulting me?

Euila sobbed against my shoulder, her tears leaking through the cotton of my day dress. I tried to shrug her away. "Pull yourself together, girl."

Euila made no attempt to move. I looked around for help: none was forthcoming. Martha Witherspoon continued to write furiously in her ever-present notebook.

The doctor approached us after finishing with the

fainting dance hall girl. She was being led out the door by her
friends, who were tossing their heads and swirling their skirts
around their ankles in anticipation of the attention they were
about to receive as they stepped through the hotel doors.
"Perhaps you should sit down, ma'am," he said to Euila.

I gave her a surreptitious shove to get her off my shoulder.

"I'm quite all right, sir, thank you," Euila said, swallowing
her sobs.

"Euila, allow the doctor to take you upstairs. This is no
place for a lady." Martha Witherspoon lifted her head from
her notebook.

"I'm perfectly…"

"You're staying at this hotel, miss?" McKnight asked.

"Yes."

"Your name?"

Euila gave it.

"Go to your room, please. I'll want to talk to you later."

"Miss Forester knows nothing about this wretched
business," Miss Witherspoon said.

"I'll decide that," McKnight said. "Why does it seem that
lately you are always around when something is happening?"

"Now see here, Inspector," a voice boomed from the
door. "That is a baseless accusation."

"Calm down, Mouse. The inspector wasn't making any
accusations," Richard said from his kneeling position on
the floor. "How did you get in here anyway?"

Mouse O'Brien crossed the lobby in two gigantic steps.
He had probably done nothing but loom over the
constable guarding the door until the nervous boy stood
aside. "I came as soon as I heard the news, Miss Witherspoon.
Are you all right?"

"O'Brien, get out of here," McKnight shouted. "Doctor,
take Miss Forester to her room. Miss Forester, wait there until
you are called upon. Miss Witherspoon, you do the same. Mrs.
MacGillivray, you may remain while I question young Angus.
And you, sir!" He was now bellowing at the cowering desk
clerk. "You can explain to me how you happened to stand
there working while a dead man lay not five feet away!"

The clerk went quite pale.

"Actually sir," Angus hurried to explain, "he wasn't lying on the floor; he was sitting in that chair until Miss Witherspoon touched him."

Euila put one hand to her mouth. Martha continued to scribble.

"Doctor, take those women upstairs. O'Brien, I told you to get out of here. Angus, you and your mother wait for me in the dining room. Lancaster, go outside and see why it seems as if every passing man and his dog is able to wander in here at will. And send someone for the undertaker. Sterling, finish examining that body, and you," he shouted at the clerk, "wait right here."

Mouse O'Brien took Martha's arm and guided her upstairs, over her protests that she was a writer and had a responsibility to her readers. Euila followed. The doctor decided that a dead body on the floor was more interesting than a wobbly Englishwoman and joined Richard in an examination of the remains. Lancaster politely suggested that if I felt the need to go home and lie down, he would act as the responsible adult while Angus was questioned. Richard lifted one eyebrow at me, then bent his head to accompany the doctor in the examination of the late, unlamented Tom Jannis.

"Thank you for your kindness, Sergeant," I said with a flutter of my eyelashes. "But I am needed here. And I think," I glanced at McKnight, who was growing increasingly agitated as no one followed his orders, "you are needed outside. Your authority will help the younger men to control the crowd."

The crowd was indeed getting quite lively. Two constables were trying to block the door while men were pushing against them, trying to see in. Several rows of faces lined the two small windows on either side of the door, Graham Donohue's first amongst them. He waved at me, hoping I would somehow be able to gain him admittance.

"Let's go, dear," I said to my son. "We'll sit in the dining room."

"I want to watch."

"Go with your mother, Angus," Richard said without looking up. "You're a witness to what happened here. You can't be involved in the investigation this time."

The dining room, the site of yesterday's aborted tea, was deserted, save for two white-aproned waiters lining the walls as if they were part of the decor. The customers had all been told to leave, but no one bothered with the staff. "Tea," I said, settling down at the biggest table in the centre of the room. A single sprig of droopy fireweed tossed into a dirty glass served as a centrepiece. "And sandwiches. Not fish paste."

"I don't know how you do it, Angus," I said as the waiters hurried away, no doubt glad of something to do. "You always manage to land in the middle of police business."

"I don't do it on purpose, Mother."

As we waited for our tea, I realized that I was making a law-abiding living just in time. My previous careers couldn't have withstood the degree of police attention Angus attracted.

I finished my fish paste sandwich as McKnight arrived to interview Angus. They didn't talk for long, and shortly after four o'clock, I hustled my son out of the empty dining room.

The lobby was empty, save for a bored-looking constable standing guard over a small wet patch on the floor. I averted my eyes.

"I'd like to check on Miss Witherspoon and Miss Forester, Mother," Angus said.

I checked my watch again. It was approaching ten past. How long would Irene wait? If I missed this appointment, would they give me another right away or make me suffer?

I hesitated. "I don't know, dear. Perhaps you'd best come with me. That killer might still be around somewhere."

He looked horrified. "Mother! I can't trail around after you."

Actually, I thought that not such a bad idea. Was I making a mistake with my son by letting him be so unsupervised?

He read my mind. "I'll be fine, Mother, if I'm with Miss Witherspoon and Miss Forrester. The Mounties will catch the killer soon."

I smiled at him. "Very well, but until then, please Angus, stay with Miss Witherspoon."

He kissed me on the cheek. Our eyes were on the same level. It seemed that he grew taller every day. I hugged him tightly.

"Mother!" Angus pulled away, flushing a deep red. He peeked out of the corner of his eyes to see if the Mountie was watching him being hugged by his mother. He was.

"Take care, dearest," I said, leaving for my appointment.

The crowd outside the Richmond had largely dispersed once the body had been removed. A few layabouts with nothing better to do lingered, hoping for a fresh flash of excitement. Graham Donohue stepped into my path.

"Fiona," he said. "This is ridiculous. I represent a prominent American newspaper, and McKnight won't give me even a hint of what is going on in there."

"Perhaps the good inspector doesn't give a fig for your prominent American newspaper, Graham. Now if you'll excuse me, I have an important meeting to which I am dangerously late."

He fell into step beside me. "We can talk on the way. That Witherspoon woman was inside the entire time. Do you think she got the whole story?"

"I don't know, Graham."

"What happened? Angus was there when they found the body, the men say. Weren't you talking to Jannis last night, Fiona? In fact, you ordered him out of the Savoy. Think that has anything to do with his death?"

"If he'd killed himself, I would consider it a perfectly natural reaction to being expelled from the Savoy. However, it doesn't appear he did himself in, so I don't see that I have anything to tell you. Oh dear, I did just tell you it wasn't a suicide, didn't I?"

"That you did, Fiona." The streets were full of mud. I had to lift my skirts to indecent heights to get from one boardwalk to another. More respectable women dragged their hems through the muck.

"Not much blood on the floor, though," Graham said

cheerfully, "least as far as I could see. But some, so he wasn't likely strangled. Must have been a knifing or a shooting. And as no one appears to have heard a shot— which would have been a pretty unusual sound around here—I'm guessing it was a knife."

"A very small knife," I said. McKnight had told Angus and me not to talk to anyone about what had happened. As if anyone in Dawson could keep such a thing secret.

"A small knife."

"Angus said it made a small neat hole in the neck. It was covered by that scarf Jannis always wore, which is why no one noticed him bleeding.

"Interesting," Graham said. "A well placed strike. Someone who knows anatomy then."

"Don't get too carried away with speculation, Graham. Everyone brought up on a farm or a woman who's attended a birth knows the rudiments of anatomy."

"You've never told me about your childhood, Fiona. Were you raised on a farm? I can see you running through fields of yellow corn and amongst the grazing cattle, your long black hair streaming behind you in the wind."

"Do I sound like my parents were farmers?"

"Your father was a horse breeder perhaps. Thoroughbreds. And you raised colts from birth and hung over the fence to watch them break records. With your long black hair streaming in the wind. Do they have racehorses in England?"

"No. Only fat ponies that pull straw-filled wagons full of apple-cheeked children at county fêtes."

It was almost four thirty when we arrived at the "dresmakers". Irene was standing outside, looking quite annoyed. No doubt she'd allowed adequate time for me to be late, yet still arrived first and had to cool her heels on the sidewalk. Ironically, since for once I'd planned to be punctual.

"Graham," I said with my most charming smile, "it would be better if you don't mention anything to the Mounties about Jannis and I having a slight altercation yesterday."

He pressed his hand to his heart. "As if I would do anything to draw their unwanted attention your way, Fiona."

"Humph," I said. Graham adored me, but he'd sell me down the river fast enough if there was a story in it.

"Mrs. MacGillivray," Irene said, "couldn't you have been on time? Maggie's a busy woman."

"Sorry, Irene," I said, trying to look contrite. "Couldn't be helped. Shall we go in?"

"Lucky for you, Maggie had an unexpected errand to run this afternoon."

"Good afternoon, Graham," I said firmly.

Never one to take a hint, he followed us inside.

The shop was small, but the south-facing windows were large and filled with panes of high-quality glass, which let in excellent light. A long table ran down the middle of the room, and dresses in various degrees of quality and completion hung from hooks around the room. Bolts of cloth and a scattering of hats lined the shelves in a waterfall of vibrant colour and texture. I sighed happily. Maggie stood beside her cutting table, tapping her toes on the floor. Quite rudely, she glanced at the watch pinned to her chest. I scarcely noticed—a stunning length of pale blue satin had captured my attention. I closed my eyes and stroked the bolt. If I concentrated on the feel of the fabric and the scent of new-cut cloth, I might be back in London, in the exclusive shop of one of the best dressmakers in the city.

"That colour isn't for you," Maggie said, sounding not at all like a sycophantic London seamstress. I opened my eyes. Instead of an indulgent patron, there was only Graham Donohue, gazing at me in an unguarded moment. Instead of a fussing lady's maid, there was Irene Davidson, looking like the cat who'd not only swallowed the cream but bought the whole dairy.

"Why not?" I asked. "It's beautiful."

"The colour of your hair and eyes and that complexion, you're way too dark to wear it. You need dark blues, navy'd be good, vibrant reds, even yellows. And black. You can get away with lots of black as well as pure white. Not pale shades. And never, ever, wear green, orange or mustard."

"Is that so?" My best evening dress was a pale green

satin. Maybe that was why I never felt particularly good wearing it, whereas I was still in mourning for the crimson Worth. "What would you suggest?"

"First tell me what you're wantin'. Day dresses, gowns?"

I wanted to shout "everything". Instead I told Maggie I was in need of one day dress and two evening gowns. We set about selecting fabric and discussing style. Maggie might not like me—aristocratic English bitch indeed!—but when it came to clothing, she was all business. Irene watched us as if she were a mother hen guarding her single chick, and Graham grew increasingly bored and fidgety, interrupting us to offer suggestions we ignored. When Maggie told me to go into the curtained alcove at the back so that she could take my measurements, he brightened up considerably.

"Have you nothing at all to be doing today, Graham?" I said.

"Nothing better than watching you, my dear."

He was staring out the window when we returned from the measuring. I had been prepared to pay heavily, and I was not to be disappointed. Maggie scribbled in her ledger, told me the total cost for three dresses, and demanded a good portion of the money up front. I dug into my reticule. No doubt the prices had shot skyward the moment I'd walked through the door.

"If you come back on Monday, the red dress'll be ready for a fitting," Maggie said. She buried her head in her ledger, and I was dismissed.

I nodded to Irene and said something silence-filling. Graham held the door open for me, but before I could step through it, a diminutive bundle of pure malevolence slipped in.

"Well, if it isn't Mrs. MacGillivray," Joey LeBlanc said, baring her teeth at me. "I've been talking about you."

"That I do not doubt," I said. "If you'll excuse us."

"I 'ear your boy, Angus isn't it, such a dear, I see 'im around a lot, is mixed up in another murder."

"Good heavens," Irene gasped. "There's been another one?"

Maggie pulled a parcel wrapped in brown paper out from under the counter. "Five dollars, Mrs. LeBlanc," she said.

"My son was unfortunate enough to be present when the body was discovered, yes," I said. With the height difference and the fact that my nose was high in the air, it was difficult to see Joey's expression. Probably malicious, as always. "But he was not involved in any way."

"That's not the way some see it," Joey said. "Some are asking why Angus MacGillivray is always around when something bad 'appens."

My nose dropped, and I stared into her ugly, beady brown eyes. "By some, I assume you mean you are spreading vicious rumour and innuendo, Joey. Which you can do all you want; no one of any consequence will pay the slightest bit of attention to the likes of you. But if you ever dare to interfere with my son…"

Joey gave me the nastiest smile I hope to ever see. "I never bother boys, Mrs. MacGillivray. No need—they come to me readily enough soon as they're able."

Before I could rip her hair right out of her head, Graham took my arm. "Leave it, Fiona. Let's go."

I allowed him to lead me away. Maggie handed the parcel to Joey. "Five dollars," she repeated.

"I also 'ear that your protégé, the ugly little Indian, is gonna 'ang for killing poor Chloe," Joey said to my retreating back. "Didn't you take against Chloe, Mrs. MacGillivray? Maybe you put 'er up to it, eh? Wonder if the redcoats 'ave thought of that? 'Course some are saying it coulda been you, Irene. Weren't you and Chloe very close friends once?"

"That's outrageous." Irene's voice broke on the words.

"Five dollars," Maggie said.

Chapter Twenty-Four

Angus tapped lightly on the door to the ladies' sitting room. Miss Witherspoon threw it open. "How dreadfully exciting," she bellowed, dragging Angus into the suite. Miss Forester lay on the settee, and the doctor was gathering up his bag. He nodded to Angus. "Shock can come on at any time, young man. If you have reason to believe your mother is experiencing the delayed effects of shock, come and fetch me, any time day or night."

"Yes, sir," Angus said, wondering why doctors were never concerned about *his* well-being. He was the one present when Jannis had toppled over, not his mother.

Miss Witherspoon placed her hat on top of her head and stabbed it with a hat pin. "Let us continue our adventures, so rudely interrupted, young Angus."

"I've been thinking, Miss Witherspoon, ma'am."

"Yes?"

"I don't want to be a Mountie, after all. I'd like to be a writer." Angus's tongue stumbled over the words. "Would you teach me, ma'am?"

Miss Witherspoon's eyes lit up. "Of course, Angus, of course. Shining the light of the truth into dark corners to reveal sordid matters some would keep quiet is the noble occupation of the writer. As we were so fortunate as to be at the scene of this dreadful killing, it is clearly incumbent upon us to follow, no matter where our investigation might lead."

"Okay."

"Euila!"

"What is it now, Martha?"

"Young Angus and I are off. Please have my notes written up by the time we get back."

"You know I will."

"Good, let us be off then."

When they came down, the last Mountie had left the hotel. The wooden floor was still damp. Angus and Miss Witherspoon avoided the wet spot.

"This means that Mary didn't kill Chloe," Angus said.

"Why do you say that?"

"Two killings in two days? They have to be connected. And as Mary's in jail, she couldn't have killed Mr. Jannis, could she?"

"Apparently not. But aren't you jumping to conclusions, dear? There is nothing to say, at least as far as I can see, that these two incidents are connected."

Angus took Miss Witherspoon's arm to help her cross the duckboard in front of the hotel. The afternoon sun was doing a good job of drying out the mud, but the streets were still treacherous. A single boot was firmly planted in the middle of the street, as though waiting for its owner to return and put his foot back in. "I know it, Miss Witherspoon, I just know it. Mary can't have killed Jannis, so she can't have killed Chloe either. We have to find Inspector McKnight and explain it to him. Come on."

Angus practically dragged Miss Witherspoon to Fort Herchmer.

*   *   *

Constable Richard Sterling and Inspector Rupert McKnight had spent the remainder of the afternoon attempting to find someone to interview about the killing of Tom Jannis. Hard to believe that in the middle of the day, in the middle of a town packed as full as Dawson, a man could be stabbed in the back of the neck and left sitting in an arm chair in the lobby of a reputable hotel, yet not a soul would know anything about it. But that was the way things seemed to be. The desk clerk had been running errands, the guests were either in their room or in the dining room, the bar of the hotel opened directly onto the street, so anyone in search of a drink would have had no reason to cross the lobby. There was no trace of blood at the lobby entrance or anywhere on the floor except around the chair in which Jannis had been sitting when Angus had first seen him and where the body had fallen. Which made it unlikely Jannis had been killed elsewhere and brought to the Richmond: he would have left a trail of blood behind him.

Jannis had been killed sitting in the lobby of the Richmond. His assailant had likely walked behind his chair, and with one stab between the vertebrae at the base of his skull, killed the man. No one had seen, or heard, a thing. No one who was prepared to speak to the police at any rate.

"If we could locate that knife, we'd be a long way to having this solved," McKnight said as they crossed the parade ground, heading back to the inspector's office. "It had to have been pretty small."

"And sharp," Sterling said.

"And sharp. Owned by someone who either got lucky, or knew exactly where to strike. Go around to some of the miner's supply stores, see if you can find a blade or tool long and thin and sharp, of the sort that might have done the job."

"You think a miner did this?"

"No reason to, but I don't know much about what sort of tools they use. I've never watched a miner work, have you?"

"I've been to the Creeks, sir. Didn't pay much attention to their equipment."

"Awful job, I hear."

"You think there's something distinctive about the knife?"

"That wound was made with a long, very thin blade. Not something anyone could grab off a butcher's block. I'd like to know if there's something like that around town, that's all. If it is a miner's tool, then every single person in town is a possible candidate to own one."

They walked in silence for a minute, each wrapped in his own thoughts.

"If the knife doesn't lead us anywhere," McKnight said as much to himself as to Sterling, "we have to concentrate on finding a motive."

"Yes, sir."

"What about that Indian fight you broke up?"

"What Indian fight?"

"Between Jannis and some drunken Indian, couple of days ago."

"That wasn't a fight. It was a bully kicking the stuffing out of a man who was in no condition to defend himself."

"Check out the Indian anyway. He might have wanted revenge."

"No Indian is going to walk into the Richmond Hotel in midday. And if he did, Tom Jannis wasn't likely to stand around talking to him. It seems obvious Jannis was killed by someone he knew, or wasn't afraid of, at any rate. He doesn't appear to have tried to defend himself; he didn't cry out; he sat there and let his killer get behind him."

"Still, wouldn't hurt to look at the Indian. Check out his movements."

"Sir, with all due respect, I think that's a waste of time."

McKnight stopped walking and turned to face the constable. "If you don't want to do it, Sterling, you can return to town detachment, and I'll find someone else to help me."

Sterling held back his rising anger. "I'd like to stay on the case, sir, but I don't think it's worth anyone's time to question the Indian. The Reverend took him back to Moosehide village."

"And left him there, I'm sure. The good reverend is unlikely to stand watch over every sad case that crosses his path. He might have made his way back to town."

"But…"

"Mining equipment stores after supper, Sterling. Moosehide tomorrow. Unless you'd rather report to town detachment?"

"No, sir." Sterling could barely get the two words past his teeth without spitting.

"Inspector, Constable, wait up!" A shout stopped the

two Mounties at the top of the steps leading to McKnight's office.

Angus MacGillivray and Martha Witherspoon were hurrying across the parade square. Martha fought to keep her skirts straight in the wind, and Angus held his cap in place with one hand placed firmly on top of it.

Angus bounded up the steps, and Miss Witherspoon struggled to keep up. "What luck!" Angus said. "We're looking for you, aren't we, Miss Witherspoon?"

McKnight opened his office door, suppressing a sigh. "What can I do for you this time, son?"

They all crowded into the office. The room was small, filled by a battered and scarred desk with a jumble of papers piled dangerously high and two visitor's chairs. Beside the cold stove, a stack of logs waited for sharp fall nights, and a carpet that had seen much better days sprawled across the centre of the room. A huge Union Jack was pinned to one wall, facing a portrait of a young Queen Victoria on the other. The wallpaper wouldn't have been out of place in a dance hall.

McKnight sat behind his desk. Miss Witherspoon verbally admired the decor before taking a chair and pulling out her notebook. Angus paced. McKnight lit his pipe and signalled to Sterling that he could do likewise. The inspector took a deep breath of fragrant tobacco before he spoke. "What brings you here, Angus?" He watched a smoke ring rise to the ceiling.

Angus looked at Martha Witherspoon, who sat stiffly in her chair, pencil posed over a fresh sheet of paper. "Well, sir, we, Miss Witherspoon and me, are wondering if you're going to release Mary now. I'd like to take her home. Mrs. Mann needs her help at the laundry."

"What makes you think I'd choose to release the Indian woman known as Mary?" McKnight said.

Sterling studied the objects on the walls. There was a photograph of McKnight sitting in the front of a group of young Mounties, a poorly-executed cross-stitch reminding him that they were all on the verge of entering the Valley of Death, a portrait of a distinguished-looking gentleman, and a bad painting of a tree. Other than the cross-stitch, there were no mementos of family.

"She couldn't have killed Jannis, could she?" Angus said. "Being in jail and all."

"No," McKnight said, "but she isn't accused of doing so."

"Well then, as the same person who killed Mr. Jannis probably killed Miss Chloe, you can let Mary go." Angus smiled, satisfied of the validity of his argument.

"We don't know that the same person was responsible for both killings," McKnight said, pulling a piece of paper from the top of the pile in front of him.

"It makes sense, sir," Angus said. "There aren't so many killings in Dawson that these two might not be related. Jannis saw who killed Chloe, and so the killer knew he had to get rid of him too."

"If Jannis saw someone killing a dance hall girl, why didn't he report it to the Mounties, Angus? I'm sorry, but your idea doesn't work."

"What about the method of killing?" Miss Witherspoon looked up from her notebook for the first time. "The similarity of both events."

"There is no similarity," McKnight said. "Chloe was bludgeoned, pardon my frankness, madam, but you did pose the question, and Jannis was stabbed. I see no similarity."

"Wasn't Chloe stabbed as well?" Miss Witherspoon said. "By a thin blade to the right side of the chest. Only when she failed to expire on the spot, we can assume, did the killer resort to more drastic methods."

"Gosh," Angus said.

Sterling leaned forward. The same thought had occurred to him, but he'd wondered how to broach the topic without stepping into the prickly McKnight's area of authority.

"Miss Witherspoon!" McKnight dropped the official paper. "How do you know that?"

She smiled out of the corner of her mouth and tapped the side of her nose. "A writer has her sources, sir."

"I'll ask you to keep your information to yourself,

madam. Police business is no concern of a lady."

"I am here in my professional capacity."

"You are still a lady, unless I am mistaken?"

Miss Witherspoon let the insult pass.

"You must see, sir. Mary can't have killed them both, so you can let her go. I promise I'll look after her." Angus was close to pleading.

"Angus," Sterling said quietly, "you can't look after an adult woman."

"My mother then. And Miss Witherspoon."

The writer looked less than delighted at that idea.

"A moot point," McKnight said. He picked up a stack of official papers and settled back into his chair. "As I won't be releasing the Indian. The two killings might have a surface similarity, but unacquainted as you both are with the mind of the common criminal, you are probably not aware, Angus, madam, that killers are often known to deliberately imitate the work of someone else. It's quite common in larger cities. Good day."

"But…" Angus said.

"I say…" Miss Witherspoon said.

"Constable Sterling, escort Mr. MacGillivray and Miss Witherspoon back to town, if you please. Then you can check the mining stores."

"Come on, Angus," Sterling said.

Miss Witherspoon tucked her notebook into her cavernous handbag and headed out the door. Head down in defeat, Angus followed. Then he stopped.

"I want to see Mary," he said.

McKnight dropped his papers back onto the desk. He'd been holding them upside down, Sterling noticed. "Most certainly not!"

"She must have the right to have visitors," Angus said firmly. "I insist upon seeing her. If you refuse, I'll find a lawyer."

Miss Witherspoon came back into the office. "I'll accompany the lad."

"Good," Angus said, "in case the inspector insists I need an adult female escort."

McKnight looked quite lost. Sterling stifled a laugh. The boy was as hard-headed as his mother.

McKnight sighed. "Sterling, give these people ten minutes with the prisoner. Then the miner's stores."

"Yes, sir." Sterling hustled Angus and Miss Witherspoon out of the inspector's office before one of them could smirk and make McKnight change his mind.

Chapter Twenty-Five

Once again my day was a mess. It was close to six o'clock by the time I'd finished at the dressmaker's and taken a furious walk through town to let off some of the steam that was threatening to boil over at the thought of Joey's ugly insinuations. If my son ever dared to cross the threshold of one of her hideous cribs! Not for the first time, I was sorry that I hadn't had a daughter, a sweet thing I could dress in pretty clothes and mould into my own image. Well, the image of the girl I'd been a long time ago, at any rate.

I went home to change into my evening gown and have a quick bite of dinner. Angus wasn't there, and I could only hope he was still following Martha Witherspoon around town. I didn't like the idea of him being on his own, not with a killer loose, but it was impossible to keep a motherly eye on the boy considering the schedule I had.

Mr. Mann was full of questions about the killing at the Richmond. He'd heard that Angus was involved, so I couldn't pretend I knew nothing about it. I explained as briefly as I could without being too impolite, wolfed down the perfectly hideous corned beef hash and escaped to my room. I looked at the green satin with different eyes. I don't know why I'd bought it—probably because the fabric looked so lovely lying on the seamstresses' cutting table—but now that I knew why I didn't like it, I felt better about wearing it. I put it on, reflecting happily that there were only a few more days until I would take possession of my wonderful new clothes. Perhaps Maggie could re-cut the green satin into something for day wear. A skirt perhaps, or the lower part of a dress, to be worn with a top more suitable to my colouring. For a few blissful minutes, I forgot about Joey LeBlanc and her nasty insinuations about my son. But soon enough, my temper returned with a vengeance.

*   *   *

Graham Donohue sat at the centre of the bar, interviewing two men who were telling him they were on the scene immediately after the finding of the body and before the Mounties showed up to spoil all the fun. I stuck my head into the back room to ask Helen to make me a cup of tea, then joined Graham at the bar. The men were delighted to make room for me.

"When you have a moment, Graham," I said, "I'd like to talk with you. Privately." I dragged the last word out, rolling it over my tongue before letting it slip through my lips. Graham almost choked on his whisky. "When you've finished what you're doing, of course," I said, to be polite.

"I'm finished." He abandoned his drink and practically pushed me across the room. He headed for the stairs, but I put a hand on his arm and slipped into the reasonably quiet alcove at the bottom of the steps. "This will do," I said.

"Fiona, I…" he said, his voice thick. He tilted his head towards me.

The alcove might be reasonably quiet, but it certainly wasn't private. A group of drinkers stared at us. "I've decided to help you," I said in a low voice, placing a firm hand on Graham's chest to stop his forward movement.

"And I'll help you, Fiona," he said. "Any way I can."

"With your story."

"What story?"

"The story you're writing about the women of Dawson who've been forced into prostitution. Do you gentlemen have nothing better to do?" I said to our crowd of onlookers.

"What?" Graham said, sounding rather stupid, which I knew he most certainly was not.

"The story you're writing for your newspaper," I reminded him. "I have decided to help."

He took a step backwards. The customers flowed around us, no one paying us much attention now that the sexual energy had dissipated as quickly as if Ray had tossed Graham out the door without his boots in February.

"Help?" he said.

"Yes, help. Why are you repeating everything I say? I want to help you. Some of the women will speak to me, where they won't talk freely with you. I suggest we begin first thing tomorrow. We can't be too early, the women will still be sleeping, but we can't be too late, as business will be starting up and then no one will talk to me...us. What would be best, do you think? Noon. Yes, noon."

"Joey won't let you anywhere near her cribs, Fiona, and the men will do what they have to in order to prevent you talking to the girls. Thank you for the offer, but I can't see as to how it will work out." Some of the colour was coming back into Graham's face.

"That's true," I admitted, twisting the necklace of fake pearls around one finger. "Not that I care much about the favours of Joey LeBlanc and her ilk. But I wouldn't want to cause the girls any trouble."

"Oh, well, can't be helped. Will you look at the time, seven thirty already! I have an appointment that can't be missed."

"So you'll have to bring them to me."

"What?"

"The girls. Are you being deliberately obtuse, Graham? If I can't visit them at their places of...uh...employment, then you will have to arrange for them to come to me. They can't come here or to Mrs. Mann's; perhaps we can arrange to rent an office where we can interview our subjects in comfortable privacy. That would be best. Look into that first thing tomorrow morning, will you."

"Fiona," Graham said.

"Yes?"

"You are the most...incredible woman."

I am not normally known for being altruistic, and I didn't really give two hoots for the prostitutes. I'd known plenty of whores in the streets of East End London, and few of them had shown me any kindness. Here, most of them were no harder up than men who came to make their fortunes on the gold fields only to find themselves working just as hard, for just as little pay, at whatever jobs they'd foolishly abandoned in the south. But there were women, such as Mary, who were virtual slaves. I'd get their stories out of them; Graham would write them up for his newspaper, and once the story was printed, the authorities would be obliged to do something to stop the underhanded bondage of women.

Not incidentally, perhaps I could run Joey LeBlanc out of business and out of town.

Graham left the Savoy so fast, he almost ran over Angus in his attempt to get out the door.

My son's face was set in lines of firm determination that I was sorry to see. Miss Witherspoon trailed after him, looking equally stern. I considered hiding under the stairs but also considered what they might do if they couldn't locate me. I stepped into the light and pasted on my motherly smile.

"Mother, I'm glad you're here."

"Where else would I be? Angus, what are you up to now?"

"How'd you know…? Never mind, you have to help us. Mary's in jail."

"I know that."

"Inspector McKnight let us see her for a few minutes. She needs clean clothes and women's things."

I dragged my son into the shadows of the stairs. Martha Witherspoon followed. All around us, men's ears were pricking up again. "Me?" I tried to whisper. "How did I get involved in this?"

"Her things are still upstairs, aren't they, Mother?"

"Yes. You can get them tomorrow. It's past time you were home."

"It isn't even eight o'clock!"

As if to emphasize his point, at that moment the orchestra staggered out onto the street to begin their nightly call for custom. They tuned up, the violin sounding rather like a cat in labour, or perhaps the bagpipes. Half of the customers—those with some musical education—winced.

"Angus, I have a business to run here. I will not be rushing about gathering up a woman's property because she was silly enough to get herself tossed in jail."

"Mother!" Angus drew himself up to his full twelve-year-old height. I stood very straight, trying to be unobtrusive about it.

"Mrs. MacGillivray," Martha Witherspoon said, her voice dripping with condescension. "Constable Sterling told us they don't even have a female attendant to look after the women in the jail. He'd suggested it once, but Inspector McKnight said he would never countenance allowing respectable women into the company of women of ill-virtue. Think of the poor woman confined in those rough men's quarters with no one but men to bring her meals and watch over her…and…and…it doesn't bear thinking about."

"I will think about it, Miss Witherspoon," I said, "tomorrow. Angus, go home." I looked at my son and saw the disappointment in his eyes and the droop of his shoulders. "I don't imagine they'll even let you in at this time of night."

"Yes, they will. The guard said we could come back anytime before his shift ends at midnight."

"Oh, all right! Come upstairs, and I'll get you some money so you can go shopping for a bit of soap and some clean linen to take to the jail. And a towel, I'm sure Mary would enjoy a clean towel."

Angus smiled again. "That would be nice, Mother. She might like some food—a loaf of bread, some cheese."

"You can purchase those things as well. Helen has put Mary's possessions into the storage closet. Ask her to get them. I'm sure she'd like her Bible."

Angus kissed me on the cheek. The men surrounding us smiled. So far from home, they loved to be reminded of the sort of quaint family relationships they'd given up to come prospecting in the Klondike.

I told Angus to ask Helen to make me a fresh cup of tea and bring it upstairs while I went to my office to get the money.

"You're very kind," Martha said.

Kindness had nothing to do with it. I hated to see that look of disappointment in my son's lovely blue eyes.

* * *

At last I got my tea, and Angus got the pathetically small bundle that made up Mary's worldly possessions. My beaming son and a rather pleased-with-herself Martha Witherspoon left the Savoy.

I'd been concerned about Angus trotting around town at Martha's heels; now it was looking more as if she were the one doing the trotting. As long as it kept him out of trouble.

The rest of the night was no more eventful than normal, although Richard Sterling didn't pop in regularly, as he usually did, to check that we weren't serving drinks to underage children, watering down the whisky, or cheating at cards. A couple of times I found myself turning with a smile when I caught sight of the familiar red tunic out of the corner of my eye. But it was always another Mountie.

* * *

It was getting close to closing time. I was not quite leaning against the back wall—Miss Wheatley would smack my palms if she ever caught me leaning—watching a man who had caught my attention. He was older than most of the men in town and was particularly well dressed in a black suit, stiffly-ironed white shirt (real white, not the sort of washed-out grey that almost everywhere in Dawson, on women as well as men, passed for white) and a black hat. The diamonds on his cufflinks glowed in the poor light cast by the kerosene lamps. He'd played a few rounds of poker, not high stakes, won a bit of money, then politely excused himself and gone to the bar to finish the evening with a drink. He said the occasional word to the men on either side of him but didn't appear to be interested in engaging anyone in conversation.

I wondered who he was and what he was doing here, both in the North and in my bar. And so I was observing him when a cheechako slid up beside him and engaged him in conversation. The cheechako, a young man dressed no worse than most, had consumed a fair amount of drink and was having trouble standing straight. The older fellow kept turning his head away, but the drunk kept on talking. The drunk shouted for another drink and poured a few coins out of a tattered money pouch for payment. I was considering asking Ray to escort the young man from the premises, as he was bothering the older one, who looked like a customer worth cultivating, when, to my considerable surprise, the older man relieved the younger one of the money bag. It was so smoothly done, I would have missed it if my eyes hadn't been following the young man's hand as he was about to put the pouch back in his breast pocket. I looked around for Constable Sterling...for any Mountie. Not a red jacket in sight. Ray was settling a dispute in the gambling room. A percentage girl sauntered up, wiggled her hips at the two men and invited the older one for a dance. He refused with a polite smile, but the young one accepted. I held my breath, knowing she was about to ask for a dollar. Instead of reaching into his jacket for the cash, he pulled a bill out of his pants pocket, and they went into the back.

The last thing we needed was for word to spread that someone had been robbed inside the Savoy. The earth had gone around the sun more than a few times since I'd worked the streets: if I got caught, I'd be in serious trouble. The well-dressed man drained his drink and shook his head when Murray offered to pour another. I crossed the room and slid into the space vacated by the drunk. "I hope you've had a pleasant evening, Mr...?"

He smiled at me, and his eyes fell to the neck of my gown. "Smith," he said.

"Mr. Smith. I don't believe you've been in the Savoy before. Are you new to town?"

"Arrived day before yesterday, ma'am."

"How lovely," I let the fingers of my left hand flutter across his chest. I danced them around the edges of his lapels and licked my lips. I looked at the cufflinks and allowed my eyes to widen in appreciation, then raised them to look into his face.

"It's getting late," he said, his voice husky. "Why don't you and me go out for some fresh air?"

"I'm sorry," I said, taking back my hand and stepping away. "I've another engagement."

His face clouded over as I backed off. I rushed into the dance hall. The caller was announcing that it was almost time for closing.

I hugged the walls so that I would come up behind the young man. "Sir, sir," I said, tapping his shoulder. He turned, and I held up his money pouch. Heavy it was too—if he'd been sober, he might have missed it. "You dropped this."

He took it from me. The percentage girl looked at me suspiciously. "Can't be too careful," I said.

"Why, thank you, ma'am," he said, trying not to slur his words. His face was unlined and his smile full of charm. An innocent corn-fed country boy. "Let me buy you a drink."

"Thank you, no," I said. "You have another dance. This one is on the house. Keep an eye on that bag. Goodness knows how it happened to fall on the floor."

Tomorrow I'd find Richard Sterling and tell him to be on the lookout for the well-dressed older gentleman with the diamonds in his cufflinks. I'd enjoy knowing he was spending a month or two in the wood pile.

I called Ray over. I described the pickpocket and told him to keep an eye out and make sure the fellow didn't step through our doors again.

My partner peered at me through narrowed eyes. "You saw this fellow pick a man's pocket and let him get away with it?"

I blew on my fingers. "I said I let him get away. I couldn't arrest him myself, now could I? I'll tell the Mounties about him. But I didn't say he got away with 'it', did I?" I couldn't help but grin. I wiggled my fingers; it's true there are some things you never forget.

Ray didn't look as pleased as I felt. "Fee, if you got caught with your hand in a man's pocket..."

"Ray," I said with a wicked smile, "I never get caught."

I walked away from my shocked partner with a swish of satin.

In the gambling room, the roulette wheel slowed to a stop. Jake scooped up a pile of blue chip, and told the room he was closing up.

Most of the girls would be gone, but as always I wanted to check on the dressing room before going upstairs. The rotten floorboard in the middle of the room moved under my weight, and I reminded myself that I'd better get it fixed before someone fell through to the foundations.

"Well, that's what Chloe told me." A woman's voice came from the other side of the open door leading into the dance hall.

"Ooohh," one of the percentage girls breathed in shocked delight, "before she were killed, you mean?"

I stopped to listen. Miss Wheatley would beat me if she caught me eavesdropping. Unlike leaning, eavesdropping was a habit I refused to give up.

"Did you believe her?" a third girl asked.

"Sure I did," the first one said. It was Betsy, one of the back-row stage performers. She sounded delighted at being the centre of attention for once. "She was right pleased with herself. Said she didn't need to put up with the likes of Mrs. MacPruneFace any longer now she had a man to take care of her. He'd offered to move her into his lodgings and all, soon as he moved out of his hotel and found a room. So it would be like a permanent relationship."

So that was what they called me: Mrs. MacPruneFace. I'd give Betsy some prunes to stew on soon enough.

"And one more thing…"

I could almost hear the assembled listeners leaning forward. I leaned forward myself. "She pretty much told me she had the goods on our fancy *Lady Irenee*."

"Oh, right. Like Irene has anything to be hiding. Butter wouldn't melt in her mouth."

"Never mind, Irene. Did Chloe say who he was? Now that she's done for, he'll be looking for another woman." She sounded hopeful.

"She said all right, but you can be sure I won't be telling the likes of you, Maxie McCoy," Betsy said.

"Why not? What do you want with him? You've got Mr. Walker," Maxie said.

"Shut up," Betsy said. "She hears about it, and I'll be out on my ear." I could assume I knew who "she" was. "I'm gettin' tired of Mr. Walker anyhow. He ain't givin' me nothing the rest of you girls don't get."

"We ain't getting none o' that from Mr. Walker," Maxie said with a squeal.

"You can have him, Betsy. Everyone knows Irene's so proper, she won't even step out with Mr. Walker. Chloe was lying. She didn't know anything about Irene that's worth telling."

"Good morning, ladies." I stepped through the door. "Looks like it's going to be a nice day. You'd best be getting home now. Some of you may have jobs to come to later."

They scattered liked a flock of painted, colourful crows when a gust of wind stirred up the scarecrow.

I grabbed Betsy by the arm. "You," I said, "can wait a moment."

"I was only gossiping, Mrs. MacGillivray," she blathered. "To impress the girls. I don't know nothing, and me and Mr. Walker, we ain't…"

"Who was Chloe's man friend?" I said. My fingers dug into the dancer's flabby arm.

"What?" Tears welled in her eyes, less, I thought, at the strength of my grip than the fear of losing her job.

"Chloe's man. Tell me his name, and I'll forget all the rest of that conversation."

"Tom Jannis. The one that was killed."

"Didn't it occur to you that you should tell the Mounties that nugget of information?"

"The Mounties? I don't go nowhere near the police, Mrs. MacGillivray."

I let go of her arm. She had a point. The women who worked for me were only one step higher on the social scale than the women in Paradise Alley. The Mounties I knew, even Inspector McKnight, wouldn't hold her social status against her when weighting her information, but I could imagine Betsy's experiences told her otherwise. When I was young and running through the streets of Seven Dials, one of the worst of the London slums, I wouldn't have told the Bobbies if I'd overheard someone plotting to kill the Queen.

"Ready to go, Betsy," Ray came through the door. He stopped short at the sight of me. "I mean, it's time to lock up."

"Oh, for heaven's sake," I said. "Ray, go away."

He went.

I turned to Betsy. She had assumed a most unattractive pout and rubbed at her arm as if to emphasize how much I'd hurt her. "I told you'd I'd forget about what I heard. Well, I lied."

Fear moved behind her eyes. No beauty she, Betsy would be looking for jobs in worse places than the Savoy if I let her go. "I never forget," I said. "You call me that name again and you're gone, do you understand?"

She nodded, and relief flooded back into her face as she realized she wasn't fired. Not this time.

Ray was standing by the front door when I came into the saloon. "I give up," I said, heading upstairs to check that the money bag was secure for the night.

Chapter Twenty-Six

I was taking off my hat, looking forward to a couple of hours of sleep, when a knock sounded at the back door. Sure that our visitor was none of my concern, I pulled a pin out of my hair. The walls of our house were so thin, Mrs. Mann's greeting and the sound of Richard Sterling's deep voice might have been coming from the room beside mine. Stuffing strands of loose hair into the few remaining pins, I went to see what on earth could be the problem now.

Richard filled the doorway, twisting the broad-brimmed hat in his hands, scraping mud off his high black boots. Angus and Mr. Mann held spoons full of steaming oatmeal halfway to their open mouths.

"What brings you here so early, Constable?" I asked.

"Good morning, ma'am. I wonder if I might borrow Angus for the morning. On a police matter."

"Sure," Angus shouted.

"Ahem," I said. "I believe you have responsibilities, young man."

"Go," Mr. Mann said. "You have duty to help police. We all have such duty."

Without even asking if he'd had breakfast, Mrs. Mann ordered Richard to sit and placed a bowl overflowing with hot oatmeal on the table. After pouring her visitor a cup of coffee, she took out a loaf of yesterday's bread and began making sandwiches.

The constable pulled up a chair, picked up a spoon and dug in with enthusiasm.

"Now that that's decided," I said, somewhat miffed at

the overriding of my parental authority, "perhaps you can tell me what this is about." I sat down. Without asking, Mrs. Mann handed me a cup of coffee.

"I'm going to Moosehide," Richard said around a mouthful of hot liquid. "This is wonderful coffee, Mrs. Mann. The porridge is good too. Any more of that toast?"

"Moosehide?" I encouraged him.

"To the Han village. Inspector McKnight wants me to talk to the Indian who was beaten up by Jannis the other day. Angus was there, and it seemed to me that the fellow might be more responsive to the boy than to a man in uniform."

"Angus was there!" I said in horror. "When a man was being beaten?" I glared at Richard.

He swallowed an overlarge mouthful of hot coffee and, trying not to spit it out, suffered as it went down his throat. I didn't have any pity for him.

"I wasn't involved, Ma...Mother. I hardly even saw what was going on. It was all over the minute Constable Sterling got there. Isn't that right, sir?"

"Uh, right."

Richard and Angus gave me identical, innocent smiles.

I huffed, not believing a word. "Will you be back by nightfall? Or, in the absence of nightfall, what passes for a reasonable hour? Angus cannot ask Mr. Mann to give him another day off work."

"Is okay for police business," Mr. Mann said.

"Is not okay for Angus's mother," I said.

"More oatmeal, Constable?" Mrs. Mann said.

"Yes, please," Richard said.

A dog barked outside.

Oatmeal pot scraped clean, coffee pot drained, they set off. Mrs. Mann pressed an enormous packet of sandwiches and slices of cake into Angus's arms.

I followed the Mountie and my son into the backyard. Mrs. Mann had already been out to get the fire started, and clouds of steam were licking around the door of the laundry shed. The brilliant blue sky promised another hot, sunny day. A raven called to us from the washing line strung between the laundry shed and the roof of the house. A big white dog lay in the scrap of weeds beside by a laundry tub. As we came out, the solid body unfolded and stretched languorously. Saddlebags were draped over the dog's back.

"Hey, you brought Millie. Great." Angus threw himself on the ground and began to scratch every available inch of the furry white body.

"Mrs. Miller, how nice to see you." I showed the dog my hand and let her sniff. I don't care for dogs—disgusting, filthy beasts. I made an exception for Mrs. Miller, usually called Millie, because she'd once saved my life.

Richard untied the dog's lead and stuffed their lunch into her saddlebags.

I watched as my son, the Mountie, and the white dog walked up the road into the yellow ball of the rising sun.

*   *   *

The Han village of Moosehide was situated on an island in the Yukon River, not much more than a mile downstream from Dawson. The natives had lived at the mouth of the Klondike River for generations out of mind, but as soon as the authorities realized the rush was on its way, they'd moved the Indians. Some of the men found seasonal employment working the mines and the steamships, but to a large extent the Han attempted to keep to the old ways, which in early summer meant preparing for the salmon migration. Under the stern guidance of the Anglican Bishop Bompas, the Han had almost no contact with whites, and few whites had any interest in disturbing them or their village.

Perhaps remembering a young Richard Sterling and all he had learned from the Cree friends of his childhood, Sterling had decided to bring Angus MacGillivray on the trip. The journey wasn't long enough to require a pack dog, but as Sterling was passing the kennels, Millie had cocked her head to one side and looked at him as though she were asking to go on the outing.

A glow of anger, dull now, but like the last ember of a forest fire, needing only a breath of wind to roar back to life, curled deep in his belly at having to go to the village to find the man Jannis had attacked. The presence of the boy and the dog would go some way towards making the trip seem more like a pleasure outing than police business.

They paddled across the river in a few minutes, Millie eagerly leaning over the side as though she were anxious to go swimming, or perhaps catch some fish. Definitely not a good idea with saddlebags on her back. Sterling told Angus to keep a firm hand on her collar.

Millie leapt joyously out of the canoe almost as soon as it touched ground. Sterling and Angus dragged the canoe up onto the shore, and the dog rushed from one wonderful new scent to another. Sterling let her enjoy herself briefly before calling her back and picking up the lead. When he looked up, a gaggle of wide-eyed, black-haired children were watching him.

"Hello," he said.

The children disappeared into the bush so quickly and silently, they might not have been there at all.

A path led from the waterline through a patch of scraggly bush that soon opened to reveal the settlement.

Moosehide Village consisted of rows of tiny cabins constructed of rough-hewn wood, packed so closely together that they put Sterling in mind of the cribs of Paradise Alley. Most of the cabins had a single window set beside the door and a compact front porch with a chair in pride of place, where the matriarch of the family watched the visitors through unfriendly eyes cloudy with age. All vegetation surrounding the village had been demolished to build the cabins. A patch of rough dirt comprised the village square.

One by one, the inhabitants of the village stopped what they were doing or stepped out of their homes to stare silently at Sterling, Angus and Millie as they entered the square. There was a large number of women and children, but few men. The women were short and small, dressed in headscarves, skirts and blouses. One woman wore a plum blouse with a frilly bib and leg-o-mutton sleeves that wouldn't have been out of place in the Savoy. The men were dressed mostly in work clothes, the children in a combination of traditional and cast-off European garments encrusted with dirt. No one smiled, and dark eyes were curtained against the outsiders. The skinny village dogs barked in warning but kept their distance.

Sterling stopped in the centre of the square, smiled brightly and held up one hand. "Hello," he said, to no one in particular. Millie wagged her generous tail. No one moved. Sterling surveyed the onlookers, searching for someone who might be the headman. A tiny, wizened woman, who looked as if she might be older than God, was sitting in a rocking chair on her front porch, puffing on a large pipe, watching everything through eyes that could no longer be surprised.

He was about to approach the old woman and offer his greetings and those of Her Majesty when the crowd of onlookers parted. An elderly white man with a full head of pure white hair and a grey beard, which flared out on either side of his chin, and wearing the long robes of the Church, came hurrying down the hill to greet them.

"Can I help you, Constable?" This had to be Bishop Bompas, long time resident of the Yukon, legendary man of God, translator of Native languages and caretaker of the Native tribes. He didn't look at all pleased at the sight of strangers in the village.

Made bold by the bishop's arrival, children gathered close, sneaking shy glances or hiding behind his skirts. Millie's tail wagged with enthusiasm. She was not a police dog—just a pack animal—and she loved people. She strained at her lead to get her nose closer to one particularly brave little girl who'd edged out from the safety of the group.

"Sorry to bother you, Bishop. I'm Constable Richard Sterling, and this is Angus MacGillivray. I'm looking for a fellow name of Charlie Redstone." Which, of course, was not the real name of the Indian they wanted to talk to, but what he used among the whites and therefore the name he'd given to the police.

"What do you want with Charlie?" the bishop asked. It was not a friendly question.

"It's a police matter, sir."

The girl edged closer. Millie wagged her tail harder.

"Charlie isn't here."

"Do you know where he is?"

Angus pulled something out of his pocket and held it out to the girl. It was a piece of candy, covered with pocket lint, but perfectly good. Several other children edged closer, anxious to see what was being offered.

"No," the bishop said.

"I know he was here on Monday. When did he leave?"

"If you could tell me what this is about, Constable? I'm a busy man, and I'm sure you understand that these people are my responsibility."

A shriek and a tiny whirlwind of brown cloth and streaming black braids flew past Sterling and the bishop. A woman grabbed the adventurous girl and dragged her away. Angry words came tumbling out in what could only be a scolding. The other children dropped back. Angus looked at the candy in his palm and tucked it away with a shrug.

"I'm not here to do your people any harm, sir," Sterling said, "but I have some questions for Charlie Redstone. Is there some place we can talk? Away from the crowd."

"If we must. Come with me." The bishop turned to the crowd and said a few words. Most of the onlookers stepped back a pace or two, but they all continued to stare at the visitors.

The bishop led the way through the village to a small cabin no different from the rest. Angus couldn't see anything to tie Millie's lead to, so he placed a rock on top of it. He was worried about what the friendly dog would get up to in the company of children who would soon be dredging up the courage to edge closer, but he didn't want to miss anything happening inside.

The interior of the cabin was close, dark and spare. The bishop sat on a plain wooden stool but did not offer his visitors a seat. "Reverend Bowen brought Charlie here on Monday. Someone in town had provided him with liquor, and Charlie drank himself senseless. Some toughs were roughing him up when the Mounties intervened. That's what Bowen told me."

"That's correct, sir."

"These people are like children, you understand, Constable, young man. They can't be trusted on their own in the white man's world."

"Seems to me, sir," Angus spoke for the first time since they'd arrived in Moosehide, "that it was the men who sold him the liquor who're the ones that can't be trusted."

The bishop glared at the boy. "Some men are always out to make money, any way they can. That's why it's up to men of the Church to keep these childlike Indians away from temptation."

"Begging your pardon, sir, but…"

"Back to Charlie Redstone," Sterling said with a look that silenced Angus. "What happened after the reverend dropped him off?"

"He slept for a day, then left the village. Gone fishing. The salmon will be arriving soon; they're busy getting ready."

"Where is this fishing place?"

Bompas's shoulders shrugged under his robe. "I don't know, Constable."

"Could you ask one of the men to take me there?"

"Certainly not!"

High pitched voices were coming closer to the cabin. A child giggled and was quickly hushed. Millie woofed softly.

"I must insist you tell me what concern Charlie is of yours," Bompas said, "before this discussion goes any further."

"The man who attacked Charlie Redstone in Dawson was murdered yesterday. I'd simply like to know where Charlie was at the time."

The bishop laughed without mirth. "Really, Constable, you don't seriously think Charlie returned to town to take revenge on his attacker?"

Sterling thought nothing of the sort. The idea was ridiculous, and this whole trip a waste of time, but he would never complain, to a civilian, that he'd been sent on a wild goose chase. "We have to consider every possibility, sir."

Angus watched the exchange with interest, his blue eyes darting from one man to the other, and Sterling regretted bringing the boy. He didn't feel that he was representing the North-West Mounted Police at their best.

"Charlie left Moosehide in the company of his mother and two ancient women he calls his aunts. What their actual relationship is, I don't know, but I do know that the ladies are a good deal older than even I am. The women have not returned, and I can assure you that no man of the Han would abandon his mother and elderly relatives in the wilderness, no matter how dire the reason. When Charlie returns to Moosehide, I'll inform the authorities. Until then, you'll have to take my word that he has gone to fish camp, and not into town." The bishop stood up, smoothing down his robe, the interview clearly at an end.

Sterling could have insisted that someone take him in pursuit of Charlie. If Charlie was with his mother and his aunts, then Sterling would feel a right fool chasing through the woods after them. Assuming someone could even be found to lead him to them, rather than on a circular journey going nowhere.

"All right, sir. I'll accept your word as a man of the Church that Charlie Redstone has gone to fish camp with other members of the village and that you vouch that he would not return to Dawson while charged with the care of his mother and aunts. Is that correct?"

Bompas nodded. "If your superiors have any concerns about this, they may speak to me directly."

They very well might, Sterling thought.

"One more thing. Have you ever encountered, or heard of, an Indian woman going by the name of Mary? She's not from around here. From Alaska, I've heard." Sterling described Mary quickly.

The bishop shook his head. "Not as far as I know, although your description could fit a lot of women. Why are you asking?"

"She was brought in from Alaska, against her will, and was working as a prostitute in town. She's been caught up in a police matter, and I thought you might have some background on her."

The bishop's face turned dark with anger. "The exploitation of these poor people is a disgrace. If this woman needs a place of refuge, bring her here."

"Thank you," Sterling said.

The crowd of children gathered around Millie scattered as Sterling and Angus came out of the cabin. The girl who'd earlier been snatched up by her mother was back. She grinned at Angus boldly and held out her hand.

"If you only have one piece of candy, Angus, don't give it to her," Sterling said, picking up Mrs. Miller's lead. "It'll only cause a fight once we've left."

The girl continued to hold out her hand, smiling timidly around a black smudge of dirt running across her nose from cheek to cheek like badly-applied stage makeup.

"Hey," he said, "didn't Mrs. Mann pack us some cake? Can I give them the cake?"

"Don't see any harm in that."

Angus pulled the lunch packet out of Millie's saddlebags and waded into the crowd of children, breaking off pieces of Mrs. Mann's fruit cake and handing them out. The children shouted in delight, and Angus's smile lit up his face.

Sterling and Bishop Bompas watched, each wrapped in thought. Once the cake had been evenly distributed, Sterling walked towards the river with Angus and Millie. A crowd of happy children followed.

The bishop did not come down to the river to see them off.

Chapter Twenty-Seven

On Saturday afternoon, while Angus was on so-called police business and I was at the Savoy, Euila called at the Manns' to leave a note inviting Angus and me to tea at the Richmond the following day.

Dawson closes up as tightly as Joey LeBlanc's purse strings on Sundays. Two minutes before midnight on Saturday, girls step down from the stage, roulette wheels stop turning, bartenders fasten the cap on the last bottle of whisky, and the doors of every business in town slam shut. The men hate it, of course, and grumble heartily. Newcomers—Americans in particular—are simply incredulous when shown the door Saturday at midnight, but the Mounties ruthlessly enforce Sunday closing, and the penalties for doing business can be severe.

For me, Sunday is one less day to make money. One seventh of the week wasted, but I'll admit I love the luxury of an entire day free of obligations to my business, my staff, and my partner. I have been known to bring the ledger home on Saturday night and work on it the following afternoon, checking over the week's accounts. Conscious of the Sunday laws, I do the books in the privacy of my room and slip the ledger under a blanket kept close for that very purpose if anyone should knock on my door.

That particular Sunday, I'd planned on not doing a stitch of work. I would wash my hair, dry it in the sun, read my novel, go for a walk through town by myself, or perhaps even venture a little way outside of town with Angus.

Anything but tea with Euila and Martha.

Promptly on Sunday morning, I sent Angus around with a note accepting the invitation.

The Richmond had replaced the armchair in the lobby with a cracked wooden one that didn't have even a cushion to protect the sitter from the hard wood. One might be poked in the posterior by a splinter, but almost anyone would prefer that to having to brush the residue of dried blood off their clothes.

Tea was served in their suite. Mouse O'Brien overflowed a delicate armchair, and as I entered the room, he leapt up so hastily, I feared for the chair.

"Isn't this pleasant?" I said, taking a seat at the circular table in the middle of the room.

The table had been cleared, awaiting the arrival of the tea tray. Martha's notebook and a stack of scribbled-upon papers were piled onto a side table beside my chair.

The afternoon was a good deal more agreeable than I'd expected. Mouse had dressed with as much care as if he were going to tea at Buckingham Palace. The patterned cravat at his throat was folded perfectly, his moustache combed until it lay flat, and his hair oiled so it almost glowed. I myself don't care for oil in a man's hair, but some women appear to (or some men think they do). Martha flitted about the room in a dress much too warm for the day—probably the best one she had—pouring tea, passing sandwiches (fish paste again!) and making cheerful chatter.

Either Martha or Euila had been wise enough to know that a twelve-year-old boy and a man only a few inches short of seven feet would consider the contents of a ladies' afternoon tea the equivalent of a scattering of crumbs, so they'd ordered plenty of sandwiches and cake. Mouse drank sickeningly sweet tea by the gallon, devoured the food, and entertained us at length—to Angus's delight as much as Martha's—about his complicated journey from New York to Seattle, where he'd happened to be when news of the strike hit, and so on to Dawson over the Chilkoot. He also regaled us with stories of his exploits on the Creeks. He was an excellent raconteur, and as he talked, Martha's eyes lit with as much intensity as a chandelier in the entrance hall of a Belgravia townhouse the night of a politician's dinner party. Mouse looked extraordinarily pleased with himself, as well as quite handsome with a touch of red in his cheeks and a sparkle in his own eyes.

Euila, on the other hand, scowled into her tea cup and added nothing to the conversation. If Martha Witherspoon and Mouse O'Brien came to an understanding, Euila would—literally—be left out in the cold.

As time to politely take our leave approached, Mouse and Angus got into a discussion about some boxing match that was scheduled to take place in a few days. Martha appeared to find the subject as fascinating as everything else Mouse said, and Euila excused herself. My eyes wandered around the room, eventually falling on the piles of paper on the table beside my chair. I picked up one of Martha's notebooks. No one protested at such boldness, so I flipped randomly through the pages. It was a rather dry list of people met and incidents witnessed. She couldn't even make the finding of Tom Jannis's dead body sound interesting. Martha didn't appear to be familiar with many adjectives other than "big" or "small". The papers lying underneath the notebook were covered in Euila's neat schoolgirl handwriting. I picked up a sheet to read, and the streets of Dawson came alive. The dirt, the smells, the sawdust covering everything, the noise made by thousands of bored men wandering the streets, the false laughter of women, ladies dragging their skirts through the mud, the desperation in the eyes of many. It was all there, albeit in rough notes and incomplete sentences.

"Isn't that right, Mother?" Angus said.

I replaced the sheet of paper. "Of course," I said, with no idea at all as to what I was agreeing with. No matter—a lady must never be suspected of not paying attention to gentlemen's conversation, however boring that might be. "This has all been perfectly lovely." I gathered my gloves. "It's time for us to be leaving, Angus." I got to my feet, and Angus and Mouse followed. Euila returned to the sitting room, and she and Martha bade us goodbye. Mouse may have lingered over Martha's hand a few moments longer than was proper, and Euila appeared to notice. The unattractive scowl settled back over her face.

"Nice tea, eh, Angus," Mouse said heartily as we descended the stairs to the lobby. He slapped Angus on the back so hard, my son took the last two steps in a running stumble. "It would be my pleasure to walk you home, Mrs. MacGillivray," Mouse said as Angus performed a wild dance in an attempt to keep himself on his feet.

"Thank you, Mouse. That would be most enjoyable."

We walked through the quiet streets. A few citizens were out getting the air, along with men who had nowhere else to be. As they did every Sunday, many of the big-money gamblers had taken the most popular dancers and a steamboat upriver to Alaska for the day, where they would be free from the stern Sunday observance of the Mounties.

Angus saw a boy he knew and asked if he could be excused. With a rushed "goodbye, sir" to Mouse, he was off.

"You have a nice boy, Mrs. MacGillivray," Mouse said.

"That I do."

"I'd like a son someday."

I hid a smile, thinking that I was fairly certain I knew what had brought that on.

"Miss Witherspoon is a fine lady."

"I agree, Mouse."

"She ever said anything to you, Mrs. MacGillivray, about uh…well about…getting married?"

"As it is for any woman," I lied, "it is her fondest dream."

Chapter Twenty-Eight

On Monday morning, a heavy knock sounded at the front door shortly after I had returned from the privy. I was the only one in the house. Angus and Mr. Mann had left for the store some time earlier, and Mrs. Mann was in the laundry shed.

"Who is it?" I said through the door.

"Graham. I'm afraid I have some bad news, Fiona."

Although I was only in my dressing gown, and my unbound hair streamed down my back, I threw open the door, terrifying images of what Graham's bad news could be rushing through my head. An accident? Another killing? Angus?

Graham froze in the doorway, his mouth half open. His eyes lingered over my red silk dressing gown. In near panic, I hadn't bothered to tie my gown properly, and my plain white cotton nightgown (with the merest touch of Belgian lace dressing up the scooped neckline) peeked out.

"What's happened?" I had no desire to stand on my doorstep and be admired in my deshabille. "Has something happened to Angus?"

"Angus? Why would…? Oh, gosh Fiona, no. Nothing like that. Can I come in?"

"If you are asking why I don't shoot you on the spot, Graham Donohue, the answer is, I truly don't know." I stepped aside. "There should be coffee in the kitchen."

He followed me to the back. I was well aware that the expensive red silk emphasized the sway of my hips and that the gold dragon shooting across my back under a curtain of black hair provided a most dramatic effect. I'd punish Graham for scaring me so then send him on his way.

"What do you want?" I said, turning after checking the coffee pot.

Graham gulped and tore his eyes away from the Belgian lace. "Fiona," he said, "you must be aware that I have always adored…"

The back door flew open. "Hi, Ma. Oh, hi, Mr. Donohue."

"Angus," Graham croaked.

I hid a smile. "Shouldn't you be at work, dear?"

"Mr. Mann forgot his lunch, so he sent me to fetch it." The big parcel was sitting in the middle of the kitchen table. "What brings you here so early, Mr. Donohue?" Angus looked at Graham suspiciously.

"Mr. Donohue has news of importance to tell me," I said. "It can wait while I straighten my appearance. Please, pour Mr. Donohue and me a cup of coffee, dear, and I'll be back momentarily."

I tied my hair into a loose knot, splashed a couple of handfuls of water onto my face and slipped into a housedress.

I was back in the kitchen in less than five minutes. Graham and Angus were glaring at each other.

"Now," I said, taking a seat and pouring tinned milk into my coffee, "what is so urgent?"

"Don't you have to be back at work, Angus?" Graham asked.

"Not immediately."

"I've received bad news from my publisher, Fiona. It seems that he isn't interested in my series of articles on the more unfortunate women of the Yukon."

"Why ever not?"

Graham shrugged and swirled his coffee around in the mug. "He doesn't think our readers would be interested."

"Nonsense. I'll write to this publisher and inform him that this is a story the readership of your paper will be most eager to hear. I'll prepare the letter this morning. How did he hear about it so quickly, anyway? We only discussed the idea yesterday."

"I…uh…that is…I told him about it some time ago. I just got the reply this morning and came right over. Someone brought the letter in on the steamboat."

Graham peered into his mug. He seemed to be concerned about his coffee. It was quite dreadful, but no worse than any other served in the North. "You needn't bother writing to him, Fiona. He's notorious for not caring about the opinions of women."

"He will have mine, nonetheless."

"Oh, Mother." Angus got up from his chair and grabbed Mr. Mann's massive lunch parcel. "Don't waste your time. There isn't going to be such a story."

"Not if we don't inform this publisher about its importance."

"Even then," Angus said. "Mr. Donohue, will you be so kind as to allow my mother to get on with her day?" He rather pointedly held the back door open.

Graham stood. "I'm sorry to disappoint you, Fiona."

"These things happen," I said. "Angus, I intend to speak to Inspector McKnight and Constable Sterling this afternoon. I'm going to send a message asking them to meet me at the Savoy at four. You might want to come along."

"What do you want with Sterling?" Graham said.

"Is it something about Mary?" Angus's eyes lit up. "Have you learned something?"

"I believe I might have, dear. You get off to work, and I promise you can hear about it when the Mounties do."

"Can I bring Miss Witherspoon? She's real interested in the case."

"Most interested," I corrected. "Yes, she can come." Once she got word of a meeting, I doubted I could keep the dratted woman away.

"What's all this about, Fiona?" Graham said, neatly slipping back into newspaperman mode.

"Good day, Graham," I said.

Angus slammed the door shut behind them.

I sat at what passed for my dressing table in front of what passed for a mirror and brushed out my hair, thinking about the cancellation of Graham's story. I was disappointed not to get the chance to mess with Joey LeBlanc. Oh, and to help the unfortunate women of the Yukon. Should I wear the blue teardrop earrings? They didn't match the dress I was planning to wear, but they did bring out the highlights in my hair.

*   *   *

Angus spent the morning in a fever of excitement. He hated working at the store, but he kept reminding himself that before much longer he'd be earning his living as a writer. A real writer like Miss Witherspoon, a writer of books, not a newspaper hack like Graham Donohue. Who, unbelievably, had managed to convince Angus's mother that he was going to expose the sordid situation of women forced into prostitution in return for their passage to the Yukon. Angus snorted, startling a lady who was examining a collection of cracked and mismatched dishes. "Is there something wrong with these?" she demanded.

"No, ma'am. Sorry, I was thinking of something else." The lady bought the plates, but watched Angus out of the corner of her eye as he took the money and wrapped her purchases in used brown paper and the end of a scrap of string.

His mother was the smartest person he knew. Why she believed a word Graham Donohue said, Angus simply didn't understand. Perhaps his friends were right when they said women weren't as intelligent as men. They needed a man to look after them all the time: left on their own, they were likely to do something stupid.

At long last, the morning's work ended, and Angus dashed home for his lunch. Then he was off to the Richmond to collect Miss Witherspoon. They spent a couple of hours interviewing anyone she could find who might know something about the two murders. Angus could tell mighty fast who truly knew something and who was prepared to string Miss Witherspoon a story to get a free coffee, pass the time of day, and perhaps later enjoy a laugh with his friends at the woman's expense. Miss Witherspoon wrote everything they said in her notebook, and again Angus wondered about the intelligence of women.

He'd come to realize that the only way he'd be able to

free Mary would be if he could find the killer of Chloe and Tom Jannis himself. The observations and opinions of everyone they'd spoken to were so vague, and so contradictory, he despaired that he would ever be able to help her.

"That was completely useless," he said, kicking at an empty blue tobacco can as they walked to the Savoy for his mother's four o'clock appointment.

"Not at all," Miss Witherspoon said, sounding quite cheerful. "I got some truly valuable insight into the minds of these men who have come so far in search of gold."

"Gold! I'm not interested in gold. I thought we were trying to find the killer so they'd let Mary go."

"Well, yes. That too," Miss Witherspoon said hastily. "That would make a marvellous ending to my book—the dramatic freeing of the innocent woman. But a hanging is equally dramatic, don't you think, dear?"

"A hanging!" Angus stopped in the middle of the street. "What are you talking about?"

"If Mary's found guilty of the killing of Chloe, she will hang. Surely you knew that, Angus?"

"But she didn't do it."

"That's for the law to decide. And for us, as writers, to record."

A cart driver yelled at them to get out of the way. Miss Witherspoon didn't move fast enough, and the hooves of the horses kicked mud all up the front of her dress. She shrieked and bolted for the boardwalk, where she tried to wipe the muck away. Angus didn't think it mattered much against the spotted-brown fabric of her dress. He didn't bother to tell her that drops of mud decorated her chin and cheek.

When they arrived at the Savoy, Murray told them that Mrs. MacGillivray was waiting in her office. Fiona sat behind her desk, drumming her long fingers against the big blue book that served as her accounts ledger.

Angus bent to kiss her on the cheek. She smelled of soap, fresh-laundered clothes and traces of smoke from the customer's cigars. It made a pleasant change from the stench of the streets and some of the men they had been interviewing. "Can you tell us what this is about, Mother?"

Miss Witherspoon sank into the couch and continued sinking, looking rather surprised at how badly sprung it was.

Heavy boots sounded on the rickety stairs, and McKnight and Sterling walked through the open door.

"This had better be important, Mrs. MacGillivray," McKnight said, not bothering to say hello.

"I would have thought any pertinent information a prominent member of the citizenry might wish to bring to the attention of the constabulary would be important." A mischievous light danced behind Angus's mother's eyes. She used big words when she wanted to be difficult.

McKnight struggled to regain his composure. "Quite correct, madam." Sterling looked at the ceiling. Miss Witherspoon scribbled.

Angus's mother let the silence linger for a few seconds. Then she said, "I heard something Saturday night that I thought you'd be interested in. It seems, according to dressing room gossip, for whatever that's worth, that Chloe had come to an understanding with Tom Jannis."

McKnight's head snapped up. Sterling stopped his examination of the ceiling. "Indeed?" Miss Witherspoon whispered, looking up from her notebook.

"What sort of an understanding?" McKnight asked. He leaned forward, as if he were about to grasp the answer.

"The girls are saying he had arranged to be her protector."

"Protector from what?" Miss Witherspoon asked.

They all ignored her.

There were lots of lonely men in the Yukon, some with a good deal of instantly-earned money, all of them looking for female companionship. Particularly when they thought ahead to the long, dark winter nights, when even the heaviest bag of gold or title to the best claim on the Creeks didn't bring a man much comfort. It was the dream of many women in the dance halls to be taken under the wing of a man with money enough to provide for them. The word "marriage" was rarely mentioned. What they hoped for was a handsome something to remember him by when winter ended and life, and everyone involved, moved on.

"Your girls know this how?" McKnight asked.

"Supposedly from Chloe herself. I can't say whether or not the wretch...uh...poor thing simply imagined his interest. Because it was Tom Jannis paying her attention, I thought you'd be interested."

McKnight said nothing. Sterling spoke up. "We certainly are, Mrs. MacGillivray. Thank you."

"Who told you this?" McKnight asked.

Fiona gave him Besty's full name. "I don't know where she lives, but if you want to talk to her, she starts work at eight."

"You learned this on Saturday, Mrs. MacGillivray? Why didn't you bring this matter to our attention earlier?"

Fiona's eyelashes fluttered. "Dear me, should I have contacted you on a Sunday? I was unsure if the police offices were open."

McKnight barely suppressed a growl.

Fiona stood up. "In light of this news, Inspector, we can conclude that there's a definite connection between the murders of Chloe Jones and Tom Jannis. And as Mary has what I understand the penny-dreadfuls call a cast-iron alibi for Jannis's murder, being under lock and key in your jail at the time, she's clearly not responsible for Chloe's murder either."

"We can conclude that, can we?" McKnight said.

Fiona smoothed down the front of her dress. Her eyes took on the colour of coal. "Well, some of us can think things through in order to arrive at that conclusion."

"Mrs. MacGillivray," McKnight said, a vein throbbing in the side of his neck, "I'm conducting this investigation. Although it was nothing less than your duty to do so, I thank you for informing us. We'll be back at eight to speak to the girl Betsy."

"You can't continue to hold Mary in light of this evidence," Fiona said.

"Good day, madam." McKnight stalked out.

For a moment Angus thought his mother was going to run after the inspector. Instead she looked around for something to throw.

"Don't try him, Mrs. MacGillivray," Sterling said. "McKnight came out of the boss's office this morning looking considerably worse than when he went in."

Fiona pulled her eyes away from the door. "I'm sorry. His officiousness does get somewhat overbearing at times, and that gets my Scottish back up. Will you forgive me, Richard?" A strange light shone in the back of his mother's eyes that Angus hadn't seen before.

"Of course," the big Mountie almost purred.

"He can be pigheaded, your inspector."

"I can't comment on that, Fiona."

Angus wondered if he and Miss Witherspoon had dropped off the edge of the earth without his being aware of it.

A bellow from the hallway brought Sterling back to his senses. "I have to be going," he said, clearly not wanting to. "Take care, Fiona, Angus. There's still a killer out there."

Chapter Twenty-Nine

So many people passed through Dawson in a day, it was likely that before the week had passed, a good portion of the population wasn't even aware of the murders, and talk of the killings died down.

McKnight and Sterling interviewed Betsy, and she confirmed what I'd told them, but it didn't seem to matter much. My son and Miss Witherspoon continued to scour the town for clues, but it was obvious—to me at any rate—Angus was the only one still attempting to prove Mary's innocence. I heard talk that the police were making preparations for a trial. If she were found guilty, Mary would hang. There were people looking forward to the event. I'd had Ray toss two men out by their ears for taking bets as to how long she'd twitch before falling still. I silenced Martha Witherspoon with a glare when she asked—in my son's hearing!—about the procedures involved in conducting a murder trial in a frontier town.

Angus continued to visit Mary every day. He'd managed somehow to talk Mrs. Mann into doing Mary's laundry and fixing an extra portion of dinner. Martha stopped going with him. Instead Euila accompanied Angus most evenings as he brought clean clothes and supper, carefully wrapped in a towel to keep it warm. I couldn't bear to think of what it would do to my huge-hearted son if Mary were to be found guilty and hanged. He'd told me Mary's explanation for how she came to be running from Tom Jannis on the night of Chloe's killing. I wouldn't necessarily have believed her, except that at the moment of being arrested and charged with murder, she'd gone to the trouble of asking Angus to send me her apologies. That in itself convinced me that she was telling the truth and that she hadn't been selling herself in the alley behind the Savoy.

As for the killing of Tom Jannis—that investigation also appeared to be going nowhere. No one they spoke to, Richard Sterling confided in me, could think of any reason anyone would want to kill him. Largely because no one appeared to care about Tom Jannis one way or the other. The hotel reported that he'd checked in a few days prior to his death, paid his bills, didn't cause any trouble (save for getting himself killed in the front lobby) and never had any visitors. There'd been one unpleasant altercation in the street with an Indian, but no one had seen the Indian in question in town since he'd gone back to his village. Jannis had been seen around town a few times with Chloe, confirming Betsy's story, but even that lead led nowhere.

That appeared to be the end of that.

I sighed with pleasure as the soft red silk caressed my shoulders and slipped over my petticoats to skim the floor. Maggie ordered me to stand on a stool, then she crouched at my feet with a mouthful of pins to set about nipping and tucking. The dress was almost a perfect fit already, an indication of the skill of the dressmaker; only a few adjustments were needed to the hem and the bosom.

I'd expected Irene to join us—if only to keep an eye on me. "Where's Irene?" I asked.

"Don't know," Maggie grumbled around a mouthful of pins. "Stand still or I'll prick you."

It sounded more like a threat than a warning. I stopped talking as her competent hands folded a sliver of fabric that would form a dart across my chest. The dress was dangerously low cut, revealing the swell of my bosom. The cut running down from the base of my throat, which I'd earned not long ago, was still red, but men seemed to find that sort of thing fascinating.

Finally Maggie grunted that I could relax.

Considering my chest was covered in pins, I took a

cautious breath as I stepped off the stool. The fabric whispered seductively as it moved around my legs. I admired myself in the cracked mirror, twisting every which way to get a look at it all. Even without jewellery, hat and properly dressed hair, I looked wonderful.

"It's beautiful," I said.

The slightest touch of a smile turned up the edges of Maggie's mouth. "It'll be ready tomorrow." The smile faded. "She was out late last night." She spat out a pin. "Went on the riverboat with some of her friends."

"You didn't go?" I asked, quite innocently, not paying attention to Maggie's grumbles as I was busy admiring myself from all angles. The dress curved into the small of my back like a second skin, flaring out inches before it reached my backside.

"You think I'm the sort that's gonna be invited to drink fancy champagne and party on that boat?"

Assuming it was a rhetorical question, I kept my mouth shut. If Maggie were to be invited along, it would be to do the cooking and cleaning.

"White next," she said, gesturing to the room behind the curtain.

"Have the police been around to question Irene again?" I asked once I'd put on the dotted white muslin afternoon two-piece and was again standing on the stool to be poked and pinned. White was the most dreadfully impractical colour in Dawson. If it rained, the streets were rivers of mud; if it didn't rain, dust and sawdust coated everything. But the white muslin was so pretty, I couldn't resist, particularly once Maggie suggested decorating the sleeves with rows of fine tucks.

"Why do you ask?"

"Just wondering. They were interested in her possible involvement earlier."

"Well, stop wondering. Irene had nothing to do with the business of that jealous bitch getting herself killed. You can get down now. The blue isn't ready for fitting yet. Come back on Wednesday."

If Irene and Maggie had been a man and a woman, I would have noticed the vast gulf between their personalities and how they lived their lives. But as they were two women, a condition of which I had no understanding, I didn't stop to consider that there was serious trouble in the relationship.

An oversight I would come to regret.

*   *   *

The following day, on my way to the shop to collect my new dress, I stopped at the Richmond. Martha was out with Angus, as usual, but Euila was in their room. She spent most of her day in their room, transcribing Martha's notes.

"I'm going shopping, Euila. Why don't you come with me? It's a pleasant day."

Euila glanced over her shoulder towards the round table in the centre of the room, covered in a mountain of paper. I pushed past her. "Goodness," I said, picking up one of Martha's notebooks. "What a lot of writing."

She took the book out of my hand. "Martha doesn't like anyone to see her rough work."

"I'm not surprised, considering what dreck it is."

Her eyes widened.

"Euila." I took the book back. "Why are you doing this? From what I can see, Martha's work isn't fit to line a cat box. You're not transcribing her notes; you're taking them and turning them into wonderful prose. You should be writing under your own name."

She sunk into a chair. "That's all right for you to say." Tears welled up in her pale blue eyes. "I'm not fearless like you, Fiona. I can't go out among men in the streets, asking them to tell me their stories." Euila blew her noise into a delicate lace-trimmed handkerchief.

"No," I said. "Perhaps not. But you can find yourself a partner who complements what talent you have rather than pretending it's hers alone." I grabbed a sheet of foolscap, packed with Euila's neat hand that was so much like my own. "This is good work. Very good. You deserve to get some recognition from it." I waved the paper in front of her face.

The tight bun piled on top of Euila's head wobbled in sad disagreement. She twisted her hands in her lap and seemed almost to fade into herself. "I can't be like you, Fiona," she said in a low, sad voice. "Fiona the Brave, Fiona the Adventurous, Fiona the Beautiful."

When we were children, Euila and I, I had been the pretty one, the smart one, the bold one, the child loved by her parents. Plain, dull Euila had been nothing but the earl's daughter, which in the eyes of everyone on the estate had meant she was better than me. Now, here in the North, neither of us with parents or servants to provide a blanket of status?

"I have a business partner," I said, after a long, deep silence, "because I couldn't possibly run the Savoy on my own. Ray Walker knows full well that neither could he. So we each take our half-a-skill and combine them into an amazing partnership."

She looked up. A touch of colour crept into her pale face.

"You could do that, Euila. Find a good investigator who can't write worth a whit, and knows it, and tell him you'll turn his, or her, words into poetry. For half the credit. Heavens, you probably don't even need a partner. If you can't interview the men, don't. You've seen enough in Dawson, make something up out of it. No one need know whether it's true or not."

A spark flashed behind her eyes. "In California and Seattle, they talk about nothing but the Klondike. I'm sure that's true everywhere. There would be a great interest in stories set here."

"Think about it, Euila." I stood up and gathered my gloves. "I'm going shopping. I'd love for you to accompany me; I've found the most incredible dressmaker."

She mumbled something about no money for dresses. I pulled her to her feet. "So watch me try on mine, and write about it later. That is the amazing thing about Dawson.

Next door to a shed selling cast-off mining equipment, you can find a dressmaker who wouldn't be out of place in the back rooms of Worth of Paris.

"I had a Worth gown once," I said as Euila collected her hat. "If I told you who bought it for me, you'd recognize his name. It lasted through absolutely everything, until a drunken fool dragged me into a fight. The poor Worth was simply not made to withstand a bar brawl over a dance hall girl in a saloon in Dawson."

Euila rarely said much, and on the walk to Maggie's, she was even quieter than usual. Thinking over my suggestion, I hoped. It must, I thought not for the first time, be dreadful to live a life that was almost wholly outside of your own control. If Euila failed to find a husband (and love be damned, suitability would be all that mattered), she would spend the rest of her days being passed around between one brother and another. And one resentful sister-in-law and another, no doubt.

Which made me think about Chloe Jones. Another woman desperately searching for someone to be her protector, someone to take care of her.

If the thing with Jannis hadn't panned out, or she'd discovered he didn't have quite the money he pretended he did, had Chloe thought she could get into Joey LeBlanc's good books? I assumed that Chloe and Irene had been more than close friends until Maggie replaced Chloe in Irene's affections. Had Chloe planned to get revenge on her former lover by revealing Irene's secret life to Joey?

Now that I was thinking of Joey LeBlanc...

"Wait here," I said to Euila. "I'll be right back."

I picked up my skirts and stepped off the duckboard. Horses and donkeys were pulled to an abrupt halt.

"You, sir. A moment, if you please."

The man turned to face me. Unlike most men I might accost on the street, he did not looked pleased at the attention. "Yeah?"

"Do you regularly lurk about behind the Savoy?"

"What the hell kind of question is that?" His clothes

stunk to high heaven of cigar smoke, and crumbs of tobacco dotted the front of his jacket. His stubby fingers were stained yellow with nicotine.

"I've seen you before. Thursday before last. You were in the alley behind the Savoy Dance Hall in the early hours of the morning. May I ask what was your business there?"

"No, you can't."

Now that I was talking to him, I wasn't all that sure this was the man I'd seen lurking in the shadows when I'd confronted Tom Jannis and Mary. I plunged on nevertheless, because I had definitely seen him in the company of another person of my acquaintance.

"Was Mrs. LeBlanc paying you that evening, or do you just like to hang around in dark alleys spying on people?"

It was unlikely this man had much experience in the criminal underworld. Instead of walking away with a laugh and a sneer, he remained where he was, while his eyes looked everywhere but at me. "I don't know what you mean."

"Of course you do." I stepped closer. "You know who I am. What's your name?"

"Black. Al Black."

"Mr. Black, you were either asked to keep an eye on your employer's former employee or you wanted to demonstrate some initiative by doing so yourself." As Al Black stood there, his eyes twitching, I decided he had probably never had a burst of initiative in his life. He was the sort of stupid low-life who could be counted on to keep frightened prostitutes in line. Confronted with a person, even a woman, with some backbone, he didn't know how to act. "Did you happen to pick anything up after we had left?"

His eyes continued to track activity on the street, and I realized he was worried in case someone saw him talking to me and reported back to his employer. I'd been wondering how to get him to talk and considered threatening to kick up a fuss by accusing him of attempting to rob me. Instead, I rested my hand on his arm. He looked at it as if it were about to bite him. "You found something in the alley, and you gave it to Mrs. LeBlanc. I'd like to know what it was. If you tell me, I'll walk away. If you don't, why, I'll congratulate you on a job well done, in a nice loud voice, and tell you that any time you have news for me you are welcome at the Savoy. Where, for you only, the drinks are always free."

That got him. His face blanched. He snatched his arm away. A lady glanced at us as she passed, but otherwise we didn't seem to be attracting much attention. I, of course, knew how to change that.

He stepped into the shadows at the entrance to a dentist's office. I followed but ensured that I was placed between him and the street. He wiped his hand across his mouth. "I saw the bitch come out the back." I suspected he intended the noun to also apply to me. "I was gonna talk to her, tell her to come back to Mrs. LeBlanc's, when he came out. He grabbed her, and she started fighting. I figured it was a nice situation. He probably wouldn't pay her, and when it was over, I'd tell her that's what would keep happening if she didn't let Mrs. LeBlanc look after her. But then you showed up, and she ran. She'd dropped something, or the man had torn it off, and I picked it up. It was a necklace, with a cross on the end. I figured I could give it to my girl."

"You didn't give it to your girl, did you?"

"Told Mrs. LeBlanc what happened, and she wanted it."

I let out a deep sigh. It was all as I'd suspected.

I backed into the street. "If I see you following me again, or anywhere near my property, I'll inform the police. Good day."

Euila was standing where I'd left her, looking quite lost in the sea of humanity flowing around her. If I didn't return, would she stand there all day, until someone told her to move? Poor Euila.

I dashed across the street. Several men lifted their hats and stopped in their tracks to permit me to pass. I gathered Euila up, and we continued on our way.

At Maggie's shop, I tried on the red gown and the white muslin dress and pronounced them perfect. Of course I didn't say that out loud; instead I found fault with the spacing of the tucks in the sleeves of the muslin and the depth of the décolletage of the red silk. Quite unlike a London dressmaker, who would have had a fit at being criticized, Maggie merely shrugged, reminded me that I'd accepted the fitting, and quoted me a fee almost as much as the dresses originally cost to fix the problem.

Graciously, I declined her offer. Maggie told me the blue dress would be ready in two days, and I proudly left with a large parcel wrapped in brown paper and tied with string.

I treated Euila to tea at the Richmond, where I ordered the manager to appear and insisted that I not be served fish paste sandwiches.

They served us cucumber and, wondrously, watercress.

That night I was a sensation in scarlet silk.

Chapter Thirty

Sadly, I hadn't found a shoemaker with the same degree of skill as Maggie had in dressmaking, and by the end of the night—also known as early morning—my feet were hurting.

Once I'd paid the dancers for their chits, I came downstairs, threw myself into a chair, kicked off my shoes and groaned.

Ray pulled up a chair and sat across from me. He picked up a stocking-clad foot, peeled my skirt back a few inches, and began to massage.

"Goodness," I said, "that's wonderful. You must want something."

His strong fingers dug into the fleshy bits on the soles of my foot and gently worked at the aches and pains. "Whatever it is you want," I sighed in delight, "you can have it."

Not-Murray carried dirty dishes out from the gambling rooms. We don't run a restaurant, but when a big spender looks to be about to leave in search of refreshment, we can have something brought out from the back in no time. That evening we'd had several big spenders.

The Savoy was perhaps the only dance hall in town that shut its doors when it wasn't a Sunday. When I'd started the business, everyone told me I was a fool to close for a few hours; the customers would leave and never come back, they said. I knew I needed to sleep sometime, and I like to keep an eye on what is happening in my own establishment. I talked Ray into seeing things my way, and rather than staying away, the customers flocked back through our doors promptly at ten a.m. when we opened. The temporarily forbidden fruit being all the sweeter.

"It was a good night," I mumbled, closing my eyes, relaxing against the hard back of my chair and giving into the delightful sensations coming from my feet.

"A very good night," Ray agreed. "That dress is what did it."

"Did what?"

"Brought in the punters. Isn't that right, Jake?"

The croupier laughed. A whisky bottle opened, and liquid sloshed into glasses. Ray allowed each of the male employees one drink—on the house—at closing. Very generous, considering his miserly Scottish roots, but it kept the men loyal. "That it did, Mr. Walker," Jake said. "Why I saw more than one man forget what cards he was holding when Mrs. MacGillivray walked through the room."

"Fellow plopped down a bag of dust to pay for one drink and forgot to wait for me to weigh it up, he was so keen on following Mrs. MacGillivray into the dance hall," Not-Murray said.

Eyes still closed, I waved one hand in the air in acknowledgement of the compliments.

"Did he come back for his dust?" Jake asked.

"Looking in a right state too. Pity—it was a heavy bag."

"Oooh, that looks a treat, Mr. Walker. Can I be next?" Ellie passed through the bar.

"It'd cost ye, Ellie," Ray said.

She laughed. "If only I'd retained my virtue."

"'Night Mr. Walker, Mrs. MacGillivray." A chorus of women's voices trilled as the group of dancers stepped out into the street. I waved languorously, still not bothering to spend all the effort that would be required in opening my eyes.

"Where can we go to now?" one of the percentage girls— a new one—giggled. "I'm much too excited to go home to bed."

"...some breakfast perhaps," Irene said. "I know a nice private place just opened up. The Imperial. It's on King Street."

"I've heard it's ever so expensive."

"My treat," Irene said. "Night, Mr. Walker."

Ray set to work on the other foot.

One by one, the men finished their drinks and followed the women out into the new dawn.

I opened one eye. "You're a good man, Ray," I said for absolutely no reason.

"Don't let word o' that get out," he said. His voice dropped, and he coughed. "I know ye think I'm a fool for her, Fee. But somethings canna be helped." His fingers kneaded my big toe. The other toes wiggled in envy.

"Irene has nothing to offer you, Ray."

"A man can always hope."

"Not always. Take my word for it, will you?" The expression on his ugly face was suddenly full of so much pain, my heart almost closed. I tried to make a joke of it. "After all, anyone wearing a dress this fantastic can't be wrong, now can she?"

Some of the cloud behind his eyes slipped aside, and he slapped the side of my foot before giving it back to me.

I took it reluctantly. "Thank you. I did need that." I patted my skirts back into place around my ankles. "I'm so tired. At a respectable hour, I'm going to go to Inspector McKnight with something I learned earlier. I'm hoping it will be enough to convince him to release Mary. It's been difficult, what with the murders and Angus so worried about her, but I…"

As if summoned by my thoughts, my son, followed by Martha Witherspoon, who seemed to have taken up the role of Angus's shadow, burst through the doors.

"Good heavens," I said. "What are you doing out of bed at this hour, young man?"

Angus opened his mouth to protest, but Martha spoke first. "It's six thirty in the morning, Fiona. A time when respectable people begin their day."

"Meaning that I am not respectable, I presume."

Martha blushed and started to stammer out an apology.

"Never mind. I have never pretended to be respectable." Well, not to people I had no interest in fleecing.

Ray chuckled and went behind the bar in search of his cap.

"What do you want, Angus?" I said.

"Miss Witherspoon has a mind to see the place close up, and...uh..."

"Unfortunately, I overslept," Martha said. "I wasn't ready when Angus arrived, so we have missed the closing. I was most anxious to interview men on their way out of the Savoy in order to get their impressions of the evening."

Ray snorted. "High literature that'll make. Sir Walter himself'll wonder why he didn't think of it." He tossed the bag containing the bar's most recent batch of takings on the table and slapped his cap on his head. "Good night, Angus, Miss Witherspoon. And thank ye, Fee. I might consider your advice."

I pulled shoes back onto reluctant feet and began to lace them. "Your arrival is quite fortunate, Angus. You can check the back rooms to ensure everyone has gone and lock the money in my desk." I pulled the keys out of my pocket, which I'd had Maggie sew into a discreet fold in the waistband of the gown, and tossed them to Angus. "Then, as a special favour, wash up the dishes so Mrs. Saunderson doesn't have to face them when she comes in. Take a damp cloth to the bar and a broom to the floor of the dance hall. Don't forget to draw the curtains and put those lights out."

"Mother!"

"Mrs. MacGillivray, I do not think..."

I tossed Martha a smile. "Wouldn't you agree, Miss Witherspoon, that if Angus wants to be a writer such as yourself, he needs to explore all avenues of life. Even mopping up a dance hall. Good night, dear." I swept out into the morning.

Never give them the opportunity to argue back.

He might be very young, but I was comfortable leaving my property and my money in my son's hands, and if the washing up and the sweeping were substandard, it would still give Helen a thrill when she came to work later that morning.

Feeling quite pleased with myself, I set off for Mrs. Mann's boarding house. My feet still tingled delightfully from the massage, but the too-tight shoes were quickly putting an end to that. I always felt somewhat naughty walking through town in evening wear when the sun was well over the horizon. I exchanged greetings with merchants on the way to open their shops, laundresses heading for work, and men setting out for the Creeks. I walked west down Front Street heading for home and my lovely bed. One or two fools new to town attempted to approach me, but I saw them off with a glance quick enough. And so I missed seeing someone scurrying in from the east—another person who had lost track of the time.

Chapter Thirty-One

As there were no more lines of inquiry to pursue in the Jones/Jannis murders, Richard Sterling had been ordered back to town detachment. Patrolling the saloons and gambling halls of Dawson might not be the way to get his career back on track, but he was beginning to think it was a good deal better than arresting proud, exploited Indian women and trying to delve into the dark heart of a murder.

He hadn't slept properly for days, haunted by the idea that he'd failed Mary and, most of all, Angus. In the afternoon, when he should have been sleeping in preparation for the long night shift, he'd woken in a drenching sweat from a dream he was unable to grasp a wisp of, pulled on his uniform, and stumbled out of the barracks into the daylight.

By early morning, the lack of sleep was catching up with him.

Outside the Monte Carlo, he stopped to exchange a few words with a constable new to the Yukon. The young man was still wandering the streets with his mouth half-open and his eyes wide. Not a particularly impressive appearance for someone representing the law. Sterling smiled to himself: he'd once been that young and naïve. He had never been outside Saskatchewan's Carrot River Valley until the day he left home to join the Mounties. An enormous lunch prepared by his tearful mother had been in his pack, a stern lecture on the evils of the world delivered by his father resounding in his ears. He'd been so naïve, he'd thought Prince Albert was an exciting town.

Inside the Monte Carlo, a woman screamed. Men started shouting, and passersby dashed from all directions towards the dance hall to catch the excitement. Sterling, followed closely by the young constable, shoved men aside, shouting, "Mounties, let us through."

A woman lay on the floor in what remained of a shattered wooden table. Her dress had flown up past her knees to reveal plump legs enclosed in many-times-mended stockings. She flailed about in the almost clean white froth of her petticoats, screaming. Another woman stood over her, fists clenched and face set in hard lines. Her dress was drab and plain, stained badly under the arms. Strands of unnaturally-black hair had escaped from her hat, and the paint on her dark red lips had flowed over the lines, making her look like the clown in a down-at-the-heels wandering circus at the end of hard day. "He's mine, do you hear? Mine!" she yelled.

"That's enough," Sterling said, stepping towards the standing woman. "Back off."

She didn't look at him. "Once she leaves my man alone, then I'll leave her alone."

"Constable, escort this lady to the street," Sterling said to the young policeman behind him.

The rookie stepped forward, "Madam," he said, as politely as if he were asking his grandmother to precede him into the church pew.

Sterling turned to the woman on the floor. He held out one hand to help her up. He could feel as much as see or hear the crowd behind him breaking up as disappointed men realized the excitement was over.

But it wasn't. The woman on the floor ignored the offered hand and with a screech leapt to her feet. She touched one hand to her head, as if she were straightening her hat, and lunged at her attacker.

Sterling grabbed her wrist and twisted. Something fell to the floor with a clatter. "Do you want to come to the Fort with me?" he asked pleasantly.

The woman looked at her hand, trapped in Sterling's

big paw, then she looked into his face, and all the fight went out of her. "No sir. Please sir, I'm sorry."

The constable hustled the other woman outside.

Sterling released the woman. "If I hear of any more fighting, it will be a trip to the Fort. Now get out of here."

"Thank you, sir." She ran, her hat tilting to the side.

Sterling dropped to one knee. The woman had been holding some sort of weapon, he was sure of it. The floor was covered in mud and sawdust, lumps of chewing tobacco and spilled liquor, and the residue of horse dung carried in on men's boots. He pulled a shiny piece of metal out from between one of the floorboards. It was about four inches long and as thin as a cat's whisker. One end was as sharp as a sword point, the other covered with a lump of fake pearl.

A hat pin. Used to secure a lady's hat firmly to her pile of hair.

Sterling got to his feet slowly, turning the pin over and over in his hand while the Monte Carlo returned to its business.

There must be hundreds, thousands, of hat pins in Dawson.

He'd searched town, looking through castoff miners' equipment for the sort of thing that could have been used to make the neat hole in the back of Tom Jannis's neck. But placer mining didn't lead itself to small, delicate instruments, and he'd given up that line of inquiry.

This hat pin, however, was exactly the right size.

The police surgeon had found a fresh puncture wound close, but not close enough, to Chloe Jones's heart. He concluded that a very small sharp knife, badly aimed, had failed to kill her, and the killer had changed tactics and bashed her head in. A similar weapon had succeeded in killing Tom Jannis with one sharp stab.

Richard Sterling would bet a month's pay that a hat pin, just like this one, had been used on both Jones and Jannis.

Not everyone would have ready access to a hat pin. Anyone could purchase one in a hat shop, but few men would be likely to do so. A man might steal one from his wife's dresser, or off the table where a whore kept her shabby collection of property while her back was turned. If it was intended to be used as a murder weapon, it would require a degree of forethought for a man to have one to hand.

Most women, however, would have one every time they were out of the house.

Chloe Jones and Tom Jannis had been killed by a woman.

Which didn't help narrow the suspects down by very much. There were more men, by far, than women in Dawson, but there still had to be hundreds of women.

Sterling put the hat pin into his pocket and continued on his rounds. It was too early to get Inspector McKnight out of bed, but Sterling would be there the moment the inspector sat down to breakfast.

Chapter Thirty-Two

My new red gown had been such a success, I was looking forward to wearing the new white muslin tomorrow. Now, if only a good shoemaker would set up business...

Soft voices could be heard from the back of the house as I came in through the front. Not wanting to engage in polite conversation with the Manns, I slipped into my room and pulled off my shoes. I tossed my reticule on the table, unfastened my hair, and ran my fingers through it, letting the weight of it stream down my back. Feeling in a strange mood, I teasingly undid the two pearl buttons that closed the top of the dress and stood in front of the cracked mirror to admire myself one more time. Maggie truly did have the skill of the angels in her calloused fingers; I imagined a lifetime of wonderful clothes that she would provide for me. Evening gowns, day dresses, afternoon dresses, tea gowns, even nightgowns and robes. Images of crimson silk, champagne satin and pristine, virginal white cotton paraded before my eyes.

My eyes opened, and I stared at myself in the mirror.

I was no longer admiring myself nor thinking of clothes.

Chloe.

Tom Jannis.

Dead, the both of them.

What was the connection?

Irene.

Chloe had told the dancers she knew something, something incriminating, about Irene. Jannis had agreed, according to Betsy—for what that was worth—to set up housekeeping with Chloe. Jannis wasn't well off, although he'd tried to keep up appearances to the contrary. It was not likely that he had enough money to keep Chloe in the style to which she would have liked to become accustomed. So what did they have to offer each other?

In exchange for his security, it was not difficult to imagine that Chloe would tell him how he could make some quick money.

A big spender with limited resources, a dance-hall girl tossed out onto her ear. Of course she would tell him. Nasty slug that he was, Jannis would be anxious to take advantage of some supposedly secret information. Once Chloe was dead, he'd come to me—the person who had the most invested in Irene. I'd spurned his feeble attempts at blackmail, so he'd gone...where?

He might have approached Ray. Ray could surely kill a rival in the heat of the moment—most men (probably most women) were capable of it. But if he could carry on with life as if all was normal after doing the deed, I'd eat my new silk dress.

The only other person with reason to fear Jannis's revelation of her secret was Irene. It would be nice to pin this on Joey LeBlanc, but Joey wouldn't cross the street to protect Irene, my most profitable employee. Joey would be more likely to have banners hung all over town screaming the sordid details in giant black print.

When Graham had interrupted us watching the dancing, had Tom Jannis been about to tell me he believed Irene had killed Chloe because Chloe, spurned by Irene, had threatened to reveal Irene's terrible secret? That she was a woman-lover, which would have made her an object of scorn to every man in Dawson, and pure poison in every dance hall—including the Savoy.

Was that why Jannis had died—because he was blackmailing Irene?

I'd seen Irene leave the Savoy. Or rather, I'd heard her while Ray was doing such wonderful things to my feet. She was in the company of one of the new percentage girls, a pretty, fresh-faced young thing, going out for breakfast. "My treat," Irene had said.

Angus. My son was at the Savoy. I'd left him alone. Under the ridiculous protection of Martha Witherspoon. Angus and Martha had been all over Dawson, talking to everyone, poking their innocent, shiny noses into everything and everyone's business.

Who had killed Chloe?

Who had reason to kill Jannis?

I wasn't wearing shoes or a hat, my hair was unbound. In my haste to fasten my dress, the over-corset caught in the eye of the lower button. I wrenched the button off in frustration, revealing enough of my breasts to have me arrested.

Let them try.

Chapter Thirty-Three

Angus pulled the curtains over the windows at either side of the front door. "I'm sorry, Miss Witherspoon, but I have to help my ma here. If you want to leave, it's okay."

Martha Witherspoon set her shoulders firmly. "Such is the lot of the writer, dear boy. Your mother is perfectly correct. Good heavens, what was that?"

"A mouse, probably. Come out when he thinks everyone's gone. Man's been sick in the back, most likely. That attracts all sorts of vermin. Never mind, Mrs. Saunderson'll take care of it when she comes in. Ma didn't really expect us to clean it up. Are you feeling all right, Miss Witherspoon? You look slightly pale."

Miss Witherspoon mumbled something about being perfectly fine and sank into the chair recently vacated by Angus's mother.

"The sick isn't so bad," Angus continued. "It mops up easily. It's blood that's hard to get out. Soaks into the wooden floor, and there it stays. Ma tells me they have a fight every so often, and some guy's usually on the floor, blood pouring out of his nose, before the bouncers can get to him. Mrs. Saunderson hates that. She'd rather have a puking drunk any day. Sure you're okay, Miss Witherspoon?"

Miss Witherspoon tossed him a sickly smile.

"I'll lock this sack up." Angus lifted the bag heavy with gold dust, jingling with coins, stuffed with bills of American and Canadian denominations and topped up with a good number of hefty gold nuggets.

"Sorry, ma'am, but we're closed right now," he said as a

woman came in through the unlocked front door. She was small and skinny. She wore a plain brown dress, caked with mud at the hem, and an unflattering hat, slightly askew. Her pale eyes darted back and forth too quickly, and the skin under them folded over and over upon itself to form deep crevices. The look in her eyes made Angus think of sadness and of loss.

"Ma'am," he said. "Can I help you?" He'd seen eyes like those before: change the colour from lifeless blue to unemotional brown and they could have been the eyes of the Indian women who'd stood perfectly still as they'd watched Angus and Sterling cross Moosehide village.

The woman shook her head. "Irene," she said. "Where's Irene?"

"Probably gone home," Angus said. "The Savoy's closed, you see."

"You should leave also," Miss Witherspoon said. "Off you go now." She moved her hands in front of her as if she were shooing away a particularly pesky lapdog.

The woman made no attempt to move; she stood still, in the middle of the saloon, her eyes darting around, attempting to peer into all the dark corners.

"Light's still on. Late for you isn't it, Fiona? Mrs. MacGillivray?" Constable Sterling walked into the saloon. "Angus, what brings you here? Where's your mother? I thought I'd better check, as she's usually long gone by now."

The woman screeched at the sight of the red-coated Mountie. She pulled a small-calibre gun out from a pocket in the depths of her dress and held it to Miss Witherspoon's head. All before Sterling could exhale.

Chapter Thirty-Four

It was a lady's gun, a pretty little thing with a stub nose and a shiny walnut handle.

"Put the weapon down, ma'am," Constable Richard Sterling said, trying to sound calm, in control, a man of authority. "You don't want trouble, now do you?"

All the blood had drained from Martha Witherspoon's face. Angus stood rooted to the spot, shock filling his face. The woman with the gun looked at Sterling then back at Martha, who sat as stiffly as one of the legs holding up the table, the gun pressed to the side of her head, and lastly at Angus.

"Where's Irene?" she said.

"Gee, ma'am, I don't know," Angus cried. "Miss Witherspoon doesn't know either. Do you, Miss Witherspoon?"

Martha Witherspoon croaked something that sounded like "no."

Sterling's heart raced; he wiped his palms on the legs of his trousers. He'd been eager to get the hat pin, and his certainty about the nature of the weapon that had killed Tom Jannis, to McKnight. It was too early to find the inspector in his office, so when Sterling had seen the light from a kerosene lamp flickering from the front room of the Savoy, he'd jumped at the chance to have a minute alone with Fiona, in order to confess how badly he felt about Angus's misplaced faith in him. Perhaps, if he were lucky, he'd be offered the opportunity to escort her home.

Instead he'd stepped into this.

The muzzle of the gun was pressed firmly against Martha Witherspoon's right temple. If this wild-eyed woman was serious, Sterling had no chance of crossing the room and grabbing the gun without it going off.

"Why don't you sit down, Mrs...?"

"Brandon. Maggie Brandon, and it's Miss."

"Miss Brandon. I'm Richard, this is Angus and Martha. Angus, perhaps you could make us a pot of tea. Everything goes better with a cup of tea, isn't that right, Miss Brandon? May I call you Maggie?"

Angus took a tentative step towards the kitchen.

"Don't you move, boy," she said. "I don't want no tea. No, you cannot call me Maggie."

"What *do* you want, Miss Brandon?" Sterling asked, hoping he sounded perfectly calm—not like a man scared out of his wits.

He took a step forward.

"Don't you move, either, or I'll finish this one off."

He held out his hands, pleased to see they weren't shaking. "Okay, okay. You want to talk to Irene? Why don't we send Angus and Miss Witherspoon to fetch her? I'll stay with you while they're gone."

"I don't think so. *You* find Irene. Tell her there's a steamboat leaving at noon. I want us to be on it. It's time to get out of this goddamned town."

Sterling didn't bother to reprimand her for her language. He couldn't leave Angus and Martha alone with this madwoman, but did he have any choice? If he stayed, they could stand here all day, or until Maggie's hand got tired. Or her patience ran out.

"You, boy." She turned to Angus. "Go sit over there." She nodded to the stools at the bar.

"But..." Angus said.

"Sit over there, boy, or I take the lady's hand off." The gun swung down and pushed itself into the flesh on the back of Martha's white hand, lying on the table.

Angus ran across the room to the bar.

Maggie looked at Sterling. "You can't make it, Redcoat." The gun returned to Martha's temple. "By the time you reach me, this lady's brains be all over her ugly dress."

Martha moaned. She looked at Sterling, her eyes wide, pleading for him to do something…anything.

"Go get Irene," Maggie said forcefully.

All he could do was to go for help. He walked backwards with great deliberation, still holding his hands out in front of him in a gesture of what—submission? friendship? What a mess. If he called for reinforcements, they'd have the place surrounded, and no one would be likely to get out without bloodshed. But he couldn't just walk off in search of Irene Davidson and ask her to handle this situation.

Strange that it was a woman who had a fixation on Irene. Men, particularly lonely men far from home, often got much too emotionally tied-up in the worship of their favourite dancer. But a woman?

He felt the door at his back and grabbed the handle. Sterling took a last look at the almost empty bar. Martha Witherspoon looked close to fainting; Angus was pale but appeared to be keeping himself under control; Maggie Brandon watched Sterling like an eagle might watch a mouse crossing an open field. He knew she was capable of doing what she threatened.

As he moved to open the door, it opened itself and slapped against his back. He whirled around to come what under better circumstances would have been delightfully face-to-face with Fiona MacGillivray.

"What on earth?" she said.

He grabbed her around the waist and half-carried, half-pushed her out into the street.

Fiona twisted, and without Sterling quite knowing how, she freed herself. "Have you gone mad?" She looked like a madwoman herself, with her black hair billowing like a storm cloud about to break and her dress half undone.

Sterling had no time to appreciate the view. "You can't go in there, Fiona."

"Of course I can. Angus is there, with Martha. And my dressmaker, although why she's calling at this time of day, I have no idea."

"Maggie Brandon is your dressmaker?"

"Yes." Fiona stepped around him. He grabbed her arm. She moved her body to break the grip, but this time Sterling was ready for her, and he took hold of her other arm as she turned.

"Fiona, you have to listen to me."

"Let go of me." Her voice was deep and dark, the look in her black eyes matching the state of her hair.

"I'll release you, if you promise to hear me out."

"You have thirty seconds," she said, as though she wasn't the one being restrained, "to tell me why my son is sitting at the bar, and I can't go to him."

Sterling released her. Fiona was a tall woman, but still a good deal shorter than he. In the back of his mind, he'd thought that something was different. Now he realized what it was—she was shorter than normal. He looked down. Her bare feet were covered with mud. Splashes of mud coated the hem of her dress—a dress he hadn't seen before, in a fantastic red. She had thrown a shawl over her shoulders, but it was slipping, revealing that the top two buttons were undone. Her face was flushed red with anger.

Attracted by Fiona's state of dishevelment and her public tussle with the big Mountie, a small crowd began to gather. "You've got her now, Constable," someone called, to cheers from the onlookers.

Sterling lowered his voice. "She has a gun, Fiona. You go in there, she'll shoot. Step one foot closer, buddy, and I'll have you arrested for using vile language."

"I ain't said nothin'."

"You will if I arrest you."

The miscreant removed himself from earshot.

Fiona lifted a hand to her mouth. "Angus?"

"Everyone's fine, Fiona, but I don't know for how long. I have to go for help."

"Irene?"

"How do you know?"

"I guessed. Oh my God. Angus." Her eyes filled with tears, and her lower lip quivered. "Angus."

Sterling wanted to do nothing but gather her in his arms and promise her that he'd make everything all right. Instead he said, "Do you know where Irene is likely to be? Can you find her and bring her here?"

Fiona looked up. "Bring her here? Isn't she inside?"

"Irene Davidson? No. That's why we need her."

"You said she had a gun on Angus."

"Irene? I didn't say that. It's some woman I've only seen around town. You said she's your dressmaker. She's asking for Irene. Maybe she has some sort of fixation on Irene, or else her man is spending too much of his time and money at the Savoy, and she blames Irene."

A light crossed Fiona's face. "Oh," she said. "Maggie Brandon killed Chloe and Tom Jannis."

Sterling felt as if his head were about to explode. What this had to do with the two murders that had rocked Dawson, and Fort Herchmer, in the last two weeks he had no idea. One problem at a time. "You, come here," Sterling saw a familiar face in the crowd. Not one of the more respectable citizens, but someone who could be trusted to carry a message.

Joe Hamilton looked pleased to be picked out of the pack. No one could quite hear what was being said between the Mountie and the woman every man in town dreamed about, but her state of frantic near-undress, and the look on their faces, was enough to keep the multitude entranced and growing.

Sterling called Hamilton closer and spoke into his ear. "You breathe a word of this outside of Fort Herchmer, and I'll see you run out of town. Understand?"

"Yes, sir, Mr. Sterling."

Sterling told Joe to make for the Fort as fast as he could. If he passed any Mounties on the way, he was to tell them they were needed at the Savoy. At the Fort he was to go straight to Inspector McKnight's office and tell anyone there that there was a hostage-taking at the Savoy.

Hamilton sucked in his breath.

"One word out of place," Sterling growled, "and you'll be lucky to be run out of town in one piece."

Hamilton took off at a sprint. The crowd opened before him.

The men were edging closer. Sterling didn't know how much longer he'd be able to keep them back. Fortunately, everyone knew that the Savoy was closed this time of day, so no one was trying to get in for a drink.

"Richard," Fiona said, so softly he had to bend forward to hear her, "what can I do?"

"Do you know where Irene Davidson lives?"

"I know something better. I know where she went for breakfast. They might still be there."

"It would help."

Without another word, Fiona turned. The look on her face was so intense, the men stood back and let her pass.

Chapter Thirty-Five

I flew up King Street, my bare feet slapping against the muddy boardwalk. I remembered the day Angus had been born and the joy amidst the pain that was the wonder of it all. I remembered that I'd felt sorry, that one time only, for his father, who hadn't been there to see what we had produced. I remembered scraped knees, exasperated nannies, expensive schools, and the dogged determination on the young face that he be the sole protector of his mother. People stepped out of my way as I ran, and no one was foolish enough to attempt to stop me and inquire as to where I was headed in such a hurry.

I burst through the doors of the Imperial Restaurant. The place was almost empty at this early hour. A sourdough scowled as he attacked a plate stacked high with pancakes. Big Alex MacDonald, who everyone called the King of the Klondike, sipped his coffee while he listened to the man seated across the table. A single bored waiter dressed in a long white apron leaned against the wall while involved in an intense examination of his ragged fingernails.

In the far corner, well away from the windows letting in the soft morning light, sat Irene, in her red-and-black silk, and a delicately pretty young percentage girl, wearing a dress that might have come out of her grandmother's closet. The remains of a lavish breakfast were on the table in front of them, not yet cleared away. Streaks of yellow egg yolk ran across the girl's plate. More precious than gold, the eggs alone would have cost Irene a fortune.

Everyone looked up as the door slammed behind me.

Irene's painted mouth opened in an 'o' of surprise. The percentage girl squealed. "Good heavens, Mrs. MacGillivray, are you all right? You look a dreadful sight."

I ignored her and stared at Irene. "You have to come with me."

She gestured to her coffee cup, still filled almost to the brim. "I haven't finished yet…"

I grabbed Irene's arm and lifted her half out of her chair. The chair clattered to the floor. "Come with me, Irene."

Indecision crossed her face. She was being accosted in a public place, for no reason, by her employer, who, judging only by her appearance, not even by her actions, had clearly gone mad. How, Irene was no doubt wondering, could she take advantage of this?

"Maggie," I hissed, not wanting everyone in the restaurant to know our business, "has Angus."

"I scarcely know what that's got to do with me."

Seeing an opportunity, the percentage girl piped up. "I'd be happy to help you, Mrs. MacGillivray."

Still standing, Irene picked up her coffee cup and touched it to her lips. I sent the cup flying. Big Alex's chair scraped on the floor. "Can I help here, Mrs. MacGillivray?" he asked.

I leaned into Irene's face. "Your friend Maggie killed Chloe, then she killed Jannis, and now she wants you, Irene, but she has my son instead. So you *will* come with me."

Irene looked behind her—the percentage girl's eyes were open almost as wide as her mouth—then back at me. She hesitated for only a moment. "I swear, Mrs. MacGillivray, you have to believe me: I knew nothing of this."

"What you knew or not is hardly my concern right now. If you don't agree to come with me to the Savoy right this minute, I will have these men drag you there. You know they'll do anything I ask."

"I'll come."

Trusting she was behind me, I headed out the door. The waiter stepped away from the wall. "You ain't settled the bill yet, lady," he said.

"Stuff it up your ass," Irene replied, tumbling into the street after me.

The percentage girl squealed again. "You're not gonna stick me with it. She said it was her treat."

I glanced over my shoulder only once as we ran back down King Street. Irene was behind me, her lovely gown streaming out behind her; the percentage girl was trying to keep up, but she was falling back, about to be overtaken by Big Alex and his companion. Far behind, the sourdough stumbled, having abandoned his pancakes to join in the chase. The waiter brought up the rear, waving a slip of paper—Irene's bill, presumably.

The crowd outside the Savoy had begun to disperse, as nothing of interest appeared to be happening. When Irene and I arrived, they turned as one and resumed their position in the street.

Two Mounties were talking to Richard in low voices. I pushed the onlookers aside, ignoring the babble of shouts and questions. Irene and I climbed up onto the boardwalk.

Richard looked into my eyes. "No further developments," he said.

A wave of relief washed over me—I hadn't dared think of what might await me upon my return.

Sterling filled Irene in on the situation. "You probably don't even know this Maggie Brandon, but people sometimes get the strangest fixation on popular perform-ers such as yourself."

The Mounties' broad-brimmed hats bobbed in agreement.

Neither Irene nor I disabused the men of their assump-tions.

"What are you going to do?" I asked Richard Sterling.

"First, he's going to request that you move back, Mrs. MacGillivray." Inspector McKnight came up behind me. "You're serving no purpose here."

"My son…"

"Is in there. I know that, madam, but there's nothing you can do. If you'll stand out of the way and let us get on with our work." McKnight was trying to be kind. And failing miserably—he made the saving of my son sound as important as clearing a drunk from the sidewalk.

"Absolutely not," I said.

"Mrs. MacGillivray," Richard said in his deep, calm voice, "you must realize that your state of dress is attracting onlookers. The fewer people around, the easier it will be for us to deal with the Brandon woman and thus rescue Angus and Miss Witherspoon."

I looked down. I'd lost the shawl I'd tossed over my shoulders, and my breasts were spilling out of my exposed over-corset. In order to facilitate running, I'd tucked my skirt into the waistband, revealing a generous amount of ankle and lower leg. My stockings were so badly torn, I was virtually barefoot.

"Perhaps you should see to your feet, ma'am," one of the Mounties said. Only once he pointed them out to me did I realize how much they hurt. Blood was leaking into the dirt of Front Street.

I'd worry about pain later.

I let the skirts drop but could do nothing about the button I'd ripped off the front of my dress. "I'm not going home to change," I protested.

Richard beckoned to Irene's breakfast companion, the percentage girl who'd followed us rather than be responsible for the extravagant breakfast bill. "Would you be so kind as to lend Mrs. MacGillivray your coat," he asked in a tone that said it was not a question.

She wore a short jacket over her dress. It was the colour of dog dirt, accented by a double row of mustard-coloured braid running around the collar and down both sides of the front. I momentarily thought that I wouldn't be caught dead in it but remembered quickly enough that that might be a possibility. I'd risk my life to save my son, if I had to.

She hesitated. "I'll buy you another," I said and slipped on the garment she quickly discarded. Perhaps she thought it as ugly as I did. She was a good deal stockier than I, and the jacket buttoned up with room to spare.

I had not failed to notice that while this exchange of

clothing was going on, the Mounties held a quick conference. McKnight stepped forward and rapped on the door of the Savoy. "May I come in, Miss Brandon?" he asked with perfect manners.

"Where's Irene?" the voice demanded from inside.

"Miss Davidson is here," McKnight said. "But I regret to say I cannot allow her to talk to you as long as you have that firearm."

"Ask her if she's ready to catch the noon steamboat," Maggie shouted.

The Mounties looked at each other in disbelief.

"Tell her to let Angus go," I said.

"Why is Mrs. MacGillivray still here?" McKnight asked no one in particular. "Did I not order you to step back, madam?"

"You most certainly did, Inspector," I replied. "In light of that order, let me say to you…"

"Fiona," Richard almost shouted, "please let us do our jobs here."

"Very well." I stepped off the boardwalk and felt something squish between my toes. Ignoring it, I crossed my arms over the hideous brown jacket. Everyone's honour having been satisfied, McKnight turned back to his men.

The crowd was growing again. Customers of the Vanderhaege sisters' bakery had sensed that something was happening and wandered over to have a look. The smell of rich coffee and freshly baked waffles gave the situation the air of a church fête in a pleasant English village.

"Fiona, what is happening here?" Men stepped aside to let Euila Forester through.

"Nothing."

"It doesn't look like nothing," she said, quite sensibly. "Martha left a note saying she was coming here to do some early morning interviews. She left her watch beside the wash basin." Euila dug in her reticule and pulled out the instrument under discussion. "She hates to be without her watch. Looking at it makes her appear to be someone with important people to see."

"Euila," I said, slowly and calmly, "right now, I don't give a fuck about Martha's watch."

She looked as if she'd been slapped. It was unlikely Euila knew what that word meant, but she knew when she'd been insulted.

Instead of taking offence, she spoke calmly. "It's obvious something is seriously wrong, Fiona. Where is Angus?"

I mutely pointed to the Savoy.

She could put two and two together and come up with four. "I assume Martha is with him?"

I nodded.

Euila slipped her arm around my shoulders. It was a bit of a stretch for her. "I'll wait here with you, shall I?"

"I'd like that."

"Do you remember the time Percy thought he'd shot himself in the foot when he and Father were hunting grouse?"

I nodded.

"He missed, fortunately, but the birdshot kicked up a jagged-edged rock that struck his foot. Do you remember all the yelling and fuss when they carried him back to the house? Percy screaming at the top of his lungs that he'd be a cripple for life, and Father shouting at him to keep quiet."

"Your mother fainted."

"She never was much good in a crisis, Mother. Poor Mother, she was never much good at life."

"I'm glad you're here, Euila."

"I'm glad I'm here, too, Fiona."

Irene joined us. She shook her head. "They won't let me talk to Martha."

"Mrs. MacGillivray, please let your friends take you home; this is no place for a lady." Sergeant Lancaster had arrived.

"Go away."

"She's upset," Euila explained.

"Damn right I'm upset."

"Your language, Mrs. MacGillivray," Lancaster said. I'd never noticed before how much he resembled Miss Wheatley at her sternest.

"My language," I said, "will be the least of your worries, Sergeant, if you don't leave me alone."

Lancaster decided to avoid a confrontation he couldn't possibly win. "I'll see if I can be of assistance." He puffed his chest up before joining the group of Mounties in quiet conversation on the boardwalk. Richard Sterling had crept under the windows, trying to peek in, but the curtains, made by Helen Saunderson, were good, unlike most of the rest of the Savoy, which would fall apart in a strong wind.

Two constables came down into the crowd and politely requested that everyone move away. "Nothing to see here," they said. The statement, of course, had the exact opposite effect. The men had been starting to break up; everyone knew the Savoy was normally closed in the early morning, so no one could suspect they were being kept out. Once I'd put the brown and mustard jacket on, the peep show was over. A few men might have the intelligence to wonder why I was standing in the street outside my own property, while the Mounties huddled in a group whispering to each other at the door, and Constable Sterling attempted to peer in the windows, but the sort of men who gathered on Front Street in the early morning weren't known for the sharpness of their intellect.

All they needed to remain in place was an order from the police to disperse.

The waiter from the Imperial restaurant stopped one of the young Mounties. "That woman," he shouted, "didn't pay her bill. Ten dollars!" he waved the paper in the air. Even over my terror for my son, I was shocked that anyone would spend ten dollars for a breakfast. "Arrest her!" the waiter demanded.

The crowd's attention turned. A low mumble began at the back of the pack as word spread that someone was asking the police to arrest the most popular performer in town.

"I'm sorry, but that will have to wait, sir," the Mountie said.

"What sort of town are you running here?" the waiter demanded. "I've told you that woman is a thief."

The crowd growled. A white-faced Euila hugged me.

The Mountie's face had gone as red as his jacket. He

looked for assistance from the officers on the boardwalk, who were paying him no attention, and then his partner, who was busy trying to send the back of the pack on their way.

"A misunderstanding. Easy to clear up." Big Alex Macdonald pulled out his billfold. "Allow me to settle the lady's account." He peeled off several bills and pressed them into the waiter's hand. The man stuffed the money into his apron pocket and walked away without another word.

Alex looked at me and gave the slightest of nods. "You men," he bellowed in a voice pitched to carry to the very back of the crowd. "Why don't we do as these fine officers suggest? The Monte Carlo's open. First round's on me."

The men set off up the street like a pack of dogs catching the whiff of a bitch in heat. True to his word, Alex followed, at a more dignified pace.

"That was slick," one of the young Mounties said to no one in particular.

Only a few onlookers remained, those more interested in the goings-on at the Savoy than a free drink. Among them, Graham Donohue, of course. I could see Mouse O'Brien tearing up the street. His collar was loose and his cravat badly tied.

"Miss Witherspoon, where is she?" Mouse gasped. He'd been running hard.

"Inside," Euila said, before I could stop her. "She's inside, being held hostage by a woman gone mad. And poor young Angus too."

Mouse pushed his way (as Mouse tended to do) past the two young constables who'd reassembled at the foot of the boardwalk and fell into intense conversation with the Mounties gathered around the door to the Savoy. Mouse gestured wildly; McKnight lifted his chin and looked authoritative; Lancaster kept glancing at me; Richard tried to persuade everyone to calm down; Graham Donohue edged forward, ears flapping.

The men all eyed each other for a few moments. I almost expected them to lower their heads and charge. Then, with a growl, Mouse turned and stalked away.

He passed two people I hadn't seen arrive. They were standing by themselves, just watching: vultures, waiting for the kill. Joey Leblanc and her employee Al Black.

Joey saw me looking at her, and the edges of her thin lips turned up in a malicious smile. Today, she was just an onlooker, hoping to be witness to my misfortune. I had no doubt that one day she'd be the instigator of it.

I'd worry about Joey another time.

*   *   *

Angus wanted nothing more than a drink of water. His mouth was so dry it made him think of the men of the French Foreign Legion, whom he'd read about in his boys' adventure stories, marching through the North African desert.

Miss Brandon had scarcely moved a muscle since Constable Sterling had left the Savoy. She twitched occasionally, and once she rubbed at the arm that was holding the gun to Miss Witherspoon's head. That was all.

Angus had gotten a glimpse of his mother in the doorway before Constable Sterling practically carried her away.

Miss Brandon ordered him to lock the door, but as he fumbled at the lock, Miss Witherspoon let out a low moan, and Miss Brandon growled at her to keep quiet. Angus didn't let the lock catch.

Since then, he'd heard a mass of men gathering on the street, and Inspector McKnight asking if he could come in, but mostly nothing but the sound of Maggie Brandon breathing and Martha Witherspoon weeping.

"I'm sure thirsty," Angus said, barely able to force the words past his parched throat. "You must be too, Miss Brandon. Can I get you a glass of water?"

"No."

"Miss Witherspoon would probably like a drink."

"No."

"We can't sit here all day, you know. My mother will be around soon to open for business."

"Once Irene gets here, we'll be gone. Boat leaves at noon. I've bought the tickets already."

"That's great," Angus said. "There's quite a crowd outside. Can you hear them, Miss Brandon?"

"Yes."

"Miss Davidson probably can't get past them. You know what a mob like that's like. Most of them with nothing better to do. My mother says they're the curse of Dawson—no money to spend, nothing to do, no interest in finding work."

"Layabouts, scavengers," Miss Brandon agreed.

"Poor Miss Davidson trying to push her way through that lot." Angus shook his head sadly.

Miss Brandon turned and fully looked at him for the first time. Wood creaked in the back rooms, but Maggie didn't notice. Her gun hand moved away from Miss Witherspoon's head so it was pointed directly at the portrait of Her Majesty hanging over the bar. "I suppose I could let you go outside and tell her I'm waiting in here. Would you do that for me, boy?"

Angus nodded. Trying to look sympathetic and friendly, he started to edge off his stool.

A shape moved at the doors leading to the gambling rooms. This time it was not a rat.

It was a Mouse.

Mouse O'Brien.

Mouse tossed a long, desperate look at Martha Witherspoon, now lying almost prostrate across the table. Then he looked at Maggie Brandon. Angus tried not to look at Mouse. "That's a great idea, Miss Brandon," he said as the man stepped cautiously into the saloon. Mouse pressed his six-foot-seven height and two-hundred-and-fifty pound weight into a loose floorboard. The board snapped.

Maggie Brandon swung around.

She fired.

Chapter Thirty-Six

Inspector McKnight was telling the assembled Mounties that it was unlikely they would be able to save the hostages. Of paramount importance, he said, was the capturing or killing of the hostage-taker.

Sterling looked at Fiona MacGillivray, wrapped in her friend's embrace. Her face was white with fear, but even with hair resembling that of one of the witches from *Macbeth*, she looked both strong and beautiful. He knew then that he didn't care one whit what happened to Maggie Brandon—he'd pay for her steamboat fare out of the country himself if Angus was spared.

Fiona felt his eyes on her, and she raised her heavy lashes. Her glance hit him like a bolt of lightning. He forced his attention back to what McKnight was telling his officers.

"When women go bad, it's a particularly dangerous thing. Their monthly cycles turn some of them into mad things."

One of the men, who'd hardly started shaving yet, asked his companion what a monthly cycle was.

None of the Mounties carried firearms. The force kept a Magnum machine gun at Chilkoot Pass, mainly to keep the infamous Soapy Smith of Skagway, Alaska, off the Pass and out of Canada. And that was about it for the firepower of Her Majesty's North-West Mounted Police in the Yukon Territory. There might be a few guns locked up in the store rooms, but if there were, no one had thought to bring them along.

Sterling stepped forward. "We have to proceed cautiously, sir," he said. "Brandon has asked for Irene Davidson. Miss Davidson is here, willing to do anything she can to help. I suggest we ask her to shout into the Savoy and try to mollify Brandon."

"We don't mollify madwomen, Constable Sterling, we overwhelm them."

"I want to help." Irene Davidson stepped forward. "Maggie only wants to talk to me."

"If you would please go and join the other ladies, Miss Davidson," McKnight said.

"But..."

"This is a police matter; the assistance of women is not required. You're only causing a disturbance and a distraction."

Richard Sterling had been demoted once; he knew he now stood at the edge of outright dismissal. "With all due respect, sir," he said, trying not to scream his frustration, "there are two civilians in there. A woman and a child."

"Nevertheless..."

Before McKnight finished his sentence, a shot rang out.

*   *   *

I was about to shrug Euila's arm off me. Time had long past for someone to do something. There was a woman in there with my son, holding a gun. She wanted Irene Davidson: I would see she got Irene Davidson. If I shoved Euila with enough force to send her floundering in the street, I could grab Irene and make a dash for the door. We'd be inside while the Mounties, gentlemen all, were rushing to assist Euila. Richard might present a problem, but if I had to, I could stop Richard Sterling in his tracks—one way or another—while Irene got through the door.

Would Irene do it?

I had no idea.

I could only make sure she had no choice.

For my plan to work, the door would have to be unlocked. Had I reminded Angus to lock it? I couldn't remember. I considered going around the back but didn't know if the back door was locked either. Ray had a set of keys, but Ray wasn't here. And there was no time to send for him.

I flexed my toes, and pain shot through me so sharply, I gasped. Euila murmured soothingly, "It'll be all right, Fiona, you'll see."

Pain be damned, I would save my child. I gritted my teeth and started to move into the half-turn that would break Euila's hold with my body, while at the same time my raised leg would knock her legs out from under her.

Before I could move, everything changed.

A single shot came from inside the Savoy.

A woman screamed.

I was so startled I grabbed Euila to keep her from falling. Then I was on my way, leaping up to the boardwalk and past the Mounties.

Only Richard Sterling moved faster than I.

Chapter Thirty-Seven

Not much care or attention to detail had gone into the building of the Savoy; the door was soft and badly fitted into its hinges. Richard Sterling threw himself against the door. Unlocked, it crashed open under his weight.

Martha Witherspoon lay across the big central table, screaming at the top of her lungs. Angus MacGillivray was running across the floor, heading for a large body lying at the entrance to the gambling hall. A big man was face down on the floor, blood leaking out from under him. Maggie Brandon still held her pistol, but she appeared vague and confused, as if she didn't seem to know quite what to do with it.

Sterling charged across the saloon; he vaulted over a chair lying overturned in the middle of the room.

Remembering what the gun was for, Brandon raised it slowly, and aimed it straight at Sterling's gut. He stopped.

"Put the gun down, ma'am. It's all over."

With a flurry of Dawson mud, red silk and black hair, Fiona MacGillivray streamed past him. "You can shoot me, you bitch," she shouted, "but you leave my son alone." Fiona ran past Brandon, who didn't even flinch. Reaching Angus, who was crouching over the body lying limp on the floor, she gathered him into her arms.

"Maggie." Irene Davidson had followed Sterling. He turned to see her standing in the doorway, the morning light around her. A dark shape was behind her, the Mountie hat unmistakeable, the features in shadow. Behind him, a cluster of officers.

Two men had been dispatched to try to get in through the back and determine if there was a way to gain access to the saloon safely and quietly. They hesitated in the doorway to the gambling hall, waiting for orders.

Martha Witherspoon looked up. Her eyes were wide with terror. She didn't move.

"Maggie, put the gun down," Irene said, her voice calm.

"I have the tickets." Brandon patted her skirt pocket with her free hand. "We're leaving on the noon boat. San Francisco is supposed to be a good place."

"A very nice place, I'm sure, but I'm not going with you, Maggie."

Sterling wanted to scream at her. To tell Irene to play along. If they could get Brandon to think she would get what she wanted and put the gun down, it would all be over.

"Not going?"

"No. I want to stay in Dawson. They like me here, Maggie."

"They *like* you," Brandon said, her words carrying the weight of the world behind them. Her head and shoulders shook like a dog coming out of the sea, and she raised the gun with steady hands. "Who the hell cares what they like. You belong with me. Once we're away from this wicked place, you'll see that all the fancy women mean nothing. You'll understand I'm the only one."

"No, I won't." Miss Davidson's voice was a whisper. "I'm staying, Maggie. Why did you have to kill them? That man? I scarcely even knew him."

"He was a sneak, always watching, listening, following people. He knew about us. He wanted money to keep quiet."

"Chloe? She was harmless."

"She had to die." Brandon started to cry. Big, fat tears ran silently down her cheeks. "That ugly strumpet fooled you; she wasn't your friend."

"She wouldn't have told. I knew how to keep her sweet."

"Oh, Irene."

Brandon's words were as light as a butterfly on the wind. She lifted the gun.

"No," Sterling yelled. He flew across the floor, kicking chairs out of the way.

Maggie Brandon put the gun to her temple. "I will always love you, Irene," she whispered as she pulled the trigger.

Chapter Thirty-Eight

I held my precious child in my arms and pressed his face into my chest. By the time I'd reached him, he'd rolled Mouse O'Brien over and was tearing open Mouse's crisp white shirt. The big man's eyes opened, and his face moved in recognition. "Nothing sadder than a fool for love, is there, Mrs. MacGillivray?" He closed his eyes. In the poor light cast by the kerosene lamp, now beginning to splutter and go out, Mouse's left side glistened bright with blood.

"Stay still," I whispered, to both Mouse and Angus. For once Angus didn't argue. He settled into my embrace, and I felt his thin shoulders shudder.

My mind didn't process the words that were being exchanged between Irene, Sterling and Maggie. I could only feel the emotion as it swirled around the room and close my heart against the scorn and the despair.

But I heard Irene's cold voice and Richard's cry of "no" and the sound of crashing furniture, and I heard the bark of the pistol, and for a flash of time all was quiet, the only sound being the sigh that marked the last breath of life as it left a body. Then Martha Witherspoon screamed at the top of her lungs, and we were surrounded by men, all shouting at once. I closed my eyes, murmured sweet nothings, and cradled my child.

And, for the first time in a long time, he was content to be held.

*   *   *

Richard Sterling fell to his knees beside Maggie Brandon.

The gun slid across the floor, and he let it go. Maggie would have no use for it again. Her body twitched as her life force departed, and her blood spread out across the wooden floor of the Savoy. Fiona MacGillivray had Angus pressed tightly against her body, and her eyes were closed.

She was all right. They were both all right. But Mouse O'Brien needed a doctor. Fast.

Men ran into the room from all directions. Sterling stood up. Irene Davidson was looking into his eyes.

He walked slowly towards her, to where she stood beneath a painting of an undressed woman. She didn't move. He stopped inches from her. "It didn't have to end this way," he said, so softly no one else could hear. "You could've talked her out of it."

Irene looked up at him with eyes that were dark and empty. She shrugged. She wore a lovely gown, but now it looked tawdry. "What's the point? You heard her confess to killing Chloe. She was going to hang; if she'd lived to stand trial, she'd cause everyone a lot of trouble first."

A Mountie shouted for a doctor. Miss Forester, yelling loudly enough to be heard over the din, demanded to be allowed inside. Someone bustled Martha Witherspoon, whose screams had settled into hysterical sobs, outside before she could turn around and look at the scene behind her.

Ray Walker burst into the room. He ran to Irene, shouting a stream of words, but his Scottish accent was so overpowering, Sterling couldn't understand a single word.

Irene lowered her eyes, turned her back on Sterling, and allowed Walker to put his arms around her. Her shoulders shook as she began to cry. Walker patted her back while his gaze took in the scene in his saloon. Fiona and Angus were still huddled together on the floor, while beside them the doctor tended to Mouse O'Brien, whose curses would have him tossed out of town if anyone bothered to take offence.

Over Irene's heaving shoulder, Walker looked at Sterling, and said, "You'll look after her." It was as much a statement as a question.

"If she allows me to."

Chapter Thirty-Nine

I allowed myself to be lowered into my chair. Plump red velvet cushions were tucked into my back, and a footstool covered in beige damask, specifically purchased for my comfort, had been placed at my feet.

I looked around the saloon of the Savoy. It was Tuesday evening—impossible to believe it was the same day as the hostage-taking and the death of Maggie Brandon. We'd been forced to close for most of the day, while the police did whatever police do at the scene of a crime. The coroner arrived and carted off Maggie Brandon with a good deal less respect than seemed proper, and the doctor left for the hospital with Mouse O'Brien, who, we were all relieved to see, walked out on his own two feet. The bullet had gone through the fleshy part of his upper arm. Messy, probably painful, but not life-threatening. And as for the mess— poor Helen Saunderson arrived for work at her usual time to find that she had to mop up not only Mouse's blood but a good portion of Maggie Brandon's brains. I wouldn't have been surprised if she'd quit on the spot. Instead she sighed and got out her bucket and mop. Something extra would be in her pay packet at the end of the week.

Before all that happened, Angus had begun to wiggle uncomfortably in my embrace and finally pushed me away. He glanced around the room, presumably hoping no one had seen him being comforted by his mother as though he were a child. Everyone had seen it, but they all pretended they hadn't. My feelings were hurt, and I reminded myself that this was the natural order of things—my son wouldn't need me much longer.

Richard Sterling offered a hand to help me up. If he held my hand for a few moments longer than was proper, I was happy for his strong warmth. Once I stood on my feet, I almost fell over. Stars streaked across the blackness behind my eyes. Sterling and Angus grabbed me and half-carried me to a stool at the bar.

"I'll ask Sergeant Lancaster to see that you and Angus get home," Sterling said.

I shook my head. Bad move: more stars.

"Where's Ray?" I asked.

"He's taken Miss Davidson home."

With all the men passing to and fro, I wouldn't have been surprised if more than a few wayward hands found the whisky bottles behind the bar. "Someone has to remain here. The sergeant can escort Angus."

"I'm not leaving you here, Mother!"

The men from the funeral parlour arrived. I averted my gaze.

"Fiona, please."

"No."

Another Mountie joined our squabbling little group. Sterling respectfully took a step back. "I'll personally ensure that your establishment is fully protected, Madam, until either you or Mr. Walker can resume your responsibilities."

"Very well," I said, giving the man a slight nod. It was Inspector Courtlandt Starnes, commander of Dawson and Fort Herchmer in the absence of Superintendent Steele.

He turned to a young constable. "Brown."

The man snapped to attention. "Sir?"

"See Mrs. MacGillivray and her son safely home." He glanced down at my feet, torn to shreds, leaking blood all over the floor. "Mrs. MacGillivray is unable to walk. Command-eer a horse and wagon if you have to."

"Yes, sir."

Angus cleared his throat. "Inspector Starnes, sir?"

"Yes, Angus?"

"I heard Miss Brandon confess to the killing of Chloe

Smith myself. So did Constable Sterling and my mother.
That means Mary didn't do it.'"

"It would appear so."

"Are you going to release Mary? Sir?"

"Immediately, son. You escort your mother home then
come to the Fort. I'll see that your friend gets a cup of tea
and is made comfortable while she's waiting."

"Thank you, sir."

And so I had been carried out of the Savoy by two husky
young Mounties and was loaded carefully into a donkey
cart, while Sergeant Lancaster fluttered about and got into
everyone's way.

My feet were an absolute mess. God only knows what I'd
run through on my mad dash, sans shoes, from home to the
Savoy and from the Savoy to the Imperial and back again.

Once I got home, the doctor—a good one, not the fool
who was always trying to check my heartbeat—tended to
my torn feet then wrapped them heavily in bandages.
Among the debris in the street, there had been a nice
sharp piece of glass, and the doctor, peering though thick
spectacles, attempting to dig out the glass with a pair of
tweezers, told me I'd be off my feet for a good while.

When he'd left, Mrs. Mann helped me out of my dress
and into my nightgown. She went to fetch the first of a great
many cups of tea, and allowed Angus into my room. My son
checked his watch and asked if he could go and see Mary.
He was very proud of that watch, Angus was, because I'd
made a great fuss of presenting it to him, telling him that it
had been my father's watch. In truth, before I had climbed
up a drainpipe and removed it from his bedside table, along
with a nice pair of diamond cufflinks, it had belonged to a
fat member of parliament who drank himself into a stupor
every night and snored excessively. I had nothing to
remember my parents by, except for my memories, but I'd
wanted Angus to believe he had a family heirloom.

I fell into a deep sleep before my door had closed
behind him.

When Angus returned, I was sitting up in bed drinking

tea. "I brought Mary home with me. She's out back, helping Mrs. Mann in the laundry."

"Good."

"I called at the hospital. Mr. O'Brien has only a flesh wound in his upper arm," he reported. "But the doctor wants him to stay in the hospital overnight, just to be sure."

"Good," I repeated, trying to fluff my pillows.

Angus sat at the end of my bed. "Miss Witherspoon is at the hospital. They say she refuses to leave."

"Also good."

He took a slice of cold toast off my tea tray. "I don't understand what happened today, Mother. Why did Miss Brandon threaten me and Miss Witherspoon? Why did Miss Brandon think Miss Davidson would leave town with her?"

I looked into my child's wide-open blue eyes. And I lied. "Miss Brandon mistakenly believed Miss Davidson had promised to make her a star of the dance halls," I said, picking at a loose thread in the quilt. "When that didn't happen, her poor confused mind thought Miss Davidson had meant she would be a star Outside. Terribly sad all around."

Angus leaned over and kissed me. "I love you, Mother."

I smiled around my tears. "I love you too, dearest."

In the late afternoon, Ray stopped by for a visit, looking extremely pleased with himself. Considering that I'd last seen him leaving the Savoy in the company of my own Lady Irenee, who had been putting on a better show than she ever did on stage, I decided I didn't want to know why he was so cheerful.

"Angus," I said. "I'll need Mrs. Mann's assistance in getting dressed. Can you fetch her for me, please?"

I shoved Angus and Ray's concerns aside and insisted I'd go to work that evening. Knowing it would be hopeless to attempt to convince me to stay in bed, they, with the help of Mrs. Mann, put their heads together and hired a cart and a sad excuse for a horse to carry me to the Savoy.

I felt rather like the Queen must, travelling down Pall Mall in her ornate carriage on some affair of state, as the single scrawny beast pulled the rickety cart through

Dawson. I waved to the cheering onlookers exactly as I'd seen Her Majesty do, with a sort of half-movement of the hand. Unlike Queen Victoria, however, I couldn't help but grin.

Angus refused to ride in the cart with me, so he walked beside, looking perfectly embarrassed at the whole affair. Richard Sterling, his face as displeased as Angus's, met us at the entrance to the Savoy.

It took me a moment to notice, but as I shuffled across the cart bench, ready to be shifted into a chair, to be carried inside by the cart-owner, Jake the croupier, and both Murray and Not-Murray, I saw that Richard's uniform jacket was pressed, brushed and spotless, his trousers ironed to a knife edge, and his boots polished to a high gloss. I opened my mouth to say something, but at that moment Murray lost his grip on the chair leg, and I lurched perilously towards the good Yukon earth. They righted me in time, and I was spared that indignity.

Shortly before eight, I was beginning to consider putting a guard on the door to keep any more customers out. We were bursting at the seams, sort of like Betsy when she put on weight in the spring but couldn't afford a new dress. Word had gotten around, as it does, that I had heroically returned to the Savoy, carried from the field of battle, so to speak. I, of course, had contributed exactly nothing towards the resolution of this morning's crisis, but men like to have a heroine, and they like me very much. So I was the designated heroine of the day. I decided to simply enjoy it for the short time it lasted. By tomorrow, all would be forgotten and something else would have drawn their attention.

Irene Davidson arrived for work wearing a cheap, overly elaborate dress of the sort most people would associate with a dance hall girl. She kept her head down and scurried for the back rooms. She needn't have avoided me: her secret was safe with me. I'd heard some of the town scuttlebutt from Angus, and a good deal more since I'd been sitting here. Maggie Brandon had gone mad, they all said—naturally enough with her being a middle-aged spinster—with jealousy at the popularity of Irene Davidson.

She'd hatched a scheme to get Irene to come Outside with her and teach her to be a dance hall star.

The Savoy had an enormously successful night. I should be injured more often. Everyone in town must have stopped in front of my chair to wish me well. I was wearing the green satin tonight, having decided it didn't much matter what I wore, as I wasn't getting out of my seat, and I had tossed a woollen blanket over my legs for the sake of decency.

My dress! How on earth had I forgotten. A blue day dress, having had the final fitting, was waiting for me at the "dresmakers shop". And all those wonderful fabrics. What would happen to them? First thing tomorrow, I'd try to salvage what I could from the remains of Maggie's business.

My cloud of admirers drifted apart for a brief moment, and Richard Sterling stepped in front of me. "I'm glad to see you looking so well, Mrs. MacGillivray. No ill effects from this morning's unpleasantness, I hope. Other than the feet, that is."

He was strangely formal. I felt somewhat formal myself. I wanted to thank him for being the first into the Savoy to confront Maggie Brandon so I could reach Angus without worrying about her attention falling on me. But I could not find the words.

"You're looking most respectable tonight," I said.

"I had an interview with Inspector Starnes this afternoon."

I lifted one eyebrow, but he didn't elaborate.

"I hope you have a pleasant evening, Mrs. MacGillivray," he said with a smile. He had a lovely smile, Constable Richard Sterling, warm and comforting, although he rarely used it. "For all our sakes."

Chapter Forty

As he passed through the throng packing the room from the bar to the doors, Richard Sterling thought back on the events of the morning. Martha Witherspoon, almost collapsing in shock, had been hustled out. Mouse O'Brien, swearing a blue streak, had walked out of the Savoy under his own power, heading for the hospital. Ray Walker had left with Irene Davidson, who was conscientiously avoiding Sterling's eyes. Fiona MacGillivray, unable to walk on the torn feet that had carried her this far, had been carried out by two extremely pleased young Mounties, supervised by Sergeant Lancaster. The men from the funeral parlour had hoisted Maggie Brandon's body onto their stretcher and carried it away, one of them complaining all the while that he'd scarcely had an hour's sleep before being dragged out of bed.

"You did a good job there, Mr. Sterling," a man said as the mass of people dispersed from the saloon of the Savoy.

"No sir, I didn't. I failed. The woman died."

"She chose to die, and so hers was the only death here today. It could have been a bloodbath."

"Yes, sir." Sterling rubbed his eyes. God, he was tired.

"You kept your head, and therefore Mr. O'Brien, young Angus MacGillivray, and Miss Witherspoon lived. I like to see a man keep his head in a crisis. Look after what needs to be done here. I want to see you in my office at three this afternoon, Constable Sterling."

"Yes, sir."

"I will be reassigning you. Your first assignment will be to find out where Brandon got that firearm and to make sure that the conduit of such weapons is plugged. Permanently. We won't abide that sort of thing in this town."

"No, sir. I mean, yes, sir."

Inspector Starnes went to confer with McKnight.

*　*　*

My feet healed quickly, although I wouldn't be going back over the Chilkoot Pass any time soon. I could get around without being carried but was limited to the distance covered by the direct route between the Savoy and Mrs. Mann's boarding house. My son seemed to enjoy looking after me, and I enjoyed his attentions. Ray continued to look excessively pleased with himself, and that I was not at all pleased about. I suspected Irene was making friends with Ray in order to try to squelch any gossip about herself and Maggie. Poor Ray.

I'd worry about that tomorrow. Today a small crowd stood at the gangplank leading to the steamboat *Queen Victoria*.

Mouse O'Brien and Martha Witherspoon had come to say their farewells. Ray Walker and Richard Sterling were there also. Mary stood close to Angus, who held on to her small cardboard suitcase. A large coloured woman was with them, wiping her eyes on an embroidered handkerchief. Yesterday, my lovely son had gone upriver to Moosehide Island, by himself, to talk to Bishop Bompas. It had been agreed that the steamboat would drop Mary off at the village, and she could stay with the Bishop and his wife while he looked for a place for her.

"I have them all, Fiona," Euila said.

"All what?"

"Martha's notes. She said she won't be needing them, and I can do what I want with them. Wasn't that nice of her?"

"Very nice," I agreed. I tossed a glance to where Martha stood, her arm tucked into the protection of Mouse O'Brien's good one. His other arm was cradled in a snowy white sling. Martha's face was flushed with the pure joy that hadn't left her for most of the week. He was still in his hospital bed, in the middle of a crowded ward, when he'd asked Martha to marry him. She accepted on the spot, and his wardmates had broken into a round of applause.

Graham Donohue had come, as flushed with the thrill of writing up the hostage-taking for his newspaper as Martha with a proposal of marriage. He hadn't asked me to read his epistle, thank heavens. This boat would carry his dispatches Outside, to where any news from the fabled Klondike, no matter how fabricated, was almost as precious as the gold itself.

Richard Sterling smiled at Euila and wished her well. Inspector Starnes had decided, I'd heard, that the town of Dawson was growing so fast, it needed a second town detachment. And, so I had also heard, newly-promoted Corporal Richard Sterling was to be in charge of it. I hoped he wouldn't be too busy with his management responsibilities to drop by the Savoy now and again.

The steamboat whistle sounded. Everyone else had gone on board. A crewman stood at the top of the gangplank, ready to pull it up.

Euila clutched her reticule to her chest. "Fiona," she said.

"I simply cannot wait," I said, "until those stories are in print. You must send us a copy the moment they're off the press."

"I will," she said, looking at her shoes. "I'm glad we met again, Fiona."

"I am too, Euila. You'd best be going, or the ship will leave without you."

She started up the gangplank, a tiny figure in a dull brown dress. What would the dreadful Percy think, his sister returning with, instead of a husband, the ambition to be a writer?

She was halfway to the safety of the boat, but I called to her. "Euila!" She placed a white-gloved hand on the railing and turned towards me.

"Write to Alistair. Tell him you saw me and that I'm doing well."

"Fiona...I..."

"Tell Alistair I remember him. Tell him I have forgotten nothing."

Acknowledgements

Sincere thanks to my great critique group, Dorothy McIntosh, Jane Burfield, Donna Carrick, Madeleine Harris-Callway, and Cheryl Freedman. Write on, women! Thanks also to Verna Relkoff of the Mint Agency for manuscript suggestions and to Jerry Sussenguth who helped with the German accent, and to the great people at RendezVous for their help and support.

I have attempted wherever possible to keep the historical details of the Klondike Gold Rush, and the town of Dawson, Yukon Territory, accurate. Occasionally, however, it is necessary to stretch the truth in the interests of a good story. The historical record says that there wasn't a single murder in Dawson in the year of the town's heyday, 1898, therefore I have taken the liberty of inventing one. A few historical personages make cameos in the book: Big Alex McDonald, Belinda Mulroney, Inspector Cortlandt Starnes, but all dramatic characters and incidents are the product of my imagination.

The reader who is interested in learning more about the Klondike Gold Rush is advised to begin with the definitive book on the subject, *Klondike: The Last Great Gold Rush 1896-1899* by Pierre Berton. Also by Berton, *The Klondike Quest: A Photographic Essay 1897-1899.*

Other reading:

The Klondike Gold Rush: Photographs from 1896-1899. Graham Wilson

Good Time Girls of the Alaska-Yukon Gold Rush. Lael Morgan

The Last Great Gold Rush: A Klondike Reader. Edited by Graham Wilson

Women of the Klondike. Francis Blackhouse

The Real Klondike Kate. T. Ann Brennan

Gamblers and Dreamers: Women, Men and Community in the Klondike. Charlene Porsild

The Klondike Stampede. Tappan Adney.

For information about the NWMP:

They Got their Man: On Patrol with the North West Mounted. P.H. Godsell

The NWMP and Law Enforcement 1873-1905. R.C. Macleod

Showing the Flag: The Mounted Police and Canadian Sovereignty in the North, 1894-1925. W.R. Morrison

Sam Steele: Lion of the Frontier. R. Stewart

Vicki Delany was fortunate enough to be able to take early retirement from her job as a systems analyst in Toronto and is now enjoying the rural life in Prince Edward County, Ontario, where she rarely wears a watch. She is the author of several stand-alone novels of psychological suspense as well as the Constable Molly Smith series (*In the Shadow of the Glacier*) published by Poisoned Pen Press. *Gold Fever* is the sequel to *Gold Digger* (RendezVous Crime, 2009). She can be visited online at:

www.vickidelany.com